Cruel in the Shadow

The Chronicles of Invernevis

Cruel in the Shadow

LORN MACINTYRE

THE BOOK CLUB
LONDON

The Book Club
125 Charing Cross Road
London WC2H 0EB

Copyright © Lorn Macintyre 1979

First published in Great Britain 1979

This edition 1980 by arrangement with
William Collins Sons & Co. Ltd

Printed and bound in Great Britain by
Biddles Ltd, Guildford and King's Lynn

Acknowledgement

The author wishes to thank the Scottish Arts Council, without whose financial support this novel could not have been written.

For my Mother and my Wife
Two Kindred Spirits

Ancient, effortless, ordered, cycle on cycle set,
Life was so long untroubled, that ye, who inherit forget
It was not made with the mountains, it is not one with the deep.
Men, not gods, devised it. Men, not gods, must keep.

Rudyard Kipling, 'The Islanders', 1902

Book One

Chapter One

On an August afternoon in eighteen hundred and ninety-nine Niall John Macdonald, newly gazetted Captain of the First Battalion Princess Louise's Argyll and Sutherland Highlanders and younger of Invernevis, was standing with one foot on the lower step of Invernevis House, and the other on gravel. He had held that posture for ten minutes, by his own reckoning, and frankly, was tired in the fierce heat trapped by the policies of trees and rhododendrons. The regimental kilt of dark Sutherland tartan clung to his bent left knee, the long badger's head sporran with its goat's hair seemed weighted with lead, the spatterdashes made his shoes hot. The plaid, held in place by hammered silver circling a cairngorm, was dragging down his left shoulder, where the crimson sash crossed his scarlet doublet, with its yellow cuffs and gold shoulder cords, its high collar with the regimental badges showing the Campbell boar's head and Sutherland wild cat linked by Princess Louise's cyphers.

The plumed feathered bonnet supported by a cane and wire cage, drooping over his right cheek, was a furnace, the tight diced band making sweat trickle, the strap cutting in under the chin. And the fingers of his right hand were long since numb in the basket hilt of the sword he had to hold perpendicular, but not as a prop, keeping it in alignment with the dirk hanging at his right side. But his face did not betray his discomfort. It had been bred to keep emotion at bay, to give orders, and not only in military life. The chin supported by the strap showed this, and the authority of the mouth was reinforced by the thick dark moustache. The forehead clamped by the diced band was high, and the dark parted hair under the feathered bonnet retreating as the thirties crept up. But the accoutrements gave the six-foot frame more bulk than it actually possessed.

There was more commotion under the black cloth hooding the tripod tilting on gravel a few paces in front of him, where pointed shoes scuffed by a pile of spent plates.

The ivy rash had spread above the dim backdrop of the sandstone porch, screening the coat of arms with its Gaelic boast: *Mairidh Sinn, We Shall Endure*, and small birds wriggled into the red leaves, seeking shelter from the heat.

Disorientated by the excessive heat and light, a bee from the hives in the walled garden was mistaking the feathered bonnet for a shaded bush, and descending in search of the flower. The new Captain tried to ignore the deepening drone, but when it collided with his left cheek he had to strike out, the sword wobbling.

The black cloth was thrown aside, revealing the distraught face of Signor Faccenda, Photographer to Society.

'How can I take zee photograph if you will not stand steel?' the temperamental little Italian in the velvet bow yelled, his goatee tilted to the relentless sky, the tripod at his feet.

A shriek of laughter came from the Captain's left, and it was infectious. His young sister Laura was shaking her gold ringlets as, hands clasped round her knees, her button boots pedalled air until she fell back breathless against wrought iron beneath the bay window.

'Behave yourself, girl, or get to bed,' a weary voice from a wicker lounger warned beside her.

Under the hoisted white parasol, Mama was weighted down under layers of grey silk. Lace foamed at her throat, and there was more on the black straw hat that was failing to save her large round face from the ravages of the sky. Kipling's *Captains Courageous* lay face-down on her ample lap, and a Skye terrier curled panting by her trailing hand, crossed paws keeping its nose from scorching gravel.

'To bed, girl, and tomorrow, bread and water,' Aunt Carlotta announced, prim and erect on the iron chair in a throat-hugging dress of white silk. The white straw hat above her

thin spinsterish face bore its circle of artificial flowers evenly.
Her hands were folded on the silver skull of her furled parasol,
and her long white gloves lay on the edge of the step near the
point of the sword her laughing nephew was trying to steady.

'Please, Cap-e-ten, one more time,' the little Italian was
pleading, the big velvet bow nodding. He made a circle with
thumb and forefinger before retreating under the black cloth.

The new Captain muttered, but struck the same posture,
worrying that the moustache might have been allowed to go
too far on that leave. It certainly amused Laura.

Beyond the photographer's black bulk was the wishing stone,
its crude circle filled with light above the shining curve of the
river, and beyond the river, on the hill above the Home Farm,
the three granite standing stones, pillars of fire. Hadn't virgins
been sacrificed there, at sunset?

'Zee profile! Zee profile!' a muffled voice was pleading.

He was looking left, at button boots swinging as his sister
shredded the long pink trumpets of honeysuckle that had
wandered from stone to iron. Aunt Carlotta still kept her spine
clear of iron, but poor Mama was panting, like the terrier by
her trailing hand, flesh submerging the wedding band. Poor
Mama just couldn't cope.

And she was thinking the same, watching her son posing,
who had only been home a fortnight. Princess Louise, Mar-
chioness of Argyll, was such a thoughtful person. Look how
she threw her home open to artists, and she was so interested
in the higher education of women. Yet she was having such
a trying time with her husband, the Duke of Argyll's heir. Oh,
clever, but typical Campbell. She could easily write to Princess Louise, explaining how they were placed, and of course
it was really *her* regiment. But Niall simply wouldn't hear of
such a letter. Maybe he was wanting away because of the
tragedy about to darken their door, though they would all have
to face up to it, as Carlotta kept saying. But why should he
want away when there was some benefit in it for him, and for
her too, thank God. He was a good son, so patient with his
sister. And he was a handsome man, taking after his father,
though taller, not so stout. She'd asked him where they were
going after Dublin, and when he said he'd heard nothing, she
knew he was telling the truth. But he did think there was a
good chance of getting back to depot at Stirling Castle, which
would put Invernevis very near. Or was he just saying that,

to please her? Because Carlotta, who was the clever one, the one who really read *The Times*, kept insisting with evident satisfaction that war with South Africa was only months, weeks away. She didn't understand the Boers, but Carlotta had assured her that they were of the brute creation, bibles in one hand, guns in the other. Carlotta knew everything, and *such* energy. So much time spent trying to train Laura, so busy as housekeeper, and yet she had started on another pamphlet on temperance. Or was it a book this time?

No, surely not South Africa and savages, after her own experiences in India. She might have to write to the Princess tomorrow, but making sure to ask after her dear mother the Queen. If only she would come their way on her next visit to Balmoral. After all, they had had her at Taymouth. Oh, they could soon put her up in the Blue Room when it was all over upstairs. But the heat: the place was like a furnace. Heat like this simply *had* to escape.

Her fingertips touched scorching gravel, then heaving hair. The light was hurting her eyes, making the wishing stone shake. Surely the Italian would be done soon. And Laura: couldn't she stop fidgeting, ruining the honeysuckle that had been so difficult to train? The palpitations were starting up again, though Dr MacNiven hadn't seemed perturbed. She fumbled in the layers of her lap, found the small heart-shaped gold box under Kipling, the other arm still supporting the parasol, but aching, aching. She was suddenly conscious of the boulder-strewn slope above her straw hat in the eerie silence. Was something about to happen upstairs? That would be more merciful, and would keep Niall at home. Her heart was making wicker quake. She popped the pill into her mouth, past the difficult new teeth. A little brandy, when she went upstairs before dinner. Oh, purely medicinal, though Carlotta would never need to find out. She would have to get the coachman to take away the bottles; it was amazing how they accumulated. But such heat and light. Just like those stagnating days in Kamptree in the Central Province, gasping in the squalid barracks for Sandy to return from manœuvres, going down on her knees to get home. Well, here they were, but what use was it when he couldn't raise his head from the pillow, when he had to be sponged down three times a day, yelling because of the sores? Only thunder could release the tension, break the tight bands round her breasts.

The flash brought down the parasol, and her elbow jarred on gravel, making the terrier show its teeth.

'Lightning,' she said thankfully, rearranging her layered skirt, Kipling face-down on stone now.

'No, Mama,' the Captain said, laughing, stepping down as Signor Faccenda's fawn-like face emerged from its black hide. His little fist held the spent magnesium torch he had decided to use because of the dimness of the porch.

And then there was a rumble from behind the mountain, like heavy furniture being shifted.

'The thunder – at last,' Mama murmured.

But poor Mama had to be denied again, for her son saw the soiled plume above the trees.

'No, Mama, an echo. Blasting at the quarry.'

Mama was very put out. 'I don't know why we agreed to the lease,' she said indignantly, her hands tugging.

'Drunken Irishmen. Worse than the iron furnace, and it was hell,' was Aunt Carlotta's contribution, her lips a thin tight line. 'Give them Home Rule and let them kill each other on their own soil. It was *your* husband who brought them here, Constance.'

'But it does bring in a good deal,' the younger of Invernevis reminded them.

The Photographer to Society was now shouldering the tripod to the gig round the corner where the horse had hooded its eyes against gravel. He came back for the spent plates.

'Remember: a dozen copies, large size,' Mama warned from her litter of silk. 'Now you may go round to the back door and ask Cook for some tea.'

'I shall bring zem myself.' And he was walking backwards, bowing, frowning because he had hoped to study his subject further over silver and Spode.

'Common little Italian,' Carlotta said. 'He'll cheat us, Constance.'

'But Colonel Hooker recommended him,' Mama groaned. 'He said he took splendid portraits. We needn't pay unless you're entirely satisfied.'

'We shall see,' Carlotta promised grimly. 'Colonel Hooker is apt to exaggerate.'

'I think I'll take a last look at the river,' the new Captain said, in case there was going to be an argument, and because he wanted out of the uniform.

'Don't be late for dinner,' Mama warned, disappointed. 'Remember it's at six.'

'I'm coming too,' Laura said eagerly, sliding from her seat, but Aunt Carlotta's look kept her back.

'Go to the school-room for the books, girl. We will read in the sun.'

Carrying one of his father's green-heart rods, he went down the lawn, in his own tartan, but with a tight knot in his round collar because Aunt Carlotta frowned on slovenliness. Though the drought had reduced the river to ripples round the massive boulders tossed from the nearby mountain in the tantrum of creation, there was always hope that he could beat his father's record, fifty-six pounds of preserved salmon mounted behind curved glass above the marble table in the front hall, where the fishing book was kept open.

The seventy yards of stepping stones of the Summer House Pool, the best on their beat, showed like the spine of a prehistoric creature that had crawled from the mountain to cool and fossilize. He crossed them carefully, and had been thrashing sluggish water with the smallest brightest fly for half an hour when Laura came skipping down the lawn. He made a sign for silence, and she sat in the octagonal summer house, its glass gone in storm. She was carrying the illustrated book that Aunt Carlotta had insisted on in return for liberation from lessons on her brother's last day.

But his sister could never settle. Soon the book of saints and martyrs was abandoned on the slatted seat and, wide arms dipping, she was wobbling across the big stones. He called on her to be careful, but the button boot failed to stretch to stone and she was splashing ashore, laughing, though Aunt Carlotta would impose bread and water.

He tugged off the boots and turned their small dark mouths to the sun. She hadn't really scared the fish. They would be resting where water still moved, cooling stone, these ghosts of the strong and beautiful of the spring run, spent fish that would become big leapers again, when next he came home.

She was making a chain of the daisies, nipping the stalks with a grimy nail, threading them with fumbling fingers, flowers losing their heads. The insubstantial chain was looped round her neck, the yellow centre steadied, to be mirrored in her skin. Her bare heels bounced off baked turf in the direction of the mountain, the insects around sounding like a chanter practising a lament.

'I saw the ghost again last night,' she announced, the daisy chain now hopelessly fankled in the gold ringlets.

He was always so patient with her.

'The green lady, the one in the picture on the landing. She came and bent over my bed, and put her hand on my forehead, like Mama used to do, only Mama's hand was warm. You know what it's like when you stick your fingers into a water-ice? That's what we're having for dinner. The new scullery-maid told me, but I wasn't to let on to Aunt Carlotta that I knew. If you don't want yours, can I have it?'

He did not want her ever to lose the lisp, the freckles round the snub nose, the gold ringlets Aunt Carlotta trained with heated iron. It could, of course, be a cheeky little face.

'If Aunt Carlotta catches you near the kitchen – ' he warned, leaving her to imagine the rest.

'But the new maid's *nice*. Her name's Maggie. Duncan the ghillie's her father. He helps me to catch minnows.'

'And Mama,' he said, seeing that his warning wasn't getting through. 'She'd be *so* angry. You mustn't upset Mama, not at such a time, with Father so ill.'

'Is he going to die?' she asked casually, decapitating daisies to clear her ringlets.

'That depends on God,' was all he could tell her.

'Aunt Carlotta won't allow me to go near him, but I looked in,' she said proudly. And, eyes flashing with the wonder of it: 'He's in a tent, on the top of his bed.'

'You didn't touch him!' he cried, getting her by the shoulder.

But the gold ringlets shook in denial, and she turned back to flowers.

'Laura, you mustn't!' he implored. 'Promise me you won't ever go near his room again – not even touch the door handle. If you don't promise, I won't bring you anything the next time I come home.'

'I want a doll,' she said, determined.

'All right, you'll get a doll, the biggest doll I can find, if only you'll promise.' His voice was hardening with irritation.

But the bargain seemed to satisfy her, and she promised. He lay back, so relieved. Her face brooded as she bent to break off another flower.

'Niall, why doesn't Aunt Carlotta get married? Colonel

17

Hooker asked her; I heard.'

He laughed at her listening at doors. 'Because she's quite happy as she is, looking after you and Mama. Isn't that enough?'

But it wasn't, apparently.

'Aunt Carlotta's cruel,' she said vehemently. 'She kills moths and gives me bread and water.'

'That's because you don't do what you're told,' he said, but without conviction.

She rolled over on to her back and shielded her eyes with a thin freckled arm. A grasshopper whirred, like the drawing-room clock when it was going to chime.

'If you didn't come back, and I was left with Aunt Carlotta – '

The twin peaks of the mountain above the house were white throughout summer. Today they stood out like two candles. The grasshopper had stopped on a blade inches from his hand.

'Of course I'll be back,' he scorned, putting his arm round her shaking shoulders. 'I'm only going into barracks, and I'll be home for Christmas.'

'With the biggest doll you can find,' she added anxiously.

'I promise.'

'It has to have long hair I can comb out,' Laura warned. 'Black hair, like Maggie the new maid has.'

And then, when the daisies were reduced to strewn petals, the stable clock which Mama had raised two summers before for Queen Victoria's Diamond Jubilee chimed five times behind the house.

The button boots were almost dry, so they went home the long way, along the river bank. At *Poll Criadha*, the Clay Pool, Laura touched his hand for stillness, wide-eyed at the wonder of small birds walking on the smooth bottom.

'Oh, they'll drown! Go in and save them, Niall!'

'Water-ouzels can't drown,' he said, laughing though she was so anxious. 'They'll come up for air when they need it.'

Casan Dubh was the black gorge where the river ran between sheer rock, trees casting chill shadows. Laura hurried him past that pool into which their uncle, the laird, beset by doubts about existence, had cast himself. *Poll Dubh*, the Black Pool, fed it, and that was no place to linger either.

They reached the hump-backed, three-spanned bridge that General Wade had thrown across the river early in the previous

18

century as part of his network for the military invasion of the Highlands. Duke Cumberland's dragoons had crossed it after Culloden because the Invernevis chieftain had been 'out' with Prince Charles Edward Stuart. Having stacked the oil paintings and furnishings on carts, the dragoons had saved the nails for straightening before scattering the stones of one of the most beautiful mansions in the west, but the heir had rebuilt.

The Macdonalds of Invernevis claimed as their progenitor Angus, son of John, Earl of Ross and Lord of the Isles. Angus was murdered in Inverness *circa* fourteen hundred and ninety by Diarmid O'Caibre, an Irish harper who cut his master's throat with a long knife. The Dean of Knoydart raged in poetry:

> By thee was destroyed the king of Islay, a
> man who dealt wine and silver; whose locks
> were fresh and crisp, thou head of Diarmid O'Caibre.

While Macdonald crones were wailing the *coronach* over Angus's washed corpse, the throat stitched with gut, the Irish harper was transported to the new lands of Invernevis. Roped between two stallions which were whipped north and south, his limbs sundered, and his screams, incorporated into local folklore, became the portent of death of the Invernevis chieftain.

They were leaning together over Wade's Bridge, looking down into *Linne Bhuidhe*, the Yellow Pool because of the profusion of marsh marigolds on its bank, near Deirdre's Bog, which had swallowed the crazed wife of the Culloden chieftain. The salmon rolled in agonizing siesta, their big backs out of the reduced water. The twenty superior pools of the Invernevis beat obligingly curved in towards the house, a sickle of water that straightened and narrowed to the salt-water loch on which the railway company had put a pleasure steamer *The Maid of Invernevis*, now beating down to the last train. At the mouth of the river, where village chapel and big house burial ground were, the salmon nets could be seen, drying on their poles like the webs of huge spiders, and above their frail membranes, by penny ferry across wide water but still Invernevis land, the growing scar of the granite quarry where two hundred Irish navvies blasted and sawed paving slabs for the

19

streets of Glasgow.

Niall's eyes went downriver, through *Casan Dubh*, where the river curved into *Poll an Roin*, the Seal Pool, though none had been seen there in living memory because of vigilant guns at the river mouth. Then *Linne na Craoibh Daraich*, the Oak Tree Pool because of what shaded it. It was a spearing place for clean-run salmon, though that barbaric method had (he hoped) been abandoned. And that pool had another name, *Ath-nan-Crodhan*, the Ford of Hooves, because an Invernevis laird threatened by a hackbut had chosen that watery path to freedom. The Oak Tree Pool emptied into *Linne Curraigh*, the Cruive Pool, where in olden times a *curragh*, or skin boat, had ferried to and fro Invernevis House in the absence of a bridge, the English rendering ambiguous, to show that some travellers were stopped by the pool, for there the stone finger (once wattle) of a *cruive* or salmon trap stuck out.

His eyes swung the two hundred yards up the sloping lawn to the house under the two-thousand-foot mountain. The three-storied crow-stepped whitewashed building of bulging bay windows and tall cluttered chimneys hurt his eyes in the sun, but when he shaded them he could make out the horizontal grey shape of Mama, like a salmon stranded on gravel. But Aunt Carlotta, being all white, was absorbed by the walls.

He looked up, above the house, to the straggling plantation where the roe-deer mustered on freezing nights, and the pheasants sheltered before being driven down for the guns. Then the sheer slope of scree, studded with sheep. The silence was uncanny, like waiting for a battle to begin, a puff of smoke, then the roar as stone landslided, destroying his inheritance, Father's white tent swept away, Mama crushed by boulders but somehow, miraculously, Aunt Carlotta surviving, straight backed, with her white parasol intact, among the ruins. How hot it was, he thought, putting two fingers inside his collar, trying to ease the brass stud. And suddenly, as he looked again, it was like a skull, the bay windows black sockets, the ivy dried blood on the forehead. His sweat turned to chill, and his knees began to give. It was no longer the present, and it was no longer Invernevis.

But Laura was tugging at his sleeve, taking him to the other side of the narrow bridge that broke the axles of unaccustomed gigs. Wade's Bridge was the boundary. Upriver the twenty pools acquired by Colonel Walter Campbell, using East Indies money, and above his beat, but on the opposite side from Invernevis House and not yet screened by young pines, his grotesque castellated mansion of Branglin still in the making, though its foundations had been laid a decade before. Yet another wing was being added, this time at the back, to accommodate his latest purchase, a motor car, and there was talk of another marvel, electric lighting, with the river harnessed. If that happened, Invernevis would sue for ruined spawning.

The hundred yards of wide turbulent water upriver beyond Wade's Bridge formed the Disputed Pool, so called because the abutting estates had never been able to agree ownership. Rather than enter into expensive litigation in Edinburgh, the arrangement was that the proprietors took it in turn to fish from alternate banks on alternate weeks. In a wrong week, a hooked Invernevis fish going up under Wade's Bridge was technically Colonel Campbell's catch, but that worm fisher with the whipless rod preferred cut lines to trespass.

'I dare you to cast,' Laura giggled.

But it wasn't their week, and well she knew it.

The river rose from a dark pass where cairns commemorated a ferocious clan battle. It was from this pass that the new railway and old drove road emerged. The rails followed the curve of the mountain's flank half a mile east of Invernevis House, and a new iron bridge, for which he had got compensation, carried it across Campbell's beat. The railway followed the river for several hundred yards before curving again to cross the moor behind the standing stones. The drove road came straight out of the pass and before crossing Wade's Bridge indented right, for Invernevis House. Road and railway converged in the village, a measured mile from Wade's Bridge, according to the small tilted pillar by Niall's brogue.

'Let's paddle,' Laura said, putting the button boots on the parapet. And, tugging: 'Oh, come on, it's your last day. Nobody will see.'

But he was twenty-seven now, and a Captain, not to mention the heir of the dying laird. Still, he was going away, and she was so insistent. He had his garters in his sporran and was rolling down his green hose when the rumbling cloud of dust at the avenue entrance revealed Signor Faccenda at the reins of the gig hired from the Invernevis Arms. At least the horse knew to take Wade's Bridge very slowly, for its sudden stop almost put the little Italian over the parapet. Though his wide-brimmed velvet hat circled in salute, the Photographer to Society evidently didn't recognize his recent subject, for the long whip in his little fist flicked, urging on, over the bridge, up to village and train. But he happened to glance down at the river and saw, with the speed of an instantaneous shutter, an image his camera could never hope to capture, but which was snapped up by memory.

For Laura was already in the Yellow Pool, her dress hitched up, curling her toes round cool pebbles, long thin legs stalking, the water like weak clammy hands round her ankles. And though Signor Faccenda hauled on the reins, the headstrong horse tore him away from the vision of the nymph wading through sunlight, with ringlets like gold chains weighing her down. What an illustration it would make for a new edition of *The Water Babies*, or, more deshabillée, for one of those poses of young girls certain gentlemen were willing to pay large sums for.

Niall was barefooted when she yelled:

'Look what I've got!'

Before he could get down she was heaving the salmon out from showering water mixed with sunlight. It thrashed in her arms like a child in a tantrum, wide tail slapping at a face on which fear and pride fought. She screamed, the big pincered jaws opened and shut, eyeball swivelling in the outrageous light and then, as stone betrayed her, it exploded back into its element, drenching.

'That will teach you,' he said, laughing through sheer fear, helping the dazed girl to the bank and, when no damage was discovered, up to the bridge where the boots stood splayed on the parapet.

'Mama said we must not be late,' he reminded her. 'And maybe I *will* leave my water-ice for you.'

Because her feet were wet, and a toe trickling blood where stone had retaliated, the button boots had to be carried, and there were the clinging scales on her sodden dress to explain to Aunt Carlotta.

In one hand he held his rod, but the other was for his sister. They went up between the irregular lines of trees said to have been planted by a drunken Invernevis laird in darkness, crumbling stone pillars and a gate off its hinges where privacy began. The wind-bowed tops of some of the oldest larches in

Scotland made a cool dim tunnel, with sunlight filtering where branches failed, patterning the leaves on an avenue pocked in the centre by hooves, rutted each side by wheels. Invisible pigeons made their soft throaty love-calls so close to scorn. His sister's sodden dress was taking the shape of a body beginning to curve and thrust at sixteen, breasts lashed into obedience by whalebone and a lace tightened in Aunt Carlotta's firm fists, her foot braced on iron, but he wanted Laura's small trusting face to stay in childhood, keeping its freckles, wide eyes of innocent wonder, so that the next time he came home, it would still be the same. The sun was burning that day into memory, trees etched against the startling blue, wayside flowers in sharp focus, but he knew that he would have to pay for it in time to come, when he tried to retrieve that day in the darkness of depression, crying: *why cannot it be the same again?* And to save something of that day for both of them, he stepped aside, drew his *sgian dubh* from his hose, and prised out bark, leaving the impression:

It made her clap her hands and dance round the tree, her shrieks proclaiming her immortality, but mocked by the mountain.

At the blind bend on the avenue, a place of sudden chill, the trees gave way to tightly packed rhododendrons, their gnarled tendrils like old hands offering blooms. Laura stopped to sniff, and over the gold-draped shoulder, inside the delicate trumpet, he could see the speckles of blood where the bee violated. The shed petals of the past had compacted into undisturbed black loam beneath, tunnels to nowhere. It was stifling, so many trumpets blaring their scents in brazen summer.

But sunlight and sky at last. To the right, the walled garden, the peaches under glass at the mercy of the mountain, the crab apples still too green to be struck from moss-upholstered boughs with the fishing rod, the bees at their conical houses, busy transforming flowers for Mama's sweet tooth. And behind the walled garden, the stables, with the diamond-patterned face of the Jubilee clock peeping from behind pines. On still days it kept the village right. The dying laird had wanted it stopped because he could not bear to count the cheerful strokes day and night, but Aunt Carlotta would allow no interference with time and change.

And then the track branching to the back door, with the green-slatted larder, zinc gauze baffling the wasps, the widening sweep of hurtful gravel to the front where Mama and Aunt Carlotta were still braving the heat-wave. He saw his sister round to the back door, where the cook would give her safe conduct, and then he went out front, acknowledging Aunt Carlotta's scolding, Mama's breathless concern, announcing that he was going up to change into his uniform, would be down for dinner in half an hour.

It was cold salmon from before the drought, and water-ices which would not survive in the large room of sombre mirrors giving up the ghosts of ancestral silver to dark brooding wood. And Mama, missing a bone, had to be slapped hard on the back by Aunt Carlotta, so cool though her sister's face was blue. Laura's laughter lost her the water-ice her brother was leaving because he had no stomach for the separation. They went out to wicker and iron again.

'Your brother hasn't come to see you off,' Mama complained, clutching silk.

'Typical,' Aunt Carlotta snorted, spine parallel with iron.

'There he is. Look.' Laura had slid from her seat and was pointing across the river to arcs of sunlight swinging down the Home Farm field below the standing stones, the hay falling like gold pages, being gathered by long-skirted women with bright handkerchiefs round their brows and Gaelic songs at their lips. 'The one on the left,' Laura said.

Niall shielded his eyes, but could not be sure.

'Go in, child, while I speak with your brother,' Mama ordered, and though Laura appealed, did as Aunt Carlotta confirmed, passing with bent head, biting a finger, into the dim porch.

'It cannot be allowed to go on,' Mama began, her hands angry now. 'Aunt Carlotta tells me he was drunk again last night.'

'And fell on the back stairs,' her informant added.

'What have we done to deserve this?' asked Mama, spreading her hands as though someone hiding round the corner of

24

the house had the answer. 'He doesn't eat with us; he eats with the servants at the Home Farm; and very often he doesn't sleep here. He *could* help here, but he works in the fields for a tenant. Aunt Carlotta thinks MacPherson's trying to make a match with his eldest girl because the ones in the village aren't good enough. God knows, it reflects on me because some will be wondering if he's our own flesh and blood – '

'Don't upset yourself, Mama,' her other son advised, staying the silk shoulder. 'Alexander will change; you'll see.'

Mama's glistening face was upturned in anguish. 'But if anything happens to you he'll get the place and ruin us in a year. After *so* long.' And, collecting herself: 'No, it's clear to me, and Aunt Carlotta agrees: he has to be disinherited. Then, if you don't have children or whatever, it goes to cousin Hubert. But nothing's been done, and here you are, going off, maybe into a war.' At the last word, a fist brought bunched lace from the silk layers.

The idea of disinheriting his younger brother had never entered Niall's mind, and it showed, especially when it came from Mama. He wasn't really close to Alexander. They had gone their separate ways early, Niall to school in England, Alexander to dodge a succession of tutors at home, following the plough instead of Aunt Carlotta's prescribed texts. Alexander hated wearing the kilt, and he hated sitting in the dining-room. He preferred old trousers and heaped plates in the Home Farm kitchen where he could use his fingers without rebuke. He had also changed his accent to suit his new environment, and was learning Gaelic. And there had been some dreadful rows with Aunt Carlotta over his drinking and easy rejection of the family faith. Women also came into it somewhere.

His train was due in under an hour, and Niall had neither the time nor the inclination to consider the implications of disinheritance. Mama's fear of him being killed was part of being the parent of a serving soldier. Not that he wouldn't welcome a bit of action. He had enlisted in '91; till '94 he had helped to garrison Edinburgh Castle; then Aldershot; now Dublin; all in the line of duty, but dull. He had been following the worsening political situation in South Africa in the newspapers, since April, when the *Uitlanders* or immigrants had sent their petition to the Queen, demanding redress for their grievances under Kruger. The Queen had accepted the petition, but Sir Alfred Milner, the High Commissioner in South Africa, clearly wanted the Boers crushed. And now two battalions of infantry had been ordered to Natal, to reinforce the British army of only twelve thousand men scattered throughout that land of dust and diamonds. There was a good chance of Princess Louise's going, since they had been there before, in '79, when they put down the Zulus at Ginginhlovo. The Boers shouldn't be any more difficult and, after all, *they* were white men, though Aunt Carlotta demurred. She wanted to see Kruger the false prophet crushed. Cecil Rhodes was the new messiah, and to show her faith Aunt Carlotta had most of her money in De Beers and Consolidated Goldfields. Her new topic was now the treacherous Captain Dreyfus.

But Mama was still going on about disinheritance.

'You are forgetting that father is still alive,' he said, to settle the matter, but only giving work for her lower lip.

'Alive, but for how long? Dr MacNiven has warned us, and for his sake as well as ours I hope it's soon. But you'd better go and say goodbye to him,' she said in a tone suggesting desertion, before the waters broke.

It was the moment he had been fearing all day, but it had to be done. He went in under the ivy, through the porch where a hollowed-out, polished tree trunk from the estate waited to receive shooting sticks, cromachs and parasols. Then into the high dim front hall, his father's record salmon to the left, on the dull wall above the marble slab with claws for feet, which had frightened him in childhood.

To his right, between the cut-glass-handled doors to dining-room and library, the wide fireplace with its fender of gleaming brass teeth, and, flanking the marble hearth, brass nymphs in flowing robes on rocky seats, inclining their braided heads to the lyres their long fine fingers were tuning. The inverted helmet of the scuttle stood beside crossed poker and tongs. Burnished metal was one of Aunt Carlotta's obsessions.

Above the fireplace, the crossed Invernevis standards with the shot-riddled linen limp along wormed poles, the coat of arms speckled with blood on these relics of Culloden. And, as a frieze round the hall, the heads of stags brought down on Invernevis lands by Invernevis lairds for a century and a half, matted hair harbouring the moth, eyes of split marbles, brass plates screwed below their shaggy throats giving the slayer's

26

name, place and date of execution. The majority were royals, but one or two hinds peeped out. Their thin delicate faces surprised by time always reminded him of Laura.

To the left, through the half-open door of the drawing-room, he could see the gold-coloured pipes of the oak-encased organ that Aunt Carlotta had had installed at her own expense, selling Consolidated shares. The idea had been germinating for years, but had consistently met violent opposition from her brother-in-law, who didn't want the drawing-room turned into a chapel, but when he had retreated upstairs she had gone ahead, and he was too weak to come down and stop the installation. Now he was forced to lie in bed, listening to her treading out 'Nearer My God To Thee'.

With the stairs about to begin, a chandelier hanging on tarnished chains, a clutter of antlers held together by circles of bone and, impaled on the horns, holders of crudely carved ivory, clotted with yellow wax. His father had made it, from stags he had brought down on the mountain, but it had proved too dangerous to refill, and the smoke had discoloured the ceiling. Aunt Carlotta had demanded it down because it was pulling out the ornate plaster, but his father had dared.

In front of him the wide staircase, brass rails holding down a green runner, the motif of Grecian urns almost faded, the ragged edges stopped by an upholstery needle supervised by thrifty Aunt Carlotta. And at the foot, where the wall turned to the gloomy door leading to kitchen and servants' quarters, the vertical coffin of a grandfather clock, the brass disc swinging to and fro in its glass guts.

The first landing was dominated by a stained-glass window, depicting a life-sized Invernevis chieftain *circa* eighteen hundred in full regalia, picked out in blue, green and red fragments, the Gaelic motto overhead. It coloured the carpet as he climbed, taking the left turning, to the passage where his ancestors in oils stared down, the earliest ones lacking because looted after Culloden, but some draped in tartan, vigilant hands on the hilts of their swords; past haughty ladies with lockets at their throats to the supreme portrait, the only real beauty that Invernevis could boast, the green-gowned Lady Anne by Raeburn, the green lady Laura claimed to meet on the stairs, under the stained-glass window, which was of her husband. Hands crossed, head and shoulders only, she posed against dramatic darkness that could not absorb the sheen of

27

her long dark hair winding round her throat, the creamy complexion luminous, the almond eyes that seemed to follow you. Only the peremptory mouth and high forehead had been passed down.

More gold-encrusted frames, getting bigger as the century progressed. His grandfather, the fourteenth of Invernevis, pacified in a sunset glen in trews and waistcoat, leaning on a long gun, and with a faithful retinue of assorted dogs, deerhound and spaniel. But, confined in three feet of canvas by a mediocre brush, his uncle, the next chieftain, stared uncomprehendingly, the black waters of *Casan Dubh* closing around. And still there was space left, though his father was too far gone to pose now.

The door of the bedroom was open in the hope that the heat would dissipate through the house. The brocade drapes of the massive four-poster had been replaced by muslin, making it look like a tent. And though the window was wide, the muslin was still in the stifling summer evening, with the river rough silver beyond. All he could see of his father was the black blur of his big beard, its angle suggesting that the face was towards the window.

He stood, not knowing how to go about it. Beyond the foot of the bed the dressing-room gaped, and under a tilted pier-glass a pair of tan riding boots were brought to attention by wide tapering insets of wood, surmounted by brass rings for extraction. They still had spurs on, toothed wheels.

'I've come to say goodbye, Father.'

But there was no movement behind the muslin, no sound in the room except the soft pulse of the carriage clock on the mantelpiece. And then Aunt Carlotta's voice was heard beneath the window, commanding Laura to behave with the feathered bonnet.

'Shut that window,' his father ordered.

He did as he was told.

'The wash-stand drawer. You'll find gloves. Put them on.'

He crossed to mottled marble, moved wood, saw the neat pile of white gloves that Mama had had sent from London. They were of thick material, for big hands.

'Now come over here.'

Only the hands were thrust through the muslin parting, but he saw sufficient to make him feel sick.

'Take the rings,' his father said, spreading his fingers. 'You won't get them when you come back.'

His heart quickened in protest, but he dared not disobey. On his bare knees by the bed, but keeping his eyes averted from what was on the backs, he tried to work the rings over the swollen flesh, the onyx with the Invernevis seal, very old, and the one on the pinkie, a gold serpent swallowing its own tail, sapphires for eyes, which his father had brought back from India.

But the rings wouldn't budge, and he was abandoning the horrible business when the voice behind muslin said:

'There's soap on the wash-stand, but *don't* remove the gloves, whatever you do.'

He dipped his gloved fingers into the floral pitcher, rubbed them on the yellow block of carbolic, crossed to smear two of his father's fingers. The rings passed off easily, but the cold salmon was coming against him.

'It would only upset Mama to wear them now,' his father advised, withdrawing his fingers. 'She does her best, God knows. But that Carlotta's a bitch. I should have kicked her out years ago. Don't hesitate, if there's the slightest trouble. And the regiment: I wouldn't know any of them now.'

Their exchanges had always been brief, to the point, Alexander being the favourite son, the one who was allowed into the library when a new fishing book had arrived, or an oiled rag being pulled through the mouth of a gun. And only Alexander was allowed on the mountain with him. Niall had been sent to Eton, to be toughened up away from Aunt Carlotta's influence, but Alexander had stayed at home. After school Niall had wanted Cambridge, but when he was still a baby the former officer of the 91st Argyllshire Highlanders had put down his heir's name for the regiment, and there was no arguing. Even when he had come of age as a First Lieutenant, his father wouldn't abdicate, though his health was failing, and Aunt Carlotta a fierce ally. But Alexander hadn't been ordered to enlist. His military duties were confined to serving as a private in the local rifle volunteer company of which his father was honorary Lieutenant-Colonel. Thirty Invernevis men, unpaid and with no commitment to serve overseas in the event of war, met at the school at weekends to shoulder rifles in some semblance of drill, and for three weeks every July they went into annual camp on the perimeter of the estate. The Lieutenant-Colonel and Alexander went, and there was a good deal of drinking after shooting contests for which the laird presented inscribed silver medals. Meantime Niall was beginning the long climb towards a Captaincy, convinced that his father's influence was behind the favouritism shown by his commanding officer. He knew nothing about running the estate, and so, when he eventually succeeded, would have nobody to learn from, unless Alexander. He suspected that if it had been possible, his father would have disinherited him and put Alexander in his place.

But his father's health could not stand the pace of horses and whisky. He had come home on leave to find the spurs static at last, and then the muslin drapes going up because of whatever disease he had picked up in the sticky heat of India when he was serving with the 91st in the sixties, before that regiment had amalgamated with the 93rd Sutherland Highlanders to form Princess Louise's Argyll and Sutherland Highlanders. The disease had done something to his skin, hence the strict quarantine, the white gloves that the gardener and ghillie wore to shift, sponge him, though that was agony, apparently. And then the light had begun to hurt, putting the precious river out of bounds. It was already at the brain, Dr MacNiven had said, but in the same breath warned how strong he was, as if Mama didn't know. He was even more of an animal to Aunt Carlotta, and she had not been near his room. It couldn't be long now.

The sky was darkening now, streaked with a burst sun behind the crooked standing stones on the horizon, the river dulling. There was nothing more to say. He dropped the sticky rings into his goat's-hair sporran, sensing that blind eyes behind muslin were following him; and at the door, emotion made him throw up his hand into a sharp salute, bringing his heels together audibly. The black blur turned.

'If there *is* war, remember: it's you or them.'

Outside, Aunt Carlotta was mustering the servants against whitewashed stone, ordering the adjustment of black gaberdine. And Roddy the coachman in his mutton-chop whiskers, high banded hat and too-tight coat was bringing round the gig with the tin trunk white-stencilled with his new rank. Symmers, the watery-eyed old butler with the drink problem discolouring his fleshy face, the swallow-tails shiny from too sedentary a time, was nearest the step. The younger of Invernevis shook hands, moving down the line, Mrs Livingstone the cook rubbing frantically at her apron before her turn came, allowed slippers because of her swollen ankles. Frank the footman, fresh from the city in a mint uniform with green piping, bowed, face surly because permission to cultivate a moustache had been denied by Miss Carlotta, who saw to such things. The maids in their starched aprons, careful curves of lace in the regulation short hair, blushed and curtsied. They were all good Catholics from the Outer Islands, Aunt Carlotta's favourite recruiting ground.

Mama was always difficult to embrace because of the surplus material lanced with pins, not to mention the *eau de toilette* so liberally sprinkled, and Aunt Carlotta only offered a plain cheek. But standing on tiptoe, Laura restored his feathered bonnet and, arms linked round his neck, lifted her button boots from the gravel. Aunt Carlotta pushed her away, and, opening a little bag she had crocheted herself, announced that she had something for her nephew. He closed his eyes and held out his hand as he had been taught in childhood. He felt something cold and when he was allowed to look saw an Iona stone rosary curled like a green snake in his palm.

'It will bring you comfort,' she assured him.

'You didn't have a wish this time!' Mama was calling, and he went obediently to the stone at the lawn's edge and linked his hands through, looking down to the Summer House Pool, then up to the standing stones before closing his eyes. But if you told your wish, it couldn't come true. Besides, it should have been under a new moon.

Then, as he was clambering on to the gig, Farquhar came strutting round the corner of the house, red tassels swinging from the deafening drones, striding up and down gravel, with the expression of a potentate at a hookah. Aunt Carlotta clapped her hands to her ears.

The coachman lifted the limp whip from its socket. As it flicked the flank, thunder crashed behind the mountain and the tense sky split in deluge, swamping Mama's hat before she could be helped indoors. Aunt Carlotta stood on sandstone, braving the cloudburst, daring the servants, calling after Laura.

But she was already running, separated from her brother by the big wheel crunching gravel, the button boots seemingly winged. She ran through downpour past the walled garden where the wheel quietened, but the rhododendron tunnel was too narrow. She darted ahead, broke off the bloom, and, as the gig passed down the avenue, braced herself against the springy bush and leapt. He had the red-speckled bloom before she dropped away from the big wheel, and he had seen the fish scale clinging at her throat.

Chapter Two

But one servant had not come out to see the younger of Invernevis off in the cloudburst, because Miss Carlotta had overlooked the scullery in her round-up.

Well past her elbows in scummed water, Maggie heard the rumble as the pipes slumped. Taking the strand of hair out of the way with a dripping hand, she lifted her head to see Laura racing the big wheel. The window was streaky, and it was only a glimpse from a distance, where the trees began to swallow the avenue, but she thought the new Captain in the feathered bonnet very handsome. The moustache put the finishing touch to the profile.

She rested her red palms on the rough bottom of the full sink and dreamed a journey by train as Laura came through the driving rain, her fists at her eyes. Her frock clung to her legs, showing how thin her ankles were in the button boots. But it wasn't that that made Maggie want to cry. She was nearing the end of her first week's work at the big house, having started on her fifteenth birthday. She had only got the post because her father was ghillie. Ten pounds a year, live in, uniform but not footwear provided, six days a week, hours as necessary, with attendance at chapel compulsory on Sunday mornings, Miss Carlotta, who saw to such things, had warned. On Sunday afternoon she was expected to visit her mother. If she proved a careful worker, she might proceed to the kitchen, and who knew, but to cook eventually. Mrs Livingstone, a stout grey-haired woman of indeterminate age, occupied that position, and she was assisted by an ambitious, unfriendly girl called Elsie, who was not from the district and who did not have Gaelic, the second language of the house, though if Miss Carlotta caught you speaking it, you were for it. It was best to keep out of Mrs Livingstone's way while she was cooking because a slap with a wooden spoon or a Gaelic swear were the least of her assaults, but when another meal was served and approved, she was all right, and even gave Maggie a cup from the cracked brown pot she kept at the corner of the range. When the scullery door was open and the sink empty, Maggie tried to watch the making of dough on the long scrubbed table, but Elsie saw and came to shut the door. Maggie tried not to cry as she listened to the low rumble of the rolling-pin, then the scrape of serrated metal as scones were cut out.

There was such a big staff, she couldn't possibly get to know them all. A good few worked outside, in the garden and at the stables, and some of them had to sleep in, though they had crofts and cottages in the village and behind the house. Miss Carlotta was custodian of their souls as well as house-keeper. Six mornings a week, at seven sharp, she appeared in the servants' hall, in a long black dress, always of silk, with a Missal in her fist, and with bunches of keys on the leather belt at her thin waist which did not require whalebone. Father Macdonald had granted her dispensation to take morning prayers while he struggled for the souls of the villagers at Mass in the chapel by the river mouth. The big table was lifted against the wall, and down on their knees on the cold flagstones, all the servants from butler to scullery-maid heard Miss Carlotta read incomprehensible Latin. Then, breaking into English, she asked deliverance for them from the multi-tude of sins to which servants were prone – lust, drunkenness, laziness, dishonesty. After she had crossed herself they could go to work, while she went to give Mrs Livingstone what pro-visions she needed, or rather, what she thought she needed. For Miss Carlotta was very careful, and always made a note of what she had given out in a little black book with a pencil attached.

Mrs Livingstone would say: 'I need curry powder,' and Miss Carlotta, having consulted her black book, would raise her voice: 'Oh, surely not so soon. You got some ten days ago. You must be putting too much in.' But when Mrs Livingstone said: 'That's all very well, but the Mistress likes her kedgeree well seasoned,' Miss Carlotta would snort, and keys jangling at her belt, would go down the stone passage to the store. Mrs Livingstone would get a small tin, and a warning to make it last. But Elsie bowed and scraped, and got on well with Miss Carlotta.

Maggie hated going to the servants' hall, but would go hungry if she didn't. Mrs Livingstone presided at the head of that long table in the cramped room, its window filled with mountain slope, and a lumpy leather sofa in the corner, by the poor fire. The cook passed down the chipped white plates on to which she tipped the small portions of meat, smothered in gravy, but still tough despite a long time in the pot. For Miss Carlotta stopped the scrag from getting to the gun-dogs, and would lift lids to make sure it was stewing for the servants.

On Miss Carlotta's strict instructions the sexes were segregated, with the girls under Mrs Livingstone occupying one half of the table, and the men under Mr Symmers, the bald old butler who smelt of drink, at the other. The plates were passed from kitchen-maid to table-maid to house-maid, and when they reached Maggie, who sat in the centre of the table, they were passed on to gardener, groom, coachman, her father the ghillie, Frank the footman, and finally Mr Symmers at the end. You couldn't lift gravy with a fork, and when Mrs Livingstone spotted you using your pudding spoon, that was the dumpling gone. You didn't dare join in the conversation, and anyway, you had nothing to say. Your face was scarlet because Frank the footman, a handsome fellow with green piping on his trousers, kept winking at you, and once or twice he came into the scullery and tried to put his arms round your waist, from behind. But you struck out with the sour cloth. And you couldn't make friends because the table-maids were so snooty, the house-maids always giggling when they weren't bruising their shins on coal scuttles. They looked down on Maggie because she didn't wear an apron and lace at her hair, and when they were huddled, whispering, they used Gaelic words she didn't know.

All she could hope for was a smile from her father as he bent to his apple dumpling on the right. He had time now to smoke his pipe after the cup of tea (if Miss Carlotta wasn't about) because there wasn't a laird fishing, and there weren't any guests. The laird was dying, the house-maids who carried the beef tea up and down whispered, wondering why the mistress took the bowl from them at the bedroom door. The laird was supposed to be blind, from a disease he had picked up abroad, before he came into the place, or so Jessie the house-maid had overheard. They quizzed Maggie's father and Ranald the gardener, who helped to lift and wash the laird, but they got nothing out of them, except a warning to mind their own business. That didn't stop them gossiping, however. The laird was finished. As for Master Niall, well, he was very quiet and (wink) very good-looking, but Master Alexander was the real charmer, carrying on with a woman at the Home Farm. Laura was nothing but 'a little bitch, always getting in the way'. And the Mistress? Well, she was scatter-brained and (whisper) getting too fond of the brandy.

Miss Carlotta was the one to watch, the one who would dock your wages if you dropped a plate, and if your apron had a crease, God help you. And if she heard you swear, you were out the door, with no back wages, and very bad references. Because Miss Carlotta was very religious. 'The holy ghost', they called her, for the way she suddenly appeared beside you to give you hell.

She didn't come into the scullery much, but Maggie tried to keep the sink clear. When the thunder came she had dropped a blue crested plate, and even though it had been cracked, she buried it in the bottom of the bin, beside the salmon skeleton. She hadn't wanted to go out and see Master Niall off in case somebody came in and found the plate, and when Miss Carlotta didn't come she was so thankful.

Having scrubbed for ten minutes, she lifted out the last pot and turned it upside down, to let it drain. Her fingertips were scarlet from scouring. It was so hot, even with the rain, but she couldn't get the window open because the paint had stuck and the cords were rotten. The kitchen door was open and she saw a glass dish in the centre of the scrubbed table, but when she went to look, seeing that Mrs Livingstone and Elsie had gone upstairs, the water-ice for which she had prepared the pail of salt, her fingers raw, had turned to mush. It made her cry.

And, as the thunderstorm broke above the mountain, another young man in the uniform of Princess Louise's was taking his leave of his mother, but instead of a feathered bonnet he wore a glengarry with two cock feathers, a green doublet, white spats and boots. His waist belt showed that he was a piper, and he carried a swagger-stick which he struck impatiently against his knee as he waited for the gig from the big house to appear.

Donald Macdonald, Maggie's brother, had been in the volunteer rifles under the laird, where his piping skills were greatly appreciated after shooting contests, when the stone jar of whisky was circulating. But he wanted more serious soldiering, and, talking to the young laird on his last leave, had eagerly accepted the suggestion that he enlist as a regular in Princess Louise's. Now, with the young laird a Captain, Donald was to be his company's piper and also his orderly. It couldn't have worked out better.

He was very like his sister, small, with dark hair and fine clear features that seemed to deny a crofting tradition. The kilt confirmed that he had not yet filled out into manhood, and in fact, in his enthusiasm to enlist, he had made himself eighteen, a year older.

He stood at the door of the croft, watching the rain sweep down the mountain. When it began to drum on his small tin trunk his mother leaned from the low door.

'Wait inside,' she advised. 'There's no sense in getting your nice uniform wet. Standing out there won't make him come any quicker.'

But though he went in beside her, he kept putting his head out, the cock feathers buckling in the rain.

'He hasn't got much time,' he muttered.

'Be careful of that watch,' his mother warned. 'Your father only gave it to you because you're a real piper now, with the young laird.'

He looked at the timepiece on his palm, a hunter without decoration. He turned it over, touched the spring and the back swung open. Though the poor light prevented him from reading the inscription on the burnished disc, he knew it by heart:

FROM LIEUT-COL MACDONALD OF INVERNEVIS
TO DUNCAN MACDONALD, GHILLIE
FOR 25 YEARS FAITHFUL SERVICE
JUNE 1898

'I didn't want to take it,' he said, the feeling of foreboding that had been with him all day growing with the crashing thunder, almost overhead now. He had spent the afternoon helping to harvest at the Home Farm, the next in line to Master Alexander, but not joining in the Gaelic songs when the line of scythes moved down, shedding hay which was gathered by the long-skirted women, crooning as if cradling children. He should have been happy, seeing that he was going into the young laird's company, as his piper, and though the Gaelic songs moved him in that landscape that he loved, with the sun in his face and sweet mown hay in his nostrils, the gathering women's shadows were sprawled on the stubble, arms wide like shot soldiers. Across the curved steel of the river, at the big house, he could see a kilted figure for a long time in the porch, and a black thing that looked like a Maxim gun being pointed at him. But perhaps it was the standing stones on the hill above, a place avoided by the locals, though the big house shot grouse there. Whatever it was, it made him feel apprehensive, the sound of stone snecking Alexander's sweep of steel setting his nerves on edge, so that he had quit, saying he had to go and get ready, though he had hours.

'You'd get the watch sooner or later,' his mother said factually. 'He wanted to be here, to see you off, but he had to go up to the big house to see the young laird off, and to help lift his father later. No one else will do it.'

'Why?' Donald wondered aloud.

'We don't speak of such things,' his mother said. 'What goes on at the big house is never discussed. But try and help Master Niall, seeing you're to be his orderly. As long as he doesn't do anything foolish, like women or drink. Let the father and Master Alexander be a lesson to you.'

But he wasn't following her. The cock feathers touched the lintel as he sheltered beside his mother, a small frail woman with worn hands and a perpetual apron. She did most of the work on the croft, milking the cow, planting and scything, and that was why he felt bad about leaving home. But Master Niall had suggested it, and there could be no refusing. On his last leave he had even given Donald a sovereign to go to Stirling Castle to enlist.

He looked down the slope at the big Welsh slates of the iron furnace streaming with rain. Its closure because of cheaper methods of smelting elsewhere had put a lot of locals out of work, and robbed the laird of a ready market for his woods. But the unemployed would rather starve than cross water to seek work among the two hundred Irish navvies in the granite quarry, blasting and hacking, squatting in hovels in which rats ran along the stained tables, sharing their thick pieces. When they got their wages on Saturday night they came over to drink and brawl in the Invernevis Arms, to accost women in the village, and on Sunday morning the track to the ferry, where the chapel was, was littered with inert figures in moleskin trousers and red neckerchiefs clutching stone jars. It made Donald worry about Maggie his sister, because the route to the ferry was past their croft. She had just started at the big house, in the scullery, but 'you have to start somewhere', his mother had said. Though Maggie was young, she was wise enough for her years.

No, it was his mother who was the worry. Her coughing had kept him awake as he lay in the low-ceilinged room that also served as kitchen and living-room. His father could remember when it had an earthen floor, with the livestock being brought in to sleep among their owners. *Casad cruaidh na caitheamh*, the slow wasting cough, they called it in Gaelic. She seemed to be shrinking, and her skin resembled the ochre washed out of the heap of spent charcoal at the furnace when it rained, staining the grass around. But she kept assuring him that she was fine, and wouldn't hear of him sending for Dr MacNiven, though he had money left.

As he leaned out to see the gig approaching, the pair of horses bending their heads into the driving rain, he put his arm round his mother's shoulders and pulled her tight. Maybe he shouldn't have enlisted, but she had wanted it, so that he could be with the young laird, as his father had been with the old one for so many years.

The gig shuddered to a halt, the big wheel spraying what had been dust minutes before. The new Captain in the cape, his feathered bonnet now in the tin trunk, smiled down and Mrs Macdonald bowed. Donald lifted his tin box beside the other and was about to climb on to the back when he remembered something. Hurrying past his mother, he emerged with the short black wooden box resembling a child's coffin which contained his pipes. He hauled himself up on to one of the facing seats and sat, steadying the black box between his feet as the whip flicked through the rain, the gig lurching forward. His mother waved, and then she was gone, but he kept looking back.

He was sodden in seconds because he had no cape. The spokes made a sniggering sound as they went down the long narrow lane flanked by hawthorn hedges, the gig rocking in the ruts, making tin collide. He raised his eyes and saw the curtain of rain pulled over the two peaks.

The road to the station turned off right before the railway bridge carried forward to Main Street. Despite the thunderstorm a good many villagers had turned out to see the young laird off. Most of them were bareheaded, hugging upturned collars and shawls to their throats as they huddled, staring at the clanking monster whose mechanics had closed the iron furnace.

The train was already ten minutes late, but that didn't matter because the laird of Invernevis had allowed the railway to trespass in return for small concessions such as a station in the village, and a moveable timetable for departures from the big house.

Hugh had worked at the iron furnace, feeding charcoal, but now he was in the uniform of a porter. He held open the door for the young laird, but as he was climbing Father Macdonald pushed his way through the people to say how sorry he was not to have managed up to the house because of a funeral in the village. He was a burly man, receding grey hair revealing a distinguished forehead above a thin, alert face, and to Aunt Carlotta he could do no wrong. He shook hands and gave God's blessing, moving his fingers rapidly between forehead and heart.

At the end of the train Donald the orderly was loading the two tin boxes but would take the pipes himself. Hugh slammed the door and, as metal clanked, the younger of Invernevis stood waving until rain and distance forced him inside. He spread out his cape before sitting at the window.

The train was running above the darkening river, making steam for the long pass. In the warm kitchen of the Home Farm above, Alexander, second son, hushed the glass of whisky on the vibrating board before plucking a card from his hand. Kate, MacPherson's dark-haired daughter, watched as her father won the hand.

Niall's face was pressed to the speeding window on the other side of the track. The storm had brought darkness, and the Summer House Pool was a black curve below, the mountain a black mass. And then, as a clap of thunder shook the train, lightning zigzagged down the mountain, illuminating Invernevis House as though a thousand lamps were suddenly turned up, dazzling the heir. Then darkness again.

But at his own third-class window further back in the train Donald searched in vain for the weak lamp of the croft.

The train whistle shrieked, not because of the dark pass approaching, but because the younger of Invernevis was aboard. In her first-floor bedroom to the front of the house

Mama heard the shriek. She was squatting in a tin bath in front of the new fire while the maid scrubbed with the brush lathered with carbolic till the spots on her mistress's back began to bleed. But Mama felt nothing but benevolence because she had half a decanter of brandy inside her, and the other half was hidden.

Several doors away, Laura heard the shriek. She was stripping for her bath, with the house-maid standing by with the big wide towel but staring, staring. The button boots had been kicked off, the salmon-scented dress was dropping when she saw the first gold hairs, curled like the spring in her father's watch.

'I can bath myself from now on,' she said.

If Aunt Carlotta heard the shriek she did not show it. She was in her nightdress, sitting at her dressing-table while Elsie the kitchen-maid, also in night attire, drew a brush down through the housekeeper's long fine hair. And as the girl glanced over Miss Carlotta's shoulder to the oval mirror, she saw closed eyes and moving lips.

Maggie the new scullery-maid had climbed to the small room she shared with Elsie, almost under the slates. She was letting her drab dress drop when she remembered that the bin in the scullery was pig-swill for the Home Farm, set off against the milk bill by Miss Carlotta. Though she was terrified, there was nothing to be done but to pull up her dress again, take the candle, and creep down the back stairs, biting her lips where a board betrayed. She kept her eyes shut, her free hand using the rough wall as a guide. Passing through the cold kitchen, the lightning was dazzling on the white table. But she went on, into the scullery where she set down the candle and, rolling up her sleeve, plunged her hand to the bottom of the swill bin. But as the broken blue crested plate bit into her hand, she heard the shriek.

Lying behind muslin, the laird of Invernevis listened to the thunder and because he had known monsoons he wasn't afraid. He knew there would be lightning too. But when the train shrieked, his head left the pillow for the first time in months because of the legend of Diarmid O'Caibre.

Donald's mother heard the shriek, but she was too worried about the milk she had managed to keep cool in the heat, but which the thunder was turning.

And as the train rumbled across the Disputed Pool, the

41

little Italian in the third-class carriage peered at the dark arches of Wade's Bridge and thought of the wading nymph. He drew back from darkness, sighing, wishing that the wonderful new process of photographing moving objects, which had been tried at Balmoral, would reach him.

Chapter Three

At the beginning of October 1899 Jan Smuts, President Kruger's brilliant young State Attorney, drafted an ultimatum. The British government must withdraw its troops from the Transvaal frontiers and send away all the reinforcements that were being shipped out.

On 10 October Queen Victoria's rejection of Boer demands was cabled to Pretoria. The ultimatum expired the following day, at five o'clock in the evening, by which time ten thousand Boers under the grizzle-bearded General Piet Cronje were massed on the Transvaal frontier.

On 27 October twenty-nine officers and over a thousand other ranks of the First Battalion Princess Louise's Argyll and Sutherland Highlanders embarked at Dublin for the Boer War. Khaki drill jackets had been issued, white spats dyed the same colour, khaki helmets and puggarees, or light scarves tried on. The tassels had been removed from all sporrans, and officers carried a claymore with a bare basket-hilt. They wore the same sporrans as the privates and, if they wished, were inoculated against enteric. And they had posed for photographs.

Captain Niall Macdonald could honestly say that he was looking forward to action after the garrison years. His stay in Dublin had been made pleasant enough by invitations to mansions in the surrounding counties. With their whitewashed walls, high stories and backdrops of mountains, some of them reminded him of Invernevis, and their hard-riding squires of his father. Riding crops were strewn on hall tables, and sodden boots awaited attention. The dark-haired Irish ladies he led on to ballroom floors were no more beautiful than those back home, and the dances he took part in under the Georgian chandeliers not unlike the Highland dances his father had forced him to learn as a boy, though Aunt Carlotta considered them to be immoral. While the ladies admired his kilt and scarlet doublet in the ballroom, Donald his new orderly had his pipes hoisted in the servants' quarters, proving their superiority against the Irish version. The new Captain was taken drives in Irish traps and was struck by the poverty of estate cottages in comparison to the ones at home. At least his father looked after his tenants, if not his family.

On that three-week voyage to the Cape boxing matches were staged to build up the men's aggression. The officers walked the deck by day and played cards in the evening, their games interspersed with brandies and tales of the Queen's shilling taken in Dublin brothels with nothing, thank God, given back. But the new Captain had no stomach for cards or conquered women. Reserved by nature, his consolation was a good cigar, a taste he shared with Jamie Mackay, a baronet's heir from Sutherland who had messed with him at Eton and was now with him as a Captain in Princess Louise's. Jamie was small and slender, with sandy hair swept back, and a thick matching moustache that failed to give masculinity to his thin pale face. It was not the salt in the breeze that was making his face contract as he stood beside his friend in the stern, and it was not the frustration of having denied himself the card school below because of mounting debts. That day a passing ship had hung a blackboard over the side on which was writ large:

BOERS DEFEATED. THREE BATTLES. PENN SYMONS KILLED.

'It'll be all over by the time we get there,' Jamie said bitterly. 'God, but we're *never* going to see action. All those years of waiting for nothing. I feel like resigning my commission, only that'll let my creditors come down like vultures.'

'Well at least we're getting a long voyage out of it,' Niall said, though he himself felt that they would arrive too late. Buller was already at the Cape, mustering the Army Corps, but from the blackboard it looked as if the Boers had already been taught a lesson. What an expensive exercise. His thoughts turned home. His father might already be dead. If there was to be no battle with the Boers he would resign his commission and go home to take over. Staring down the long bright avenue left by the churning screws, he could see his homecoming clearly, though he was thousands of miles away: Laura's button boots scattering gravel as she ran beside the big wheel to the ivy-encrusted porch where poor flustered Mama and calm Aunt Carlotta would be waiting, the object of their suffering and anger already underground. He would rescue Alexander from MacPherson's clutches at the Home Farm, restore the estate which had suffered in his father's long illness, and to keep in touch with military matters assume command of the rifle volunteers. But first he wanted to do battle in South Africa. Action would help to erase his father's spite in pushing him into the army. Mama would have to manage somehow, till he got home, and if he didn't – he spiralled the spent cigar to the darkening sea before following a dejected Jamie below.

The troopship *Orcana* put into Cape Town on 17 November. The new Captain had hardly time to raise his eyes to Table Mountain before the battalion was hurried north in two troop trains across the Great Karroo, hundreds of monotonous miles of scrub interspersed with occasional clusters of *kopjes*. The soldiers left the sliding doors of the box cars open and sat with legs dangling, the new Captain staying with his company because he wanted to get to know them. The red and yellow earth was cracked, like many mouths crying out for rain, but the clarity of light caused by the ever-blue sky astonishing. Vultures drifted above the unyielding *veld*, and springboks bounded, shying away from clanking metal. And there, sniffing where no wind was, stood the beautiful oryx, delicate as his sister, with its long straight horns and black banded head, its ranks thinned by white hunters. The Highland soldiers crowded, gasping at the giraffe, laughing at the waddling ostrich, comparing it in Gaelic to quaint old women of their villages. Their tongues tried to identify, their minds to retain bustard and hyaena, so that, if they ever got home again, they might tell their grandchildren at fireside *ceilidhs* that they had seen a sunset '*coltach ri famhar deth bhalag luachrach*', 'like a giant mushroom'.

When they pulled into De Aar at daylight on the morning of the 19th, they learnt of the battle round the tin-roofed huddle of Ladysmith, called after the lovely Spanish woman that cavalryman Harry Smith had snatched from the sack of Badajoz. Vice-Commandant Lukas Meyer's brilliant deployments had confused the British, caught unaware in the dawn by four thousand rifles firing, backed up by a 'Long Tom', a gun that sent a shell six miles. The angry-eyed General De Wet had pushed the British back to Ladysmith and siege. Eight hundred prisoners had been taken by the Boers, who had two hundred dead. The British had lost twelve hundred that day, to go down in history as 'Mournful Monday'.

Princess Louise's men brooded as they silently observed an old Highland ritual preparatory to battle, the shedding of sporrans, the stitching of khaki aprons on the fronts of kilts so that the drab *veld* would absorb them. Captain Macdonald and the other officers surrendered their swords and Sam Browne belts, taking up rifles and adopting the same equipment as their men. Reduced to one rank, the battalion was now ready for the fray, but was forced to cool its heels in that dusty camp, for summer was coming to South Africa, when at Invernevis the winter winds were whipping spray from the loch and filling the corries with snow.

Jamie was in an intense state of excitement, pacing about, eyes animated, forehead shining with sweat as he struck out at persistent insects.

'I wish they'd move us so that we can get a crack at them.'

'You may get more than one chance,' Niall said from his shaded seat by the bell-tent. 'I hear Methuen's furious about the Boers using dum-dum bullets.'

'Dum-dum? What make's that?'

'Home-made, with a file. When it hits you it spreads out all over the place and – well, you can imagine for yourself. The international conference banned it in July, so that shows the morals of those we're up against.'

'I'll get my shot in first,' Jamie said grimly.

'You won't, unless you put on your helmet.' He called through canvas to his orderly, who was tidying the tent. 'Donald, get Captain Fraser some water.'

Several days later the battalion was sent forward by train to the Orange River Station to rendezvous with the rest of the Highland Brigade. The heat stretching his clean-shaven skin over his lean face, Major-General Wauchope the Brigadier asked after his 'old friend' the laird of Invernevis. The new Captain knew how much his father respected Andy Wauchope, veteran of three Colonial wars, with wounds to prove it, though Aunt Carlotta despised the Lowland coal-mine owner, calling him a 'jump-up'. Rather than refer to a disease whose name he did not know, the Captain said that his father's health was failing fast.

'Great pity,' the Brigadier said, putting his hand on the son's shoulder in sympathy. 'There wasn't a braver man in the British army.' It sounded like a prompt.

But before the Highland Brigade could assemble, Princess

Louise's were once again entrained, this time to reinforce Lord Methuen, whose diminished force was approaching the Modder River to relieve besieged Kimberley. It was dark before the camp at Witkoplaagte was reached, and already the featureless South African terrain was defeating the Highlanders, some of whom had been stalkers and poachers. The two companies left behind at Klokfontein to unload the baggage at the railhead lost their way, and so there were neither food nor blankets for Princess Louise's men. But the officers of the Yorkshire Light Infantry shared their tea and bully beef, jesting about haggis shooting. No food set on the Invernevis table by Mrs Livingstone tasted as good as those chunks of meat.

Even if there had been blankets the new Captain could not have slept with the excitement of battle. Jamie had two cigars left, and they wandered together from the camp fires and the grunts of men curled up on cooling sand, into a darkness perfumed by peach trees. Niall's nerves were tuned like a *clarsach* to the night, striking the deepest chords. It was that same feeling of perfection he had experienced on the avenue on his last afternoon at home, with Laura's wet dress clinging to her ripening body in the thunderous atmosphere, and trees, sky and water in harmony. The thought of death in the battle to come did not distress him. This was the moment for which he had been trained and tuned for eight years, the moment of redemption when he would challenge his father's preference for Alexander, prove that he was capable of leadership, of lairdship. He would lead his company resolutely, fire straight and true, without reflection because he wanted to live in preference to the Boer who fired filed bullets and leapt on his pony at the sight of a bayonet. He *had* to live, to get home to Laura, to save her from Aunt Carlotta's assaults, to take his rightful place as laird, a place history had assigned him. But he would not repeat his father's failings by being too friendly towards the tenants, by coveting whisky and women.

And Jamie was also keyed up for the battle, taking short quick puffs at his cigar as he walked beside his friend. He was determined to throw all he had into the fight. It wasn't a medal he was going for; it was an escape from the monotony of his existence, a vindication of wasted time. The possibility of death didn't disturb him. He was heir to an estate he wasn't interested in; he had huge gambling debts; he had a domineer-

47

ing mother who had never allowed him his manhood; and he had a sickly sister, about whom the dreaded word tuberculosis was now being used sparingly.

'What are you thinking about?' Niall wanted to know, beginning to circle.

'About my sister Mary Rose. You met her, remember, in Edinburgh in '94, when we gave the Centenary Ball in the Assembly Rooms. She's a beauty, but she doesn't keep well. I was thinking how well this climate would suit her. She wanted to come out as a nurse, but mother wouldn't hear of it.'

Niall vaguely remembered a girl not unlike Laura being introduced to him in the press of a thousand people. 'Funny, but I was also thinking about my sister,' he said. 'It's strange, but we've been friends for so long, yet we've never met each other's families.'

'We'll put that right, after this war,' Jamie said, in a voice that could promise nothing.

The new Captain trampled his cigar butt into sand and went to his tent. Donald had made a bed up for him, but he could not sleep. He sat outside, his hands locked round his knees, staring up at the stars, flashing like countless rifles firing eternally. Somewhere a hyaena gave out its derisory call.

At four-thirty they were on the move, fires trampled out, the hungry dusty men of Princess Louise's still cheerful because of the promise of breakfast and a bathe at Modder River Station. They were part of a force of eight thousand under Lord Methuen marching on the Modder, where Methuen, on the evidence of spies and cavalry, believed that there were 'probably no Boers at all', or at the most four hundred defending the demolished railway bridge. Once the river was crossed and the Boers cleared, Kimberley lay ahead.

They moved through the peaceful dawn, with the blue hills of Magersfontein coming into focus in the distance. The plain they were crossing was wide and flat, with dark bushes broken by poplars, and here and there the dramatic white of farm buildings, a green-girded *kraal*, or stock enclosure. Hares and buzzards were flushed as they swished through the grass. The new Captain was remembering early-morning grouse drives over the Invernevis moor, above the standing stones, with the dogs going ahead, raised paw in the frozen stance of pointing.

The men behind the new Captain of 'A' Company were joking about poaching, their words cancelled by the clatter of the armoured train that had accompanied them from the Orange River and which moved backwards and forwards, as if undecided about the dawn assault.

But where was the Modder? According to Methuen's maps, they were now about three miles from it, on a gentle slope leading to a huddle of houses and a clump of eucalyptus trees, with a long line of bushes. If they could not catch the glint of water, they saw Modder River hamlet on the opposite bank, beyond the broken spans of the railway bridge.

Methuen now ordered a general deployment, and a slight change of direction to the left, with Princess Louise's deployed in two lines, extended about six paces' interval in reserve of the firing line. Where there had been jokes, there was now silence as the new Captain's company moved down towards the river, with Rimmington's Mounted Guides on the extreme left, hooves lifting through scrub, and in the far distance, the 9th Lancers containing the right of the advance.

The silence and inactivity of the enemy under the brightening sky made the new Captain nervous. He could just make out Methuen's mounted figure going forward to choose a house for his headquarters, his binoculars sweeping as he waited for his staff to canter up. Methuen thought he was looking at the line of one river, whereas there were two. About a quarter of a mile above the broken railway bridge the Modder received its tributary the Riet. Their junction formed a crude Y, with the flat area between the wavering arms known as the Twee Riviere. On the tongue of land where the two rivers met stood the Island Hotel in shaded pleasure gardens, a favourite picnicking place for the people of Kimberley.

Having breakfasted, General Cronje went out to the verandah of the Island Hotel and watched the British advance through binoculars. It was certainly impressive, a dust-shrouded front three miles wide on either side of the railway line, presumably to make the fording of the Modder easier. But its movement to the right worried him: was Methuen going to cross the Riet by Bosman's Drift and trap the Boer force on the Twee Riviere? Cronje sighed with relief and lowered his binoculars as he saw the British swing to the left, towards the Modder.

But Methuen's binoculars were still sweeping the peaceful scene.

'They're not there,' he said to Colville as the Brigadier of the Guards rode up beside him.

'They're sitting uncommonly tight if they are,' the Brigadier answered.

At that moment the unseen trenches in front opened up, and somewhere on the right front a pom-pom began. The British had walked straight into a brilliant ambush that might have become a massacre, had the Boers had the nerve to maintain their fire. Despite the distance and the extended order, casualties were heavy, the air choked with bullets. Princess Louise's were over two thousand yards from the railway bridge when the firing began, but they kept advancing another two hundred precarious but precious yards till the Boer fire faltered. But the British firing line had halted, and the battalion was ordered to lie down preparatory to moving up in support.

Princess Louise's were to the left, facing the Modder, but the Guards, on the right, facing the Riet and forming the firing line, were halted eight hundred yards from the river by the Boer fire and the barbed wire enclosing the local racecourse. Advance was impossible, so they lay down in the leafless scrub, or tried to find shelter behind ant-hills. The sun climbing in the ruthless blue would take the temperature to around one hundred and eight degrees, soldering kilts to the backs of knees. They had to lie on their rifles, to stop metal sticking in case they got a chance to use them. Men who could no longer bear the thirst would perish trying to crawl back to the water carts, and soldiers would snore through the battle, cheeks on the scorched soil.

On the left, Princess Louise's men had some cover from a slight rise in the ground, but not from the sun. The new Captain of 'A' company pushed back his helmet to save his neck. The noise was deafening as sixteen British guns pumped thousands of shells towards the river bank, stripping foliage, shattering buildings, and the answering pom-poms came flapping and cackling like the geese at the Home Farm. He shielded his eyes from sun and smoke. In the first seconds of the attack the crew of the Scots Guards' Maxim had been annihilated, and now, on the right, the gun pointed like an

50

accusing finger at the Riet, on whose opposite bank, on the Twee Riviere, Boer guns blazed. And there were more Boers on both sides of the Modder.

The situation was utterly confusing, and his men were complaining as blisters as big as fists began to rise on the backs of their splayed legs. In retribution for the wreckage of their hills by Highland boots, ants began to invade kilts.

Where were his orders? They couldn't lie there all day, in the scorching sun. At least with the Boers you had a chance. So, giving a quick signal with a hand, he began to crawl towards the river, with the action of a swimming frog, the sand burning through his kilt, the breech of his rifle blistering his palm. It was like the rare days when he had defied his father's cynicism to go stalking on the mountain, inching over hot sharp rock as the suspicious stag sniffed, then turned its trusting heart to the sights. And even when his finger failed him, there was always Duncan the ghillie to guide him, make him go on. But he was out on his own now, at the Modder, a hundred men crawling behind, relying on his judgement. Even a few men getting across the river would be good for the morale of the thousands static to centre and right, he realized, and if it was true about the bayonet, the Boers would run. The answer was to get as close to the river as possible and work upstream, to link up with the other companies of the battalion.

It was slow, painful going, stones lacerating, arms and legs aching, but the thought of water behind the line of trees made him determined, and the men's stomachs were beginning to grumble. Crawling was taking too long, so they began running, crouching, dropping when bullets came. At three hundred yards from the river he began to turn upstream, realizing they were now dangerously isolated on the extreme left, a suspicion confirmed by fierce firing breaking out from a tree-enclosed farmstead and *kraal* to the left, putting them supine again. It blocked the way to the river and would have to be rushed with the bayonet.

At that moment, General Pole-Carew with other companies of Princess Louise's about half a mile up the river was reaching the same conclusion, his binoculars surveying the Boer stronghold. Since it was sylvan, it offered excellent cover for snipers. Sweeping the *veld*, with lenses that the sun repulsed, he saw 'A' company under Captain Macdonald on the extreme left go flat. He swung again, saw with horror Methuen manifesting through the heat-haze, visiting various parts of the firing line instead of directing operations from his nominal headquarters at the Ganger's Hut, three miles up the railway line.

There was a shallow *donga* or gully running down to a spinney by the river bank, and if that could be taken, the Boers in the farmhouse and *kraal* would be cut off from retreat across the Modder. Lord Methuen, on whose orders the fate of eight thousand men, mostly static, hung, insisted on leading in person a charge of thirty men of two companies of Princess Louise's down the *donga* because he knew that if the battle was to be won, it would only be on the left, by crossing water. Miraculously, the elderly gaunt Guardsman whose own regiment was being repulsed at the Riet returned breathless, unscathed, but with the Boers still in possession. He had now learned why he could not see the Modder from three miles away: the *veld* shelved into a natural thirty-foot trench.

Meanwhile, on the left, Captain Macdonald was ordering his company to fix bayonets and charge. Their boots ploughed through sand as they approached the farmhouse and *kraal*, men stopping with shocked mouths when a bullet found its mark, but their Captain shouting encouragement, with no time to consider the possibility of being killed, straightening in defiance, surefooted as when running down Invernevis lawn as a boy, to the Summer House Pool, with a rod in his hand, on and on, among the trees now, branches whipping his face, a face at a window, the firing dying with fixed steel seen, through the farm buildings in pursuit as they fled to the river, big slouched hats becoming wheels.

Even if he hadn't been on a sandy slope he wouldn't have stopped, for it was like racing the rabbit before it went underground. Shin-high scrub impeded, but he was raising his rifle, shouldering it without stopping, steadying the sights. The Boers were already splashing through the shallows, reeling like drunk men. The new Captain stopped, and without thought or feeling shot one of them in the back, watching him fall, arms wide, face-down into the river, the current rolling him over, showing the spreading stain on the waistcoat, carrying him away.

His men were now around him, firing at the sodden figures

scrambling up the opposite bank, seeking shelter in the few crude houses their comrades were holding, but after bullets by the dozen were sent through the shattered windows, there was silence. A crossing was now possible, so sending the others back to garrison the farmhouse, the Captain kept thirty men.

Encouraged by the charge, Captain Mackay, with parts of two companies, plus detachments from other regiments, was converging on the river. There was no way but to wade the three hundred yards. Captain Macdonald was first in, walking till it reached his waist, the strong current trying to tear off his kilt, the sun blisters agonizing on the backs of his legs. And then came Captain Mackay to join sweaty hands and form a chain which spread out and across as the soldiers entered water, their rifles slung round their necks. As he waded he thought of Laura in the Yellow Pool, stalking the salmon, her dress hitched up. But the Modder was much deeper, three times as broad, and with every movement there was the danger of Boer snipers picking off the men from the bushes on the opposite bank. And Jamie's nervousness was transmitted through his hot firm grip.

But at last they were clambering up sand, grasping bushes, turning to help a few men up as reinforcements before making for the houses the Boers had vacated. Having gone through the wrecked rooms to make certain there were no snipers, the two Captains mustered as many men as they could and proceeded in open order along the bank, through the shelter of thick oak scrub and trees, a place of shade, but not to pause.

General Pole-Carew had now crossed the river to direct operations. The hamlet and farm of Rosemead was easily overrun, Princess Louise's swinging to the right, to threaten the whole Boer line from flank and rear. And then occurred one of these impulsive actions so understandable but so dangerous in such a stifling, sniper-ridden war zone. Having sent the Boers scattering, Princess Louise's men ran down to the river and, throwing themselves down on the sandy slope, began to drink and drink, despite the dead horses and dead Boers being brought down. And though he realized the risk of infection, the new Captain had his fill. Water bubbling and spilling through Invernevis heather was never sweeter.

But the cost of slaking the thirst was time lost and companies scattered. Pole-Carew tried to muster them in the brushwood, to press upriver. But the Boers had crept back to snipe, and now there was an obstacle in the way of Princess Louise's, a fort-like farm with high mud walls and prickly pear. A detour left was too far, and British guns were sweeping the ground to the right. There was no way but through a narrow passage into a small yard.

The new Captain had been suspicious, but when he saw the six-foot-high barbed wire fence with one small gate, he was convinced it was a trap. But was the way back any safer? About twenty men had been ushered through when a shell fell, the blast sending the Captain reeling against stone. He was stunned, there was smoke and confusion, but he saw two decapitated men of his company still on their feet, clutching at each other like drunk waltzers.

It was one of their own shells, for at the moment an additional British battery had emerged out of its own dust cloud across the Modder. It had travelled fifty miles in twenty-eight hours in answer to Methuen's summons, and though the crew were footsore, having walked to save the horses, they went into action immediately, close to the river to give support to Pole-Carew's party.

More men were pushed through the gate before a second shell arrived. The new Captain was searching about frantically, not knowing what he was looking for, but knowing that the fire from friendly guns across water *had* to be stopped. He broke a window with his rifle butt, tore down the red curtain, sent one of his men up on to the roof to wave it. But the trees prevented it from being seen. And now came a hail of shrapnel from their own naval guns, ricocheting off stone to lodge in Highland flesh, as well as cross-fire from the Boer guns. They were forced to fall back on Rosemead, where the new Captain with ten men threw themselves into a farmhouse.

The afternoon dragged by with desultory guns, and about seven o'clock the Boers galloped off, but the new Captain and his handful of men were ordered to continue to hold the farmhouse, in case the Boers came back in the dawn to re-take it. The rest of Princess Louise's was collected and bivouacked about a mile from Rosemead dam, but only to find that the transport was not being allowed to join them. For the second night they were without food or blankets, this time after a strenuous battle. The Highlanders began to grumble until, at nine, a stray wagon yielded tinned meat, biscuits and rum.

But in the farmhouse the new Captain was already sleeping, slumped on a broken chair, dreaming. The Boer he had shot in the back had turned to look at him before the impact had sent him sprawling into water. That bearded face became his father's, breaking surface in the Summer House Pool, but horribly blistered.

Before dawn the battalion crossed the dam to the sound of pipes, and the naval guns began to bombard the Modder River Station. There was no response, however. The tremors jolted the new Captain from his uncomfortable chair. He went outside to watch the dawn's grey curtain lifting on the theatre of war, revealing dead horses and men strewn over the shell-pitted earth as far as the eye could see.

They went through the stripped trees, in a dawn without birdsong, past the Boer trenches littered with spent cartridges and empty gin bottles glaring in the sun. He had never felt such depression, such disgust at man, but Princess Louise's grimy-faced battalion was happy, roasting chickens and sucking pigs over broken-up chairs. Though he had no appetite the new Captain broke the hot flesh in his fingers and found the wish-bone. It was snapped with Jamie, who got the smaller part, and who kept repeating:

'Damn it, they've gone, and I didn't get one. Did you?'

And now, as the count began in that sad ruined landscape, it was seen that Princess Louise's had suffered most. The new Captain went among the wounded of his company, offering words of encouragement before they were lifted away.

For a fortnight the battalion lay at Modder Camp, but it was no holiday after the victory. Outpost duty was a necessity because of the stealth of Boer snipers, while a low-level deviation bridge was constructed till the permanent railway bridge could be repaired. The cavalry horses were exhausted, the ammunition train almost empty. But there were recreations. After the day's digging at fortifications, sweating men stripped naked, running without shame to the river, ploughing sunlight and spray, splashing, cupping water and calling out: 'Chateau Modder, full of body!' Shielding his eyes with his palm, tongue moving over parched lips, Jamie stood watching the naked bathers until aware of Niall at his side.

And there was a congratulatory message from Lord Methuen after 'one of the hardest fights in the Annals of the Army'. Methuen himself had been wounded, but not seriously. The other units of the Highland Brigade were arriving, and by 9 December it was complete. With his wound healed, and his force of thirteen thousand, he was convinced that he was now strong enough to complete the last stage of his advance for the relief of Kimberley. But the fortnight the British force had spent in camp had allowed six thousand Boers to gather in opposition on the ridge of which the rock-bound *kopje* of Magersfontein formed the centre. Unlike Modder there should be no confusion caused by faulty geography. The ground between Modder Camp and Magersfontein Hill had been thoroughly surveyed by Major Benson of the Royal Artillery, and by cavalry patrols. Methuen would bombard Magersfontein Hill with all the heavy artillery he possessed, and next dawn, rush it with bayonets. The steel tip was to be the Highland troops.

At three o'clock on the afternoon of 10 December while the Boers were at prayer meetings the Highland Brigade left the Modder Camp, led by General Wauchope, Methuen having heliographed to Kimberley that help was on its way. Its sparse grass spiced with mimosa that clutched at kilts, the *veld* stretched to the cluster of *kopjes*, the nearest of which was the two-hundred-foot Magersfontein Hill, on whose slopes Methuen's artillery was unleashing its full force, that horrifying weapon the lyddite shell hurling the red earth and ironstone boulders fifty feet high, turning the hill into a volcano leaking yellow-green fumes.

Princess Louise's men were inactive, lying with the bulk of the Highland Brigade behind Headquarter Hill, two miles from Magersfontein. The nearby howitzers wailed like banshees, and the slopes of the distant hill rose in spouts. Watching the bombardment, Captain Macdonald was remembering the rumour that Wauchope had expressed serious doubts at the briefing. If, as Wauchope apparently believed, the Boer force was stronger than Methuen supposed, then they should all be dead by now, blown up with the rocks among which they were crouching. But supposing both Methuen and Wauchope were wrong? Supposing there were a huge number of Boers, but entrenched *elsewhere*, nearer to Kimberley, ready to launch a massive counter-attack?

The failure of the Boer guns to respond to the pounding made the new Captain nervous, and his men were restless. Rather than hang about, they wanted to get into the thick of

56

battle because Modder had been a tonic. At the Modder the heat had made the inactivity of the Guards intolerable, and now it was the turn of the Highland Brigade, with rain falling steadily, saturating kilts and uniforms, reducing visibility over the *veld* where British guns were blasting rock with a sound that reminded the Captain of the granite quarry across water from Invernevis. The bivouac tent that each soldier carried in addition to a blanket and one hundred and fifty rounds of ammunition was no protection against the teeming rain, and the Captain could not take shelter in case urgent orders came through from Methuen, who was holding his last war council, sitting on the box seat of a wagon as he watched Magersfontein Hill erupting. When the bombardment ceased about five, Methuen was no wiser as to the number and position of the enemy. But the enemy now knew he was on the move, and De la Rey's field-works were to prove 'one of the boldest and most original conceptions in the history of war'.

Still no orders for the Highland Brigade, and once again no provision made for a hot meal. They were not allowed to smoke or light fires. The grumbles of 'A' company turned into angry Gaelic, and though their Captain could not translate, he had heard the tinkers using the same tone to Aunt Carlotta when she refused them food at the back door. He heard Methuen's name mentioned, and saw heads shaken, but did not enforce his authority. He too was hungry and depressed, without the consolation of a cigar. Watching the heavy rain clouds banking to the north-west, he wondered if the dawn attack would now take place. The descending darkness was bringing a feeling of foreboding, the same as he had experienced on his last day home, when he had seen the house as a skull from Wade's Bridge. He didn't really believe in such things, and he wasn't very religious. Though born into a centuries-old Catholic family that had included fanatics such as the Culloden chieftain, he had managed to escape Aunt Carlotta's iron enforcement by being away at school in the south, and when he was home on holiday his father seemed to take delight in mocking his sister-in-law's devotions. As a boy Niall had used his Catholicism to drive away shadows from his bed, until he had become acclimatized to that gloomy house, with Mama, who had tried table-turning and been stopped by Aunt Carlotta, saying you just had to accept such things if you were an old family with an old house. But when

Laura's flaw had become apparent, he felt betrayed by his faith, angry at Aunt Carlotta's avowal that it was 'the Lord's work, which we dare not question'. Manhood had brought him to accept his Catholicism as part of his heritage, to be guarded and passed on, like the heirlooms in the glass cases in the drawing-room, but like them, having no immediate benefit for himself. But now, as darkness descended on Magersfontein Hill after the indecisive day, he found in his numb fingers the Iona stone rosary that Aunt Carlotta had given him the day he had departed from Invernevis. Before Modder he had not considered the possibility of death, but now, in the eerie South African night, he sensed that death was out there, on the dark *veld*, circling like a vulture ready to descend in the dawn.

For confirmation had come through that there was to be a dawn assault, and at eleven-thirty the hungry men of the Highland Brigade got up from their bivouacs and fell in. The Brigade was in quarter column, the plan being to get within charging distance of the supposed Boer position on the south side of Magersfontein Hill, and then to deploy. The Black Watch led, followed by the Seaforths, Princess Louise's men, and the Highland Light Infantry. They moved off half an hour after midnight, a tight rectangle of ninety-six lines, four thousand men contained by rope-connected guides on the left, with General Wauchope leading, carrying his old claymore like a Highland chief marching to Culloden.

The terrain was treacherous. The day's deluge had turned the burning *veld* into cold slimy mud sucking at boots. Large ironstone boulders grazed Highland knees, prickly mimosa broke the weave of kilts. Men stumbled over ant-hills, almost bringing down others in the tight cordon. And now a thunderstorm was beginning, louder than lyddite rupturing rock. Moving in the roped mass, the Captain was comparing the advance to walking along the bank of the Invernevis river, in darkness, at Deirdre's Bog, and the image of his home was reinforced by the flickering lightning and the violet rays of Kimberley's five searchlights, known as 'Rhodes's eyes'. Not only did the lightning momentarily blind, causing men to stumble, knees lanced by two-inch thorns: it also interfered with the compass of Major Benson, who was directing the advance because he had reconnoitred the ground. At two o'clock a change of direction had to be made to the right to counteract the erratic needle, ironstone and the metal of four

58

thousand rifles in alliance with the lightning.

Dawn comes early to South Africa, and there in front was the grey emerging shoulder of Magersfontein Hill. Deployment was twice suggested by Benson, but Wauchope wanted to push on before the sky brightened, so that they were as close as possible to the enemy. At four o'clock the order to deploy was at last given, but with the Black Watch striking a thick barrier of thorn bush, through which they pushed in twos and threes where gaps were found. Since it was impossible to deploy in the middle of the bushes, Wauchope decided to postpone the movement till the whole Brigade had passed this obstacle, which meant another four hundred yards' advance.

When the Black Watch and Seaforths had cleared the scrub, but the rest were still shoulder to shoulder in quarter column, Wauchope ordered a halt and deployment outwards. The Seaforths moved to the left of the Black Watch, Princess Louise's to the right, and the Highland Light Infantry in reserve. Mustered by their Captain, 'A' company had begun to extend, more and more men becoming grey shapes at fifty yards' distance, when a bright light flashed on the hillside in front, followed by several rifle shots.

It was as he turned that an extraordinary sensation seized Captain Macdonald. The image of Invernevis House was already in his mind, with the thunderstorm, and now, as De la Rey's brilliantly concealed trench on the level four hundred yards in front opened up a terrific fire, he had the impression that he was hurtling in a train above the Invernevis river, towards the mansion lit by a million lamps. And the train seemed to be leaving the rails, going up into the sky, towards the flashing stars, before it began to break up.

The darkness was ringing with contradictory orders – to lie down, to fix bayonets and charge – but the Boer guns were both deafening and blinding. The Black Watch were driven back on the Seaforths, and they in turn on top of Princess Louise's. The Highland Brigade sounded like a giant accordion being compressed, groaning. Friendly bayonets turned, friendly boots trampled as the guns under Magersfontein sprayed. The shout to 'retire!' became a screamed chorus, and the tightly packed Highland Brigade fell apart, becoming running bodies thudding into each other before they fell shot.

The Captain of 'A' company still faced the blinding guns,

but it was not an act of courage. Thorn bushes would not let go of his kilt, and barging men veering into the night beyond the range of the rifles prevented him from turning. Then he heard the pipes, and thought it was a dreadful dream he was awakening from at Invernevis. But it was not Farquhar circling the mansion in reveille: Donald Macdonald his orderly had hoisted his pipes in the fast breaking dawn and, prodding the bag, turned to face the hail of bullets, his steady fingers finding the regimental tune 'The Campbells are Coming', striving to stop retreat becoming ignominious rout. Then, as if an old score was being settled, the Captain heard 'The Invernevis March' succeeding. It sent a thrill down his spine, but as he turned to shout encouragement he saw the wailing tree of the pipes collapse in the lightening sky.

Inspired by this act of defiance, other pipers of the Highland Brigade began to lend their noisy encouragement to stand firm and fight. Invisible hands seemed to clasp the Captain round the waist, freeing his kilt, pushing him towards that hill which Boer rifles were turning into a blinding beacon, his mud-clogged boots stubbing ironstone, but going on, discharging his rifle where light flared.

Then a bullet from the ground-level trench struck his left kneecap and his boots stopped, his body swaying in surprise. As a child he had waded into the Summer House Pool to retrieve a bobbing ball, his body shocked into gasps by the coldness of the water despite summer, but gritting his teeth, going on because the ball would not be replaced and because, sitting on a horse at the front of the house, with Alexander up beside him, his father was watching him. He was up to his knees when his foot snagged, sending him sprawling into the greenness, the slanted stone biting at his kneecap, his blood coming swirling to the surface, like red tangled wool. He could not look at the knee but had waded ashore and limped up the lawn to show father and brother that he was a big boy and was not crying, though the wound smarted and spilled.

But this time, under Magersfontein Hill, the pain of the wound saturating his hose down there in brightening dawn was beyond the power of his open mouth to express. Though it was no longer being played, 'The Invernevis March' was ringing in his ears as he swayed there, Kimberley's five-rayed searchlight like a giant palm pushing him back.

Laura was running beside the big wheel on the narrow

avenue and he was screaming at her to get back, get back, though no sound came. A web of muslin was enmeshing him, winding round and round, though he tried to tear it away, like tearing sticky willies from his kilt on boyhood walks. But the web kept on being spun out, kept on tightening, up his chest, round his throat, over his eyes. The massed pipes seemed to scream at him as the web fankled his feet, making him fall back as rifles spat and the stars went out.

Chapter Four

When Niall opened his eyes he was on his back, and for a few moments he was confused, imagining he was lying in the meadow across the Summer House Pool with Laura. It was so peaceful, lying there, letting the mind empty into arched blue. Then he saw the war balloon drifting aimlessly, and vultures circling. Canvas on stone was supporting him, and the slightest movement of his left leg was agony. Or was it one of those dreams you carry into consciousness? The Inver-nevis chieftain present at Culloden had been crippled when his horse was cannon-balled from under him. Laura always cried for the horse.

He could turn his head, however. Right and left men were sprawled behind ant-hills and bushes, kilts exposing the backs of their thighs, mess tins struck into silver by the sun. Pipes were wailing somewhere. He began to cry at the sight of so many dead till he saw one slithering forward a few feet through the sand, the backs of his hands lizard-skinned. Then he realized that the assault was continuing. Guns pounded like the late train from the south gathering speed in the pass for the gradient towards the standing stones.

But he was airborne now, being hurried away by two crouched figures of the Royal Army Medical Corps, past pith helmets like stopped tortoises. When they got him out of the firing zone they lowered him gently and applied improvised splints, using a discarded rifle and a scabbard well padded with grass taken from a corpse. Ironstone in his fist absorbed the pain.

And then he was on the move again, towards the ambulance wagons drawn up at the collecting station, soiled canvas red crossed, cool when he was slid underneath. A kilted man from the dawn fusillade was shouting for light till his hands found his face. Most of the water from a skin bottle dribbled down stubble. It was even more harrowing on the jolting ride to the field hospital, with a needle trying to broach a strong Highland vein, administering morphia to an already disowned arm.

The Captain bit his lip and closed his eyes, negating the pain in his left knee because he was now travelling up the Invernevis avenue on a gig with suspect springs, with Laura running ahead, her bare feet miraculously avoiding exposed stone, floating up the avenue, under the flashing canopy of the trees, up and up, her dress clinging to her curves, arms wide, on and on, until the blind bend –

It was evening, and he was in a bell-tent in the field hospital with other wounded officers, peaked canvas trapping the heat of the day, flies stotting, seeking an exit. The nurses moved quietly, distributing brandy, beef tea, arrowroot and condensed milk to repudiating stomachs. The Captain turned his face away from the swimming spoon. Jamie had just come into mind. What had happened to him under Magersfontein, when the stars had fallen, exploding? And Donald his orderly, with his loyal pipes? Very likely they were both dead. And his company? Wiped out, probably, like the flies the nurse was swatting. Very few could have survived in that fire. And he began to see the devilish cunning of the Boers. Oh, how wrong Methuen had been in lobbing lyddite! Instead of massing on Magersfontein Hill, they had dug a trench at its foot, in the open, the ground-level ambush meaning that most bullets would find a mark, crippling. These weren't the rules of war. And Princess Louise's had been in the thick of it. Kimberley would fall, and the war drag on, with more troops having to be sent out. He hoped they could fix him up quickly so that he could get back into the field, but the pain in his left leg was warning him that serious damage had been done. Besides, he was now feeling sick and shivery, from the soaking he had got, waiting behind Headquarter Hill, he supposed, then lying wet, wounded. He called for a basin, but the nurse wasn't quick enough.

He had pooh-poohed an inoculation for enteric at Dublin, but now he was developing it, bodily functions taking him by surprise, sweating so heavily that it was like lying in a river, relinquishing his weak hold on time. It was like a magic-lantern show, with the bright slides changing in rapid succession, but without continuity. The Summer House Pool was swollen in spate, but with the stepping stones covered, the standing stones on the horizon guns pointed at the sky as the thunderstorm flashed behind, discoloured clouds billowing like smoke. The Home Farm was in siege, being shelled by the big house, and he had to get across to its yellow squares to rescue Alexander. Wade's Bridge was shattered arches, and beyond, rails running into sky above the Disputed Pool.

A rope had been slung across the river and he was wading, holding on to it. But his father had lifted his kilt and whipped his bare buttocks with a cartridge belt, so the cold water was agony on the weals. The water was up to his waist now, so cold that it stopped his breathing. Sound and light in the sky deafened and blinded, but he had to get across, to bring Alexander back.

Then his brogue struck a submerged stepping stone, his hand leaving the rope, and he was falling forward with wide arms, his head going under, spinning, into *Cruibeag*, the Small Pool, where a gaff impaling his left knee was used by his father to drag him ashore.

After the nurse lifted him to the bitter cup he lay down again. Now it was not his father but Aunt Carlotta lying behind immobile muslin, and not Mama but Laura nursing her, bringing her a bowl of shuddering carrageen between both hands, her face twisted idiotically as Aunt Carlotta's mouth searched for the spoon; and then the scene shifted to the back stairs, where his father's spurs bit into wood, his shoulder braced against cracking plaster as he molested Elsie from the kitchen, empty sockets where his eyes should be.

Things were blotted out for a long time till he opened his eyes, found himself in the meadow across the Summer House Pool, lying on his back beside Laura. If this was death it was sweet, with the sun on his face, the scent of flowers, the sound of insects. All pain, all anxiety had drained into the earth, leaving his mind a *tabula rasa*. But why was the blue canopy going peaked, dirty grey, and who was that moaning? What could be upsetting Laura in such peace, when he wouldn't be going away again?

'Aunt Carlotta can't touch you now.'

The nurse stayed his shoulder, telling him that they were going to move him.

He was leaving Invernevis again, travelling by train over the Disputed Pool, the mansion lights flaring and fading, metal busy beneath him in the dark pass which went on for a long time before he emerged into quietness and coolness.

The nurse in the base general hospital was welcoming him back to life with champagne.

'What's happened?' he asked in panic, knocking the glass aside as he tried to sit up.

'The worst's over,' she said.

But he had seen the white mass of his leg, and in his anguish appealed for enlightenment.

'It's healing well.'

He caught her wrist, would not let her go until she had told more.

'A bullet in the knee, but it's been removed. And you had a *very* bad attack of enteric.'

It was all coming back: blisters, a Boer rolling in a river, the guns pounding, ironstone erupting, lights in the dawn, pipes stopped.

'Have you heard anything of a Captain Mackay, Princess Louise's?'

'Nothing. He's not here.'

'What about Donald Macdonald, my orderly?'

'I wouldn't know. This is an officers' ward, and *I'm* your orderly. But you must sleep now, and gather your strength. You've been through a lot.'

But he could not sleep. His leg throbbed, and he was thinking about Invernevis. They would have been notified that he had been wounded, but they would not know how badly. Mama would be frantic with worry, what with Father, if he wasn't already dead, and with Alexander no help, wasting his seed at the Home Farm. And Laura would be inconsolable, believing him dead, leaving her to the mercy of Aunt Carlotta, the only one who would be calm because of God's unchallengeable will.

And Donald his orderly, the ghillie's son? Was his playing of 'The Invernevis March' under Magersfontein Hill when it erupted a hallucination caused by the agony of a leg still supporting him in the torrent of Boer fire? Or was it for real, with a bullet rupturing the bag? Because if it was Donald's mother would be heartbroken, and he would be blamed for taking the boy out, though it was his father's rifle volunteer company that had given Donald a taste for soldiering.

He thought of the evening the gig had picked up Donald and his black tin box outside the croft, in the thunderstorm, and how he had almost forgotten his pipes. It seemed so long ago, too far back for memory to focus on, a time watches couldn't count. The gig rumbled backwards, over Wade's

Bridge, to the big house. He had a hazy image of posing for a photograph for Mama's album, his bent left knee aching as it now ached, only it was now straight, a grotesque white pillar outside the bedclothes.

His father. He wondered if there was still life behind the muslin. But if you didn't know what a man was dying of, you didn't know how long he might live, lying there in the breeze from the river, a long grey shape like a diseased salmon returned to its home river to die, but too weak to move upstream, into darkness.

He himself was now immobile in a wooden hut, with the South African sun streaming through the windows, laying open coffins on the bare wooden floor. Baffled by glass, mournful flies came back, busy where blood was. Their chests and limbs swaddled in bandages, men reached out moustached mouths to the cigars and champagne the nurses were holding, a spoon glinting near bandaged eyes. The nurses had white caps, like Mrs Livingstone and her assistant wore because hygiene was a virtue to Aunt Carlotta. They had white armbands, with red crosses. They had aprons, like the Invernevis maids, and a bow bunched neatly behind, like Laura's should have been. They had white starched cuffs, like Nanny used to wear, and they made you feel a child again, dampening down your brow with a sponge, holding your wrist in light fingers as their little watches tracked the pulse. And why had they all got such pretty faces? Why were they always so cheerful where ergotine was being injected, ice sucked to stop bleeding lungs? In a night lit by hanging lanterns they flitted insubstantially between beds where men moaned, calling out names and places in childish voices before the sheets were lifted over their faces. There was always a red cross out there, in the centre of the ward, at the table lit by the circle of the lantern.

His long white hands roughened by heavy surgery, the young doctor from Edinburgh inspected his leg and said it was 'coming along nicely', but by the time the Captain had formulated his question about returning to his company, the doctor had moved on.

Then it was Christmas, midsummer in South Africa, and they received the Queen's gift of a small tin of chocolates bound in red, white and blue ribbon and bearing her portrait. He would have liked to keep them for Laura, but the heat

66

melted them. But Mama would like the tin. In the decorated ward small glasses of whisky and cake were distributed, held by nurses where eyes and limbs disallowed, the richness repudiated where bullets lodged. Cigar smoke hazed and mellowed the antiseptic atmosphere, and an addict with a bandaged face caused amusement by demanding that a hole be cut.

'*Slainte!*' the Captain shouted to the man across the corridor, a Major in the Black Watch.

'Thank God for the water of life!' the Major shouted. raising his left arm because the right was missing.

Those who were strong enough were swung on to chairs beside their beds, and a melodeon compressed between healing hands made music for the carols the circle of nurses in the centre sang, backed up by basses and tenors from the beds. The sound and the bright faces of the nurses made the Captain's heart ache for the Invernevis Christmas of blazing logs, flaming puddings studded with silver threepennies, with his father presiding at the head of the massive mahogany table, wearing an absurd paper hat, his health as yet unruined by whatever was festering in his powerful body, his black beard and piercing eyes like those of a cynical prophet as he defied Aunt Carlotta by drinking large glasses of red wine and, worse, offering Alexander a taste. His father was probably dead, festivities stopped, black everywhere. And even if he had been told that his heir had been wounded before he died, he would only have said: 'Bloody fool to let them get him first.' Only death would have satisfied him, because that would have allowed Alexander to succeed.

His father didn't like him because he was Aunt Carlotta's favourite, though he had never wanted to be, trying to keep out of her way when he was home from school, but always getting approving pats on the head and a second helping of pudding. Death under Magersfontein Hill might have been better, because even though his father had passed on, Aunt Carlotta still had to be lived with. Neither she nor his father had allowed him to make independent decisions, and both treated him as though he were still a boy. He had been forced into the army, to spend eight tedious years in barracks, and now that he had been involved in war, he couldn't say that he had learnt anything. He couldn't say that he was a deeper, finer person. Oh, he had wanted war, but it had disillusioned instead of elevating because the Boers were dirty fighters. In the military manuals he had been schooled in, you always saw your enemy in the light of day. There had been no mention of colossal guns that could send a shell six miles, or ground-level trenches hacked out of rock and active in the dawn. They would blame Methuen, but what could he do against such an enemy in a war in which you had to resort to shooting in the back because they fled from hand-to-hand fighting?

New Year was brought in with another nip of whisky, and where limbs would allow, hands linked between beds for the singing of 'Auld Lang Syne', though the Astronomer Royal had decreed that the new century could not begin till 1 January 1901. His stretched hands gripping others brought back the human chain across the Modder, only there he had the use of his legs, with Jamie beside him, instead of a Lieutenant with shell-scorched face, his shocked body making his bedsprings audible throughout the night. That was why brooding on a broken leg and thoughts of death were cowardly. He had life; he had hope; and he had Laura at home, waiting.

January was stifling heat and a plague of insects. He pestered the doctor, but wasn't to be allowed up yet. To keep the convalescing quiet, a pile of newspapers was brought into the ward, so that they could read the reports on the battle for the relief of Kimberley. Special correspondents, including Winston Churchill, had been sent out, and there were elaborate maps of the battlefields. Under the heading of 'Black Week', the press grouped the three battles of Stormberg Junction, Magersfontein and Colenso. The Captain was shocked to read that his father's old friend General Wauchope had been killed at Magersfontein, 'still clutching his claymore, like a Scottish chief of old'. Princess Louise's had suffered particularly heavily at Magersfontein. His own name was among the wounded, for Mama to have hysterics over, and, to madden Aunt Carlotta, the information that he was the son of 'Major Alexander Macdonald of Invernevis, a distinguished soldier of the 91st Highlanders'. He had always had to live in his father's shadow. But, thank God, there was no mention of Jamie.

And then he read: 'We note the bravery of Piper Donald Macdonald, 'A' company, Princess Louise's, who did his best to give the disorientated force encouragement and direction by striking up the regimental tune, but was killed by a bullet passing through the bag.' It was what he had feared, but it was still a shock, and he lay there for several minutes, remembering. But there was no use in brooding: that was a hero's death, the kind his father applauded.

He returned to the papers, to read that Lord Roberts had been appointed Commander-in-Chief, with Lord Kitchener as his Chief-of-Staff, which would surely bring the war to a speedy conclusion. But just imagine: the Boers had scooped out twelve miles of earth and ironstone under Magersfontein Hill, curving like an open razor.

Having exhausted the battle reports, he turned to the other pages of *The Times*, whiling away the afternoon by reading the small advertisements. Life seemed to be going on at home, with theatres where women danced, estates to let 'with fine shooting', plenty of servants.

Then, as he was about to pass the paper on to the next bed, his eye caught the Deaths column, something that Aunt Carlotta always read, thin iips moving.

> At Invernevis House on 10 December 1899,
> in his sixty-seventh year, Lieutenant-
> Colonel Alexander Macdonald, sixteenth
> of Invernevis.
> South African and Indian papers please copy.

He let the paper slide from his bed and lay for a long time with his eyes closed, seeing the work of Aunt Carlotta's steel pen in the intimation. He had died on the day of Magersfontein, yet by an eerie error of editing he was treated as being alive by the war correspondent on another page.

He heard the rustle as the nurse picked up the paper and moved quietly away, assuming he had fallen asleep. But he called her back.

'My trunk, under the bed. You'll find a white sporran. Please get it.'

Down on her knees, she slid the trunk out, disturbing Donald Macdonald's neat packing. When she placed the sporran on his chest he thrust a hand in and groped, extracting the two Invernevis rings, still sticky with carbolic. He slipped them on, and, though they were too big, left them.

Learning that he had now succeeded, the doctor yielded to his questions that night. The bandages could come off soon, but it would be a couple of months before he was up, with a game leg for life because the Mauser bullet had shattered the kneecap.

Book Two

Chapter Five

When the train emerged from the dark pass his face was close to the glass and he was horrified to see the blaze, certain that the mansion under the mountain was on fire, but when the rumble of the Disputed Pool bridge began, the emerging moon showed the silhouette of the mountain, giving him his bearings. The blaze was on the same side as Invernevis House, but down by Wade's Bridge, and he could lie back again, having remembered the custom of the welcome-home bonfire, the same as he had got at his coming of age.

Clad in crumpled tweed acquired in London, his game leg rested on the opposite seat of the gas-lit compartment which he had reserved, to save embarrassment. The tin trunk was in the van, supplemented by two new leather suitcases stamped with the black letter I. And a London goldsmith had reduced the circumference of the two heirloom rings. They were tight on the flesh now, on adjacent fingers of the left hand.

Because of complications caused by surgery to his leg he had been forced to stay months in hospital at the Cape. He had followed French's flank march, and shared in the ward's jubilation when Kimberley was relieved on 15 February, and Ladysmith on the 28th. Even more emotional was the victory of Paardeberg, after ten days, with General Cronje, mastermind of the Modder defences, surrendering to Lord Roberts. But the Captain's happiness was muted by the fact that Princess Louise's had again suffered heavy casualties. Among the wounded was Captain James Mackay, 'who distinguished himself in the fighting'.

He had left Cape Town on 5 June, the day that Lord Roberts had entered Pretoria. Instead of going north to Invernevis, the new laird had lingered in London, residing in Brown's Hotel and retaining the daily services of a masseur in the hope that his hands would move a knee the doctors said would be permanently straight. When there was no improvement after two months, he decided to obey Mama's urgent letters and head home, but as far as possible dispensing with the walking-stick.

Though the weak lamps of Invernevis village were approaching, he was not at ease. He had written to say that he was invalided out of Princess Louise's, but he had not told them that it was with a game leg for life. That would only have caused speculation and exaggeration, and he preferred to show them that he was still mobile, though by an ungainly movement.

The gig was waiting for him at the station, deserted because most of the villagers had moved down to Wade's Bridge to welcome him. Roddy the coachman shook his head sadly as he helped the new laird up. He had nothing to say because he had helped to put the old one into his coffin.

They went down the steep brae into the damp autumn landscape of audible trees, with the new moon among moving clouds, and the pin-pricks of the navvies' shacks at the granite quarry across water. The monotonous clop-clop and Roddy's stubborn silence made the new laird sleepy. He shivered and dreamed a log fire, with Laura running laughing through wide doors. There was no shame now in going home for good. His father was dead, and hadn't Lord Roberts telegraphed that the war was over, with President Kruger's departure for exile?

The briars of the hedges were making mournful harps of the wheels as they approached the Macdonald croft, the landscape falling away to the left, past the ghostly peak of the iron furnace, to the shore where waves shifted shingle with more sad music. The croft was in darkness.

'How is Mrs Macdonald?'

'Dead,' the coachman said abruptly, his whip a parabola.

'When?' Invernevis asked hoarsely.

'About a month after the boy went away with you. She

should have been dead months before, Dr MacNiven said. Riddled with cancer, she was.'

So the second black box on the back of the gig containing the ruptured pipes would have to be taken up to the big house.

They were running above the river now, the Summer House Pool swollen in the momentary moonlight, the mansion lights brightened by the bulk of the mountain. Upriver, the growing flare of the bonfire, and moving shadows. He was now beginning to feel nervous, wishing he could avail himself of his new cigar-case. But the gig was turning, taking Wade's Bridge, the two horses hesitant. Overhead, an arch of saplings bound with greenery, and the word FAILTE, Gaelic for welcome, picked out in flowers nurtured under glass. It came into his mind that it was like driving through a giant wreath.

But it was not a time for gloom. The brutal man with the leprous sores had had his day, and he was now Invernevis, the mode of address taken from the land because the two were inseparable. It was strange, the series of identities he had had to learn to live with, to shed like snakeskins: the boy, the younger of Invernevis, the officer, and now the laird. That was why Farquhar was now pushing through the crowd, making the night air resonant with 'The Macdonalds' Welcome to Invernevis', his brogues stamping time on the hump of the bridge, and the villagers pressing behind him, cheering, waving improvised torches of windblown branches. Crackling flames from the pile beside the unhinged gate climbed into the sky, the avenue's leaf-strewn tunnel revealed, the mountain amplifying the welcome.

He sat on the gig, on the centre of the bridge under the arch, overcome as they pressed forward, but not far enough to jog the piper who stood between them and the bowed heads of horses which had pulled coffins as well as chieftains. But as Roddy came round to help him down, the sound died, the chanter falling from Farquhar's lips, the bag expiring in a groan. Spent torches trailing sparks were cast towards the Yellow Pool.

They shrank back into the shadows, watching the left leg nearly throwing him off balance as he took the hump of the bridge. Some women were sobbing, men muttering in Gaelic.

'It's all right, I can manage!' he shouted in assurance, slapping the leg, and then Father Macdonald was coming forward to fill the awkward silence, to take his hand and say how grieved they were about his father, but how happy to have him home as laird. The priest then turned to face the crowd, his profile commanding in the firelight. He made the sign of the cross.

'Let us pray for our new laird,' he ordered. And then, when he had bowed heads, he continued in English: 'We thank you, Lord, for sparing him on the battlefield. We pray that he will have a long life of health and prosperity, and we pledge our loyalty at all times.'

They murmured 'Amen' with him, and as the pipes ranted again, silver-mounted ivory circling the flames, Invernevis moved among them, taking hands, giving thanks. Old women blessed him in Gaelic, gripping him in the pincers of arthritic fingers. Men saluted and called him 'sir' after they had removed their caps.

As he swung towards the last of them standing in the shadows on the other side of the bridge, he recognized the stocky figure and clean-shaven face of Duncan the ghillie.

'I'm so sorry about the boy,' Invernevis said, stuttering as their hands locked. 'He showed great bravery. You should be very proud.'

'I've another son, sir,' the ghillie said in a factual voice.

'And your wife, too.'

'It was merciful, sir. She only hung on to see the boy safely away, and she was gone before we got the news.'

But it did not sound like a rebuke.

'And how's the fishing been?' Invernevis asked, to fill silence.

'They're spawning now, of course, sir, but I'm hoping for a good spring run.'

Then the gig was beside him, and he was being helped up by many hands.

'We would like you to accept this as a tribute of our respect and loyalty,' Father Macdonald said, handing up the open black box over the big wheel, the silver rose-bowl resting on satin.

He insisted on standing up to say his thanks, knowing that it would be sterling, and that they had all contributed.

'Seeing it's a special occasion, I've allowed them whisky for a toast,' the priest said.

A lantern was placed on the trestle table under the trees,

the stone jar inverted, the glasses passed round, including the women. The priest raised the whisky to his lips, shouting: '*Slainte* for Invernevis!' and the people clashed glasses and repeated the Gaelic greeting.

The whip touched, the horses turned, moving up the avenue, leaving them to drink and dance in celebration till the fire was ashes, the stone jars empty. The tunnel of autumn foliage closed over Invernevis's head, blotting out the moon, the gig lamps wavering on thick trunks, metallic leaves held against the spokes by the wind. The pipes grew fainter, and as the gig took the blind bend he suddenly realized how cold he was. He might have taken whisky, but did not want Aunt Carlotta sniffing in disapproval.

The shrivelled rhododendron blooms brushed against the gig lamps, scattering petals which the wind took up. Tendons clung and whipped back, leaves rustling. Then the sky was beginning again as the gig made gravel noisy by the bay window where a solitary lamp welcomed on dark wood. Aunt Carlotta was a silhouette in the porch, her cheek turning to be kissed, her skirt whispering on stone as she turned in. When she saw the way he walked into the hall her face did not change as she crossed herself, saying it was 'God's will'.

He was looking around.

'She's upstairs, lying down,' she said.

'Laura? Isn't she well?' he asked in panic.

'No, no, your mother. She hasn't been herself of late.'

'Not herself?' He was even more confused.

'You can go up,' she said, nodding to the stairs. 'Your sister's with her. I'll see to dinner.'

Stick in one hand, the other grasping the banister, he heaved himself up, certain he was going to find something serious. He turned into the passage where the oil paintings were brought from the shadows by a lamp on a table, and as he swung along, the corner of his eye registered the anomaly. There was a faded square where Lady Anne by Raeburn had hung.

He stopped so quickly that he had to balance against the wall, his hand rocking the adjacent frame. His first thought was that the picture had been stolen or damaged, and Aunt Carlotta hadn't wanted to break the news. It was quicker to ask Mama than to struggle down again, so he knocked and pushed open the door.

Heaped with widow's weeds, Mama was sprawled on the bed, arms wide, noisy mouth open like a stranded fish's.

At the bottom of the bed, Laura sat erect in a high-backed chair, the way Aunt Carlotta had taught her, training her with small biscuits. Her hands were folded on her lap, one button boot hooked behind the other as she sat staring at the grey wall above Mama's bed. But how she had changed. She looked unkempt, like a tinker child, her dress dirty, her face smudged, golden curls straggling as she sat staring, slack-mouthed, at the wall.

He was wondering what in God's name had happened when she became aware of his presence. There was a scream; button boots flew over the carpet; hands locked round his neck, hoisting; his cheek was wet. She babbled on, demanding the black-haired doll that he had promised in the meadow across the Summer House Pool on the afternoon he had left for war.

He took her wrists and lowered her gently. But he had only taken a couple of steps towards the bed when she shrieked with laughter, doubled over, slapping her knees.

'Your leg! Your leg! Why are you walking funny?'

He turned to the distended face, at knee level now, and for the first time in his life felt like striking her.

'Stop it, you little fool!'

Wide-eyed, slack-jawed, she straightened.

'This is no time for games. What's wrong with Mama?'

But he needn't have asked. As he turned he smelt it, though he was still a few feet from the bed, and as he moved closer, his toe stubbed, setting glass going.

'It's Mama's medicine,' Laura said in that high voice apparent maturity had not changed. 'If I don't give it to her, she won't get well.'

He was looking down on the wreck of his mother, wide-mouthed, lacking teeth, sparse grey hair stranded over her shoulders, the cheeks sunk in, almost the double of his dead orderly's mother. Mama shared with Queen Victoria the distinction of diminutive hands. They were grimy, the nails broken.

'Her medicine,' Laura repeated, pointing to the dressing table where a bottle and glass waited on tarnished circular silver. 'When she wakes up I've to give it to her. If I don't have it ready she makes an awful noise, and then Aunt Carlotta – '

The girl was crying now, confused by her brother's new contempt for games. He put his arm round her shoulders and led her to the bed, sitting beside her, where Mama's scored palm lay.

'Now, Laura, you do love me, don't you?'

That question was answered with anguish.

'And I you, so we trust each other. The last time I was home I promised you I would bring you back a doll, and I've kept my promise. All I ask in return is that you tell me the truth, as you've always done. How long has Mama been sick, like this?'

She found breath between sobs. 'Since father went to hell.'

He was towering above her, hauling her up by the wrists. 'You wicked, wicked girl!'

'I'm not wicked; father was wicked,' she said earnestly. 'Aunt Carlotta said he was a wicked man and was sent to hell for his sins. She said he would burn for ever.' Her eyes widened, voice dropping confidentially. 'On the night he died, the dogs made a *terrible* noise, like someone screaming.'

He lowered himself, putting his head into his hands; and had his game leg not been aching with the exertion of the stairs, he could easily have been convinced that it was a nightmare. The woman behind him was in an alcoholic stupor, the girl beside him incoherent. Only Aunt Carlotta had the answers. *Someone* had to have them.

He was at the door when he said: 'Laura, I want you to come here.'

The boots came, but they stumbled, disorientated.

'I'm not going to give you a row, my dear. You did your best.' It was hard for him to keep the words together as he hugged the bent head.

He led her into the passage and showed her the space. 'Now, Laura, you remember the beautiful lady who hung here?'

'Yes, yes,' she said, shoulders shaking with excitement. 'The lady who's the ghost, the one I meet on the stairs.'

'Never mind the ghost. Where's the picture?'

She didn't hesitate, because she had nothing to hide. 'Mama gave it to a man, and he gave her – look, I'll show you.' She ran into the room, thrust a hand under the pillow supporting

Mama's head, and as she brought the little canvas sack, tipped the sovereigns into her palm. 'Aren't they lovely? Mama's promised me one if I'm good and have her medicine ready before she wakes up.'

The game leg hit plaster as he went down, across the hall of treacherous rugs and into the drawing-room where Aunt Carlotta sat at her desk, using a steel pen on the proofs of her latest temperance tract. When she saw his face she folded her small steel spectacles, laid them on the black type and went to the sofa by the fire.

'Such a terrible time. I'm quite worn out, but God will give me the strength to see it all through. When? Since he died, night and day. She never stops. But I can't blame her. It was an appalling end, and we had to give them drink before they would agree to lift him into his coffin.' The memory made her cross herself. 'Like a leper, but not one God would touch. The beasts of the field are cleaner, but I'll spare you the details. So she began to drink, a bottle a day. Getting it? Oh no, I wouldn't allow her to go into the village, but someone is fetching it for her, and I'm certain it's that coachman. The Raeburn? Oh, she sold that to a dealer from Glasgow for fifty pounds, to get money for drink, because she's too shaky to sign a cheque and, anyway, I *dared* Richardson the lawyer. For fifty pounds, and it was gone before I noticed. Oh, I tried to get the name of the dealer, but she couldn't remember. His kind don't leave cards. And one afternoon when I went down to take tea with Father Macdonald – I had to have some respite, you understand – I came back to find your mother in here, with a grubby little man, and these glass cases open. A gold watch had already gone for five pounds, but I managed to get it back, after I'd threatened him with the constable. And that's not all: Campbell was to get the Disputed Pool for one hundred pounds, but I soon put a stop to that.'

'And Laura dragged into it all,' he moaned.

But Aunt Carlotta snorted. 'That girl's become too much of a problem. Quite uncontrollable. She goes into the kitchen, and you don't know what she's saying. I think we must consider a home. I understand from Father Macdonald that there's a good one in Edinburgh, quite reasonable – the money, I mean.'

Had he not been so tired after the journey and depressed after the revelations he would have quarrelled violently with her. But she had saved the heirlooms and the Disputed Pool, if not the Raeburn. That really broke his heart. Fifty pounds for an heirloom that was insured for thousands.

'And Alexander?' he asked wearily, wanting to get the bad news over.

Aunt Carlotta's eyes were glinting. 'A dis-grace. Oh no, he hasn't lived here since you went away. This place isn't good enough for him, apparently. MacPherson's got him where he wants him at the Home Farm. More men went out to South Africa after Magersfontein, but he wouldn't go. Oh no, *he's* too cowardly.' She turned dramatically. 'But I'm forgetting, you haven't seen the will. Your father's last act of spite against this family was to leave his debauched second son eight thousand pounds, mostly in brewery shares.'

She was watching for his reaction, and he could not conceal his anger. There had been a good deal of money when his uncle had the place, because he was a recluse with simple tastes, but his father had spent so much on horses and sporting gear. The estate would need every penny. Yes, it seemed like spite, giving Alexander the wherewithall to bring the family into even more disrepute by his conduct. It brought back Mama's idea of disinheritance.

But Aunt Carlotta was not quite done.

'Eight thousand pounds, but not his money, because my sister did bring *something* to that nightmare of a marriage. Money that should have gone to you, but you'll get the little I have. I've written to Richardson about the will, to see if it can be challenged.'

But before he could express his disapproval at her interfering in estate affairs in his absence Symmers came in to say that dinner was served. He followed Aunt Carlotta into that large room of double bay windows, one looking up the avenue, the other across to the river. Two lamps were burning on the massive mahogany sideboard, made into four by the long mirror behind. A place had been set for him at the head of the table, at that chair with the curving arms and claw feet kept empty during his father's illness. The familiar room from that outlook felt strange. The heat of the fire, with its ormolu clock on white marble, never seemed to reach the table, and the light was always poor, despite the lamps supplemented by a pair of candelabra making the reflections of silver cutlery look like fish in a dark pool. Oil paintings, too big or not part of the limited series in the passage above, land-scapes mostly, hung from brass hooks gripping the oak moulding under the embellished ceiling, too high for lamps or candles to show. The locked rack of the tantalus with its two decanters was out on the sideboard, beside a silver cigar-box and a silver-sheathed match-box. For Aunt Carlotta's attitude to temperance was not absolute: though she sniffed at it, she knew that gentlemen had to have their brandy and cigars after dinner, and Father Macdonald indulged. But she would not tolerate drinking and smoking among the servants and the villagers, and it was to them that the teachings of her temperance tracts were directed.

He noticed that the regimental presentation to his father, a silver stag's head carrying a bowl in its horns, had been removed from its customary place as centrepiece, a simple rose-bowl on a black stand in substitution. More than curiosity made him ask.

'It was an ugly thing,' she said dismissively. 'I had Symmers put it in the silver safe. Don't you recognize that bowl?'

He leaned forward, but could not read the inscription in the weak light.

'It's what the tenants gave you when you came of age,' she said.

'Well, I've got a spare one now,' he said.

But Aunt Carlotta wasn't amused. 'No imagination, that's what's wrong with them. You try and make them see the light, but they cannot.'

He noticed that there were no other places set at that long table which could wind out to accommodate twenty, the chairs ranged against the walls.

'Isn't Laura wanting dinner?'

Aunt Carlotta was lifting the brimming spoon, and it was steady as she answered him. 'I don't allow her to eat here any more. She keeps dropping her cutlery and upsetting bowls. It does get on the nerves, and it marks the surface.'

'And where *does* she eat?' he asked angrily. 'Surely not in Mama's room?'

'In the nursery,' his aunt said calmly, taking up more soup. 'There's no carpet there, so it's only a matter of mopping up.'

He wanted to say it, but decided it was not the time. Laura *must* be treated as one of them, otherwise there would never be any improvement. Hadn't Dr MacNiven said as much?

And she would have to be kept away from Mama. It wasn't good for a young girl to see things like that. It was time she had a governess, or a companion: he would see to that himself. And Mama would need a nurse, though it would be expensive. He was the master now, and such decisions were his responsibility. Aunt Carlotta tried to help, but she sometimes went too far.

Symmers's unsteady hand came out of the shadows to take his new master's cold soup, slopping it over the plate's crested rim. The stag which had been shot on the mountain had been well hung, and knife and fork easily parted the streaky red meat, but he had lost his appetite.

'That will be sufficient, Symmers,' Aunt Carlotta was saying, waiving the savoury. 'You may leave the coffee in the drawing-room and go down to the bonfire.' A fork wagged. 'But I warn you, come back drunk and you'll definitely be dismissed this time.'

And when the old butler in the shiny tails had bowed himself out, she continued:

'I warned them about gossip, but it always gets across the river. They're saying now in the village that your mother hasn't taken her clothes off since he died. Even if it were true, what concern is it of theirs, who also sleep in their clothes? I blame that scullery-maid Macdonald. She's too quiet, and the quiet ones are the most dangerous.'

'Maggie, my orderly's sister?' he said incredulously.

'And daughter of your father's ghillie, who was left one hundred pounds in *his* will, for what I cannot imagine.'

'He helped Mama to wash and lift father,' his son reminded her.

'These were no more than his duties, seeing there was no one fishing,' Aunt Carlotta said. 'It was a will drawn up in spite. Prepare yourself for a shock.'

'Then I suppose I'd better see it, if you'll excuse me,' he said, rising. 'I shan't take coffee.'

'I've left all the papers on the desk, but it's still to be cleaned out. The keys are there, but I couldn't bring myself.'

The library, which was adjacent to the dining-room, lacked a bay window, but was still spacious, facing up the avenue. There was a large leather-topped desk in the centre, the swivel chair in front of the fender. One hundred and fifty years of books had accumulated haphazardly on the floor-to-ceiling shelves, some, like *The Gentleman's Magazine*, given space because it was too much trouble to stop the subscriptions in the days of poor posts. The majority, like Cadell's massive edition of the *Waverley* novels, had been purchased by his uncle, whom Niall's father had succeeded, and whose name was Niall's middle one in deference. John, fifteenth of Invernevis had remained a bachelor, despite tradition's demands for direct descent. A recluse with a brilliant mind, he had spent most of his time in the library, even taking his meals there, and sometimes sleeping on a camp bed when a problem was too pressing to take upstairs. Educated at Cambridge and Heidelberg, he had taught himself Gaelic, and even followed it back to Pictish script, spending days translating a single sentence, writing to Celtic scholars in a language they could not understand, until one dawn of birdsong he had sought clarification through *Casan Dubh*. When his brother Alexander took over, the library stank, and the drawers of the desk were crammed with unconnected papers as well as the dehydrated contents of crested blue plates he had been too absorbed to consume.

The new laird stopped on the threshold, struck by the recollection that he had been allowed in on very few occasions. His chief memories – and these, being from childhood, were hazy – were of his father's spurred boots standing on the hearth, and the thread of the chair squeaking as the burly man with the close-cropped head and large beard swung this way and that, lost in thought of another life overseas, no doubt. Alexander was usually in the room with him, sitting on a stool by the fire, looking at the engravings or early photographs in the latest fishing or stalking book, the expensive predecessors piled on the shelves, rejected because they had no new skills to offer. His father was always gruff with him, asking him what he wanted, and when the excuse didn't work, advising him to go back to Aunt Carlotta while Alexander sniggered and prodded flaming wood. And when the swivel chair was empty, Alexander was allowed to swing in it, knees drawn up while his father smoked and drank by the fireside.

He lifted back the chair, eased his game leg under the desk, and turned up the lamp, picking up the blue stitched document from the pile held down by an anemone trapped in domed glass. Written in a clerk's copperplate, the long preamble stated that the document was the last will and testament of

Lieutenant-Colonel Alexander James Macdonald, sixteenth of Invernevis, who, 'being of sound mind', was making an arrangement that made his elder son drop the document in disbelief. He was only to get the life-rent of the estate, which was put under three trustees: Father Allan Macdonald, parish priest of Invernevis; Mr Walter Richardson, Writer to the Signet, Charlotte Square, Edinburgh; and Colonel Thomas Godfrey Hooker, late of the Lancers, c/o his club. And failing his elder son's ability to furnish a male heir, the estate was to be conveyed to Alexander, 'beloved' second son, his heirs and successors.

He read it again to make certain, seeing his father's warped mind working from the grave. He hadn't disinherited, but he had constricted, like a crushing Indian snake. The life-rent amounted to being passed over, the appointment of trustees implying that he wasn't capable. He was being treated like a minor, or an imbecile. It was a malicious will, designed to set brother against brother, but with Alexander preferred, and he had appointed as trustees people he had hated, but who were staunch friends of Aunt Carlotta's. So even as life-renter and not laird Niall was being forced to take orders from her, because she would twist the trustees to her will. Father Macdonald depended on her patronage for creature comforts that Rome denied; Colonel Hooker, old soak, was in love with her; and Richardson was merely weak, dazzled by breeding. The heir wasn't to be allowed his manhood, his right to make decisions, though that was what his military career (forced on him by his father) had trained him to do. Did his father hope that Aunt Carlotta's inevitable interference would make it impossible for him to bring a bride to Invernevis, thus allowing Alexander to succeed, with eight thousand of brewery shares behind him?

And there was more, with Mama, who had endured so much, made parasitic on him by her annuity, the first three hundred pounds of income from an estate her husband had dissipated. Laura was to be granted a home at Invernevis House for life, with a sufficient income to keep her, though putting that in was another slur on his elder son's character. Aunt Carlotta was to get as 'keepsake' 'my bone-handled riding crop'.

There followed a list of bequests to estate workers, and servants, and he was surprised to see that the ghillie, the coachman, and the butler got a hundred pounds each. Mrs Livingstone the cook got nothing.

The will was dated two years before death, when he was still on his feet, which meant that a challenge wouldn't succeed, though the disease had been showing then. And of course the trustees would defend, not wishing to relinquish the power vested in them, with lucrative expenses.

He laid down the document and leaned back in the chair. He was opening his cigar-case when he noticed the next letter on the pile. It was a small note, addressed to his mother from Dr MacNiven. It was difficult to read, and had to be held close to the lamp.

> I put paralysis on the death certificate, to
> save you further suffering, but we both know
> it was syphilis.

He had heard that word before, whispered by brave men in the mess who had wandered from the brandy decanter to the brothel. He understood its origins, but had closed his ears to its symptoms. Now the lamp was mobile, ranging the shelves in search of an encyclopaedia, and though it was years out of date the volume he carried to the desk made him break off reading.

For the muslin curtain was being torn aside, revealing the sores, the ruined eyes of a disease that could be transmitted by touch. No wonder the bequests to servants were so big. Poor, poor Mama. No wonder she was drinking herself into unconsciousness. Aunt Carlotta had left the doctor's letter under the will out of hatred, but who could blame her, since she had such high principles? It was an outrage against life. He had only loathing now for a man he had hardly known. But thank God Laura was untouched.

He left the uncut cigar lying on the open volume and wandered to the window. Through the trees he could see the bonfire flaring as it was fed more wood, the reel of the pipes accompanying the spiralling flames and dancing shadows. He had been gelded by his father and wished that he had fallen at Magersfontein. He had no power but *had* to keep things going, for their sake as much as his own. A good many of the families had come to Invernevis with the first chieftain, had fought and died for the succession, first at home, then abroad.

84

Though the river might divide mansion from village, there was no spiritual division. The tenants were one big family, depending on the laird, the man at the centre, as the wheel depended on the hub to keep going. By his father's will he had been put on their side of the river, to fight with them against the trustees in case they raised rents or lowered wages, in order to keep the big house going. It was a vicious circle, his father forcing him to fight himself and his own inheritance, hoping, no doubt, that he would surrender to Alexander. But that wasn't going to happen. Despite Aunt Carlotta he would get a wife and an heir, but not rushing recklessly into marriage, as his father must have hoped by leaving such a monstrous arrangement. There was not going to be another Magersfontein. The new century called for a new beginning so he held Dr MacNiven's note to the mouth of the globe till it began to curl and go black. When it burst into flames he used it to light his cigar.

But when he picked up the next paper his confidence changed to outrage. It was the copy of a letter from Aunt Carlotta to Munro the undertaker, instructing him to open a layer in the enclosure behind the chapel, since Lieutenant-Colonel Macdonald was *not* to be buried with the Invernevis chieftains in the chapel proper. Aunt Carlotta had broken centuries of tradition, something she had no authority to do, and something he himself would never have done, despite the horror of his father's disease, and despite the fact that he himself had broken tradition by appointing trustees. And she had cunningly placed her instructions next to the doctor's letter and the will to justify the shift. He stood there, by the lamp, seriously considering exhumation, but his father had been buried nearly a year, and there was a danger of infection if the coffin was lifted. He would have it out with Aunt Carlotta. He was the laird, despite the trustees. A new beginning was even more necessary.

Down at the bonfire Maggie the scullery-maid was having the same thoughts, hoping that his arrival home would bring changes. When he had stopped to speak to her father she had hidden behind a tree. She was so sorry about the leg, but thought him more handsome than ever, a real gentleman. Not that she had had any dealings with his father. Miss Carlotta was the boss, and she had made Maggie's life a misery, suddenly appearing in the scullery to pick up plates and put them back in the sink, claiming they weren't cleaned properly. And on the day when news of her brother Donald's death at Magersfontein had come through, so soon after her mother's passing, Maggie was standing crying in the scullery when Miss Carlotta came in, pushing her towards the sink, shouting that work was good for grief.

Her life had been hell after the lawyer had told her father that he had been left a hundred pounds by the old laird. Miss Carlotta had come in with blazing eyes, saying that some people didn't care what they touched, as long as there was profit in it. Maggie hadn't understood that reference to her father helping to lift and wash the laird, and that had made it worse. Miss Carlotta was in such a temper that she had knocked against a plate – one from the crested dinner service – and when it smashed on stone, shouted that it hadn't been properly balanced, and would be docked from wages.

When Miss Carlotta had swept out in her angry dress, Maggie had gone to the servants' hall to give vent to her upset against her father's shoulder. Having petted her, he told her to return to her sink.

'Stick in, lassie. Your mother set her heart on you making something of it here, and if you were to be sacked it would be a terrible disgrace.'

So she had endured, and held the plates under water twice as long. Miss Carlotta kept appearing to criticize, and at the half year Maggie's wages were ten shillings short. Though she was shocked, she didn't query it. But Miss Carlotta wanted to explain.

'Five shillings for the dinner plate you dropped, the other five for unsatisfactory work. If you don't get a grip of yourself in the next month, you're back down the road to the village, girl. I have another girl in mind, but not from these parts – a good worker and a *good* Catholic.'

And when she gave her wages to her father in place of her mother, Maggie explained the shortage by saying that she had written to Signor Faccenda, asking for a photograph of the new laird in his army uniform.

'And what address did you put?' her father asked, shifting the lamp to see her face.

Maggie knew that she was going very red. 'Just Glasgow,' she said. 'Signor Faccenda, Photographer to Society, Glasgow.'

'And you expect *that* to reach him, girl? Glasgow's a big place, and ten shillings not easily come by. Don't start imagining we're well off because I was left a hundred pounds by the old laird. That money's being put aside, to put up a stone for your mother, and one for Donald, though he isn't buried here. And Hector will have to get his chance.' He shook his head incredulously. 'A photograph of the laird, and you only a scullery-maid. Well, I suppose that's what you call loyalty.' But his rare smile went and he added: 'Don't get above yourself, girl.'

But the new laird had been wounded and wouldn't be coming home for a while yet. When she went up to her bed Maggie prayed that he would come home soon, safe and well, because Miss Carlotta had found a new line of attack. Everyone in the servants' hall knew that the Mistress was drinking heavily, and the house-maids were always mocking Laura lisping: 'Mama's medicine.' It gave Elsie from the kitchen, Miss Carlotta's ally, a good laugh. But Maggie kept quiet at the middle of the table, chewing her tough meat. The only other person in the room who didn't laugh or make a reference to the drinking was her father.

Then one morning Miss Carlotta had almost taken the scullery door off its hinges, screaming (the house-maids upstairs heard her) that it was Maggie who was spreading the stories in the village about the Mistress sleeping in her clothes, and drinking straight from the bottle.

'But I've never been to the Mistress's bedroom, and I'm hardly ever in the village,' Maggie protested, astonishment giving her the power to reply.

That only made Miss Carlotta worse, and her long thin throat was throbbing as she shouted: 'You little slut, daring to betray the trust I've placed in you, taking you into this house when God knows where you would have landed up. You will leave at the end of the month, without back wages.'

It was still two days till Sunday, and Maggie was exhausted, her back aching from bending over the sink, her hands raw, stomach nauseated by the floating scum in pots that took so long to scour. She started to cry, finding release for the pent-up feelings of months, her mother's death, her brother's, the young laird wounded, Miss Carlotta's unfairness. Her back was to the sink, her head bowed.

Then a remarkable thing happened. Miss Carlotta put the

ball of her palm under Maggie's chin, and, lifting it, said in a voice Maggie had never heard her use before:

'You know, you're quite pretty when you cry.'

With which she went, leaving Maggie utterly confused, wondering what cruel trick Miss Carlotta was playing on her. Was she to clear out? She didn't know. Not till the end of the month, she'd said. What was the meaning of it all? She'd finished the dishes for the moment, and would go upstairs, to tidy up.

But Elsie's bare arm barred her way through the kitchen. 'Is this you slinking back to bed, now that Miss Carlotta's taken a fancy to you? Oh, I saw it all right. Well, it won't last, so get back in there because there'll be plenty of tins coming through from the baking.'

Maggie didn't know what she meant, but she went back to the sink, and Miss Carlotta didn't come back, so the sacking stood. But on the night of the bonfire, when she expected to be kept back for the dinner dishes, Mrs Livingstone told her she could go down.

'You're young, but let's hope it's the first and last home-coming you'll see,' the cook said.

Maggie would never forget these words. They were in her mind when the new laird limped over Wade's Bridge to come and talk to her father. He had given her permission for a five-shilling contribution to the silver rose-bowl fund which Mr Symmers the butler had collected, though Frank the footman had said that the money would go to empty a bowl, not buy one.

When the new laird had gone up the dark avenue with the gleaming silver on his knees, leaving her to listen to the pipes and watch the dancing, she felt sure things would be better. Miss Carlotta had certainly quietened down for the home-coming.

Chapter Six

Miss Carlotta had had the dead man's room fumigated with sulphur candles in preparation for the heir's homecoming because tradition dictated that the big bedroom in the picture passage was the laird's, connecting with his wife's. The muslin drapes had been torn down, the horse-hair mattress and bedding burned by the ghillie and coachman. But Miss Carlotta was still not satisfied. The two house-maids had had to scrub out the room on their knees, and wash down the furniture before waxing it. The window was then left open for a week.

The dead man's clothes had been left in the massive wardrobes in the dressing-room. The new laird went through the wardrobes with Duncan the ghillie. He would have liked to have kept the kilts, to have sent them to Perth to be cleaned and taken in, but the thought of the heavy dark Macdonald tartan lying next to bare skin made him cautious. Besides, he didn't yet know if he had the courage to wear a kilt with the game leg.

So the wardrobes were emptied, and all the clothes piled in the middle of the floor, shirts for a bull neck, hose for brutal calves, and several pairs of breeches, with the leather inside the thighs well rubbed. The trees were saved, but the big brogues put out. All the stuff – and there was masses of it – was of the finest quality, with the labels of Princes Street and Piccadilly. He knew he could get quite a bit of money from the second-hand clothes shops specializing in gentlemen's wear, but the idea of other people in his father's clothes made him decide that burning was the best solution.

He had to grope in the dark recess of the wardrobe to get at the last garment, a regimental doublet for a dress kilt. It had hardly been worn, and he had to borrow the clasp-knife the ghillie used for gutting fish to hack off the crested silver buttons before throwing the doublet in the heap. But the buttons of the 91st Argyllshire Highlanders could go in the glass case in the drawing-room, beside the snuff boxes, breastplates and medals.

All that remained was the pair of riding boots standing

under the tilted pier-glass. The spurs had too many bad associations to save, and the boots were already splayed on the pile when the ghillie said:

'I could use them, sir. They're good strong boots.'

'But they're far too big for you, Duncan,' he said in surprise.

'I could put paper in the toes,' the ghillie said, sitting on a chair to unlace his own boots. He hooked his fingers through the brass rings and pulled out the wooden insets. Then he was struggling into the tan boots, pulling his plus-fours down over the top and standing up to stamp and say: 'There you are, sir. Very comfortable. Just a wee bit at the toes.'

When Invernevis stooped to pinch leather there was a good inch. 'You're welcome to them, Duncan,' he said, smiling. 'Only I wouldn't advise you to let my aunt see you wearing them. You know how strict she is about dress, and they don't exactly go with the plus-fours.'

'I'll wear them on the river, sir. I'll put tackets on the soles to give them a good grip.'

The riding boots were removed, the clothes and brogues taken down the back stairs. They were carried to that area behind the walled garden reserved for burning, soaked in paraffin, and a match dropped. Invernevis could see the black smoke from the library window as he stood drinking coffee before getting down to his desk. There were so many letters to be written, and the black-bordered ones expressing sympathy at his father's death had to have priority, since they had lain for almost a year, Aunt Carlotta avoiding hypocrisy by not answering them. The lawyers would have to be written, to be told that he had now taken over, and would welcome an early meeting at Invernevis, since his leg put Edinburgh out of bounds for the present. And he would have to write to the Captain-General of the Queen's Bodyguard of the Royal Company of Archers, asking if he might take his father's place when the sovereign visited Edinburgh.

He had been up to see Mama that morning, finding her full of remorse over her drinking, but inconsolable when she saw the game leg, crying that it was a curse on her, first with Laura, then Alexander, then her husband, and now herself and the heir.

'What did I do to deserve this?' she wailed, and though he knew it was dramatics for more drink, he felt so sorry for her, lying there in the widow's weeds that had obviously not been off for a long time. She had made herself into an old woman in the space of a year. The grey hair hanging in strands from her big skull was like a man's; her mouth and hands twitched as she spoke, and he could feel her body making the bed vibrate.

'Just a little whisky, then I'll sleep,' she said hoarsely, with the look of a gun-dog about to be whipped. 'If I can get off to sleep I'll be all right. Where's Laura? Why is it so dark? Oh, Niall, I'm so afraid.' She clutched at his arm. 'These black people at the window, what do they want, climbing up? Have they come to take me away?'

'There's no one there, Mama,' he said, lowering her shoulders.

'One small whisky,' she pleaded. 'That's all I want, then I'll sleep. I promise I won't ask for any more.'

'No, Mama, because you've got to make a start some time. I know it's going to be hard, but you'll have to find the strength. You'll feel terrible for a few days, then you'll be all right, able to come down and help Aunt Carlotta.' He knew the symptoms, having seen them in a Major raving on a camp bed in the Dublin barracks, having to be held down with trunk straps in case he swallowed his own tongue after a week night and day of poteen.

But when he repeated that there was to be no more whisky she began to scream and pound the pillow with her fists, like a child in a tantrum. There was nothing to be done but to slap her quiet. All his instincts were against slapping a woman, and especially his own mother, but they would be hearing her in the servants' hall. Then Aunt Carlotta would come up to make matters worse. One sharp slap was sufficient.

He had never seen such a look of astonishment. She touched her cheek as if in disbelief at what had just happened to her, and then, turning her face away into shadow, she bit her fist and began to sob, the way Laura did. The sound accompanied him to the door, but he dared not turn and relent. She would have to lie there, sleepless behind drawn curtains, making the bedsprings audible with her twitchings until the drink had been sweated from her system. Maybe then she would manage some food, if the neat whisky hadn't burned her insides.

And then there was the problem of Laura. Aunt Carlotta

had acted as governess, to save money being wasted, saying the girl would never be able to read or write. All she did was to sit in the school-room, pretending to study the illustrated books of saints and martyrs that Aunt Carlotta had imported from Italy. She was now too old for a governess, but he wondered if she shouldn't have a companion, a girl of her own age and the same background who would help her into womanhood. But if such a girl could be got, Aunt Carlotta would say that her nephew no longer trusted her with his sister. Perhaps it would be wiser to leave things as they were for the moment, but he would have to spend as much time as possible with Laura.

There were practical matters to attend to first. The junk of the years had to be cleared from his father's desk, the drawers tipped out on to tooled leather circled where tumblers of whisky had sat within reach. There were sterling silver Devon minnows to trawl for salmon, and bullets, their contents emptied into the stags whose heads hung in the front hall. Tight bundles of paper were bound with grubby tape. He was going to toss them into the fire, but it occurred to him that some of the frayed yellowing documents might refer to the estate. But when he broke the rotten tape and fanned through the papers, he found they were old accounts for sporting equipment and trophies. Some of the sums staggered him: one hundred guineas for a made-to-measure saddle, five guineas for a silver medal for a rifle volunteer company shooting contest. Since they were all receipted, he consigned them to fire. Another bundle was a series of letters from a woman in Argyle Street, Glasgow. The spelling was atrocious, but the meaning behind the wavering pencil plain. She had been a maid at Invernevis in the eighties, but had been sent away to have his child. The letters begged him to honour his part of the bargain by sending on money, and at the top of each letter, in red ink, he had written: '2 guineas sent'. But there was no such reckoning on the last letter. Barely legible, it stated that since the child had died, he was released from his obligations. 'For mysel, I would rather go on the streets than be biholden to you.'

He kept prodding with the poker in case any fragments survived to fall into the hands of the maid who raked out the fire in the morning. The sooner such a brute passed from memory, the better.

92

The last bundle dated from Indian days, before he was born. He knew that he had no right to read them, but curiosity about that part of their lives made him break the band. They began in courting days, and in her neat handwriting, addressing him as 'Dear Major Macdonald', his mother recorded an elephant ride, 'very frightening because of the height, but when it is a Maharajah's, all you can do is to hang on. Carlotta was her usual calm self, however.' A tiger that her father had shot 'looked very pathetic, stretched out. He is going to take the skin home, for the hall, but I shan't walk on it. Carlotta doesn't like animals, anyway.' Kamptree, no date, but Friday. 'My dearest, you looked so handsome last night, at Colonel Gordon's Cremorne. I wish you'd teach me the sword dance, tho' I don't suppose it's for women.' 'Dearest, I must warn you that Papa is most opposed to you, and so is Carlotta. You are supposed to have a wicked reputation, but even if it's true (which I don't believe) I find it *exciting*.' 'Darling, I will be walking on the left side of the Soldiers' Garden, carrying a pink parasol. But only for *five* minutes, as Carlotta will be sent to spy.' Two lines, scrawled. 'Papa is dead. Col. Gordon is here, but you *must* come. Carlotta only prays.' 'Darling, I talked to Col. Gordon and he said YES, we may, because he thinks you a good soldier, and me a poor soul. But Carlotta will have to come too, as she can't go back to England alone. You'll understand.'

Kamptree, to Major Macdonald, on manœuvres. 'Sandy, I *hate* these barracks. The sanitation is disgusting, the heat and flies awful. And the servants so disrespectful – I feel another Mutiny will break out at any minute. I want to go back to England. If your brother won't put us up, mine will. It's all right for Carlotta. She's busy converting the natives to Catholicism, getting dozens of rosaries sent out. But what use is that when they can't count? *Please* come home soon.'

'Sandy, I had another Indian woman at the door last night, saying you molested her daughter on a rush mat, and her sister *at the same time*. Twelve years old. I tried to give her money, but she pointed to my pearls and wouldn't go back into the hills till she got them. Carlotta was there, and there was a *terrible* row. She swears these things are *true*, but I said you were being blackmailed. It's the *third* time in two weeks. You'll *have* to come home and put a stop to it, otherwise Col. Gordon will get to know.'

'Sandy, how could you? Ten years old, though I admit she looks older. But why, and *black*? It's not what it does to me, it's the danger of disease. I didn't have any money, so Carlotta had to give me some, which means she'll go on and on. Please: resign your commission. Let's go home.'

'Sandy, I fail to understand what it is about you, and you supposed to be a gentleman. I don't know, I turn my back but Carlotta says it's a *sickness* of the soul. Depravity, she calls it. Yet I still love you, which makes me silly, I suppose. But I console myself with the thought that it can't – daren't – happen in England. Come home soon. Constance.'

Where hers ended, his began, and though the son was sickened, he read on, his hand trembling by the lamp. 'Miss Constance, the pleasure of your company at the Cremorne, please. I shall do the sword dance again, specially for you. Yes, one could get a bad cut on the foot from the blade, but the secret is to side-step quickly. When I fail, will you bandage my foot? Yours Certainly, Alexander Macdonald. 'PS. My regards to Miss Carlotta who does not like me, I fear.'

'Darling Connie, Five minutes in the Soldiers' Garden was sufficient because memory can stretch it into hours. You looked lovely, the Rose of Kamptree, a new variety of bloom. As I explained, since I don't know the wicked crimes your father is accusing me of, I can't defend myself. But I'm a man, with all that that implies. Worse, a Highlander, so don't expect me to sit around, sipping Indian tea. As for Carlotta, she hates my guts, why, I don't know, and don't care. It's probably to do with religion, something you don't have much time for, out here, when you're putting down Mutinies in which white folk are dismembered. Until Thursday, your Sandy.'

'I'm sorry about your father, but he hated me, and there's an end to it. I'll come, but you must keep Carlotta at bay. Howling prayers doesn't help. Sandy.'

'Darling Connie, I had my interview with Col. Gordon and heard all the old stuff about officers not being allowed to marry. However, when I was handing in my sword he gave in and said it would settle me. Agreed. As to Carlotta coming along, I'll endure, for your sake, but only if she keeps her Hail Marys to herself. I'm not going to make a declaration of love because you *know*, Rose of Kamptree. Always, Sandy.

'Connie, I know the barracks are hellish etc. but there's no chance of going back home till my imbecile of a brother decides to hand over or commit himself. If the servants give you trouble, go to the Colonel, and he'll kick their backsides.'

'Connie you fool, Don't you realize how *dangerous* it is putting down about Indian girls on paper? *Of course* it's a pack of lies. Your dear sister probably put them up to it. If any more come, tell them you'll put the soldiers on them. But I'm too busy for such petty problems. Sandy *will* come home as soon as manœuvres are over.'

'Connie, All right, I admit it. I got drunk once or twice in the Mess and went down to a brothel, which officers have been doing since time began. How was I to know they were twelve or ten, or whatever age they claim to be? And as for your sister Catty saying it's a sickness, her trouble is that she's never experienced LOVE (I mean physical as well), though I suspect she would like to, hence her reason for hating me. She'll never understand what's between us, which is why she can't separate us. ——ing little Indian girls can't harm us, especially when I know you don't care very much for that side of things, so necessary for some men. Lust isn't a disloyalty. I had a letter from my bro. the laird, part in Gaelic (which I bloody well can't read, far less speak) in which he goes on about the Futility of it all. He's definitely off his head which means that I have a chance of getting the place and you out of that hell-hole. If that happens I'll make it all up, but Catty *can't* come. PS. I hear they might restore the Highland dress to the regiment which means I'll be able to do the sword dance properly. You remember, Rose of Kamptree. Yes, Yours, Sandy.'

There were several others, but he did not read on. The horror of his father's sexual predilections was mitigated by the honesty and tenderness he had shown towards his partner. He would not have believed his father capable of such affection, and he had not realized that there was such a bond between him and Mama. The crumbling bundle of letters had opened his eyes to human nature more than war had done. He had never had a woman himself, so he didn't know, but he saw it wasn't all black and white. They were opposites, obviously, and yet they had stuck it out together. She had forgiven him his Indian indiscretions, and yet thirty years later the full horror of them had brought heart-break and

95

back-break at Invernevis. No wonder she was lying upstairs with the dt's. Not that tenderness excused his father's reprehensible conduct, for it was easy to lie in a letter, and Mama was a trusting person. She must have felt such relief when they sailed from India, and yet – many things were puzzling him, but one in particular: if he had hated Aunt Carlotta so much, why had he brought her back (or allowed Mama to bring her) to Invernevis? Surely he *hadn't*, with her also. No, it was inconceivable: she must have a hold over him. Threatening to publicize his Indian indulgences if she wasn't taken? It wasn't likely he would ever find out. And did it matter now?

Had he kept those dangerous letters out of sentiment in his desk, or hoping that his heir would read them and re-evaluate him? Aunt Carlotta must have come across them when he was in South Africa, but they didn't look disturbed. But what to do with them? Despite the awful contents, they were really heirlooms, revealing one chieftain's character, as much as the oil paintings and the items in the glass cases in the drawing-room. If he threw them into the fire, future generations would judge Alexander, sixteenth of Invernevis, by local legend, saying that he had given his poor wife a terrible time. He was denying his father a fair hearing by burning them, but to keep them would cause embarrassment and shame, perhaps.

It was as if he held his father's soul in his hand, a pile of crumbling papers that fire would take a second to consume. He would be destroying history, settling old scores, the sneers, the life-rent, Alexander the chosen one. Though it was daytime, the room felt eerie, as if his father had left the letters to test him, and was sitting in the swivel chair, watching, waiting, seeing if his decision would prove his worth as a laird.

He dropped the letters back into the drawer, slammed it shut and twisted the key. After that he needed a brandy, sitting by the fire, thinking. He would have to assert his position with Aunt Carlotta, show her that he was the laird despite the trustees. The best strategy was to get to know the servants, most of whom had been appointed by his aunt, and with whom (the younger ones at least) he had had little contact in the years of military service. The way Mama was, he was going to have to depend on their devotion and discretion.

Best to begin with the woman who had been feeding him

since infancy. Mrs Livingstone was trundling a rolling-pin when he went through. She was flustered seeing him, rubbing the flour from her palms, trying to straighten her linen cap. He explained that his leg wasn't that bad, and he listened sympathetically as she described her swollen feet. She might have to retire before she intended. He said he was sorry but he would see her right.

He had a few words with Elsie the kitchen-maid, who seemed to him a shifty girl, never looking at you as you spoke. Yes, she was quite happy, and learning a lot from Mrs Livingstone. But he had seen Elsie pulling shut the scullery door when he came in, so he went through.

The resemblance to her dead brother was remarkable; the same pale skin, black hair, but she was smaller; pretty, he thought. Her back to the sink, she was so embarrassed that she could not speak, and when he said: 'I was so sorry about your brother; a very brave man, you know. And your mother also, of course,' she bit her lips and nodded.

'If there's anything I can do, do let me know,' he said vaguely.

'But I'm leaving at the end of the month, sir.'

'Leaving? Have you got another post?' Colonel Campbell came immediately to mind. The brute had stolen Invernevis servants before, by offering more money and more modern conditions at Branglin.

'No, sir, I was sacked. Miss Carlotta sacked me, sir.' It was all coming out. 'She said I was spreading stories about your mother, sir. Oh, I *wasn't*, sir.'

And she was crying. He had never been in such a situation with a servant and was unsure of himself. First he pushed the door shut.

'Now I think there may have been a misunderstanding, Maggie,' he said gently. 'My aunt's had a lot to cope with when I was away. Don't worry: I'll speak to her and put things right.'

'But I don't want to stay if there's going to be trouble, sir.' She was very upset now, and he felt it was getting out of hand.

'There won't be any trouble,' he told her, trusting his tongue. 'It's just a misunderstanding.' To reinforce his pledge he put his hand on her shoulder. When he saw the emotion he had aroused he retreated, back to the door. He had made a mess of it. He would have to learn how to handle tempera-

mental servants, especially young women. But that was something you could only learn by trial and error, apparently. It
was different when you were the laird's son, wanting help
with a shoelace, or with assembling a rod. Now he would
have to be both strict and natural.

But the worst part was still to come. Aunt Carlotta was
positively indignant at dinner, though Symmers was hovering
somewhere in the shadows.

'I've always considered the servants to be my responsibility,
and your father was quite happy to have me as housekeeper,
because he was getting me on the cheap.'

He did not doubt it, which let her anger run uninterrupted.

'Don't you see? You're undermining my authority over the
servants. They simply won't *obey* any more. I *know* that
Macdonald girl's trash, believe me. I've had her kind before.'

He didn't like that at all, but kept his temper.

'If you dismiss her, we'll – or I'll – be the talk of the village.
I can just hear them saying: he takes her brother out to get
killed, now he's sacking the sister.'

'And why should *we* care what they say in the village?'
Aunt Carlotta wanted to know. 'They owe their well-being to
this house, and the way they repay us is to spread wicked
gossip. Which that trash of a girl took to the village in the
first place.'

But he was going to stand firm, knowing that if he won,
the future would be easier.

'She *will* stay. That's the least I owe to the family. Don't
forget what her father did for mine. And she lost her mother.'

Which made Aunt Carlotta throw down her napkin and
stamp off, shouting over her shoulder that he was going to
turn out as bad as *him*. She kept to her room for several days,
and made the footman and ghillie drag her dusty trunks from
the attic. She sent for Elsie to help her pack, having let it be
known through the house-maids that she was leaving because
of the wicked stories the scullery-maid had been spreading in
the village.

But something happened that was to empty her trunks and
give her another subject for spite. She had come down to the
drawing-room to collect her temperance proofs from the desk
when Symmers the butler closed the door behind him. He
stood looking at his shoes, working his hands.

'Well, what do *you* want?' she asked sharply. 'If you've

been sent to announce dinner – '

'No, ma'am, not dinner.' He was having difficulty with his words.

'Drunk again,' she said contemptuously. 'Well, before I go the least I can do is to get you sacked.'

'No, ma'am, it's nothing like that.' (The threat was not new to him.) 'It's just that I thought I should come to you first. You see, Master Alexander's in the hall, wanting to see the Master.'

'Oh, *is* he? We'll soon see about that.' And, as she was sweeping through the door he was holding open for her: 'You did right – for once, Symmers.'

Since he was standing in the shadows, it took her several seconds to locate him, lurking just inside the door, by the marble table with the fishing book. She took the centre of the hall and drew herself up, determined that the house would hear.

'So you have the audacity to come back *here*, you scoundrel. Did I not make it clear that there is not, and never will be, a place here for you? You forfeited that right for good when you crossed the river to live at the Home Farm. You are nothing but a reprobate, following in your father's footsteps, and he was Satan to me. You have chosen Gomorrah; that means you have forfeited the right to cross this threshold. And before you inherit this house, I will burn it. If you don't get out this instant, I'll have the footman throw you out. To the likes of you, the Master is *never* at home, not even if you used the back door.'

Sitting at his desk in the library, Invernevis could not help hearing her every word. Her first sentence let him guess the object of her anger, and he had sat on, shocked, until he realized the servants would hear.

He threw open the door.

'What's going on out there? This is outrageous – '

But the anger he intended was lost in laughter from above. There, on the landing, Laura knelt, face pressed between the rails, fists gripping.

'Alexander does look funny!' she shouted. 'Oh, I know, I know! It's Hallowe'en!'

A small stocky man with a fair moustache, he was in ploughman's clothes, shapeless jacket, legs lashed with twine, large tacketed boots.

'Get to bed, you idiot!' Aunt Carlotta screamed up. And then, to her nephew: 'I'm going to get the footman to throw him out.'

'No,' he said firmly, holding the library door open. 'He wouldn't have come unless it was important.'

And Alexander, who had not uttered a word, went in while Aunt Carlotta stormed off, shouting for her trunks.

He stood beside the desk, awkwardly, until told to take an arm-chair by the fire, Invernevis swinging round on the swivel chair.

'I'd better stand,' he muttered. 'My clothes aren't clean.'

'Never mind that,' his brother said impatiently. And, when he was poised on the edge of the chair: 'And what brings you up here, at this hour?' He saw no point in concealing his bitterness. 'Are you worried about Mama?'

'You saw in the hall why I couldn't come,' Alexander said. 'She really *hates* me.' He shook his head, as if in disbelief.

'Do you blame her? You weren't much help when I was away, yet Father left you all that money and the estate, if I don't have a son. All she got was an old riding crop, and I needn't remind you how much she hates horses. The point is, she sees you going the same way as him. And why, for God's sake? Because you're a second son, like he was? But you *knew* there was always a place here for you. Did I ever give a different impression? Did Mama? And Laura: you've never bothered with her. That's the bit I find hardest to accept. By ignoring her you've treated her as if she was – '

'What Carlotta just called her,' Alexander said. 'I never thought of Laura like that. It was just that she was always wanting to be with you, so I kept out of the way. But it's Carlotta who's been making all the trouble in this family over the years. You *know* how much she hated Father.'

'Do *you* know what disease he died of?'

Alexander shrugged. 'Something he picked up in India, Mama said. But what does it matter? He's dead.'

'And left you a good deal of money,' his brother reminded him. 'Much more than a second son would normally get.'

'Look, Niall, I didn't brave Carlotta to talk about Father or his money. I'm here because I'm in a spot.'

'Well, since it can't be money this time, what then?' he asked wearily.

'A woman,' Alexander said, his roughened hands twisting

his cap. 'I've got a woman into trouble.'

Invernevis groaned. Then he swore. He knew the kind of woman it would be. Shades of his father.

'My God, this is the limit. Haven't you done enough to tarnish the family name?' He turned to face his brother. 'Well, you know what you can do: you've got money.'

'What has money got to do with it?' Alexander asked angrily. 'Will you let me explain? It's Kate MacPherson at the Home Farm.'

It took him several seconds to absorb the information. It couldn't be worse. He had seen the girl once or twice, when she brought eggs up to the house, but he hadn't paid any attention. What a fool Alexander was, getting caught like that by MacPherson, who would certainly be looking for a wedding so that he could boast of his relationship to the big house. Well, that wasn't going to happen. It would be the biggest scandal for years in the village, and some would gloat.

'I was going to suggest that you follow Father's example by giving her some money and sending her away, but MacPherson would never agree to that. The only thing you can do is to brazen it out – deny it's yours.'

Alexander's look was more puzzlement than anger. 'But it *is* mine, and I want to marry her.'

Which brought his brother to his feet, to grope in his pocket for his cigar-case, and instead of cutters, to use his teeth and spit leaf at the fire. When the match had spurted and his cheeks stopped sucking he lowered himself again. At least the action had made him see the light.

'I know your game, the same as I know *his*,' he said, pointing the cigar. 'You obviously hoped I wouldn't come home from the war. That would have been the best solution, wouldn't it? You've done this deliberately, so that you could have a family before me. Then if anything happens to me, you get the place, and have heirs to continue it. *His* will didn't specify that *you* had to have a son. And you choose a tenant's daughter, to embarrass me and this house. No doubt he put you up to it before he died.' He appealed with his hands. 'Don't you see what he's done by the will? We're supposed to tear each other to pieces, the way his gun-dogs go for meat.'

'You've got it all wrong,' Alexander said angrily. 'It's got nothing to do with getting the place. I asked her to marry me because I love her.'

101

'In which case you're mad,' his brother said contemptuously. 'All right, you've a good chance of getting the place by the terms of his will, so why not marry someone from your own class? You could come home and live here for the time being. I'd make it all right with Aunt Carlotta. Then, if I had a son, you could be compensated. I'd make sure you got the Home Farm, if that's what you want.'

'I'm going to marry Kate MacPherson, and I *won't* be coming back here,' Alexander said resolutely.

'Totally mad,' his brother said, shaking his head. 'Oh, it sounds very romantic, the aristocratic ploughboy and the farmer's daughter, but it won't work out because whatever silly ideas you have you're still one of *us*, by birth and breeding. Don't you see: they set a snare for you at the Home Farm and you've walked straight into it. They'll take every penny off you, and you'll *never* get a divorce, because they'll know the estate could be coming to you. Father was far too wily to get caught like that. Oh, he had his pleasures all right, but he always came home.' He leaned forward. 'Listen, deny it. Tell MacPherson he can't prove it's yours.'

Alexander was agitated. 'I didn't come here to ask your permission to marry, because I don't have to. I came to ask a favour. No, it doesn't need to be a favour because I'm willing to pay. I'd like a piece of ground – on the other side of the river, at Wade's Bridge – to build a house and settle down.'

Invernevis received this request in an explosive silence, his eyes widening with each word. 'This is outrageous,' he said, his voice kept low by shock and anger. 'So it's true: you do want to embarrass me, to show the village that though you're the second son – and Mama and Aunt Carlotta – ' But he could not finish.

'Haven't you done enough?' he asked after a while, almost pleading. 'Haven't I enough on my hands with Mama and Laura? I'm warning you, if we go any further down, we shan't be able to recover. And five hundred years will be for nothing. Father was bad enough, but at least he *stayed* here; you seem to be so intent on becoming a villager. What will happen to the tenants if we're brought down by your behaviour? Have you asked yourself that? You'll be destroying what you apparently prize so much.'

'I don't have any quarrel with you, and I'm not trying to harm you,' Alexander said earnestly. 'I'm only asking for what *you* want, for me to settle down. I can't, in this house. Oh, I know you can't approve of the woman because she's not one of *your* class, but if you met her, you'd find she was perfectly decent. I got her into trouble and I have to do the right thing by her. Even Carlotta would have to admit that that was moral. Half an acre, so that I can build: that's all I'm asking, and I'm willing to pay. By the river because I like it down there, and we would have privacy. I've got the money to build. Not a big house, six or seven rooms.'

His brother was watching him thoughtfully, stroking his chin, bemused by the incongruity of breeding and appearance. The cigar had relaxed him, and he felt he was in control of the situation. In fact, he was beginning to feel sorry for his brother, whose eyes at least showed his sincerity. He wasn't wicked; only a fool for himself, but every family had its black sheep. And could he be blamed, considering he had spent the formative years with his father? But it wasn't that simple. He was the laird, and there were certain rules.

'All right, I agree.' But, holding up a cautionary hand: 'There has to be give and take in this. You get the land; I get your agreement to disinherit yourself by renouncing your share of Father's will – the estate, I mean. I don't need to go into the reasons, except to say that if things didn't work out for me, it wouldn't be very appropriate, the Home Farm inheriting Invernevis House. If you agree, the estate will then go to Hubert, our cousin, in the event of me not having a son.'

But Alexander didn't need time to consider the choice. 'Yes, I'll agree to that. I've never thought about inheriting the place, and wouldn't have wanted it, even if you had been killed in South Africa. I've made enough of a mess of things already. That's why I want to get married, to settle down and make a go of it.'

Invernevis was astonished by his brother's instant rejection of his inheritance and wondered where the trick was. But they shook hands on it. 'You sketch out the bit of land you want, and let me see it before you get plans drawn up. Then I'll get the lawyers to give you a title. But remember: the house will have to fit in with the surroundings. It's very beautiful, down there by the Yellow Pool. And it'll be seen from here.'

'It won't be anything grand,' Alexander assured him. 'Just a villa. I'm going to plant trees so that it can't be seen from the road. Oh, I forgot to say that I'm sorry about your leg.

And Mama: give her my love.' He stood awkwardly, working at his cap till his brother opened the door and looked out.

'You're safe enough. Aunt Carlotta isn't about. But I'd go quickly, just in case. No, no, not by the back door; it's quicker by the front. Well, good night, and let me know when the wedding is.'

When Alexander had gone, and with his cigar almost finished, Invernevis wondered if he hadn't been a damn fool. Sentiment had got the better of him, as it had never done with his father. True, he was going to relinquish his claim to the big house, but they would be practically living on his door-step, and there would be a lot of talk. And he still had to get the consent of the trustees to the bargain.

An interesting idea was beginning to take shape. He already had a factor, MacKenzie, a drinking crony of his father's who lived in a grace-and-favour house in the village, but who was hopelessly disorganized and who could no longer be entrusted with estate papers because his failure to settle accounts on time had caused summonses to be served on Invernevis House. Now why couldn't Alexander take over the factorship, collect the croft rents and go round the farms to see that everything was in order? He must have learnt something at the Home Farm, and he was well liked, which meant that they would trust him. Invernevis would work on the idea.

His confidence in his own judgement was strengthened when he went in to dinner, to find Aunt Carlotta down for the first time in three nights, but even as Symmers's shaky hand was ladling out soup at the side table she was attacking.

'Such effrontery, coming to the front door when he's not even welcome at the back. And you so *weak*. Instead of having him thrown out, you take him into the library, and gave him whisky, no doubt. Well, what did he want? His room back?'

Invernevis asked Symmers to leave before he answered, and before he had finished explaining about the wedding and the site by the river Aunt Carlotta had thrown down her spoon with such violence that it dented dark wood.

'Wickedness!' she shouted, throwing aside her napkin as she got to her feet, and, wagging a finger at her nephew: 'That awful man your father has left evil in this house. I sense it everywhere I go, your mother, Laura out of control, that scullery-maid and her lies. I like to think of myself as a good Catholic who doesn't believe that the dead come back, but in his case I'm beginning to believe that even hell wouldn't have him and that he's back here.'

The exertion had left her breathless, and she balanced her bent body on her hands, the candelabra flames wavering.

'You didn't allow me to finish,' he said. 'He'll get the site by the river, but he's going to disinherit himself. That's the bargain, and he's agreed to it.'

At this news Aunt Carlotta lowered herself, but keeping her eyes on him.

'I should think so. But surely he could have been cut off without getting a foothold so near this house? Marrying a farm girl just because he's made her pregnant. What will people think of us? And a child with blood from both sides of the river: it's grotesque. I hope you're not going to let that trash MacPherson get the better of you in this. Well, I know what I'm going to do: I'm going to speak to the trustees, to see if there isn't a way of cancelling his lease.'

'You mustn't interfere in estate matters,' he warned her. 'Besides, his lease has years to run yet. No, we'll just have to accept it,' he said, wanting his next course.

'*Accept?* I shall never accept such a situation.' She straightened her back against slatted wood. 'I was going to leave here before *he* came, and though I've more reason for going now, I'm going to stay to fight this. You haven't been laird long, and already you've made some very bad mistakes. I'm going to stay to try and undo them, and to make sure you don't make any more. Oh, yes, *you* say I've no right to interfere, but I have. I've given my life to this place and this family. I came here with your mother because I saw what a terrible mistake her marriage was, but would she listen? I took all the blows, but I didn't mind that so long as you children could have some sort of life. Oh, I knew it would be difficult because you had *his* blood in your veins as well as ours. But the struggle hasn't been worth it, because God took his vengeance with Laura, and now your brother – '

And for the first time in his life he saw his aunt crying. He couldn't be sure if they were tears of rage or grief, but he went to stand by her, his arm round her shoulder.

'It'll all come right. You'll see,' he tried to reassure. 'Alexander wants to do the right thing by the girl, and he wants to settle down. That's a start.'

'He'll never change,' she said, dabbing her face with a small square of lace. 'And every time I look out of a front window or see that brute MacPherson, I'll be reminded. Don't you see? You've got the worst of the bargain. You could stop him from inheriting by having a son, but by giving him that site you can't stop his bastard sept from living in the shadow of this house for generation after generation. If it was being under trustees you were worried about, I have some influence with them. They want rid of him as much as we do.' And she called Symmers to take away the cold soup.

Maggie stood at the scullery sink, waiting for the dinner dishes to come through. They were late, and she'd been on her feet since six that morning, but she didn't care. Her arms in cooling scum, she stared out into darkness, smiling. The Master had touched her. He had actually *touched* her. And she wasn't going to lose her job. He had believed her that she wasn't a carrier of tales. He would protect her against Miss Carlotta's tempers. Her father was right: best to get on with her job quietly, to take great care with the dishes, the crested plates especially, and maybe in a year or two she would be moved into the kitchen. Because now that the Master was taking an interest in her Elsie might be more friendly.

So many stars. Though the big brass taps dug into her breasts, she craned forward, pressing her face against the cold black pane. A maturing moon was tangled in the avenue's bare branches. It was a lovely night for a walk, if it wasn't so eerie. Yes, she was going to save up for a photograph of the Master.

'They're damned late tonight,' Symmers grumbled, pushing her aside, pouring Miss Carlotta's cold soup into the sink. 'And I was going to go down to the Arms for a refreshment.'

A measured mile, mostly uphill, from Wade's Bridge, main street, Invernevis, ran for one hundred and fifty yards, thirty broad feet of dust, compacted or disturbed according to the climate and the frequency of wheeled and hooved traffic. After the railway bridge was crossed, the blacksmith's was on the right, a huddle of splayed boards leaking light and sound where springs that had succumbed on Wade's Bridge were given back their resistance. Behind the shack, on summer nights, an amended form of quoits was staged, with horseshoes being tossed at iron pins driven into the ground. Bets were placed, and the old laird had often been a participator, riding boots splayed, one eye closed, his steady hand invariably giving him the contest. He converted his winnings into stone jars from the nearby Arms which he shared with the other competitors, the vessels passed without wiping, and with a good many crudities between mouthfuls.

Beside the blacksmith's was the tin-roofed post office, where a tapping key transmitted telegrams south – coffins for the village, stores for the big house. A local wag had christened it Ladysmith, because it was a shanty, and because Mrs Mac-Quade, who manned the key, sat in angry siege behind the metal grille, sending with her finger and circulating with her tongue.

Then came two or three low cottages, the perks of retired estate workers, their lintels at the brow level of an average man, their windows two feet of embedded glass screened with mobile muslin. Behind the cottages, in a sandstone villa moated by weed-choked gravel, MacKenzie the factor lived in a hopeless muddle of papers, convinced that he was still responsible for the smooth running of the Invernevis estate, though that duty had long since been transferred to Edinburgh. All he did was to go round on a gig on rent days, taking whisky where it was offered.

On the left side of the street, coming from the railway bridge, was the store, satisfying most of the simple needs of the village when home produce fell short. In its fly-flecked window, death notices and a pyramid of blown tins. On fine evenings worthies with clay stumps in the corners of their mouths, caps over eyes, thumbs hooked in open waistcoat pockets, leaned against its bright granite before gravitating to the station for the arrival of the late train from the south.

At the end of main street, still on the same side, a track turned up to Father Macdonald's rhododendron-screened residence, to school and cemetery, then moorland. Main street itself ended in a T-junction with the road to the south, and there stood the Invernevis Arms, a droving inn that had neither expanded nor modernized to meet the demands of the railway. It was a long whitewashed building of rotten red woodwork, basically a bar and six attic bedrooms, let out to those who could afford to pay Campbell's extortionate daily rate for fishing the Branglin beat. The laird of Invernevis was the feudal superior of the Arms, and the licensee was Carmichael, a massive bald-headed man with a short temper who had been a policeman in Glasgow, but who had been

107

retired early, for causing grievous bodily harm, some locals alleged, though not to his face. His convex stomach stretching the frayed sleeveless Fair-Isle pullover, Carmichael kept order with his fists when his tongue failed.

The pub of the Invernevis Arms was the focal point of the village, at least for the men. Low-raftered, its one deep-set window failing to attract light from the west, it consisted of a short curving counter, its surface hollowed by elbows and stained with slopped drink. In front of it, flanking the open fire of sluggish peats, several rickety tables and benches stood on bare floorboards. Apart from the functional clock facing the counter, Roman numerals cased in mahogany, the only other object on the smoke-dulled wallpaper was a large mirror, its gilded stag advertising MOUNTAIN MONARCH blend.

Here hard information was exchanged, rumour rejected or confirmed, some of it to be taken home to wives to distract from the drunken condition of the carrier. In that way news circulated the village, though the women adapted and distorted in the transmission. But the pub clientele had one rule, unwritten because the village had little use for that skill: Gaelic to be the sole means of communication, to perpetuate the mother tongue and to exclude Carmichael from confidential conversations.

There was standing room only most nights, the noise a mixture of Gaelic argument, the pump squirting pints, the click of dominoes, and on Saturday night was added the raucous Irish brogue, demanding more drink or redress as Carmichael towered in front of a battery of bottles, eyes sweeping.

Alexander came in every night, punctually at seven, to buy his large whisky with a sovereign and to sit in a corner with four or five crofters, discussing beasts or cultivation. Out of deference to the laird's brother these men of indeterminate age in shapeless tweeds broke their own rule by conversing in English, and listened politely, eyes twinkling above their pensive pipes as Alexander expounded the theories he had picked up at the Home Farm. But when he was slaking his throat with neat whisky, they corrected him gently, not meaning, of course, any offence to MacPherson, who was 'a good enough farmer, in his own way'. Alexander nodded gravely, becoming more animated as he fumbled in his waistcoat pocket when Carmichael (who only crossed the counter for fights) brought across the laden tray to the sign of the raised finger. The crofters searched their tweeds for coins, but Alexander wouldn't hear of it, so they settled back, sipping smoke and liquid fire. Farming was the sole topic, and there was no friction. Though they knew from their own women folk that he had put MacPherson's daughter in the family way, it wasn't only instinctive manners that made that subject taboo. It was irrelevant to the conversation; it had happened before, with Alexander's own father; and a peculiar prudery among old, experienced men outlawed sex and such like among humans as a topic of conversation in the pub.

So Alexander drank and debated with the crofters throughout the week, but on Saturday nights he had to raise his voice to be understood above the moleskinned contingent, sodden with salt spray from the ferry, filling the pub with sound and stench, jostling for resting places at the counter, then banging glasses to be refilled. And though they couldn't read the labels on the bottles, they knew when they had been short-changed, and waited in menacing silence until mine host had made good the deficiency from the drawer under the gantry. When they learned from Carmichael that Alexander was the brother of the quarry owner, they crossed to his dim corner, slapping him on the back, saying they were all 'God's chuldren', putting big whiskies into his fist and standing over him till he had drained the glass and was ready to return the compliment. They carried Alexander's glass to the counter as though it was a chalice, and insisted on Carmichael filling it without first washing it, and when it was brimming with the whisky Alexander had bought, they tossed it back with an Irish Gaelic toast.

Alexander was drunk most nights when Carmichael roared time, pointing an accusing finger at the clock, giving them two minutes before the constable came prowling. The crofters hoisted Alexander to his feet, put his cap on his head and steered him towards the door, but giggling like a girl, he always insisted on a moment's halt to buy a half-bottle for the road home, and though it was after time Carmichael always served him.

The crofters steadied and slowed Alexander going down the brae, and at the bottom there was a halt while the half-bottle was consumed by being passed from hand to hand, the mouth being wiped with a sleeve before Alexander received it. The empty was tossed into a hedge and he linked arms with them, head back under the hard stars, ruining the Gaelic song they were singing.

Though they shared his drink and saw him a good part of the way home, to the Home Farm, they treated him with the respect due to someone from the big house, calling him 'Master Alexander', despite his insistence on 'Sandy'. And when he pulled to a halt to relieve himself, they turned their backs. The big house lights were still showing as they saw him safely to the gate of the Home Farm, but neither residence came up in conversation, nor did his reason for crossing the river. He wanted them to come up to the Home Farm for a last dram, saying that MacPherson would be pleased to see them, but they declined politely, saying they had beasts to bed.

On the Saturday night after he had been to see his brother, to tell him that he was going to get married, and to ask for the building plot by the river, Alexander was in his usual clothes in his usual place in the dim corner of the pub, clay pipe in one hand, glass in the other as he explained how much he was learning about farming from MacPherson.

'I'll learn a lot more, after I get married. MacPherson says he'll have more time to teach me.'

The crofters received this news in silence, looking at each other without changing expression.

'Well now, a wedding. I suppose we ought to congratulate you,' one said quietly.

And they shook hands over the clustered glasses.

'Oh aye, there's no doubt that MacPherson knows what he's about. He'll not buy unless he can fatten up and sell at a big price,' another said, bland eyes on Alexander.

'And what he doesn't know about breeding isn't worth knowing. That man could cross anything.'

The whisky coming out on his forehead, Alexander nodded in serious agreement.

'Mind you, things can go wrong in the crossing,' the first crofter said. 'I mean, you expect the pedigree to come through, and sometimes it doesn't.'

Alexander was taking it all in, not conscious that they were all watching him.

'Aye, it doesn't do to cross sometimes,' the second crofter said. 'If you've got a pure strain, better to keep it that way.' He leaned over the table, watching to make sure Carmichael couldn't hear. 'Now I remember your father had a stallion, a better beast I've never seen. Well, it broke out of its box at the big house stables one night and came charging down to the village. It mounted Iain Dubh's mare, and it was never the same again.'

'The mare?' Alexander said, puzzled.

'No, no, I'm talking about the stallion. It was no use after that, and your father had it put down. There was a foal, but it was a queer wee thing, neither one thing nor the other, no use for working, and no use for showing.'

'I've never heard that one before,' Alexander said.

'And why should you have? You were probably only a boy then.'

But the conversation was curtailed by the arrival of the Irishmen, barging in, calling for Power's best Irish before they reached the counter, slapping the locals on the backs, greeting them in a harsh difficult Gaelic. Carmichael was the wary umpire in the uneasy alliance between the two Celtic races whose physique as well as language differed. The locals resented the Irish intrusion, but Carmichael had his takings in mind. If he could make a quick killing out of the quarry, he could retire to the south and civilization. So, leaning over the counter, he stopped animated Gaelic exchanges from developing into scuffles. Though he didn't understand one word, the flushed Irish faces were sufficient.

In Alexander's corner the conversation had switched to a shouted consideration of milking methods, with Alexander miming MacPherson's way of tugging teats while the crofters watched, smiling, then demonstrating how they did it, and their fathers before.

'You have to take as much as possible out of the beast without hurting it, Master Alexander. The way MacPherson does it, he causes damage.'

At the counter an Irishman was emptying his fourth glass. He was well over six feet, in rolled-up ragged shirt sleeves despite the December frost, his biceps bulging through shaping granite. A small metal cross on a chain gleamed among the copper-coloured hairs curling at his collarless throat. One eye – the right – had been permanently closed by a granite chip, giving his bearded face an expression of ominous malice, his grey bullet head close-cropped because of lice.

He hitched up the studded leather belt at his moleskins and

asked Carmichael for a drink on credit.

'I'll pay you next Saturday, as Mary is our mother,' he said, making a pious sign.

Carmichael balanced himself on his palms and confronted the customer who equalled him in stature. 'You know damned fine I don't give tick. I've had too much trouble from you lot before.'

'But the locals get it.'

'They're different. I always know where to put my hands on them. But you: you could be gone by next Saturday, killed in a blast or sacked.'

'Oh, so that's the way it is,' the Irishman said, nodding slowly, lips pursed. 'We're not honest enough for you, but you'll still take our money. That's bad enough, but the way you talk about us gettin' killed, or being sent away, you would think we was animals.'

The noise around subsided suddenly, the Irishmen putting down their glasses and looking at each other, the locals watching Carmichael.

'I've told you, that's the rule, and I'm not breaking it,' Carmichael said, not moving. 'And another thing: Mary might be your mother, but she damned well isn't mine.'

The Irishman looked at the tiny glass in his fist and inverted it on the counter. He turned away, fumbling with his moleskins.

'This is what I think of this place,' he announced, and, legs splayed, he urinated into the fire.

As dense stinking smoke bellowed, chairs and benches toppled, glasses smashing, the two races locking. Clay pipes were being trod to powder as Carmichael swung his legs over the counter, wading in with fists and feet, swiping locals as well. Small stocky men jumped on big Irish backs, trying to throttle with plough-hardened arms till they were pitched overhead, among splintering wood. Grey heads butted rock-hard Irish bellies, buckles drawing blood. The lantern that shed light from the rafters was hit by a forehead and swung crazily, shadows flailing the brawlers, blood showing lurid. The noise was deafening: Irishmen with bruised shins roaring like animals in pain, the locals moaning, hugging gashed skulls on the bare floorboards as studded Irish boots trampled and swung.

Paralysed by drink and incomprehension at the beginning of

112

the fight, Alexander found himself on his feet, being pushed forward by the crofters, then going back at great speed as an Irish fist found his midriff. Though without breath, he got to his feet again, but only to go over to an Irish boot. To save himself, he crawled under a smashed table.

The noise had spilled out into the night, to be amplified by frost-bound main street, bringing shawled women in laceless brogues and in some cases bare feet, stumbling and screaming towards the loud lighted window an Irish fist was broaching for fresh air. The women crowded, beating wood with raised fists, wailing for their men, but an Irish back shut them out.

The pub was wrecked, strewn with splintered wood, glass and inert bodies of both sides. A chair raised to a skull had brought down the gilded stag on the mirror, and the clock, minus its pendulum, was yapping on. And still they fought.

Then the constable came running, struggling into his tunic, a shrill whistle stuck in his scarlet face. He pushed the wailing women aside, ordering them home, then raised his lead-weighted truncheon to the door. But the Irish back would not yield.

'There'll be murder done!' a woman was screaming, her face at the shattered window.

Roused from his sleep by the noise, Father Macdonald was coming down main street in a long black coat buttoned to the throat, and a rounded black hat. As he approached the lighted window, the women fell back, silent, bowing.

'This is the priest here!' he shouted through the shattered glass. But it had no effect on the fighting.

'We'll need to break the door down, sir,' the constable said.

'No, no, there's enough violence,' Father Macdonald said, unbuttoning his coat at the neck. He removed the large silver cross and chain which Miss Carlotta had given him and thrust it in his fist through the broken window.

'In the name of God, stop, I say!'

The din seemed to leak away, and the door swung open. As the priest stepped inside with the cross still in his fist, Irishmen and locals turned away, with bowed heads. His boots crunching glass, but avoiding the prostrate, he went to stand in the centre, raising a hand to steady the rocking lantern as he surveyed the wreckage.

'This is outrageous,' he said, addressing them in English. 'The whole village disturbed, the women and children put

113

into a state of alarm.' He looked from locals to Irishmen. 'This is not the work of men. It is the work of vicious destructive animals at each other's throats. Does Scripture not teach us that we must live in peace, despite our differences? It would have suited some of you better to take your energy out to South Africa and apply it against our *real* enemies, the heathen Boers. Because the most important thing which you have in common and which should unite you is that you are all Catholics. Yet here you are, brawling so near to the Sabbath. I do not know if there are any arrangements to hear Mass at the quarry, but I do know this: Mass will be held here at seven tomorrow morning, and I expect all the locals to be there, injured or not.' Then he noticed Alexander slumped under the broken table, limbs spreadeagled, sleeping apparently. 'Master Alexander!' he said, shocked. 'This is no place for the likes of you. Are you hurt?' And he went forward anxiously, kneeling down.

Alexander opened one eye and regarded him with a silly, stunned smile. Some of the locals saw and sniggered.

'I shall have more to say about this,' the priest said, rising to retrieve his dignity. 'Now go home and attend to your wives and families, and pray that your sins of destruction and debauchery will be forgiven. And if you Irishmen do not go quietly to the ferry, it will be a matter for the constable.'

Father Macdonald went and stationed himself at the door. In one hand he held up the big silver cross, and in the other his inverted black hat. As they began to file out, he thrust both out towards them. Embarrassed, the locals put their lips to the cross as they fumbled in their tweeds for small coins for the hat. But the Irishmen closed their eyes and, as if in ecstasy, kissed the cold silver before turning out the pockets of their matted moleskins to show the priest that they had nothing to give.

Alexander was being helped to his feet by the crofters with whom he had been drinking before the fracas. They turned him in the direction of the door. Seeming to forget the priest's presence, he stopped at the counter and was about to ask for his usual half-bottle carry-out when Carmichael shook his head quickly. They steadied Alexander in front of the cross. The light from the now-stationary lantern made it flare, losing its form, becoming a blinding blur. The priest was pushing both cross and hat in front of him, his face grave, but Alexander shook his head and stumbled out into the night while those who were accompanying him kissed and gave.

Carmichael was showing a rare smile as he went towards the priest. An Irishman had clutched the hem of his pullover in an attempt to bring him down, and the bright pattern was running.

'It's good of you to make them pay,' Carmichael said, reaching out for the black hat. 'This is going to cost me a pretty penny to put right.'

But Father Macdonald regarded him with cold eyes. 'Oh no, you mistake. This money is for the church. It does not put right the damage they have done to their souls by tonight's behaviour, but it will help the fabric of the chapel.' He held out the hat to Carmichael. 'No, you can sort all this out of profits, and you won't feel it. And I suggest you begin by putting five pounds into this hat in penance for the spiritual damage you have done tonight.'

'But I'm not a Catholic,' Carmichael protested.

'All the more reason for you making a contribution.' And, seeing Carmichael still hesitant: 'May I remind you that I am a trustee of the estate, and it will be partly on my recommendation whether you continue here as tenant. Both the laird and his aunt will be very angry about tonight's proceedings.'

'It's blackmail, that's what it is,' Carmichael said angrily, but he leaned over the counter and took five sovereigns from the drawer. They dropped chinking, shining amongst the predominant copper.

Outside, the constable was using his truncheon to herd the Irishmen towards the ferry, and where there was hesitancy, weighted wood collided with bone. The locals were dragged home by irate wives, their wounds ignored. The crofters who were Alexander's friends wanted to see him part of the way home, but met opposition from their women until they took them aside and whispered in Gaelic about the impending marriage. The women went their own way, heads together, the brawl forgotten.

Though he still felt sick, Alexander had recovered his wind in the frosty night. He wanted to hide behind the Arms, to get a half-bottle when the priest had gone, but the crofters persuaded him to make for home. They went with him down the brae, holding him by the sleeve in case his boots gave way on the ice. Though there were no half-bottles or linked arms

115

on the level ground, they walked close beside him, loud in their praise.

'Man, but we were right proud of you, you gave such a good account of yourself in the fight,' one said. 'I saw the way you went for the big fellow. Aye, Sandy, wouldn't your father have been proud to see you. Of course we couldn't do much, because we're getting old.'

'Maybe, but we didn't disgrace ourselves,' another said. He was chuckling. 'It was the way you stood up to Father Macdonald that got me. He had no right, making us kiss the cross in public and taking our money.'

They left him with a unanimous 'Good night, Sandy!' at the gate of the Home Farm, and he went up the steep stony track to find Kate sitting up for him by the kitchen fire, her black hair combed out, wound round her throat, and a shawl over her nightdress. The dying peats could not conceal the pronounced curve.

'It gets later and later, especially on Saturday night,' she said wearily, and when he was seated at the table, out in the darkness: 'Well, what's the excuse this time?'

He told her about the fight, and how it had taken Father Macdonald to break it up.

'But you weren't in it!' she cried in alarm, and when his silence confirmed: 'Come over here, I want to see if you're hurt.'

He barged against chairs to come and sit at her feet, and when she had drawn flame with a poker, she raised his head and saw the bruise darkening round his eye.

'Oh my God, I'll need to get a piece of steak before Mother sees it!'

He detained her gently by the wrist. 'It's nothing. It'll be away by the morning.'

'And you look so white,' she moaned, holding his head against her belly. 'Is this what the village has come to, with these Irish animals? If your brother cared about his people, and not profit, he would shut the place down.'

'They're not animals; they're just like everyone else, under their moleskins,' Alexander said dreamily, suddenly remembering what was strange about the walk home: the crofters had called him 'Sandy' for the first time.

'Oh no, they're not like everyone else, and neither are you, under these ploughman's clothes,' Kate said emphatically. 'You shouldn't be going to the pub. You're not only letting yourself down, but your family. Oh, I *know*: that's all finished with. So *you* think, but it never will be because you're their flesh and blood. I might be carrying your child, but that doesn't stop me from saying that you should go back home, make it up with your brother and aunt. I'm not the first or the last local girl to have a baby out of wedlock, as Father Macdonald calls it. I can manage; my mother at least will understand.'

He had her tight by the wrist now, and was on his knees. 'You don't know what you're saying. You haven't been up to the big house, except to deliver eggs. The way Carlotta treats me, you'd think I was an animal. And Niall's so stiff and formal, as if he was still an officer. Listen.' He knelt, trying to put his arms round her waist. 'We're not going to let my family make us quarrel. It'll all turn out all right, you'll see. I *want* to marry you, and I *want* more children as well as this one. The new house will be up by next summer, and we can settle down by ourselves.'

'It's not the house, it's the people in it. Oh God, I wish you could see yourself,' she said in anguish, ruffling his hair. 'You think they accept you down in the Arms, but they don't. They only want to boast that they've been drinking with the laird's brother. I gave you two sovereigns when you went out. How much have you got left? There, you see, and *you* certainly didn't drink that amount.'

'They're decent people,' Alexander said defensively.

'In some ways,' she conceded. 'I'm one of them, and I don't trust them because they're so cunning, praising you to your face, then pulling you to pieces behind your back. I suppose I'm like that myself, though I try not to be. But if they don't trust each other, how on earth are they going to trust you? Because, you see, they think it's only a phase with you, and that when you do decide to go home, you'll trail everything back to the big house. Don't you understand? They want the village and the big house to be separate. If they aren't, how can they respect the big house?'

'Well, if I spend money, I get to know a lot about farming,' he said, trying to deflect the conversation from the big house.

'But my father will teach you for nothing, though God knows what good it will do you – unless you're going after a farm of your own. Are you?'

'I haven't thought about it,' he admitted.

'No, that's just the trouble; you don't really know what you want. But you know what you *don't* want, and that's responsibility. At least your brother accepted his.'

'It was easy for him. Carlotta thinks the world of him.'

'Anyway, we'd better get to bed,' she said, seeing the conversation becoming circular.

She helped him through to the bedroom they now shared with her father's blessing after the wedding had been agreed. She removed his boots, pulled off his trousers. Her back was turned to him in case he bumped the child in the night, and he lay in the darkness, listening to the low river amplified by frost and thinking of the Irishmen, huddled in the boat of dragging oars crossing to the quarry, sleeping in their moleskins in their rat-infested shacks. He didn't feel angry at the punch that had left him with a sore stomach. Instead, pity, and admiration, almost, for their strength.

Then the silver cross was being held out again to him as the moonlight came through muslin. He strained towards it, but it shimmered into oblivion.

Chapter Seven

Following the fashion of Prince Albert, dead spouse of her beloved Queen, Mama insisted on a Christmas tree in the front hall. Invernevis was anxious about fire, but Aunt Carlotta (who thought such decorations pagan) took upon herself the responsibility of snuffing the candles before she went upstairs for the night.

Laura was ecstatic, dancing about and clapping her hands when the tree was hauled in from the plantation above the house. When she tried to help, clutching at branches, needles showered, which made her even more excited. She knelt to help Ranald the gardener plant the sawn stump in the tub of black soil, steadying it with both hands and shrieking when it began to topple.

Aunt Carlotta scolded and chased her, but she came back to take the decorations out of the boxes, getting the tinsel streamers hopelessly fankled, wound round her button boots and, in trying to step clear, making matters worse. Her brother freed her, making her spin round and round, unwinding the silver shackles, their laughter giving momentum to the game until Aunt Carlotta began to shout:

'You're worse than she is!'

Mama sat watching, the high chair by the hall fire swallowing her. Carlotta had successfully opposed her nephew's idea of a nurse, saying she would keep an eye. Though the widow's weeds had been ripped off and replaced by a new set after a harsh bath of bristle and carbolic, Mama was still getting supplies. But now she was more cunning, hiding the bottles. One had jammed a cistern; another had turned up among the sticks in the hollowed-out tree. Aunt Carlotta had not tracked down the carrier from the village, but the coachman was still the prime suspect, and she insisted on frisking the pockets of his greatcoat before he was allowed over the back door.

Mama had made herself old and hunched with her addiction, and now she depended on a stick. Dr MacNiven had warned her about what she was doing to her heart, but as she sat watching the Christmas tree going up, there was a peppermint under her tongue, and the comforting knowledge that there was still· some left in the bottle inside the Indian vase on the stand outside her bedroom door, a place they would never think of looking.

When the high parts of the tree had been decorated Invernevis turned towards the library, to finish some letters for the morning post. As he was reaching for the handle an explosion behind made him duck, bringing back the horror of Magersfontein.

Laura stood in the middle of the hall and round her button boots were strewn the silvered slivers of the bauble she had been balancing on her palm, running in circles, pretending it was a star in motion. There was silence. Laura stared down open-mouthed at the beauty she had broken. But Aunt Carlotta was coming crunching, to take her by the shoulders and shake her.

'You little fool! I thought I told you to go up to your room, out of the way. Well, just for that you'll go and get a shovel and pick up every last bit. If it gets into the paws of the dogs, you'll know about it.'

Laura stood, looking at her brother in mute appeal. It was one of these moments memory would photograph. He saw the hem of the drab dress above the splayed boots, different from the day of the lifted salmon, the limp arms by her side, the jaw slack. The effect was that of a puppet dangling on strings. One cut would make her crumple. And at that moment he knew for certain that he was all she had, that it was he who controlled the strings.

Aunt Carlotta was watching him too, but defiantly, daring him to challenge an authority she had worked so hard to re-acquire after her cancelled departure. But he knew he could not give in to her, not at such a time, with servants watching and Christmas dazzling his little sister. Mama was changed in one way at least. It was time now to solve the problem of Laura.

'No, Aunt Carlotta, because if she picks up the bits she'll cut her fingers. But she'll go and get a brush and shovel, and be more careful in the future. Because if you break nice things, Laura, you can't expect to have them replaced.' He tried to put irritation into his tone, as a concession to Aunt Carlotta, but Laura was looking at him and she knew. She skipped through to the kitchen for the brush and shovel, leaving her aunt scowling while Mama, warmed by flame and surreptitious brandy, dozed in the high chair, a queen falling asleep over ceremonial.

Invernevis saw that he had won, and he went back to his letters, but with the worry that if anything happened to him, Laura would be at the mercy of Aunt Carlotta. At least the estate was no longer at the mercy of Alexander, since after much argument Aunt Carlotta had agreed that he could have his site in return for disinheritance, and the trustees were bound to accept. It troubled his conscience, but there was no alternative, and it turned his thoughts to marriage. His military career had ruled that out, but now he would have to get out and about more in society. Not that there was much chance of meeting a suitable woman in their part of the world, and besides, there was the impediment of the game leg which Mama had not got used to.

Marriage. He savoured the idea over a cigarette. To bring another woman into the house would be very difficult. Aunt Carlotta would not want her authority challenged. But no woman would want to move into the present set-up, he thought wryly. Mama was an embarrassment, and Laura – he hadn't thought of her in that way before, but he could see that a stranger would wonder, since Laura was his sister. And would it be fair to Laura to transfer his attention? But more than ever he needed an heir.

Brooding on marriage brought his thoughts back to his brother's wedding. The invitation for the first week of January was propped against the clock on the mantelpiece, but he had already declined. The best man would come from the village, from the Arms, no doubt, but Invernevis had already written to the Edinburgh silversmiths for a canteen of King's Pattern, sterling, but without a monogram. To seat six. That should be sufficient for the size of the dining-room, from the plans he'd already approved. Aunt Carlotta's invitation had been consigned to fire the moment it had come into her hand, with the protest that it was a calculated insult. Mama wasn't pleased at what the marriage would do to her dignity in the village, but she wanted to attend because of the prospects of drink. But Carlotta soon put paid to that by answering for her. And as for Laura, she wasn't even consulted.

So Christmas had come, which meant presents for the servants. Aunt Carlotta had already closeted herself with the

Army & Navy Stores catalogue, her steel pen marking the practical. Invernevis would have liked to go to Edinburgh to shop and spend a few days at the club he'd just been elected to, not being able to join it in his father's lifetime because of the latter's conduct. But he was worried about leaving Mama and Laura. Instead, he wrote to a Princes Street store, giving the approximate ages of the ladies and asking for their help.

Christmas activity increased, with the large baskets of logs beside the principal fireplaces constantly having to be replenished from the pile behind the house, and scuttles of coal lugged up the back stairs, bruising shins. Mama left her bedroom door open and her two Skye terriers ran riot with Laura, until Aunt Carlotta sent the three back upstairs. Relying on the feel of fruit in a palm instead of scales, Mrs Livingstone had already made the plum puddings, embedded with the meagre number of silver threepennies that Miss Carlotta had brought through in a little canvas sack, proclaiming economies. The speckled cannon-balls cooled and matured in the slatted larder at the back door.

Invernevis sat in the library, wondering over a series of cigarettes whether or not to hold the tenants' dance that year. It was a long-established custom but had lapsed in his absence in South Africa, on account of his father's death. Should it be reinstated? It was an opportunity to meet all his tenants for the first time, to thank them for their past loyalty to his father, and to look forward to his own future. He dared not consult Aunt Carlotta because she would demand its cancellation, out of fear that Alexander would come with a Home Farm party, including his wife-to-be, who was apparently already showing signs. And there was no use in asking Mama. She was still in widow's weeds, still getting a supply of drink despite her sister's trackings and interrogations. Oh, Mama would want the dance, for the same reason as she had wanted Alexander's wedding, never mind the disgrace.

No point in asking Laura, because she would dance round, clapping, demanding company and music. And if there wasn't to be a dance, she would cry for days.

He raised the matter with Aunt Carlotta when they were alone at dinner, telling her casually, as he was about to leave the table for a cigar, that the dance would be held. Would she see to the preparation of the drawing-room, please? The same precautions, the more vulnerable pieces of furniture taken to

122

safety, the glass cases locked and covered, the sofas pushed against the walls and the carpet rolled back. And there would be the usual buffet in the dining-room. Nothing elaborate: a haunch of venison and whisky.

She looked at him as though he had taken leave of his senses.

'Out of the question. The trustees have warned us about money. And have you forgotten the trouble I've got – your mother, your brother, your sister? I simply couldn't cope, and Father Macdonald would never allow it.'

This was always her trump card, but he wasn't beaten. 'But they missed last year's dance because of father's death.'

'And a very good thing, too. Father Macdonald said there was much less drunkenness in the village last year. They use the dance here as an excuse for a fortnight's binge, so we can help him by cutting it out.'

'But we have to show our appreciation,' he protested.

'Do we? Isn't it the other way round? We put roofs over their heads, at ridiculous rents, and give them good jobs. We even have to bury some of them. And the way they show their gratitude is to spread wicked gossip and get drunk in this house. If that's their way of showing respect, let them keep to their side of the river. And have you forgotten about the dreadful brawl in the Arms a fortnight ago, with your own brother involved? Father Macdonald risked his life stopping it.'

'I quite agree, it was deplorable, but holding the dance lets them see that *we* can still hold our heads high,' he said. It was like playing a fish. 'And if you're worried about Alexander coming, he wouldn't dare show his face here.' He sighed. 'It's a great bother, though – all that furniture to be shifted, and food to be prepared. And you get the brunt of it.' She was hooked now, he felt, and it was time to strike. 'But there's a good reason for holding the dance this year. I see from the papers that the war's going badly, and they need more men to go out. I'm going to use the dance to do a bit of recruiting.' He said this in a tone which suggested that he was going to trick the village, which made Aunt Carlotta's lips tighten in satisfaction.

'It's a great pity your brother won't enlist,' she said, leaving the rest to him. She sighed to show the burden of it all. 'All right. I'll explain to Father Macdonald.' But her nephew doubted if the priest had even been consulted.

The male servants had to lift back the heavy pieces of furniture and roll up the carpets, the maids dust and polish. Miss Carlotta locked the glass cases of heirlooms and pocketed the keys before having boards placed to prevent breakage, because some fool was bound to lean on them. She carried the most fragile ornaments herself and locked them away in cupboards with keys from the big bunches at her waist. The French porcelain clock on the mantelpiece with naked nymphs forming a triumphal arch for time was put into darkness, the delicate movement stopped. Snuff boxes and silver trinkets were cleared from tables because they could so easily be pilfered. The silver-framed photographs, mostly heart-shaped and amassed by Mama, were wrapped in newspapers and stacked away because Miss Carlotta could not see why the family should be on common view. The illustrated books of Italian saints and martyrs which she had distributed over the tables were gathered together and borne away from grubby fingers and minds that made too much of nakedness, when the real theme was the adoration of the blessed virgins, the sacrifice of the chosen one.

Laura got in the way of the feather dusters, making Mama's terriers worry them, and her button boots interfered with the progress of the polishing cloths over the floor. The kneeling maids didn't mind; the dancing girl with the droll mouth gave them a breather, but Miss Carlotta was furious, striding to grip her by the arm and propel her towards the door, shouting: 'A telling's no use. It's a good thrashing you need, girl, to teach you. Now get up to your room out of the way and take these dogs with you, or I warn you, there'll be no Christmas for you.'

But Laura didn't go upstairs. Without knocking she brought the dogs into the library and sat cross-legged on the rug in front of the fire, taking tangles from coats with her fingers while her brother's nib scraped and ash accumulated on his cigar. He didn't find her a distraction. She made no noise, except to prod the log with a poker, trying to get more heat out of something that was almost consumed. When the blackening wood spat back, making the dogs snarl, she giggled and hugged them.

'Watch. They might bite you. They're temperamental,' he advised.

'What does that mean?'

It was a silly word to have used.

'Is Alexander going to get married?' she asked after a long silence.

'Yes, he is,' he said, surprised that she knew. 'Listening at doors again, were we?' But there was no anger in his voice.

'Aunt Carlotta says he got a girl into trouble. The same kind of trouble as I get into?'

'No, not the same,' he said, smiling sadly. 'Far more serious trouble than you'll ever get into.'

'Niall, will I be able to get married one day?'

Her back was to him, her head bowed to the stretched dogs. The question startled him, and though he had long since answered it in his own mind, it returned to torment him with its implications. How could anyone tell her, least of all him? There she sat, already a woman externally, but in mind and emotions forever a child. Dr MacNiven had warned Mama not to expect an improvement, since something within that lovely little head had been permanently damaged at birth, preventing her from developing beyond a mental age of ten, though the body would go on on its own. Though she was capable of bearing children, he supposed, she wasn't capable of rearing them because she was a child herself, and always would be. A sudden thought filled him with horror: suppose she was to be molested, by one of the Irish navvies from the quarry, say, and to have a child. It would outgrow her mentally by the time it was ten. He could think of no greater crime. Her fate was to spend the rest of her days with her own flesh and blood, relying on them for protection, having nothing to call her own, except an armful of dolls, remaining a child while those around got older and more and more short-tempered. Maybe in that she was fortunate, he thought, turning in the swivel chair to touch her hair. To remain innocent and vulnerable for the whole of life was as much a triumph as a tragedy.

'I don't think marriage would suit you,' he said. 'And, besides, I wouldn't want to have to share you with anyone.'

Despite Dr MacNiven's diagnosis, she could come away with something surprising.

'But *you* might get married.'

Rather than lie, he hugged her.

By Christmas Eve the public rooms were ready for the

125

tenants' dance on Hogmanay, but Miss Carlotta's duties were still not done. She had to go through to the kitchen to make sure that Mrs Livingstone had prepared sufficient food, and to sample it.

The deer carcass that Duncan the ghillie had dragged down the mountain slope hung on hooks over the open fire. It was as tall as Maggie, and all day the scullery-maid had been standing beside it, turning it at regular intervals so that it would be evenly done. The fierce heat and physical exertion had exhausted the girl, and yet there was still an hour's turning to bring the venison to a golden brown colour and satisfy the cook's prodding fork. The roasting flesh scorched Maggie's palms, and the burden squeaking on its swivel made spreading islands in her armpits as she leaned over livid coals, sweat from her face sounding as it fell. She was hanging on to the braced iron spit like a person too tired to jump for execution, and the hot carcass burned through her dress with a queer, almost pleasurable feeling, like moving hands.

As Miss Carlotta came in, Maggie was thinking that she would rather be poor backward Laura, if it meant liberation from such labour. The growing heat of the carcass under her hands made her remember the effort of moving her mother in the bed under the coomed ceiling.

'Is it still not done?' Miss Carlotta asked irritably, inspecting the laden table in the centre that bore the lunch for the next day – the colossal turkey, free gratis from the Home Farm, that Miss Carlotta would have thrown in the bin, was wastage not a mortal sin; the plum pudding twice the size of a skull, with a plume of holly; the fish and blanc-manges for Mama because drink had destroyed her digestion.

On the shelves at the side was the food for the tenants, loaves, mince pies, small simple cakes, with Miss Carlotta lifting, to check that the mincemeat quota had not been exceeded. Elsie went with her, since Mrs Livingstone's feet, which had been complaining for days, had swollen to the point where they would not even accept slippers. She slumped at the end of the table, tippling tea.

'Oh yes, ma'am, we only put two eggs into the cake mix,' Elsie was saying proudly.

'I'm glad to see *somebody* obeys me in this house,' Miss Carlotta said.

'We're only waiting for the venison,' Elsie said, looking

significantly towards the fire where the scullery-maid laboured, shoulder to the carcass, clasping it as if in a too-quick waltz.

On her way across Miss Carlotta picked up a knife. She pushed the girl aside, sliced at the flesh, put the sliver between her teeth.

'Underdone,' she pronounced. 'We may like it that way, but they will not. It will need more than an hour. And do keep turning it, girl.'

Where she had cut was a trickle of blood which stained Maggie's palm as she applied her shoulder again, hiding her face because of the tears.

Miss Carlotta then went upstairs, but not to bed, though it was past nine. The hamper containing the servants' Christmas presents had been carried up to her sitting-room, and they still had to be wrapped in brown paper and labelled with a black pen.

Laura was on the stairs, on tiptoe, her face pressed to the stained-glass window of the chieftain.

'Why aren't you in bed, girl?' her aunt asked savagely, finding the victim she had been searching for all night. That scullery-maid had deserved a good telling-off, but Mrs Livingstone had been there, tired, touchy.

But the girl didn't turn. 'It's the moon,' she said breathlessly. 'It's a different colour through all the bits of glass. Does that mean that it's going to snow? Because I *want* it to snow – for Christmas.'

'It's not going to snow, you stupid girl. It's a fine clear night. And if you don't get to bed this instant, there won't be any Christmas for *you*.'

And then Laura remembered. 'I've to hang up my stocking!' she shouted, fists trembling at her shoulders.

'You will not hang up your stocking. You're a woman now and it's time you learnt that there is no Santa Claus. Things do not simply come out of the sky, girl. For what *you* get, you are indebted to other people – to myself and your brother, and, God knows, it is a struggle. You are going to have to learn that when we give you things – food, clothes and our constant attention – we expect something in return. That something is obedience. And there are no miracles like Santa Claus in this life. There is only one father, at Christmas and all the time, and he expects us to give, not take, so that we might get grace and salvation. These are the best presents, but you have to earn them. So get to bed. Your presents will be on the tree down there in the morning, with the others, and you'll get them with the others.'

Laura was crying before Aunt Carlotta had finished and now, shoulders drooping, she led the way up the dim stairs, button boots dragging, a world without snow or suspended stockings incomprehensible to her. She would have gone downstairs to ask her brother to restore these things, but Aunt Carlotta was blocking the way, herding her to her room, along the bare passage, and when she was inside that drab room without fire, she threw herself on the bed and let the pillow absorb her unhappiness. It wouldn't be the first time she cried herself to sleep, fully dressed, and especially when Niall was in South Africa. It wasn't worth it, trying to be good, trying not to break things, not to get in the way. Something had been dying inside her since Niall had gone to war, leaving her with Aunt Carlotta, who was always hitting, and Mama, whose medicine, always ready when she wakened, only made her sick. It was like a fire in a grate, so far down that more coal wouldn't make any difference. If she forgot to turn the key, Aunt Carlotta came to take away the small lamp and leave her in darkness, lecturing about the price of paraffin, the menace of a backward girl having a lamp burning beside her bed all night long. But she wasn't afraid of the dark. There were things in it only you knew and didn't have to share with anyone – a rat scraping behind the skirting, then coming out and playing in the moonlight, harming no one, though Ranald the gardener put down wire cages. You gave it cheese you had taken from the dining-room, after they were finished, when Symmers was too busy draining Niall's glass to notice. But the green lady, the one in the picture that went away when Mama was taken sick, didn't come any more to lay her cold hand.

Death. The word was like a draught disturbing the curtain. She had peered round the door several times at the canopied bed housing her father, the way caterpillars were wrapped up, before they became winged things. And just as she had broken open the cocoon she had found in the garden to expose the grotesque creature, neither caterpillar nor butterfly, so she had pulled aside the muslin to see something that was no longer recognizably human. The eyes in the suppurating face were turned towards her, but there was no recognition. The

128

mouth hung slack. It was a face from her world, as when she held the mirror up and wondered why her mouth wasn't the same as Aunt Carlotta's, or even Maggie's.

In the room above Laura, Maggie was having much the same thoughts as she stepped out of her stinking dress and lowered her hot face to the cold cracked basin. The carcass was at last cooked, and her father would lift it down in the morning. She was so tired that the icy water didn't shock her face. As she sat on the edge of the bed, tugging off her boots, she remembered the small socks she used to hang above the fire in the croft, using the Missal to hold them on the mantelpiece. She was a child then, sleeping in the kitchen with her mother, and it still made her face burn to remember how she had cheated, lying watching the fading peats, fighting to stay awake so that she could witness the seeming impossibility – Santa Claus coming down the chimney.

Only once had she managed it. Her mother had a heavy cold, and to sweat it out of her system had piled on peats and taken a toddy. She wrapped herself in a blanket and lay down beside her daughter, the sweat soon breaking, and her chest noisy, keeping the girl from sleep. She could see the dark shapes of the socks above the gleaming peat. The big fire alarmed her because she was sure that Santa Claus would get burned as he climbed down, dragging his sack. Should she nudge her mother and warn her? But before she could decide her mother was rising, a dark ghost creeping to the fire. To her horror Maggie saw her opening the kist by the fire and, stretching up, her hands like claws, put something into a sock, making it sag at the toe.

She had always loved her mother, but now she could have crept up behind her and pushed her into the fire. Only once before had she felt such disillusionment: when her mother had told her that the fairies would no longer trade a coin for a tooth left under the pillow. But as her mother came coughing back to bed, having put the single present in the one stocking, Maggie's anger evaporated into tears at the vision of coarse hands skimping, giving the others the best bits from the tough fowl. And she also saw coins counted out on the grained hand above the furrowed brow when MacKenzie the factor came round for the rent, not much since her father worked at the big house, but a great deal out of small wages, with four mouths.

As Maggie knelt by the bed on Christmas Eve in the big house, putting her palms together, her mother was first in her prayers, and then her brother, lying somewhere in South Africa, too distant to comprehend. The bed was cold, and Maggie could not sleep. It was also eerie because Elsie's bed was empty. She had gone in her nightdress to wash Miss Carlotta's hair, then brush it out when it dried. That took a long time, and once or twice Elsie had wakened Maggie, creeping in as the Jubilee clock chimed the small hours. If Elsie slept in, Miss Carlotta didn't say anything, though Mrs Livingstone was angry. But Maggie would have to be up before six, to help light the fires in the kitchen, and there would be a huge pile of dishes to do till late at night.

But the next day's chores didn't seem to matter because the Master had been so nice to her that day in the scullery, promising her that she wouldn't be sacked. And he had touched her. If she thought about his hand, a tremor came.

To counteract the freezing cold of the attic room, eerie with Elsie at Miss Carlotta's, Maggie sought sleep by trying to visualize the Master's face. But the smooth clear cheeks turned into the veined golden flesh of the stag carcass, which, gathering momentum, began to whirl like a dancer, and soon became a black blur.

Chapter Eight

For the first time since coming to the big house, Maggie slept in, and it had to be on Christmas Day. Elsie had crept out without wakening her, and by the time she got downstairs Mrs Livingstone had the stove and open fire going, helped by Elsie.

'You'll catch it, my girl,' the cook warned, transferring her attention to the porridge pot. 'Miss Carlotta's been through looking for you, and she wasn't half mad.'

Which made Elsie smile as she cracked eggs into a pan.

'Miss Carlotta said there wasn't to be any Christmas dinner for you,' Mrs Livingstone continued. 'So get into the scullery and scrub the sink.'

And as bristle hissed on chipped stone, Maggie remembered that no one had wished her a merry Christmas, like her mother used to do.

Laura had been up for ages, lighting the lamp herself, though it wasn't allowed, and – horror of horrors – carrying it to the marble wash-stand, its wick smoking, the cold bare boards under her soles. She shrieked with delight as her fingers broke the membrane of ice in the pitcher, but when she ran to pull back the curtain there was only blackness. As her face touched the bowl of icy water, her eyes shut tight, the dining-room clock struck six times under her heels. It was too cold to splash, she decided, and as for the tablet of cheap soap – but Aunt Carlotta would lift her hair and look behind her ears, so some show had to be made.

And then the dress, the one with the blue bow that Aunt Carlotta had laid across the clothes-horse, warning that it had taken an hour with the iron. If she hurried, she could escape the accursed corset. It wouldn't be the first time she had rolled it up and kicked it under the bed. If you laughed in it, it hurt, and then Aunt Carlotta would say: 'We'll have to pull it tighter, won't we, girl?'

Aunt Carlotta did not approve of jewellery, but seeing it was Christmas Day, she had left out a single strand of paste pearls. Laura had trouble with the catch, and it was some time before she thought of swinging the open bit round to the front, so that she could see what she was doing in the mirror. Even then your hands didn't correspond to their reflection.

But for her feet, it was still button boots.

Invernevis heard her go by as he shaved, stirring the badger's hair brush, the ivory-handled open razor rasping and dipping to shed hair-flecked soap in the china bowl. It should have been a dress kilt for Christmas Day, but he hadn't the confidence, the left leg having settled into a permanent straight line. So it was a tweed suit, white collar and a tie studded with a pearl. And lastly, the gold hunter threaded through the waistcoat.

Miss Carlotta had been down since before six, the hem of her silk gown, high-throated and pinched at the cuffs, sweeping the stone of the kitchen floor as she awaited the descent of the servants, and when the little inverted pendant watch at her modest bust showed six-thirty and the scullery-maid still not down, she voiced her anger, standing over Mrs Livingstone's swollen splayed legs as she used her hands to rake warm cinders from the deep throat of the stove, piling them on a newspaper while Elsie fetched coal and kindlings. And having issued strict instructions that there was to be no Christmas dinner for the late riser, Miss Carlotta sallied through to the drawing-room.

There were now rows of wooden chairs on the space cleared for dancing and in front of them, the portable altar she had had made in the south, not trusting the estate joiner. Father Macdonald was going to hold the Christmas Mass for the servants there, a facility denied her in years past by her brother-in-law, who said that the public rooms weren't for worship, and who warned her to keep to the servants' hall. But the previous year, with the brute dead, and his heir away at the war, she had established the pattern. Mostly from the servants' hall, the chairs had been set out by the piper and ghillie. The front row, segregated by three feet of bare floorboards, was for the family. Two chairs, without the comfort of cushions. The room was cold, but there was no question of a fire, since they had to be alerted to how lucky they were for the gift of life.

She sat down at the organ and tested its tone, satisfied that the dampness that had broken out in Laura's bedroom above hadn't got into the pipes. Father Macdonald's wheels came

132

crunching, and having personally delivered the Lord's blessing, he was taken up to her sitting-room to change into his vestments. As the whiteness went over his head, she unhooked the bunch of keys from her waist, unlocked the cupboard and took out the silver-gilt chalice and supply of wafers, the vessel wrapped in linen, the wafers in an air-tight tin. The cork was tight in the wine bottle, but it came out. Downstairs again, she got the candles going on the altar, using the most delicate sticks from the silver safe. When the inverted pendant watch showed seven, she hurried into the hall, lifted the padded stick and began to beat the large circle of wrinkled brass she had brought from India.

The crash almost sent the slippery plate from Maggie's fingers. She thought it was the breakfast gong, making her realize how hungry she was, but then Mrs Livingstone called through to say it was the Christmas Mass in the drawing-room, and would she hurry because she had already angered Miss Carlotta by her lateness.

Invernevis had come down, and Symmers the butler was marshalling the staff in the hall, lining them in order of seniority, with Mrs Livingstone at the head, and Maggie at the tail, against the door going through to the back. Miss Carlotta was already seated at the organ, stiff-spined, testing by tugging and tramping, little steel spectacles secure on her nose, though she knew the music by heart.

Invernevis led the way in, followed by Laura. There was no chair for Mama, for though her sister knew she needed absolution, it was too much of a task to get her up and dressed so early. Besides, communion meant wine.

When they were all seated and still, Miss Carlotta watching them in the mirror screwed to her right, above the keyboard, the white-vested priest came in and went to the altar between organ and congregation, holding up both hands for bowed heads.

'This Mass is being offered for the glory of our Lord, whose assistance and blessing we beseech in defeating the barbaric Boer, so that peace and prosperity might be restored to our Empire. It is also being offered that those who have gone into darkness may have an opportunity of repenting of their sins, and that the sinners in our midst might be led on to the path of righteousness.'

Invernevis was certain that the references were to his father and brother, if not Mama also, but no one else in the room had raised their heads. Except Laura. As the priest launched into interminable Latin, she could not resist peering through her splayed fingers. What did it all mean? And the people were answering back, which you didn't dare do with Aunt Carlotta.

'*Glória Patri.*'

She was back in the school-room, sitting at the desk, Aunt Carlotta's mouth making munching movements as she read out stories from the Bible. The language was funny, and Laura couldn't follow them. Cain? Imagine a person being called after a stick. She wanted to go out and play, but when her attention wandered to the window, Aunt Carlotta leaned over and rapped her knuckles with an ebony ruler.

Laura would put her hands up to her face, to try and tell her aunt how confusing it all was, and that she would rather hear the stories the tinkers told at the back door. Because one day, when Laura was hopping about the front hall, the toe of her button boot kicking a piece of slate from square to square on the carpet, Aunt Carlotta had heard her chanting a Gaelic song. Though her aunt did not know the meaning, the sound was sufficient to send her into a terrible rage, the well of the stair making her voice like a man's.

'Where did you learn that? I demand to know where you learnt that, you parrot!'

The tinkers had told Laura not to tell, saying that Gaelic was magic, so she had to endure more shaking.

'The Queen's English is your language, do you hear? I have taught you to speak properly, and you will continue to do just that, though your vocabulary will never amount to much. But at least we can understand you. Gaelic is the language of the servants and the village. It's an ugly language and if I hear you saying so much as one more word again, I'll put you to work in the scullery.'

Which would have made Laura quite happy because she liked putting her hands into hot water and seeing how long she could hold them in without crying out. Somewhere behind her in the Mass Maggie the scullery-maid sat, the girl she sometimes knocked on the window to. But Laura didn't dare turn round because Aunt Carlotta was watching her in the mirror.

*'In illo témpore: Pastorés loquebántur ad ínvicem: Tran-
seámus usque Béthlehem, et videámus hoc verbum, quod
factum est, quod Dóminus osténdit nobis. Et venérunt fes-
tinántes, et invenérunt Mariam, et Joseph, et infántem
pósitum in praesépio.'* ['At this time: the shepherds said to
one another: Come, let us make our way to Bethlehem and
see for ourselves this happening which the Lord has made
known to us. And so they went with all haste, and found
Mary and Joseph there, with the child lying in the manger.']

Bethlehem. Now there was a word she knew, though it was
hard to say without lisping. She folded her hands on her lap
and crossed her ankles because she liked that story. It always
came before the distribution of presents from the tree. Now
what was it last year? She had to close her eyes and concentrate because she got mixed up between Christmas and her
birthday, which was in the summer, because she remembered
the heat, the strawberries and cream Mrs Livingstone had
slipped to her. Aunt Carlotta chose all her presents, and it
was always something to wear. This time she wanted a puppy
she could keep in her own room and feed from a saucer.
Nobody else would be allowed to stroke it, or take it for walks.
It would sleep in her bed, though Aunt Carlotta said that
an animal's proper place was outside. She was sure her dolly
wouldn't mind sharing.

Bethlehem. There was a stable, with a baby in it. She spent
a lot of time at the stables behind the house, pushing open
the half-doors and holding out fists of hay to the horses. The
way their lips moved over the palm of her hand when the
hay was all gone made her legs weak.

She hugged the horses; she whispered into their ears and
stroked her cheek along their velvet skins. It was so peaceful
in the stable, with the swallows' nests stuck to the rafters like
the opera boxes in Aunt Carlotta's book on the treasures of
Italy. And below the boxes, on the cobbles, the dried bouquets
of their droppings. If the swallows could get back from
Africa, why couldn't Niall?

And as her mind flitted, the gruff old coachman would
appear at her back.

'Sent to spy on me by your aunt, eh? Go on, clear out.
You're upsetting the horses.'

This day he was really angry, his eyes bulging, raising his

135

hand as if to strike her, and as she stumbled away, her button boots made glass sound on stone in the pile of hay by the door. Before he could stop her she had lifted the bottle, seen the amber medicine that Mama drank. And she had listened at enough doors to know that Aunt Carlotta suspected the coachman of bringing the stuff from the village.

'I'll not tell, honest,' she said, retreating backwards, over the cobbles. 'I'll not tell if you let me come and talk to the horses.'

He stopped, stroked his chin and smiled, the first time she had ever seen his face nice.

'And I thought you were daft,' he said. 'All right. Don't you say a word, and you can come up here. I won't tell your aunt.'

He knew she would keep the bargain. She knew it was an easy one to keep because poor Mama needed her medicine, but Aunt Carlotta didn't want her to have it. But she was now being pulled to her feet by her brother because the priest had announced a carol, indicating with his palms that they must all rise, the organ beginning.

Books did not need to be handed out because 'Silent Night' had been sung every Christmas since Miss Carlotta had come to Invernevis. Besides, some of the servants had difficulty reading English. The carol filled the cold, high-ceilinged room, the baritones of gardener and ghillie swamping the subdued sopranos of the Island maids, Miss Carlotta's feet tramping, striving to give the organ ascendancy, pulling the black knobs, opening up the gilded pipes. Though she did not know the words by heart, Maggie moved her lips because Miss Carlotta seemed to be watching her in her wing mirror, and in the front row Invernevis was uncomfortably conscious that his aunt's steel-framed eyes were also on him, demanding more volume. He couldn't help but think of Colonel Campbell at the controls of his new car.

Beside him, at shoulder height, Laura's lips were moving, but not in cadence with the singing, and her eyes were out of focus. The sound, which had the same effect on her skin as rubbing against a horse, had put her into one of those temporary trances which were a frightening feature of her mental condition. Her hands hung slack by her side, her mind empty. Words like minnows had shoaled away, darting this way and that, beyond reach. And then, as the carol reached the crescendo of the last adoration, they sat down, and her eyes allowed the world again.

But the most difficult part was coming.

Since Miss Carlotta would not allow an altar boy from the village, the priest had to perform communion single-handed. The little silver bell from Miss Carlotta's dressing-table was tinkled twice, and he spread his hands over the bread and wine.

'Hanc igitur oblatiónem servitútis nostrae, sed et cunctae familiae tuae, quaésumus, Dómine, ut placátus accipias: diésque nostros in tua pace dispónas, atque ab aetérna damnatione nos éripi, et in electórum tuórum júbeas grege numerári. Per Christum Dóminum Nostrum. Amen.' ['And so, Lord, we thy servants, and likewise thy whole household, make this peace-offering which we entreat thee to accept. Order our days in thy peace, and command that we be rescued from eternal damnation and numbered with the flock of thy elect: through Christ our Lord. Amen.']

Laura was thinking of the conjurer Niall had taken her to see in the school on one of his leaves. Dressed in black swallow-tails, but with white gloves, he had shown the audience an empty top hat and then pulled a white dove from it. Laura hadn't believed it was real till it had begun flying about the room, beating its wings against glass to get away. The conjurer had laughed, but now the priest was striking his breast, calling out a list of names. 'Barnabas, Ignatius, Alexander.' Was he angry with her brother because he had given the girl at the Home Farm a baby, which was what it sounded like at the library keyhole? Aunt Carlotta was certainly angry, and had shouted at Alexander.

'Dómine, non sum dignus ut intres sub tectum meum: sed tantum dic verbo, et sanábitur ánima mea.' ['Lord, I am not worthy that thou shouldst enter beneath my roof, but say only the word, and my soul shall be healed.']

As he spoke he rang the bell three times, and Aunt Carlotta slid from the organ stool, to go and kneel in front of the altar, teeth parted to receive the Host that the priest passed down, murmuring:

'Corpus Dómini nostri Jesu Christi custódiat ánimam tuam in vitam aetérnam. Amen.' ['The Body of our Lord Jesus Christ preserve your soul for everlasting life. Amen.']

Invernevis followed his aunt, but was excused kneeling because of his game leg. And then it was Laura's turn, the moment she always dreaded, though there had been so much training, kneeling on the bare boards of the school-room as Aunt Carlotta held out the small salted biscuit, making her raise her head. She was warned that it was a mortal sin to chew the Host, because that would cause Christ more agony, like the nails that had been driven in. She knew that pain, when nails came through her boots. The wafer had to be swallowed without touching the teeth, but when she closed her eyes and gulped, it always stuck and Aunt Carlotta hit her on the back, shouting, making her do it again.

As she rose to go for communion at a prompt from Niall's right hand and Aunt Carlotta's glaring eyes, a button boot hooked over her brother's game leg, and she fell on her knees in front of the altar, a splinter driven in, making her bite her lip and wince. But the priest, who seemed so tall in his white vestments between the candles, was leaning over, holding out the Host, and Aunt Carlotta stooped by her, holding a silver salver under her chin to catch the dribbles. Her tongue was out, eyes shut tight as the wafer passed between her teeth, but she could not gulp. The priest's two fingers were almost in her mouth, waiting, but her heart was hammering. Then as Aunt Carlotta's shoe sharply prodded her thigh, she swallowed.

But the wafer had stuck to the roof of her mouth, and as she pushed in a finger to dislodge it, Aunt Carlotta slapped down her hand. Furious, her brother leaned forward and pulled her back to her chair. Surely to God the priest could make special dispensation.

The servants began to file up, the butler first, Maggie last. She had seen what had happened with Laura and she was so nervous that instead of risking the wafer sticking in her throat, she kept it under her tongue all the way back to her chair, Miss Carlotta's suspicious eyes following her.

'Dominus vobiscum.'

'Et cum spiritu tuo,' the servants responded, not knowing what they were saying, even after so many years.

But it was not the end. Father Macdonald had withdrawn

138

upstairs, but Miss Carlotta was now at the altar, lecturing.

'The tenants' dance will take place on New Year's Eve, as is the tradition in this house, and when you have finished your duties, you may join in. As you are all aware, I do not approve of drink, but I am told that it is the custom to have it at this dance.' She looked significantly at her nephew. The steel spectacles glinted in the altar candlelight as she continued: 'However, it is only to be taken in the strictest moderation, and if I discover that any of you are the worse from it, you will be dismissed instantly. I hope I make myself clear. Now all that remains is to wish you a merry Christmas on behalf of the family.'

At this point Invernevis got to his feet, to his aunt's obvious annoyance. Turning to face the servants, he thanked them for their support and loyalty while he was away at the war, when the circumstances were 'difficult', but he hoped that the year to come would be better in every way.

Symmers the butler opened the applause, and conveyed the servants' traditional thanks to Miss Carlotta and the Master for looking after their welfare and giving them Mass.

They filed out, Miss Carlotta leading the way, but they were not going to their duties. It was the housekeeper's practice to distribute the presents immediately after the service, to get them out of the way, and to strengthen the recipients' gratitude, to God if not her. So once again they had to line up in order of seniority, with the butler next to the tree, and the scullery-maid at the end, by the door. Miss Carlotta's procedure was to unhook the presents from the tree and hand them one by one to the laird for distribution. She had loathed it when the rank presence beside her was her brother-in-law in his habitual riding boots, a cigarette between his fingers near the inflammable tree as he passed the parcels, sometimes tossing them, and sometimes slapping the buttocks of the blushing recipient.

But now it was her nephew standing beside her, shaking hands before he passed over the present, Symmers murmuring his thanks in his usual bland way, though he knew by the feel that it was the perennial pair of black socks. And the females held out their hands, curtsied and accepted the shapeless parcels of Army & Navy Stores woollen underwear. After an hour you were 'itching to get out of them', as Mrs Livingstone, who always received the same, said.

They shuffled forward and when they had their presents, turned back to their duties. The line diminished, the tree becoming bare at the bottom. Miss Carlotta's mouth seemed to be twitching towards a smile as Elsie the kitchen-maid's turn came, and her parcel was longer than the others.

Only Maggie was left, standing back, with Invernevis beckoning her to come forward, and Laura hauling at her arm. But as she came, her face burning, Miss Carlotta turned away and began to mount the stairs, regally pinching her silk gown to prevent herself tripping.

Invernevis was aghast, and Laura stood, slack-mouthed, still gripping Maggie's arm. But Aunt Carlotta was already turning up into darkness, to take coffee with Father Macdonald, her head in the same fixed position.

And then Laura found her voice, shouting: 'Aunt Carlotta, Aunt Carlotta, Maggie hasn't got her present!'

But it was too late. A door was already shutting.

Invernevis was both angry and embarrassed. There was nothing left at the bottom of the tree, and he felt certain that this was his aunt exacting vengeance for Maggie seeking his protection. So he felt responsible. But what was to be done? Silence could only confirm that it was a snub.

But Laura was giving him the few seconds he needed in which to make a decision that would save both Maggie's face and his aunt's. For, jumping up and down, his sister was pointing to the top of the tree and saying excitedly: 'She can have my present,' though she didn't know which parcel was hers.

Maggie was wishing the floor would open. She couldn't retreat to her scullery because that would mean passing through the kitchen, and Elsie would be there to gloat. And she couldn't run up the front stairs to her bedroom. Apart from the fact that they were strictly prohibited by Miss Carlotta, trespassing bringing instant sacking, the Master barred the way. So she stood by the tree, her face, she knew, scarlet.

Invernevis was all too well aware of her agony, made worse for him by the memory of the brother he had recruited. And Laura was now jumping off the bottom step, trying to pull down the higher presents. She would topple the tree if not stopped.

'Go and wish Mama a merry Christmas,' her brother ordered. Holding Maggie lightly by the elbow, he led her to

140

the library, wondering with each awkward step how he was going to deal with this situation, since the girl was close to tears. He pushed open the door, let her into the warmth. She stood awkwardly, and he was instinctively making for his chair on the other side of the desk when he realized that that would be too formal. So he went to stand by the fire, clasping his hands behind his back to conceal his nervousness, and keeping his eyes on the carpet as he cleared his throat for speech.

'I'm truly sorry about my aunt forgetting you. It must be because she's had so much to do, and forgot to add your name to the list, since you're new.' It didn't sound convincing, so he tried to strengthen it. 'It's a big staff to look after, you see.' No, that wasn't any good, because he was apologizing for the wrong thing. 'Anyway – ' he coughed unnecessarily – 'I must make this oversight up to you.' His fingers were already in his waistcoat pocket, searching for a gold coin, but he suddenly remembered the scandals involving his father, servant girls and money. 'Now, I'd like you to tell me something you really want – *want*, not need – and I'll send away for it today. It'll be a week or so coming, but better late than never, what?' And he tried to make a joke of it. 'Take your time. You can tell me later today.'

But he realized how impossible it was. He couldn't make the situation worse by mentioning cost – 'something within reason, of course' – because he didn't know what limit to set. If the girl got a more expensive present than the rest, that could cause envy and speculation, and if his aunt came to hear, it would make things even worse. No military decision he had had to take had caused him so much uncertainty. He was angry with himself. If he couldn't deal with such delicate situations, he wouldn't be much good as a laird. Damn Aunt Carlotta: she had put him in an impossible position.

All the time the Master was talking Maggie kept her eyes on his desk, trying to listen while admiring the silver ink-wells, the little gold cutter for cigars, the notepaper in the holder. It all seemed so neat and orderly, unlike the corner of the dresser Elsie allowed her. How on earth had the anemone got inside the clear, scone-shaped glass holding down the pile of papers? Nobody wrote to her, and she wasn't very good at writing, so there was no use in asking for one of the slim silver pens, though they were lovely.

141

As he spoke her eyes roved, like a child at a toy-shop window, and by the time he had finished she had made up her mind. There was no need to wait; she could have her present now. She picked up the silver-framed photograph of the newly gazetted Captain in full ceremonial dress.

'Can I have this, sir?'

He was so taken aback that his heel struck the fender. Was it some kind of joke? What on earth could the girl possibly want with a photograph of him, and an old photograph at that, the one that had taken so long but had turned out such a disappointment because of the feathered bonnet shading his face? When the account came from the little Italian, Aunt Carlotta had refused to pay.

But when he saw the flush spreading up the girl's neck he knew, because he remembered that day in the scullery when she had been so upset over Aunt Carlotta sacking her. His contacts with women – and these were society women – had been restricted to rare formal occasions. Except with Laura, of course, when he had to comfort her after Aunt Carlotta had been scolding, but that was different. But a servant? What *did* one say? Did one simply ignore it as being a fantasy that would pass? His father had taken full advantage, but Maggie came from a good family, her mother having been in the kitchen before her marriage to the ghillie. She wasn't the type of girl to try to trap him. Too quiet and shy, despite Aunt Carlotta's estimation. She was due a present, and the way she was clasping the photograph, he couldn't very well take it from her. And not only because he could not risk a scene. The girl's eyes convinced him that she wanted the photograph very badly. Maybe for the silver frame, to put a photograph of her brother in, if there was such a thing.

It was a dangerous situation, but he tried to keep it light, to save the girl as much as himself. 'Very well, if that's what you want, but I was thinking of something better.'

But she was already retreating to the door, stuttering her thanks, the photograph against her bust, as if he was about to change his mind. And he might have, had she not shut the door, for he was beginning to realize the implications when Aunt Carlotta missed it from the desk. He slumped in the chair by the fire. My God but he had made a mess of it, the same way he had made a mess of handling Alexander. He wasn't going to be any good as a laird, if the most junior servant girl could get round him. Maybe that was why his father had been so hard, not giving an inch, tying him up with trustees. But then, there were the scandals with the servant girls. They would say he was going the same way as his father. Maggie was pretty enough, with her black hair and pale complexion, but she didn't interest him in *that* way. He simply felt sorry for her because of her brother and mother, because Aunt Carlotta was so hard on her. It was his aunt who had put him into this position, and now he had played straight into her hands. She would ask where the photograph was, and if he told the truth, she would think there was something between him and the scullery-maid. That would explain why he didn't want her sacked. Oh God, what a mess. And what if the girl displayed the photograph in her room?

But Maggie had no intention of doing that. As soon as she was outside the library door, she unbuttoned her dress and pushed the photograph inside, arranging it at her shapeless waist. Her heart was pounding. It was a *far* better present than any Miss Carlotta could give, and besides, he had given it with his own hands. In a nice frame, too.

The front stairs confronted, and for a moment she considered running up them and hiding the present in her room. But the danger was heightened by the sound of Miss Carlotta and Father Macdonald coming down, talking, saying something about 'sinners needing a lesson'. She hurried through to the scullery, deciding that it would be safer to keep the photograph about her person in case Elsie went through her things in the bedroom. Keeping it on her would give her all day to plan a place, and if a safe one couldn't be found, she would just have to take the photograph out of its frame and carry it about with her at all times, since the silver corners dug into her skin.

She passed safely through the kitchen to her sink because they were all in the servants' hall, having their breakfast and opening their parcels, the young maids holding up the shapeless woollen knickers and making wry faces while Frank the footman, with his new black socks stuffed in his pocket, urged them to try them on there and then.

'You can always swop with Farquhar,' the footman said, pointing to the morose piper who had received yet another pair of black garter tabs for his hose.

'That bloody woman must think that I'm going to play at

funerals for the rest of my life,' he complained bitterly. And to Frank: 'No, you put the knickers on. You're the toff from the city.'

Maggie's father had received a thick pair of socks, with reinforced heels, and he was glad of them because they were long enough to be worn under the old laird's leather riding boots that the heir had allowed him to salvage.

'And what did you get, Elsie?' Mrs Livingstone wanted to know.

Her question made them all look down the table to where the kitchen-maid sat, but there was no sign of her parcel.

'The holy ghost must have crept in and taken it back,' Frank said. But his tone changed when he added: 'Maybe she's given it to Maggie.'

'I don't believe in opening a present in front of others,' Elsie said angrily. 'It's supposed to be a secret. And what you've just called Miss Carlotta is blasphemy.' She rose and picked up the parcel, which she had been keeping behind her legs, against the chair. And to the footman, before she went out: 'Your tongue's going to get you into trouble one of these days, and I for one won't be sorry to see you going down the avenue.'

Mrs Livingstone tried to shrug off the behaviour of her assistant, but the laughter had died. Though there was still tea under the cosy, she cleared the maids back to their duties.

Frank waited till he had the ghillie alone. 'I'm sorry about what happened to Maggie. A bloody shame. That woman's a spiteful old bitch. Always getting at the girl, and that Elsie – '

But the ghillie held up a hand to show that he was not going to break his old established rule about not discussing his employers, or what went on at the big house. All he would say was: 'You're new here, boy, and you've a lot to learn about loyalty if you want to get on. There's an old Gaelic proverb: the noisiest bird always gets snared.'

'But she deliberately hurt Maggie,' Frank said angrily.

The ghillie's narrowed eyes regarded him above the briar stem of his pipe. 'And how do *you* know it was deliberate? Maggie's the newest one here; Miss Carlotta might easily have forgotten.'

'You know damn fine she didn't.'

'Don't swear at me, you young pup, or I'll put you through that wall.' He rose, balancing his fists on the table, leaning

144

over menacingly, speaking with his pipe between his teeth. 'Maggie doesn't need the likes of you to get on in life, and if you go making trouble for her you'll have me to deal with.'

Father Macdonald had gone to say the third Mass of Christmas Day to the villagers, but would be returning to the big house for lunch. There was only himself and his aunt at breakfast, but Invernevis did not want to spoil the day for Laura, so he said nothing about Maggie's missing present.

'Mama feels stronger,' Aunt Carlotta announced. 'She will be coming down for lunch.'

'And Laura will be here also,' her nephew reminded her.

'I hope she conducts herself better than she did at communion. Father Macdonald is *most* upset.'

'She was just nervous, that's all,' her nephew said, seeing no gain in confrontation. 'Perhaps she should stop taking communion.'

'She has to take communion, otherwise she will not get salvation,' Aunt Carlotta warned. And, leaning across, her knife wagging: 'You must not encourage the idea that because she is backward, she is exempt from the laws of this world and what lies beyond. Father Macdonald *will* continue to hear her confession because she has sins, like the rest of us.'

Invernevis transferred his anger to the triangle of toast, smearing on Home Farm butter so forcibly that burnt crumbs scattered round his plate. No, he didn't feel like Gentleman's Relish.

Aunt Carlotta's kipper was now a skeleton. As her finger hooked through the arched handle of the breakfast cup, she announced: 'Poor Father Macdonald. Do you know, the quarry manager had the audacity to ask him to go across and give *them* communion today.'

'And is he going to go?' her nephew asked, hoping that they might be deprived of the presence of the priest at Christmas lunch.

Aunt Carlotta looked at him as if he was mad.

145

Book Three

Chapter Nine

The only difference between Christmas dinner and the other
meals of the year in the flagstoned kitchen of the Home Farm
was that a white cloth covered the scarred boards, and glasses
with stems instead of thick tumblers were set out. Otherwise
it was the same assorted cutlery, tarnished forks and discoloured bone knives, not even from the same set, and there
were the same assorted chairs, some with suspect backs.

The growing flames of the piled peats were reflected in the
horse brasses and scarlet show rosettes arrayed round the fireplace, and the brass jelly-pans balanced on the mantelpiece
gleamed like gold. An oil lamp was stationed on the big
chipped sideboard, and another on the centre of the table
because the low ceiling and the single window overlooking the
river discouraged light.

The sweet peat smoke mingled with the smells of cooking
and the farmyard odours wafted in under the draughty doors.
Two black and white collies slumped sighing on the hearth,
and when the kettle made a slow whistle, they jerked up their
heads.

Impressive in black, with a gold chain of substantial links
crossing his midriff, MacPherson stood at the head of the
table. He was a big man, with bushy white eyebrows giving
his fleshy face a querulous look, the only hair on his massive
peaked head being white curled patches like ram's horns above
his ears.

He stood over the huge turkey with the bound feet, making steel spark on steel, then testing the big blade on his thumb. He sawed at the breast, lifting the tender white meat on to a willow-patterned plate which he passed to Alexander, who was sitting on his right.

'Got to keep your strength up, eh?' he said, winking.

Alexander blushed at the light laughter from below. He was wearing a tight-fitting, high-buttoned black suit and a rounded white collar, making him look like a boy despite the moustache.

'I would have taken a leg,' he said defensively, lifting the glass of whisky by his fist.

And when MacPherson's daughter Kate, who was sitting opposite Alexander, raised her eyebrows at the heaped plate being passed to her, her father said jovially:

'Aye, lass, but remember you're eating for two now.'

That caused more laughter down the table, and Kate smiled, folding her hands on her distorted floral dress. At the other end of the table, Mrs MacPherson, grey-haired, face deeply lined after so many children and chores, shook her head sadly at her husband's crudity. He saw her and retaliated.

'It's nature, isn't it, woman? Damn me, if it wasn't the byre would be empty. *They* don't have to produce certificates before they calve, do they?'

No one dared answer that, so the plates were passed down from sons to other daughters, the dark meat going to the two loonies who sat on either side of Mrs MacPherson. Huge-headed, with mobile faces and slack mouths, these residents of the hay loft were always laughing to themselves. Today they were in their best clothes, too big jackets that Mac-Pherson had passed down.

'For Christ's sake eat with your cutlery on one day of the year!' MacPherson bellowed at the loonies. He pointed the carving knife. 'Any more nonsense, and there's no pudding for you.'

They began to cry. Mrs MacPherson petted the two fifty-year-old skulls simultaneously with: 'Now, now, sonnies,' and proceeded to cut up their meat for them.

'Just look at these potatoes; like bloody snowballs,' Mac-Pherson was saying, heaping Alexander's plate. 'Mind you, it's not the goodness of the ground,' he added hastily. 'It's my good manure.'

147

'Please, Father, not *now*,' Kate said, wincing.

'Farming doesn't stop just because it's Christmas,' her father warned. 'And Sandy wants to learn all about farming, don't you, son?' He sat down. 'Now let's see if this bird was worth the chase round the yard the bugger gave me,' he said, picking up knife and fork. 'Aye, you had some neck on you,' he said, addressing the carcass.

'Say grace first, Donald,' his wife demanded.

'Grace? Oh aye,' he said gruffly, meat already in his mouth. 'Father Macdonald might be listening at the door. Sandy'll say grace for us. Try it again in Gaelic, son.'

He stood up awkwardly, and while they bowed their heads, gave thanks. The two loonies sniggered but were hushed by Mrs MacPherson.

'You're coming on fine, Sandy,' MacPherson acknowledged. 'Still a wee trace of the accent, but that'll go in time. You'll soon pick up the language.'

'He hears plenty of it in the Arms,' Archie the eldest son, a tall thin youth with a nervous twitch, said.

'Instead of making smart remarks, you should give your mouth work with your knife and fork, to fatten you up,' his father said savagely. 'Otherwise you're not going to be much good at running this place after me.' As he spoke he tilted the whisky bottle between himself and Alexander. 'A meal's no good without a good dram.'

'Then why aren't we getting one?' Donny, another son, demanded.

'Because you can't hold the stuff. It'll take you all your time to deal with that white wine. *Slainte.*' His glass clashed with Alexander's.

'Don't give him too much,' Kate implored. 'He should be going up to the big house to wish his folks a merry Christmas.'

'He's stopping right here,' MacPherson said menacingly. 'And you keep out of it: this isn't woman's business. Just you get food down for what's in your belly. Sandy doesn't want to go near the place, do you, son?' And, without waiting for an answer: 'Merry Christmas, by Christ! More like a wake, with the priest and that bitch Carlotta. And he didn't get a very warm reception from his brother the last time he went, did he?' he said sarcastically, turning to his daughter.

'That's his aunt's way. You have to make allowances.'

'I'm not talking about his bloody aunt,' her father said

angrily. 'I'm talking about his brother, the laird.'

'Drop this conversation,' Mrs MacPherson warned, noticing how embarrassed Alexander was.

'But he did get the bit of ground by the river,' Kate persisted, ignoring her mother. 'If that's not being generous, I don't know what is.'

'Oh, there's bound to be a catch in it somewhere,' Mac-Pherson said. 'He'll be looking for you to give up your claim to the estate. Never do that, son.'

Alexander was about to say something, but Kate spoke quickly the first thing that came into her head.

'This turkey's very tender.'

It wasn't worth replying to, and besides, Mrs MacPherson wanted her say on another matter.

'They tell me the Irishmen are getting worse. You'll have to be careful, Master Alexander. Remember what Kate's carrying.'

'Sandy can look after himself,' her husband said proudly. 'Didn't he show that, in the pub the other week? A few more months of this food and hard work, and he'll match anybody in the district. Just like his father. Now *there* was a character,' he said wistfully. 'Many a bottle we shared in this very kitchen. Funny how history repeats, isn't it?' Then he remembered something. 'Just a minute,' he said, his chair scraping. He groped audibly in the dark recesses of the fireplace, bringing back a bent poker which he laid beside Alexander's plate. 'Your father did that.'

Alexander looked, but did not touch the twisted metal.

'So the next thing's the wedding,' MacPherson said, eating again. 'Everything in hand, woman, eh?' he shouted down to his wife.

'No, the next thing's the tenants' dance at the big house,' Kate said quietly.

'Aye, well, you'll not be going to that in your condition,' her father said gruffly. 'Not that you've anything to be ashamed of,' he added hastily.

'But Sandy can go,' she said.

MacPherson wiped his mouth and shook his head slowly. 'No, Sandy's place is here, with you. Isn't that right, son?'

He nodded, and received more whisky.

'Aye, I'm fair looking forward to the wedding,' MacPherson said. 'Nothing fancy, of course. The main thing is for everyone to enjoy themselves. But I'll have to watch the spending. The rent's high, and it'll go higher if the trustees have their way. That bloody Carlotta's got far too much say for a woman.'

'But I'm still worried about the dress being white,' Mrs MacPherson said. 'Father Macdonald won't like it at all.'

'She's my daughter and she's got as much right to be married in white as any woman,' MacPherson said angrily. 'And if the priest makes trouble, there won't be any more bags of potatoes or lambs.' He turned again. 'And you, Sandy? Is it going to be the kilt?'

'He doesn't like the kilt,' Kate said.

'Let him answer for himself,' her father warned. And he waited.

'As Kate says, I don't like the kilt because I had to wear it all the time as a boy,' Alexander said uncomfortably. He fingered his lapel. 'This suit's fine.'

'Good lad,' his future father-in-law said, clapping him on the shoulder. 'Just you wear what you feel most at home in, and don't listen to them women. They're just like that Pankhurst bitch; they'll have the trousers off you before you know it.' And he laughed, slapping the table, making cutlery jump.

'Mrs Pankhurst's a very brave woman – ' Kate began.

But her father held up a warning hand. 'Now before you begin, think about that woman in the big house across there, and remember what a little power can do to your sex. Oh, I don't mind women getting a share of the hard jobs, but power – that's different. That's why I've no time for Queen Victoria. She should get off the throne and give it to the Prince of Wales. Now *there's* a man.' He looked down the long board at his wife, and there was affection as well as irritation in his voice. 'Well, woman, you didn't do much ploughing, but I saw to it that you had plenty to do in here, what with carrying them and rearing them, and I made sure there was plenty for the churn. That's the way it should be. You remember that, Sandy. Let them do the breeding and the butter-making inside. We'll concern ourselves with putting the bull to the cows, and getting the milk.'

There was a diversion at the bottom of the table, where the two loonies were fighting over the wish-bone, with Mrs MacPherson patiently interceding, explaining that they could share, and folding their pinkies over the prongs.

'Now close your eyes and make a wish,' she ordered them.

Their eyes screwed tight, mouths working, they tugged till the bone splintered, sending them toppling from their chairs, which brought MacPherson to his feet, roaring:

'Right, you buggers! Back to the hay loft with no pudding. And you, woman: why do you encourage them when you know they've got nothing up top?'

'They've a lot more than many folk,' she said, steady eyes on her husband.

'I think I'll go and lie down,' Kate said, suddenly standing.

'Is he kicking, eh?' her father asked, leering.

'I'm tired. It's the woman's burden,' she said.

'I'll help you through,' Alexander volunteered, rising, unsteady on his feet.

While MacPherson watched with satisfaction, he took Kate's arm through to the bedroom.

'Take good care of her – them, I should say – Sandy!' MacPherson called.

Alexander stopped at the door, watching the loonies who were about to take a tearful departure being comforted by Mrs MacPherson.

'Seeing it's Christmas, won't you let them stay for pudding?' Alexander asked.

'Oh, all right, son,' MacPherson said, shrugging. 'But they better bloody behave.'

Kate sat on the bed, and asked Alexander to swing her legs up. She lay like a corpse, arms by her side, stomach grotesque. He went to stand by the small window, pulling aside the muslin. It was growing dark, and the lights of the house across the river were brightening.

'You should have gone up to see them; your mother at least,' Kate said, her voice seeming to come from a great distance.

'I told you before; there's no way past Carlotta.'

'That's because she feels you've let her down by coming here. I told you before, and it still stands, though the wedding's fixed. Go back across there and I won't think any the less of you.'

'No, I'm staying,' he said stubbornly.

'You let Father give you too much drink.'

'It's Christmas.'

'It's always Christmas with you, Sandy,' she said wearily. 'One of these days you're going to wake up and find your stocking empty.'

'You're beginning to sound like Carlotta, treating me as if I'm still a boy – a bad boy.'

'Oh, you're not bad,' she said, as he groped towards her distended silhouette. 'Only foolish.'

He climbed on beside her and put his ear to the floral dress. 'I wonder if he's speaking Gaelic yet.'

'Why Gaelic, and why a he?' she said, holding his head there. 'If speaking Gaelic means a life like this, I'd rather it be English. And I'd rather it be a girl, because they don't inherit, like men, though, God knows, I'm a poor example to my sex.'

'I don't follow you,' he said, frightened in the darkness, where something moved inside her.

'It doesn't matter,' she continued, as if speaking to herself. 'I was only trying to say that being on this side of the river isn't as romantic as you seem to think. Look at the way my father pushes people around. Thank God you stood up for the loonies.'

'I'm fond of your father,' he murmured.

'So am I, but you're not one of the family, though he treats you like one. The way he talks to you, you'd think he had no sons. You call it affection; I've another name for it. And for one dreadful moment in there I thought you were going to tell him that you'd given up your claim on the estate.'

'I don't see why I shouldn't.'

'Walk in there just now and tell him, and you'll see a different side to him, one you won't like. But what's the use in talking? You're far too trusting. Imagine giving the money you inherited to my father to keep for you.'

'But I get some when I need it. If I had the control, it would be gone in next to no time, and we need it for the new house.'

'Oh, you get it when you want it, to go down to the pub to spend it on drink, mostly for others,' she said bitterly. 'I'd rather a croft than all this trouble. And that pendant you gave me for Christmas: it was far too extravagant. I didn't dare wear it today. Instead of giving me something, you should have got your sister a present.'

'I wanted to,' he said quietly. 'I was going to give her one

152

of the kittens from the byre, but Carlotta would only have got it drowned.'

'The best present you could have given her was a visit,' Kate said critically, 'even although that meant apologizing to your aunt. Poor wee Laura. She's not had very much out of life.' She was silent for several seconds. 'Sandy,' she said, clutching his hand. 'Hasn't it occurred to you that this baby could be like Laura?'

He did not answer, but she felt him stiffen beside her.

'If it was, it wouldn't make one bit of difference to me. Would it to you?'

'No,' he said hoarsely, his boots pointing to the dark window, the big house lights ghostly behind the muslin. He had never felt such fear, and when he put his hand on her stomach it felt like a boulder.

At the front of the house across the river Laura was sad. Once against the promise of Christmas Day hadn't been fulfilled because of Aunt Carlotta's insistence on peace and propriety. True, she had been allowed to sit at the big table with all the silver, instead of taking her meal on a tray in the nursery, but the treat had been spoiled by Father Macdonald's presence. He was such a solemn man, and when he was speaking, Aunt Carlotta's eyes dared anyone to make a sound. It seemed to Laura that there were vast spaces of dark wood between the five persons at the table because Aunt Carlotta had insisted on an extra leaf, though Symmers had said there was plenty of room. And the shining ranks of scalloped silver on either side of her place confused Laura, who was used to eating only with a spoon. She waited until Niall had chosen, but the big soup spoon seemed so heavy, and when she tried to get it into her mouth, she slopped and Aunt Carlotta halted in her talk with Father Macdonald, who sipped from the side of his spoon and tilted his plate forward. When Laura tried, soup went over the crested rim and Aunt Carlotta said: 'Once more, and straight to bed without pudding, girl.'

Mama had come down, but only to keep her face close to the plate, making clacking sounds with her teeth as she chewed fish. Father Macdonald pretended not to notice, but Aunt Carlotta on the other side gave one of her looks. Mama was sulking because she had asked for wine, but Aunt Carlotta wouldn't allow, though Niall and the priest got some. Niall at the head of the table was only answering in short words.

The only moment of excitement was when her brother poured brandy over the Christmas pudding and applied a match. The blue flames shot up and Mama screamed, staring with wild eyes, her mouth working. But the flames died down and the horn-hilted knife was plunging, releasing steam. Laura chewed each mouthful carefully, hoping for a silver three-penny, but there was only fruit. Mama got one, however, and had to be slapped on the back by Niall, and when the coin stotted over the table Laura giggled and Aunt Carlotta turned her face away. Father Macdonald tried to make a joke, keeping the threepenny, 'as an offering', he said. 'Better late than never.' Aunt Carlotta didn't laugh.

But it wasn't so bad in the drawing-room afterwards. The presents had been taken down from the tree by her brother, and she helped carry them into the drawing-room. Father Macdonald got an advance copy of Aunt Carlotta's latest temperance tract, but though he shook hands and said thank you, he didn't smile. Laura's present from her aunt felt soft and interesting until the wrapping was torn away, revealing yet another pair of button boots. She could have cried, but Aunt Carlotta said: 'Be grateful, child. Many people get nothing for Christmas. They'll strengthen your ankles.' But the hated boots were cast aside when Niall's present was opened. Two silver-backed brushes and a heart-shaped mirror, with the letters LM interlocked on the shields, the silver smooth, the brushes so soft, like the coats of Mama's Skye terriers.

'Are they *really* mine?' she kept asking her brother. He nodded and smiled, but Aunt Carlotta was very angry.

'That's far too good a present for her,' she complained. 'Five minutes, and that mirror will be broken.'

'What does it matter, so long as it pleases her?' he said calmly.

There would have been a scene in front of Father Macdonald had Aunt Carlotta not opened her nephew's present at that moment and discovered a gold crucifix and chain.

'It's so delicate,' she murmured, letting it slip through her fingers. 'I shall keep it for special occasions. And what did *you* get?' she asked, going to investigate the figure askew on the sofa by the fire.

But Mama was having such difficulty with the satin ribbon, though it was arranged in a loose bow. Aunt Carlotta was

154

well used to cutting up her sister's meat, so she removed the wrapping. But the present was embedded in cotton wool, and Mama couldn't manage.

'What *is* it?' she asked, when it was at last on her palm.

Her sister required to study it before committing herself.

'I think it must be a watch,' she announced dubiously, feeling for the catch on the smooth gold object into which Mama's monogram had been cut.

Laughing, Niall had to show them how. He sprung it open to reveal a cameo profile of Queen Victoria, formidable in the closing years. 'A special keepsake,' he said.

Mama was like a child with a toy, though she could not master the catch, worked by pressing her monogram.

'The dear Queen,' she kept repeating, caressing gold. 'I must write to her daughter.' And with a resolve that everyone thought had been swamped by drink: 'No, Carlotta, *you* will write to Princess Louise and tell her what a terrible time I've had. Tell her – '

They propped Mama up with cushions in the corner of the sofa and let her talk on, clutching the memento of one who had failed to call. Her son left his presents to the last. First he opened Mama's, which was a silver-cornered visiting-card case stamped with the letter I and containing a supply of fifty, the scroll writing stating his lairdship. He went to kiss Mama for the gift, but she stared blankly, since Aunt Carlotta had chosen it. And from his aunt there was a Missal with mahogany boards and brass clasps, with a plate on the front: *Niall Macdonald, seventeenth of Invernevis.*

Laura was in an agony. How could her present match these? She had gone to a lot of trouble, giving Mrs Livingstone the gold coin she had got from Mama, and getting the cook to write to Edinburgh. Now Niall was unwrapping it. Oh yes, he seemed pleased with the gaily coloured box of cigars, with the picture of the jester, and he was coming to her to whisper: 'You really shouldn't. It's far too much. You're just spoiling me.' She could see the tears in his eyes, and to save him from having to say anything she threw her arms round his neck.

Aunt Carlotta, who disapproved of smoking, was clearly not pleased, and would have said something had Father Macdonald not accepted one of the cigars, much to Laura's annoyance. Rather than lose the priest to the library, Aunt Carlotta gave permission for cigars to be smoked in her presence, and while the priest puffed blue smoke, she resumed their discussion on temperance, with special reference to the village and the rampaging Irishmen.

'It *has* to be closed down, otherwise murder will be done,' she said decisively.

But the major part of the priest's subsidy came from the big house, and he was watching Invernevis closely.

'I wouldn't go as far as that, Miss Carlotta,' he murmured. 'But I would say they should be contained on their own side.'

'Contained? But you *can't* contain wild animals.'

'Meaning that they might swim over, like stags?' Father Macdonald suggested, hazarding a joke, but seeing his mistake immediately. And to correct it: 'No, the trouble lies at the Arms. Carmichael doesn't care how much drink he gives out, or at what hours, so long as there's profit in it. And I'm not only talking about the Irishmen.'

'Then *there* is your answer,' Aunt Carlotta said triumphantly, challenging her nephew with her eyes. 'Evict Carmichael, and you have solved the problem on both sides of the loch at one stroke.'

Invernevis nodded, but not enough to give them confirmation. It was beginning to sound like a trustees' meeting, and it was spoiling his cigar. The decisions on the future of the quarry and the Arms could wait. He lay back on the sofa and let them talk. Beside him, Mama had sunk into the cushions, her nostrils noisy, the memento of her monarch slipping from her grasp.

Behind the sofa, Laura sat cross-legged, her new button boots on in concession to her aunt. They hurt, but that didn't matter, since leather stretched. The heart-shaped mirror from her brother was propped against the wall, and, a silver-backed brush in each fist, she drew the soft bristles through her hair. But the ringlets always reformed, snapping back into place like the bell springs on the board in the kitchen.

If the drawing-room was reasonably peaceful, there was hilarity in the servants' hall where the Christmas dinner was well under way. Despite Miss Carlotta's strictures, drink had been smuggled in, and bottles of sherry, port and whisky stood in the centre of the table. At the foot Symmers the butler was well away, lolling in his chair, a paper hat perched on his balding head, mouthing the Gaelic songs the others were crooning, though he didn't have the language. Mrs Livingstone

156

had been persuaded to have some sherry, and she was flushed and giggling. The two carcasses of the Home Farm chickens in front of her had been picked clean, and the plum pudding reduced to a scatter of raisins.

Frank the footman was drawing a wish-bone through his white teeth, stripping and sucking it dry before hooking his pinkie round one branch. He leaned over the ruins of the food and offered the other branch to Elsie the kitchen-maid. She hesitated, but hooked her smallest finger.

'Now close your eyes and make a wish,' Frank ordered.

The bone splayed and cracked, leaving the footman with the larger part.

Elsie was angry. 'I don't believe in that superstitious rubbish,' she said, tossing away the piece of bone.

'Oh, I wouldn't say that, dear,' Mrs Livingstone beside her cautioned, and launched into memory. 'I was at a big house outside Edinburgh before I came here, and one day after the chicken came through from the dining-room the cook picked up the wish-bone and ran it under the tap. She asked me to pull it with her. Now I've never told anyone this before, but I didn't like her, so when I pulled the bone I wished I would get another job, with my own kitchen. And I got the chance of this place within six months, so it *does* work. Of course it's like the stone at the front of the house: you're not supposed to tell your wish at the time, otherwise it'll not come true.'

'I'll need to try that stone,' Frank said.

'Oh no, you won't,' the cook said emphatically. 'Miss Carlotta doesn't allow servants out at the front, far less using the stone. Besides, she's like Elsie: she doesn't believe in such things.'

'Yes, Elsie seems to have a lot in common with Miss Carlotta,' the footman said.

'And what do you mean by *that*?' Elsie wanted to know, raising her voice.

'Nothing, dear, he's tight,' Mrs Livingstone said, covering the girl's hand. 'You'll need to watch you don't get gout, Mr Symmers,' she called down the table.

But the old butler only grunted before draining his glass.

'Give us a tune, Farquhar,' Frank shouted to the piper, who was sitting on the sofa, taking whisky with the gardener.

'And bring Miss Carlotta through?' the piper said. 'How dare you disturb the peace of Christmas Day with that pagan instrument,' he mimicked, and the maids at the table laughed and clapped, small sherries having gone to their heads.

Only two people in that stifling room, with the fire banked high, refrained from drink and laughter. Elsie sat tight-lipped, letting her tea get cold as jokes about Miss Carlotta flew thick and fast. Maggie's father sat in the corner by the side-board, frowning as he drew on his short pipe. He was watching the footman, who had banged with a spoon for silence.

'We've had enough Gaelic songs,' he said. 'It's not fair to those who don't know them.'

'Well, one of the girls will give you lessons,' the piper called out, but Frank ignored him and waited till the laughter had subsided.

'Here's a better song,' he announced, and, straightening his jacket, began to sing. Everyone agreed that he had a pleasant voice, but was the song really suitable for Christmas?

> 'Goodbye Dolly I must leave you,
> Though it breaks my heart to go,
> Something tells me I am needed,
> At the front to fight the foe,
> See, the soldier boys are marching,
> And I can no longer stay –
> Hark! I hear the bugle calling,
> Goodbye Dolly Gray.'

All the time he was singing, swinging his elbows as though marching, Frank was smiling down at Elsie, who bent her scowling face to her spread nails.

There was silence when he finished, the maids nudging each other, puzzled.

'You don't mean to tell me you're going to join up?' Mrs Livingstone said, shocked.

'Of course not. It's only a song.'

But the ghillie was getting to his feet. 'Aye, it's only a song, and you're only a fool. You haven't the guts to go out and do something manly for once, instead of strutting about in that fancy uniform. I know your type; let others go and get killed so that you can sit here in comfort, drinking and mocking them.' He turned at the door. 'We don't want your kind in these parts. Gaelic's far too good for the likes of you.' And

158

before closing the door behind him he said something to the
piper in Gaelic.

The footman was still on his feet, his fists clenched by his
side in the embarrassed silence. 'What did he say about me
just now?' he demanded to know.

'It had nothing to do with you,' the piper said angrily. 'If
you must know, he said he would see me later.'

'Liar,' the footman said, shaking. 'That's a cowardly thing
to do, talking about a person in a language they can't understand.'

But Mrs Livingstone was intervening because of the butler's
incapacity at the other end of the table. 'Sit down, Frank. It
was a silly song to sing, seeing Duncan lost his boy in the
war. And his wife gone too. You must make allowances.'

'Allowances?' Elsie said, sneering as she stood up. 'There
won't be any allowances made for him.' And she went out,
slamming the door behind her.

'Now you've upset Elsie,' Mrs Livingstone said anxiously.
And, addressing the whole company: 'You'll need to watch.
What happens in here gets trailed back to Miss Carlotta.'

Though there was drink left, the party was spoiled, and the
maids began to move their chairs.

'Not so fast, you lot,' the cook cautioned. 'We'd better
clear up this mess. You can't expect Maggie to do it, seeing
she didn't have a bite, so we'll all have to muck in. And that
includes *you*, Frank, *and* Mr Symmers.' But when she went
down to give the butler a dunt on the shoulder, she could not
rouse him. She prised the glass from his fingers and turned to
the gardener.

'You can help Frank to carry him to the sofa. He'll need
to sleep it off, and this place will need to be kept locked in
case Miss Carlotta comes through. Now let's get these bottles
out of sight, and the dishes through to the scullery.'

Having been hard at it since morning, Maggie was now
doing the lunch dishes, her hunger pangs forgotten. She had
jammed a chair against the door, and the Master's photograph
was propped between the big brass taps as she plunged in
greasy plates and withdrew them, gleaming, stacking them
carefully because the best crested ones were always used when
Father Macdonald came. The tureens with painted apples for
handles had to be lowered very carefully into the greasy water,

otherwise they would hit the bottom of the sink and crack, which would mean at least two months' wages. And there were so many pieces of silver cutlery to clean. The forks had to be scrubbed with a soft brush between the prongs because Miss Carlotta would inspect them for black stains. Likewise with the scallop patterns on the handles. Periodically Miss Carlotta came through to hold the silver cutlery up to the light and look for scratches. They were all monogrammed I, and if it didn't stand out distinctly, the piece of cutlery was dropped back into the sink, with special instructions for its cleaning. When all the pieces, from soup ladle to spoons, were washed, they were taken through on a tray to the butler, who counted them carefully in his pantry, making certain he was getting back the number of pieces he had issued. If they tallied, they were put under green baize in the silver safe, and the key returned to Miss Carlotta.

Maggie was humming a Gaelic air as she took the coffee spoons in her fist and thrust them into cooling water. She looked at the Master's picture and smiled, and began talking to it as she would never have dared to his face, telling him how kind and thoughtful he was, and how much the moustache suited him.

'I think you've put on weight since you came home,' she said.

The thrill it gave her made her open her fist underwater, releasing the coffee spoons. She groped frantically, but only located four. There should have been five. Though it meant waiting on more kettles from the stove, she pulled the plug out, letting the scummed water run away with a slurping sound, waiting to see the missing spoon at the bottom. But to her horror she saw it caught in the whirlpool, being sucked away. She snatched at the slender crested handle, but too late: it plunged down, rattling, and was gone.

She rested her elbows on the sink and put her face into her hands. That was all she needed: the butler would report the missing spoon, and Miss Carlotta would go crazy. And the Master wouldn't be pleased because they were very old spoons, like the rest of the silver. The only hope was that Mr Symmers would be too tight to notice when he put the silver away that night. But that would be dishonest. It would be letting her father as well as the Master down.

She put the Master's picture back inside her dress and pulled

160

the chair from the door. Better to go through to Miss Carlotta and own up. Maybe she would be let off with paying for
it out of her wages. It would be very dear, a pound perhaps.

She was tidying her hair when Frank put his head round the
door, startling her.

'I've saved you some sherry,' he said, setting the small glass
on the draining-board.

'I can't. My father's against drink.'

'Take it, he'll never know,' he urged. 'And besides, you'll
be helping to save Symmers's liver.'

Tempted, she looked at the dark liquid in the slender glass,
and she was reaching out when she had a clear mental picture
of her mother's face. She burst into tears and, accepting the
shoulder the footman offered, blurted out about the lost
spoon.

He pushed her gently away and looked thoughtfully at the
sink, going down on his knees to inspect. Then he went out,
and when he returned it was with a pair of pliers and a
bucket. She watched, wondering, as he lay on his back under
the sink, grunting as the pliers strained at the butterfly nut.

'You're dirtying your uniform,' she protested.

'That doesn't matter. Some bugger's painted over this nut.'

Then metal began to squeak, and the nut at the bend came
away, releasing a foul-smelling black liquid which missed the
basin and splashed on his sleeve, making her groan. But he
stayed where he was, pushing two fingers into the pipe and
feeling about. When he pulled them out he had the coffee
spoon, and when he had replaced the nut, he ran the spoon
under the tap before handing it to her.

Maggie was so relieved that she stood on tiptoe to kiss his
cheek, and the footman was putting his arms round her waist
when the mournful organ sounded from the drawing-room.
Miss Carlotta was determined that the whole house would
receive *Panis Angelicus* as darkness fell.

Maggie broke free from the footman's hold and fussed at
his sleeve with a wet cloth, sponging. The day that had begun
so badly was having a happy ending, and she would go
upstairs early to admire the Master's picture by candlelight.

But Frank seemed angry, pulling his sleeve away.

'I don't think you like me,' he said sulkily.

'What makes you say that?' she asked, surprised. 'Of course
I like you, and you've just saved me from an awful row.'

161

'Then prove it.'

'Prove what?'

'Prove that you like me by drinking that sherry I brought through for you.'

She was no longer frightened. She picked up the glass and drained it at one gulp. As the sharp liquid hit her throat it made her cough and splutter, bringing tears to her eyes. But they were both laughing.

'Now you're no longer a member of Miss Carlotta's temperance band,' he said. 'Elsie's the only disciple left.'

Mama had been helped up to bed, but without her Victoria memento, which had slipped from her fingers during sleep and gone down the side of the sofa. It wouldn't be discovered till years after her death, by a maid yet to be born spring cleaning. And she didn't miss it that night because her mind was on the new bottle for which she had given the coachman a guinea and which was under her pillow. She wouldn't even need to leave her bed.

Laura was in her bedroom, having been sent up early by Aunt Carlotta. She didn't mind that night: the key was turned, and once out of her dress and new button boots, she could sit on the edge of the bed, brushing out her hair and, shifting the lamp to the edge of the cabinet, holding the heart-shaped mirror to her body, the booming music from below making her shiver.

Aunt Carlotta's late organ recital didn't really bother her nephew. He had put a new log on the library fire and was sitting, savouring another of his sister's cigars, smiling at the pleasure the vanity-set had given her, and smiling too when he thought of Maggie and his picture. Being a laird was giving as well as receiving.

Her exhaustion changed to euphoria by the sherry and the relief at recovering the silver spoon, Maggie was cleaning the sink for the morning when Mrs Livingstone called her through.

'Leave it, girl; you've done enough for the day, God knows,' the cook said, her swollen feet in front of the stove. She set down the cup of tea and swung open the oven door, using a cloth to transfer the covered plates to the big table. With the mysterious look of a magician, she whipped off the top plate to reveal breast of chicken, potatoes and vegetables. 'I kept it for you.'

162

Though terribly hungry again, Maggie looked at it dubiously.

'If it's Elsie you're worried about, she's gone up to Miss Carlotta,' Mrs Livingstone said. 'Now you'll find a knife and fork in that drawer, and take a spoon too, because there's plum pudding. Christmas isn't the same without plum pudding. Now sit down and take it while it's hot.'

Aunt Carlotta's organ recital crossed the icy river, and was heard by the loonies in the Home Farm hay loft, playing with the tin watches their second mother had given them for Christmas. But still in his clothes and boots, Alexander was asleep, though Kate's eyes were open, her hands on the moving bulge.

Chapter Ten

As nine chimed from the stable clock on Hogmanay, the tenants began converging on Invernevis House for their annual dance, some coming in gigs and carts, but mostly on foot. It was a clear cold night, with the moon turning the Summer House Pool to streaked gold. An owl interrupted the eerie silence as groups of tenants took the road above the river, its dust compacted by frost, the men swinging lanterns, the women holding the hems of their long dresses clear of their shoes, stumbling because they were not used to such attire. The frosty air made their laughter audible, and there was a good deal of joking, for most of the men had already had a dram or two, to conceal their nervousness at going up to the big house, with a new laird in residence.

At Wade's Bridge they paused to look over the parapet into the dark water of the Yellow Pool, and one wag announced: 'Aye, I should have brought my gaff,' until his wife nudged him and reminded him it was spawning time. The line of lanterns stretched back into darkness, and it was halted and moved to the side from time to time by an oncoming gig or cart, hems tangling in the brambles.

As the avenue yawned, the lanterns brightened, and roosting pigeons burst from bare branches. The hard rutted surface was sore on unaccustomed shoes, and because of the shadows and snapping branches which might have been roe-deer there was less laughter. Besides, the big house was now rearing, all its bottom windows illuminated, light reaching out to the gravel and the crooked wishing stone. In front of the porch the brass on the dim lamps of Father Macdonald's trap gleamed, the horse like stone between the shafts. All other vehicles had to go behind the house.

The laird was standing in the porch, waiting to receive his tenants. Though confidence was still unsure, custom had forced him into full Highland dress, dark, high-collared velvet doublet, with square crested silver buttons, lace at his throat and cuffs, goat's-hair sporran, diced hose and gleaming shoes with silver buckles and, at his right side, hanging from the belt with the engraved silver buckle, a long dirk hilted with a cairngorm.

As the tenants mounted the steps, he shook hands and wished them the compliments of the season. Once that had been got over with, Miss Carlotta was waiting in the hall, to nod and make sure that Symmers the butler (who seemed to have been at the bottle) was not mixing up the cloak-rooms.

Moving into light and the commanding presence of Miss Carlotta, the women were clearly embarrassed by their clothes. Some of the gowns had come from the big house, Miss Carlotta having weeded out her own and her sister's wardrobes for charity sales at the outbreak of war. But the laird's aunt was too well bred to betray any sign of recognition when silk garments, too big or too tight, were trailed past. Anyway, the majority of the skirts were home-made Macdonald tartan, the wool having been spun in the crofts.

The men were in their Sunday best, black high-buttoned suits surmounted by white collars, some showing brass studs, thick watch-chains, mostly silver, across their waistcoats, the toecaps of their boots gleaming. They piled their black hats in the hollowed-out tree as they filed in, to stand about the hall. A few were wearing kilts, but with bone-buttoned jackets instead of doublets, brogues instead of buckled shoes.

The double doors of the drawing-room were wide open, revealing the bare expanse of floor, heavily waxed to stop boots scarring, the oil lamps on stout surfaces round the walls, metal circles clipped to the mouths of their globes to save the high gilded ceiling from smoke. The organ had been cordoned off with a rope lashed round the backs of chairs in case anyone tried a tune or set a glass down on the light oak. In the far corner to the left four men in shirt sleeves were sitting in a semi-circle of chairs, tuning two accordions and the same number of fiddles, the raucous notes reaching the hall where the tenants stood awkwardly about, some pretending to admire the frieze of stags' heads, muttering in ambiguous Gaelic at the sporting skills of the late laird, others peering into the dining-room. Two tall glass lamps stood on the sideboard, stripped of its silver for security's sake, the long mirror behind shedding light on the table, extended to its limit and now white because Miss Carlotta had insisted on covering it with two layers of old blankets before spreading the frayed cloths. The cold haunch of venison lay on a metal tray. A bone-handled

165

fork with two long prongs was stuck into the meat, and beside it a matching knife with a long broad blade. Mince pies, shortbread and cakes were piled, and a black bun in the shape of a log bore a sprig of holly. Stacks of white plates, most of them with small cracks like veins, had been taken from the servants' hall, along with bundles of cutlery, the forks tarnished, the bone-handled knives discoloured through careless immersion in water.

At the other end of the table were the drinks. Aunt Carlotta had absolutely prohibited whisky, on account of its cost and effect, but had allowed a large Sheffield-plated bowl of steaming punch, with a ladle protruding. Fruit floated on the surface, squeezed lemons tricking the palate, masking the fact that it had been well watered down. A barrel of beer with a tap and a bucket beneath was propped on blocks at the edge of the table, the floor bare for the inevitable splashing. Thick glasses were stacked.

The musicians were now playing a recognizable tune, and Miss Carlotta, assisted by Father Macdonald, was herding the tenants into the drawing-room where Murdo the blacksmith, more massive in black, was waiting to announce the first dance.

Laura was sitting at her dressing-table, brushing her hair and examining the result in her new mirror when the first strains of music floated up. She was late. The mirror clattered on mahogany as she dived for footwear. Hoisting the hem of her lilac frock with its parallel frills down the front, she fumbled with the buttons of her new boots.

At the top of the house Maggie was also dressing. She had ironed her black Sunday dress and starched the cuffs, but it still looked shabby, with its severe shoulders and row of little black buttons down to the waist. She'd always wanted a bright dress with a touch of lace, but her mother would never hear of it, saying that girls who wore fancy clothes always got 'into trouble'. Clothes were for work, not pleasure, and if one worked hard enough, there should be no time for pleasure.

But just look at Elsie, whirling, admiring herself in the mirror in a grey silk gown that was Miss Carlotta's Christmas present and that only needed a little letting out at the waist for the perfect fit. And not only that; she had a little silver spangled bag to go with it, also from Miss Carlotta.

'There's the music,' Elsie said, having one last critical turn in the mirror. 'You'd better not keep Frank waiting for the first dance.'

But Maggie let that remark go. She didn't feel like going down among these people, though she knew all of them. She'd rather go to bed, though she wouldn't be able to sleep because of the music and pounding feet. She was so tired after the festive season preparations, the skin of her hands scarlet, raw to the touch because of having to scour so many big pots with sand and vinegar, using her bare palm to caress the copper because Miss Carlotta insisted that it was the only way to avoid scratching. Dragging herself up to the cramped room under the cold slates, Maggie found it more eerie than usual in her utter fatigue. She had the feeling that something terrible was going to happen in the house that night, but she didn't know what, or to whom. It was the kind of feeling that her mother had sometimes reported, and Maggie prayed that that wasn't to be her inheritance. She was glad when Elsie came up to take over the gloomy mirror with her dressing, though the sight of silk aroused envy. She could stay in the room with a candle burning, and the Master's picture for company, but Miss Carlotta insisted that *all* the staff attend, to show the village what a well-organized and harmonious house it was. She couldn't possibly take the picture downstairs with her, in case it fell out of her dress during the dancing. It was under the pillow, wrapped up in her nightdress, but was it safe? Now that Elsie had gone down, she'd have one last look at it before putting on her stout Sunday shoes.

The subject of her picture was still at the door despite the frosty night, shaking hands and exchanging festive greetings. His leg was hurting from standing so long, but he had a duty to do, and Aunt Carlotta was hovering in the hall to make sure he completed it. Women too old to dance but determined to preserve the continuity of the occasion gripped his sleeve with bent fingers and gave him their Gaelic blessings from toothless gums. Young women touched his hand, blushed in the dim porch and passed in.

The tenants had filed into the drawing-room to occupy the chairs arranged against the walls, the men on the left side, the women on the right. A waltz was announced, to give the tenants time to warm up after their long cold walk, and because Miss Carlotta preferred slow dignified dances. The older couples took the floor while the young men, their numbers depleted by the first call to South Africa, stayed fidgeting in their seats, waiting for each other to cross and select from the opposite line of young women, laughing to conceal their nervous expectation.

As the elderly experienced dancers, some in high collars and long dresses, turned under the dim gilded ceiling, the young began to join them until almost everyone in the room was dancing, some with grave precision, others with the awkward feet of navvies, hoping their clumsiness would not show from the sidelines where critical old women huddled and nodded.

Laura was now downstairs in the hall, peering round the door, but the dance was too slow and complicated for her, so she amused herself by humming while pulling pine needles from the tree. She was hungry, but Aunt Carlotta was now on guard at the dining-room door, making certain that no one (and particularly the butler) sneaked an early drink. When Elsie came through, Laura gasped, recognizing her aunt's gown, and she also saw her aunt's nod of approval as the kitchen-maid passed towards the dance. Laura bit her lip. Why hadn't she been given the discarded gown? And why was Elsie always in and out of her aunt's room, when she wasn't allowed? Several times Laura had heard someone leaving late, and had got up to investigate, opening her door a little. The first time she had almost screamed, thinking that the candle-carrying figure in the long nightdress was a ghost. She wanted to tell Niall, but was frightened he would accuse her of making it up, like the time she'd told him she'd seen the green lady on the front stairs, the one from the picture that Mama had sold. No use in telling Mama anything because she just gave you a silly look and started to mumble. If only she would keep her teeth in.

Then Maggie came through, in her black dress, and Aunt Carlotta gave her such a look as she passed, keeping her eyes on the floor. Laura let the pine needles fall as she ran up to her, pulling at her arm, making a great fuss because she'd found someone she could talk to, someone she could go into the dance with. And as Laura pulled at an embarrassed Maggie, she knew her aunt was watching her, but not able to check her, because there was her brother coming in from the porch, and he was smiling at her.

'Have a good time now,' he said to the two girls as he headed for the library for a much-needed brandy.

His words made Laura giggle all the more, and drag Maggie towards the drawing-room. But the effect on Maggie was to make her legs weak. He was even more handsome than he was in the picture, and she began to wonder frantically if it would be safe under her pillow.

All the tenants to the number of over a hundred were now assembled in the drawing-room, the majority of them dancing. Fiddles and accordions had speeded up, stamping boots making the stout boards vibrate, the aged spectators clapping on the dancers, the thunderous noise spilling out into the hall where Miss Carlotta stood, guarding the dining-room, her hands crossed, high collar supporting a face registering its disapproval at such disruption at a trying year's end.

But Laura was entranced, standing inside the door with Maggie, watching the high-kicking young men clapping their hands and whooping as their partners whirled. To Laura it was something wild and primitive, like a Home Farm horse plunging and prancing in the meadow across the Summer House Pool, or a salmon leaping and thrusting upriver. Her palms paced the pounding feet. She was desperate to join in, but dared not with Aunt Carlotta watching at her back. How wonderful it would be to break free, to do as she felt for once, like all these people, generating so much joy, brows beaded with sweat, more than ankles exposed as dresses whirled. But always there, at her back, was Aunt Carlotta, with her strict list of the things young ladies should not do, warning her that she would have to be doubly careful because she wasn't normal.

There was a pause to allow the dancers to gather breath, to let the bare-armed, splay-footed musicians replace moisture from the jugs of water under their chairs. It was another of Miss Carlotta's rules, in case the music got out of hand, encouraging suggestive dancing, but the players had their own supplies of whisky in their instrument cases and would avail themselves at the interval for food. Meantime they had to watch, for Father Macdonald was sitting beside them, arms folded over his black vestment as he supervised the dancing.

The music was starting up again, the couples rotating, revealing Frank the footman dancing with Elsie. His hair was plastered down and he was dressed in a tight-fitting pearl grey suit, the rounded collar of his dazzling white shirt linked by a pearl-mounted pin. As he held Elsie closer than arms-length, his back bent, and his shining ankle-hugging boots twisted expertly, executing the turns.

Laura stood open-mouthed, staring at the daring display, but Maggie stepped back awkwardly, dropping her eyes from the dance. She was turning to go out for air when she saw Miss Carlotta standing in the centre of the hall, a statue of grey silk, throat and wrist hugging, staring into the drawing-room. It was a look that would haunt Maggie for the rest of her life, and which age and experience would help to explain, but not entirely. For it was a look in which love and hate were hopelessly mixed, the staring eyes having a queer hunger which the compacted mouth seemed to deny. There was no doubt in Maggie's mind that the dancing servants were causing Miss Carlotta's trance, and in particular Elsie, who now faced her benefactress momentarily, her head thrown back, her teeth exposed as the handed-down dress spun above her crossing feet, showing the epitome of big-boned virility, like the basket-carrying girls in the advertisements in the society magazines that sometimes found their way from drawing-room to servants' hall. And, as Maggie allowed her eyes to stay with Miss Carlotta, it seemed from the house-keeper's small heaving bust that she was struggling for breath.

But as the dancing servants swept out of the frame of the doorway, Miss Carlotta awoke to the fact that the scullery-maid was staring at her. The look she gave to the girl as she turned towards the dining-room seemed to convey the warning: 'This is all your fault. This is another thing you are going to pay for.'

Maggie's daydreaming fear of future reprisals was disturbed by Laura tugging at her hand, with the exclamation of sudden revelation:

'If nobody wants to dance with us, let's dance together.'

'No, because it's not natural,' she said, but leaving her hand with Laura as consolation.

'Not natural? What does *that* mean? Oh, come *on*,' Laura pleaded, tugging.

And for a moment Maggie would have done it, to spite Frank and Elsie, who were now the centre of attraction. Other couples had sat down to admire the solo performance, the young men wishing for Frank's feet, the women for Elsie's dress and energy. But some of the older ones were muttering and shaking their heads, even though Father Macdonald, sitting by the band, was smiling, his clapping hands urging them to faster skills.

'Come on,' Laura pleaded.

'It would only make your aunt angry,' Maggie said, unable to take her eyes from the two dancers. 'So angry that she would send us both to bed.'

'There's no fun here. I'd rather go to bed,' Laura said bitterly.

But her mood was transformed by a movement on the dance floor. The servants' feet had defeated the sawing fiddles and splayed accordions and now, on the last note of the dance, Frank had Elsie by the waist and was lifting her from the floor as though she were a doll, but a doll whose underclothes were showing. As he turned her in the air and set her down, the music was replaced by thunderous applause, with Laura racing across the floor, grasping Frank's hands, wanting him to dance with her, pulling him this way and that, her button boots skidding. The footman was angry and embarrassed, looking around for someone to come and rescue him, while Elsie stood by, weak with laughter. The audience began to laugh at the silly girl until Father Macdonald, noticing Miss Carlotta coming towards the door, stood up and announced it was time for food and drink.

As the tenants pushed their way out, Maggie struggled to Laura, leading the tearful girl to the side.

Sitting at the library fire, his second brandy balanced on his bare knee, Invernevis heard the music stopping, and then boots hurrying towards the dining-room. He should have put in an appearance in the drawing-room, but had kept to the library because walking about drew attention to his game leg, and would only elicit embarrassing expressions of sympathy. Dancing was out of the question for good – not that he had ever enjoyed such social occasions. He had kept to the mess while the others were out on the town, and even when it was the turn of the officers to serve the men at Christmas dinner, he had been embarrassed. He preferred the quiet life, but that could get boring. A new year was coming, and he would have to be more active. It didn't do, being indoors all day, with women. The presence of his father's record salmon in the front hall and the fishing books which he took from the shelves some evenings after dinner had revived his boyhood interest in a sport that his father had never encouraged him in, though Alexander was always getting new rods and tackle. Fishing would take him out of doors, away from the women, and particularly Aunt Carlotta. It wasn't easy, living with three women, all of them problems. Aunt Carlotta seemed to want to be laird as well as housekeeper. She read the estate papers he left on his desk, and she was always telling him what to do.

'If that tenant won't pay his rent, I'd put him out. Give one charity, and all the rest will be looking for it.'

Yes, Aunt Carlotta would have to be put firmly in her place in the coming year. And Mama: well, she was still getting drink, though God knows from where. Maybe a nursing home would be best, where they could watch over her all the time. It would be expensive, but well worth it, even if the whole of her annuity had to go; and that wasn't to say that she would be there for the rest of her days.

And Laura. She was the biggest problem, poor soul, now that she was a woman. But that hadn't made Aunt Carlotta any kinder towards her. One thing was certain: whatever happened, he wasn't going to send his sister away to an institution. No, it would be better to have another woman in the house, someone to take an interest in Laura but at the same time not antagonize Aunt Carlotta. After all, the money she was going to leave him would give him some independence from the trustees.

He was again thinking of marriage. It was something he couldn't keep putting off, now that Alexander had agreed to disinheritance. But what chance was there if he didn't get out and about more? What chance anyway? No woman would visit the house because of his father's reputation, and now that he was dead, there was bound to be speculation as to the diagnosis. And even if the fear of contamination was overcome, and the rutted avenue braved, there was Mrs Macdonald, tippling behind a silk screen, her teeth loose.

No, it might be wiser to look further afield, to go regularly to his Edinburgh club, attend the meets of the Royal Company of Archers, now that Archers' Hall had been refurbished. He was bound to make friends, get invited to their places. He would have to be careful, of course; it wasn't simply a question of proposing to the first woman who seemed to be suitable. Other things had to be looked at. There had to be

mutual feelings, mutual love for a place as remote as Invernevis. And the woman would have to be very understanding,
to get on with his mother, his sister and his aunt. It was the
kind of situation that could scare off a woman. After all, the
laird's lady would want to be in charge of her own house.
And most women hated heavy drinking in their own sex.
Laura could be trying at times, so you needed a great deal
of patience. But then, the way his mother and Laura were, a
woman would think there was something unstable in the
Invernevis family, and wouldn't want to become a part of it,
for her own sake, and for any children that might come. And,
of course, he wasn't taking into consideration the reputation
that Alexander had acquired, which must have spread beyond
Invernevis. Other aristocrats had got women into trouble
(witness the Prince of Wales), but they hadn't married them.

He felt trapped by his own family, and was having another
brandy in consolation before braving the dance when there
was a rap at the door, and the handle turned without
announcement.

In his black suit with waistcoat and watch-chain, Mac-
Pherson from the Home Farm looked prosperous, though the
working boots were somewhat incongruous. Invernevis flushed
angrily, but accepted the strong grip given with the farmer's
gruff festive greeting, with the remark: 'Well, we'll soon be
related.' The offer of a brandy was immediately accepted, and
while it was being poured MacPherson went uninvited to the
other chair by the fire, planting his boots on the fender.

'Aye, it's a pity you can't manage to the wedding,' he began,
taking the glass. 'But, of course, you're so busy with the
estate.'

Invernevis heard the sarcasm clearly, and his dislike of the
man increased.

'Not that anyone's been pushing Sandy, you understand. It's
what he wants, and he's got himself a good-looking woman,
though I say it myself. Of course, I can't settle much on her,
because farming doesn't pay in this part of the world, what
with one thing and another. Anyway, I expect they'll make
out fine.'

The familiarity about Sandy maddened Invernevis, but he
felt he had to fill the silence before there were further hints
about rents.

'I gave them the site by the river.'

173

'Aye, but it'll be a while before the house is up, so they'll stay with us in the meantime. I'll be keeping an eye on the builder myself. They wouldn't think twice about cheating him, even though he *is* the laird's brother. I keep telling Sandy to stand up for his rights, but he's too nice a fellow.'

Invernevis was getting very angry with the innuendoes. For once he was in agreement with Aunt Carlotta: MacPherson was a nasty piece of work, always wanting something done for nothing on the Home Farm buildings, though his rent was ridiculously low, because he had been a horse-riding and drinking companion of the old laird's. MacPherson had a son to succeed, so there was no chance of him giving up the lease. There was a rent review in the summer, though.

'Aye, it's going to be a good wedding,' MacPherson was saying. 'Mind you, I'll probably find that the bills will ruin me when they come in. Not that I grudge it, you understand. Sandy's a fine lad, and she's a good girl. He only needs to get the chance, and he'll make a go of it.'

Invernevis winced at such familiarity from a tenant. But what could he do? MacPherson had arranged it all very cunningly, encouraging Alexander to go up to the Home Farm, then mating him with his daughter, as you did with gun-dogs, only in the human case there was a serious discrepancy of pedigree. Obviously Alexander hadn't yet told his father-in-law that there was now no chance of Kate, or whatever she was called, succeeding to the big house. Let MacPherson sweat.

'Well, it was very good of you to come and see me,' Invernevis said, rising to show that the interview was over.

MacPherson drained his glass and set it down on the mantelpiece. 'Well, we'll be seeing a lot more of each other from now on, I expect.' He turned at the door. 'How's your mother? I've been hearing she's poorly.'

'Oh, she's quite well,' he said casually.

'It would be the strain of the bereavement,' MacPherson said knowingly, nodding. 'Aye, he was a fine man, your father, the strongest man I've ever seen, and not a bit of side to him. Many a dram and a crack we shared at the farm. Sandy's the image of him.' And, seeing the look on the new laird's face: 'Anyway, I'd better go and see what like your dance is.'

He went, leaving Invernevis smarting, wondering how much of Alexander's money MacPherson had had. Well, if that was

174

the kind of person his brother was putting his trust in, it was better that the disinheritance papers were signed as quickly as possible.

The dining-room was still crowded, with tenants pressing over the table, waiting with palms under the knife for the slices of venison and transferring them straight to mouths. Mince pies were snatched away, exposing the cracked plates, fruit and crumbs trampled, though Miss Carlotta presided, clapping her hands above her head and calling for a civilized approach. When she saw an elbow leaning on the sideboard, she jolted it.

The noise was deafening, women flushed with punch talking all at the one time in Gaelic. Most of the men were congregated round the beer barrel, anxiously watching the tap for a sign of slackening flow, knowing there was not a second barrel. The beer frothed and overflowed, spattering into the enamel pail, and when the barrel failed, the pail was tilted and the slops shared out.

The raucous Gaelic interrupted by a shattering beer glass made Miss Carlotta clap her hands over her ears and rush from the room. There were circular stains on the sideboard, and food between the floorboards. They were animals, and like animals would not answer while they were eating and drinking. There was nothing for it; the dancing would have to begin again, to entice them from the dining-room before they got really drunk and wrecked it. And those with weak stomachs would be sick. She shuddered as she swept across the hall, into the drawing-room, snapping her fingers at the musicians who were drinking from the supplies in their instrument cases. My God, they were mad to allow the village to overrun them like this, she thought. She would have to put her foot down; it was definitely the last dance, no matter what her nephew said. And to add insult to injury, there was that brute Mac-Pherson striding in, to boast of his relationship to the big house. Father Macdonald was well out of it. She was thankful she had sent him up to her own sitting-room, so that Elsie could give him tea. What a help Elsie was at such trying times!

When the band began playing again they swallowed what they were taking, shouldering their way out, Laura leading the way, a squashed cake in her fist. Maggie had been standing in the bay window, keeping well out of the way of Miss Carlotta, watching Frank carve a thick slice of venison for Elsie, and, having smeared mustard, hold it to her mouth. Laughing, she had allowed herself to be fed, bit by bit, but Miss Carlotta had not seen. Maggie would wait in the dining-room till the dance got under way again.

Most of the dancers had returned to the drawing-room and were milling about the floor, waiting for the blacksmith to announce the next one. But Invernevis was there, stooping to whisper to Father Macdonald, who nodded, rose and rapped for silence.

'The laird wishes to say a few words about a very important matter, so listen carefully.'

Invernevis cleared his throat as faces swung towards him. 'First of all, I welcome you to the house, and I do hope that everyone is having a good time.' He paused. 'However, in our happiness we shouldn't forget others less fortunate. Most of you will know that at the end of last month, when Lord Roberts was handing over command in South Africa to Lord Kitchener, he announced that the war was over. Now that isn't quite true. I'm not for a moment suggesting that Lord Roberts was telling a lie. No; the fact is that a Boer gentleman called General De Wet has been continuing the war more or less on his own, and is proving very difficult to catch. It isn't all that serious because he doesn't have a very big force, but it is annoying. In order to catch him, and to bring the war to a speedy end, more volunteers are needed. Now I know that a good many men have already gone from this parish, and some have laid down their lives. The whole country is as proud and grateful as I am, and I am confident that others will answer this call. A soldier's life is a hard but fascinating one, and you get the opportunities to see countries that you would not otherwise see. South Africa with all its animals is a very fascinating country, and some of you will be surprised to learn that while we are shivering here, it is summer out there. And the conditions are good. It's my opinion, and the opinion of the military authorities, that Highland soldiers have the best chance of catching De Wet because the countryside isn't all that different to our own part, and because Highland soldiers have the strength and courage to conquer, as they've proved throughout history. I would therefore ask the young and able-bodied among you to consider this matter carefully, and if you decide to serve your Queen and country – and there

176

can be no higher service – to come and see me after the festive season, when I'll send you through to Stirling to see the authorities. I say Stirling because I would like to think that you would want to enlist in Princess Louise's Argyll and Sutherland Highlanders after you have had a taste of soldiering. And don't be put off by this.' He slapped his thigh. 'That was because they were waiting for us. Now we've got them on the run. Anyway, I shan't hold up the dancing any longer. Thank you.'

The priest led the applause, which came mostly from the women and older men. The young men were looking at each other with uncertainty, and some young wives and sweethearts gripped arms tighter. Since an atmosphere of gloom was descending on the dance, Father Macdonald gave the blacksmith authority to call an Eightsome Reel.

While Invernevis was speaking Maggie was walking slowly beside the long table in the dining-room, trailing her fingers through stains and crumbs. The beer tap dripped on the floor behind her, and in the centre of the table the venison haunch, which had taken so much of her strength in the turning, had been hacked down to bare bone. On the opposite side of the table old women crumbled cakes in their seized fingers, coughing where a raisin lodged. With their thin wrinkled faces protruding from shawls, they reminded Maggie too much of her mother in her last days. Some of them, and especially Betsy with the pronounced eyes, were said to have the power of second-sight, meaning that they saw future events, and especially funerals. Her mother had never liked Betsy.

Maggie was suddenly aware of the coldness of the room and the inquisitive eyes of the old women. She hurried out, heading for bed, knowing she wouldn't be missed now. The grandfather clock at the foot of the stairs showed it was after eleven. She stood staring at the pendulum swinging behind the engraved glass door, going from side to side with a mournful sound. It would soon be another year, but there was nothing to look forward to, with her mother dead, her brother dust in a distant land of strange animals. Why was the Master asking other young men to go out and get killed? What had events in the world got to do with Invernevis?

As she contemplated the clock swinging in another year, a hand on her shoulder made her cry out.

177

'And why aren't you in dancing?' the Master wanted to know. 'What interest can you possibly have in the works of an old clock?'

Even if she hadn't smelt the brandy, she could have guessed from the brightness of his eyes. Was he leering at her? For a moment she felt frightened, being alone with him in the hall, but then she remembered her mother's saying that it was a gentleman's privilege to get tight from time to time, as he held her arm and turned her around, leading her towards the drawing-room.

'I'd give you a dance, if it wasn't for this leg.' But it wasn't an intimate tone: it was the tone of a well-mannered man made confident by brandy on a night for celebrating.

He stood behind her in the doorway, blocking her way to bed. Though the tenants were lined up and impatient to get the Eightsome Reel started, there were still shortages in sets. A boy in his first cut-down suit asked Maggie to dance, but she shook her head quickly. Then Frank the footman came pushing, catching her by the hand, and despite her protests that she couldn't do the dance, he pulled her towards the set where Elsie waited with a new partner.

The recruitment for the sets, conducted by Father Macdonald going round, had produced full quotas, and young men who were not sure of the steps waited opposite smiling partners. At a signal from the MC the music began.

Standing in the doorway, Invernevis marvelled at the intricacy of a dance he had been forced to do as a boy but which he had never mastered, invariably moving the wrong way, or facing the wrong partner. The majority of his tenants seemed to have an instinctive sense of movement and timing. Clasping hands, they rotated in a circle, with one of the set in the centre, fist on waist, other arm raised, toe tapping ankle and floor till it was time to link arms and whirl the next person into the centre. As they danced to the strident accordions, they whooped encouragement to the dancer in the centre.

Invernevis had never seen such spontaneous enjoyment, had never heard so much noise generated, not even when his dusty company had cast off their uniforms and plunged into the Modder, gulping the pollution of dead horses and Boers. Kilts spun and legs kicked from under long gowns, and then the circle was speeding again, outstretched arms straining, the women with their heads thrown back, squealing for more

178

speed, more speed until one set crashed into another, steadied itself with laughter, and was off again, like a huge wheel out of control. And there was Maggie, the shy scullery-maid, being whirled on the braced arm of the footman, looking into each other's eyes as they turned, parting to make the circle again, round and round, brogues thudding in the centre. It made Invernevis feel old and envious, kept back from liberation by convention and a game leg.

And then he saw Laura darting across the floor, into the dance. She ducked under the clasped hands and stamped in the centre, arms raised, the button boots kicking recklessly, body shaking as though suspended on invisible strings. She broke the circle, whirling on the arm of each of the eight, the boots going so fast and so wildly that they seemed about to send her sprawling, and when she had been whirled by the last of the set she was propelled towards the next set, to tumble into the centre, beginning her kicking and turning again.

Those who were sitting out the dance were on their feet, to watch her, and some were even standing on their chairs. The old women pushed and craned, eyes bright with the scandal of it. The musicians were standing up to get more power, the accordionists splaying their bellows to their limits, the fiddlers pressing with their chins as they sawed with long sweeps, sweat beading their foreheads as they urged the erratic dancer on.

MacPherson from the Home Farm was doing the same, standing up beside the priest, his huge hands coming together in applause, boot stamping as he shouted: 'Come on, lassie, show them the stuff you're made of!'

But as Laura was released towards another set, where Maggie's arm saved her, Aunt Carlotta was shouting and pushing past Niall.

'Stop this exhibition this second! Stop, I say!' And she shook a fist at the musicians.

'No, leave her,' her nephew said in a mesmerized voice, his arms barring her way into the room.

It was like a colt tumbled from the womb, seeking the world on splayed legs, tottering and skidding, but going on, determined, till suddenly it found the freedom of movement, bucking and prancing, whinnying in a weak high voice as it went this way and that across the meadow, falling but always finding its legs again in the sheer joy of living, seeking a strength and co-ordination it could never have because the womb that had given it life had also damaged it.

She had broken up the sets until the dance revolved around her, speeding in a huge circle now, yelling encouragement and laughing. She was in the centre, whirling Maggie on her arm and she wouldn't let go, going faster and faster, ringlets floating, teeth showing as though she were in pain, eyes focused on the dim gilded ceiling above, hypnotizing her to new speeds, and the stains spreading in her armpits, the button boots a black blur.

Maggie was screaming for release, but she could not break free. It was like being linked to a runaway horse. A frieze of faces flashed nauseatingly, the music seemed to be bursting her ears, her mouth was wide but no sound came. Her fear was spreading to the circle. It stopped suddenly, and so did the accordions, splaying in crescendo, the fiddles scraping to a halt, but Laura was still whirling, eyes closed now, smiling as if at peace in such speed.

And then she let Maggie go. The scullery-maid skidded and stumbled across the floor, saved by the braced arms of Frank. But Laura, like a star out of control, was careering across the floor, eyes closed, arms outstretched as though she were blind, groping for a barrier that was not there, plunging through space, sliding to rest, sobbing, her arms clasped round her brother's game leg.

They broke the grip and carried her up to bed, but she was already asleep in MacPherson's strong arms before her room was reached.

The dancers had had enough, and some of the young women were frightened by Miss Carlotta's staring eyes, her inability to get speech. She was led out, leaning on Father Macdonald's arm, Elsie going ahead for the smelling salts.

It was almost twelve. The lamps were turned down and they formed another huge circle, but this time subdued and immobile, standing there with clasped hands, counting the strokes of the Jubilee clock. And when it was 1901, the new century, according to the Astronomer Royal, accordions and fiddles played, the circle contracting as they swung clasped hands, chanting 'Auld Lang Syne'.

Though she was still weak, Maggie took her place in the circle, supported between Frank and Mrs Livingstone, who had come through from the kitchen for the finale, her feet disallowing dancing. Laura's dance had given Maggie a fright, but she had enjoyed the night. The Master had been so nice to her, and so had Frank, though Elsie had been his first choice. But no doubt Miss Carlotta would blame her for encouraging Miss Laura.

As 'Auld Lang Syne' ended and the lamps went up again Invernevis was horrified to see that he had been holding Mac-Pherson's hand in the circle.

'That sister of yours is some lassie,' the farmer said, shaking his head in wonder. 'Aye, she certainly takes after her father. Mind you, it's a pity Sandy couldn't have been here, but he wanted to stay with Kate. It's been kicking a lot, and it might come early, you see.'

Invernevis wasn't really listening to MacPherson because the episode with Laura had frightened him. He hoped she hadn't damaged herself, dancing like that. The new year had got off to a bad start, with Aunt Carlotta so angry that she'd had to be helped upstairs. That was the three women in the house in bed, and the mess of the dance still to be cleared up.

Taking advantage of Miss Carlotta's absence, some of the maids were going outside with the young men who had got the most dances out of them. Frank pleaded for a stroll up to the stables, and Maggie was tempted, because the night air would clear her head. He was still persuading her when her father crossed the deserted floor of the drawing-room, telling her to get to bed.

And across at the Home Farm, Alexander had got so drunk that he had had to be carried to bed before the Jubilee clock rang in the new year. Kate held his head to her protesting belly while the two loonies took a leg each.

Chapter Eleven

The snow came on the third night of the new year, stealthily drifting on window sill and avenue. Letting out the dogs in the dawn, Mrs Livingstone discovered a white wilderness. But Laura did not rush downstairs to join the capering dogs on the front lawn, to scoop up snow and send it showering, shrieking. She had been in bed since the Hogmanay dance, and when the maid opened the curtains to show her the new world, Laura asked that they be shut again, since the light was hurting her eyes. At her brother's insistence Dr MacNiven was sent for. His gig braved the drifting avenue, and having examined Laura by lifting an eyebrow and locating the pulse at the thin wrist, he could find nothing wrong, which only confirmed Aunt Carlotta's opinion. She stood over the bed with crossed arms.

'Get up, girl. The maids have enough to do with your mother.' And she pulled the bedclothes down.

But Laura lay curled up, her feet hidden in her nightdress, an arm over her eyes.

'Please, Aunt Carlotta, let me lie here,' she pleaded. 'The light's hurting my eyes. I won't be a bother, I promise.'

'Lie if you like, but there'll be no trays sent up,' her aunt warned, heading for the door. 'Your brother wants you to eat in the dining-room from now on. These are his orders, and I'm not going to disobey.'

The door slammed, leaving Laura to haul up the clothes and hide her face in the pillow, trying to get relief through sleep. But the lights of the dance still whirled in her head. She had tried to stand up, but couldn't without support, using the wall to guide her to the water closet where she was sick, but frightened to tell. And when she got back to bed her shivering made the springs sound.

'It's sheer laziness,' Aunt Carlotta told her nephew. 'A spoilt brat, playing on people's kindness. I warn you, this is what it will be from now on. Far better to put her to a home, where they're used to dealing with the likes of her. It's bad enough having your mother in bed most of the time, but she at least has a reason. No, I can't cope with your sister any more. You would expect an improvement, now that she's a woman, but she's getting worse. And her exhibition at the dance was disgraceful.'

Invernevis wasn't convinced by Dr MacNiven's opinion, and as for Aunt Carlotta nagging about a home – never. He had planned to have a week in Edinburgh, at his club, but decided to stay, to keep an eye on Laura. Every hour when the stable clock struck louder than usual in the cold atmosphere, he found himself opening her door and peering round. But the ringlets were buried under blankets.

He had to find something to occupy his mind, so he decided to rearrange the rods and guns in the long glass cases in the library. Maggie's father helped him. The weapons were mostly the old laird's, damascened shotguns whose butts had been specially tailored to that brutal shoulder, and because of his son's height and stance they did not feel right, the shortened barrels tilted as he aimed out of the window at an imaginary quarry in the silent white landscape, with the river below subdued by ice. The same with the green-heart salmon rods, which they took out to the hall, the ghillie assembling, his master casting a non-existent line. The rods had been shaped as natural extensions to his father's short powerful arm, and they lacked the whip his son liked. It was decided: he would have to get guns and rods made to his own requirements when he went to Edinburgh.

Providence and sentiment prevented him from giving his father's sporting gear away, or selling it. No, his rods and guns would remain locked in the cupboards, along with the short rods, rook and pea rifles of his son's boyhood, to become heirlooms, along with the banners crossed on the wall of the front hall, the snuff boxes and spurs in the glass cases in the drawing-room.

'Of course, if you wish to use any of them, you need only ask,' Invernevis advised his ghillie, putting the cupboard keys on the small bunch he carried on a gold chain.

'No, sir, I've got my own gun, a good one.' And, giving his new master his first lesson in mature sportsmanship: 'Your father used to say: never let anyone else use your rod or gun. Get one that suits you, keep it in good condition, and you've got a friend for life.'

Invernevis stayed in the library, to scan fishing books and

smoke cigars, listening to the wind soughing in the wide throat of the chimney. But as he looked at illustrations of rainbow trout stretched out in death, thoughts of Laura kept breaking surface. Then he had an idea which made him close the book with a thump and pace excitedly, letting the cigar grow cold on silver. Once the war was over, he would take her to South Africa. He stopped to savour the vision: Laura in a white dress in the dusty landscape, mesmerized by the sight of giraffe and locust cloud, breathless at sunset. He would take her to the Modder, allow her to wade, show her Magersfontein, let her handle ironstone. They would stay at the Island Hotel on the Twee Riviere. She could exhaust herself running through the pleasure gardens by day, shaded from the sun's splintered mirror, and in the evening sink her crooked white teeth into peaches before sleep, cheek propped on a fist, smiling in dreams of delight to come. No Aunt Carlotta to spoil things, as she had done in childhood, sitting beyond the high-tide mark, parasol unable to shade that thin stern face shouting the hazards of the loch. He would insist that Aunt Carlotta stay at home, but he would take one of the maids to attend to Laura. Maggie, perhaps? She wasn't trained for such work, but Laura seemed to get on well with her, judging by the time she spent at the scullery window. No, it wasn't going to be a dream conceived in winter by radiant logs. As soon as De Wet was run to earth, and the peace signed, he would write to Thomas Cook, asking for an itinerary.

But a blizzard stopped the sending or receiving of letters, and for a week he was without newspapers. The avenue was blocked, snow scaling the tree trunks. Not even Father Macdonald's trap could get through to hear Aunt Carlotta's confession as she sat on a stool behind a silk screen in the drawing-room, coy as a young girl, getting Hail Marys for trivia. Mama was the worst affected by the white siege. The horses were confined to the stables, the snow too deep for the coachman to wade to the village for the daily supply. Though she was an immobile mound in a bed kept continually fired by two stone bottles, Mama was desperate. There was nothing to be done but to send surreptitiously for the butler, slip him something and ask him to search the cellar – if he himself hadn't drunk the stock. He produced two dusty bottles of claret, and, having made him draw the corks, Mama dismissed him. The wine went to vinegar under her bed, but she kept on drinking it until the bottles toppled to join the others.

Maggie's scullery was freezing, but at least there was the consolation of hot water for her arms. Small birds rapped their urgent Morse on glass, but she couldn't open the window. The hopping robin made her daydream. Mrs Livingstone believed that the souls of people returned as birds. What if that was her mother, tapping on the other side of the glass, begging instead of ordering?

And there was hot water at the top of the house. Miss Carlotta encouraged the servants to bath once weekly, on Sunday night, cleanliness being next to godliness. Maggie lugged one of the big tin baths up to her room, then three big kettles supplied by Mrs Livingstone. The water was scalding, but she gritted her teeth as she stepped into the cloud of steam and sat down slowly, the heat making her gasp, turning her skin scarlet. Once she was settled she began to scrub, using the bristle brush with the long handle on her back, lathering it with carbolic, scraping until she was raw, making sure that she was getting at all the sweat, plunging her head in, her fingernails working through the scalp. And when she was satisfied that she was clean, how wonderful it was to lie back in the bath, neck against the high rim, knees drawn up, holding up the Master's picture, hot water and admiration making her short of breath.

Then, horror of horrors, footsteps on the stairs, Elsie coming up for the night. To thrust the picture under water would be to ruin it, but what else was to be done? As the door handle turned, she skited the picture across the floor, under her bed, where it clanged against iron.

There stood Miss Carlotta, looking down at her. Though there was only a candle, and a floating scum of soap concealed her nudity, Maggie crossed her hands.

Miss Carlotta's mouth twitched before she spoke, and her stare did not shift.

'At least you're clean, girl.'

Her voice and eyes frightened Maggie. She had seen that glazed look before, when Elsie was dancing. The hard lines of the features seemed to dissolve and reform into beauty, or was it a trick of the steam?

And then Miss Carlotta was stooping in audible silk to the scrubbing brush, plunging her hand into the water, groping for the soap, lathering bristles as Maggie braced her toes against tin, too terrified to tell that she had already scrubbed her back.

For that was what Miss Carlotta was doing, bending over her, working the brush, but with a gentle circling motion that made Maggie tingle and relax. She was a child again, being bathed by her mother in front of high banked peat, her elder brother banished from the room, the towel warming over the back of a chair. She was burning underwater, wanting Miss Carlotta to keep on, to go lower, but knowing there was something wrong, something unnatural in the act because Miss Carlotta was breathing heavily, and because, when the hairs had started coming, her mother had made her bath herself.

The brush was now at the base of her spine and coming round, tickling and at the same time so pleasurable, so that you wanted it to stop, and to keep going, in the same breath. Her toes curled on tin, Maggie's body was building up towards spasm – the same thrill after she closed her eyes, having looked at the Master's picture for a long time – when Miss Carlotta suddenly rose from her knees and threw the brush into the water by Maggie's legs before the door slammed, making the flame waver above the saucer.

Maggie lay sobbing in the lukewarm water, baffled and frightened. Miss Carlotta seemed to have taken a sudden liking to her, perhaps because of something the Master had said. She hadn't uttered a word while Miss Carlotta was working the brush, so why had the housekeeper rushed out as though she was offended? But at the back of her mind Maggie knew there was something bad in it because of the sensations the circling brush had aroused in her. It was a sin, the same as when you touched yourself under the blankets, and yet Miss Carlotta was such a strict Catholic. It couldn't be that. It was just that she had tried, but couldn't bring herself to be friendly, couldn't bear to scrub a servant's back. A servant brushing out her hair was different, though.

When Maggie groped under the bed to retrieve the Master's picture, she cried because the glass was cracked and the frame dented. She buried her face in the pillow and wished she was dead.

In the days following Miss Carlotta didn't come near the scullery, but Maggie could hear her in the kitchen, ordering a tray to be made up for Miss Laura, but saying in the same breath: 'Of course I don't approve of this. There's nothing wrong with the girl. No, Mrs Livingstone, definitely no pudding. If she wants some, she can come down.'

And when the tray came down untouched again, Miss Carlotta ordered that the soup be reheated and sent up in the evening, or until such time as it was accepted.

'She'll be glad to take it yet.'

But Laura wasn't interested in food. Once the maid had taken away the tray and blown out the small lamp she left the rumpled blankets and groped her way along the wall to the window, getting behind the curtain and standing there, barefooted in her long white nightdress. The white lawn sloping to the river under the moon hurt her eyes. The hole of the wishing stone was filled with a membrane of ice, and below it a roe-deer left black punctures in the whiteness as it searched for branches to strip, stopping to sniff suspiciously and survey the house. But instead of excited jumping and rushing downstairs to shout what she had seen, Laura looked beyond its small horns to the standing stones above the Home Farm. Her eyes fell short and they became black blurs in the whiteness.

She turned towards the bed again, feeling her way back. It wasn't the coldness made worse by Aunt Carlotta's prohibition of fire; it was the pains in her head caused by looking, things going out of focus and disintegrating, like a waterfall striking stone in a heat-haze. But she wasn't going to tell her aunt about the pains because she would only accuse her of lying. If they got worse, she would speak to Niall, the next time she heard him at the door.

Even with only one blanket it was so hot, as if it was summer, leaving her with such a thirst. She put her head under the clothes and dreamed a water-ice, but then the pain began again, blotting out, making the sound of a spate in her ears. She was in the black waters of *Casan Dubh*, being spun round and round, choking, carried down, slipping past the stepping stones, out to the loch, to drift on her back, eyes closed against the sun's glare. She knew she was going to die, but she wasn't going to tell anyone, not even Niall. It was her last, her greatest secret, to be hugged, like the puppy they had denied her. She burrowed, becoming her own fire.

Snow continued to cut off the village from the big house, and Mrs Livingstone was getting desperate for supplies. Milk

187

could not come from the Home Farm, and the sack of oatmeal was dangerously low. The cook scrabbled in the slatted larder, producing scrag ends until the ghillie spotted Laura's roe-deer behind the house and brought it down. Once gralloched, it should have hung until maggots showed, but Miss Carlotta overruled aristocratic taste. As an alternative to venison, and to give the ghillie something to do, she sent him down to the front lawn to shoot rabbits.

Invernevis was getting fidgety as the cigars in Laura's Christmas box went down to single figures, and most of the fishing books looked at, if not read. He was wanting papers to see how the war was going. Besides, the snow was keeping away the recruits he had called for at the Hogmanay dance so that De Wet could be caught. He tried to deny tobacco by bending wire into hooks and dressing them with feathers, a jeweller's glass screwed into his eye at the library table, but the products were not tempting enough. It was no use; he would have to go upstairs and make Laura tell him what was the matter.

He sat on the edge of the bed, in the darkness, holding her hot hand, urging her towards expression.

'It's the pain,' she said eventually, in a small voice that he had never heard before. 'When I look at light, my head hurts. At least, that's what it used to do. Now it hurts all the time.'

'Try and describe the pain,' he said despairingly.

'It's just a pain. Like toothache, only higher up.'

'And when did it start?'

'The night of the dance.'

'You must have hit your head,' he groaned, sensing the worst. '*Try* and remember.'

'I didn't hit it. It just started up when I was being carried up. My eyes first, and then my head.'

And then a terrible question had to be asked.

'Did Aunt Carlotta hit you?'

No answer.

'You know you can trust me, Laura. Tell me and I promise not to say a word to a living soul. I always keep my promises, don't I? I *did* bring you back a doll.'

'She didn't hit me, she didn't,' she pleaded.

'All right, but I had to ask. Now, is your head hurting at this moment?'

'It hurts awfully,' she moaned, holding his hand tighter and sitting up. 'Oh, I wish my head could come off like Dolly's.'

He heard the struggle for bravery in her voice.

He laid her back gently and rose. 'Don't worry, I'll get Dr MacNiven first thing in the morning,' he vowed. 'Now you must try and sleep.'

'But he told Aunt Carlotta that there was nothing wrong with me, and she'll only give me a row,' Laura said, panicking. 'She says it costs money.'

'I decide who's to come to this house, and how the money's to be spent,' he said angrily. Then, patting her reassuringly: 'Please try and sleep.'

Downstairs again, he sat at his desk and wrote a short urgent note to Dr MacNiven, then cranked the bell handle, waiting impatiently with the envelope. Mrs Livingstone shuffled through to say that the maids had gone to bed, but she was roasting venison.

'Tell Roddy I want him.'

'Oh, he's away to bed too, sir. He didn't think he'd be needed with the snow.'

'Then who *is* about?' he asked impatiently.

'Well, Duncan's in the servants' hall, cleaning his gun, sir. He won't get home to the croft tonight.'

'Send him through.'

A few minutes later the ghillie appeared, wiping his hands with a rag. 'The frost goes for the barrels, sir,' he explained.

'I want you to take this letter to Dr MacNiven first thing in the morning, as soon as it's light.' And to enforce the urgency: 'It's about Miss Laura. She's not at all well.'

'I'm right sorry to hear that, sir,' the ghillie said with genuine concern. 'I could take a lantern and go just now.'

'No, no, if it started snowing again you'd only be in trouble. But first thing in the morning, please. You can't walk, of course. But take the gig, it's got bigger wheels; and a shovel too. You'll have to bring the doctor; I doubt if he'll risk driving himself in such conditions. And one other thing: if my aunt's about when you leave, don't tell her where you're going. It'll only worry her.'

The ghillie nodded knowingly.

The next morning at nine the gig brought Dr MacNiven, his black hat bobbing through the white landscape, the horses stepping high, hauling wheels that sometimes stuck and had to be shovelled clear by the ghillie, wearing his late master's riding boots for protection. Miss Carlotta heard the creaking

189

wheels, but before she could get through to find out, the doctor was upstairs, examining Laura while her brother paced the hall.

It seemed ages before Dr MacNiven came down, his face giving nothing away as he followed Invernevis into the library, refusing a chair as usual.

'She complains of pains in the head, as if she'd fallen, but I can't find any bruises. And she hasn't eaten for days, which doesn't help. It's very strange,' he added, scratching his balding head. He had been in practice in Invernevis for nearly forty years, and had complete faith in the old remedies. Not for him the new textbooks with their fancy theories. There was only one thing to be done. 'I'm going to bleed her,' he explained. 'That should relieve the pressure in her head. So I've left leeches, and I'll come back in a couple of days.'

The thought of leeches sucking at his sister made Invernevis squeamish, but he trusted the doctor, who had tried his best with his father.

'But you must make her eat,' Dr MacNiven urged. 'A good bowl of broth works wonders, especially in such weather. And maybe a little pudding, to encourage her.'

'I'll tell my aunt right away,' Invernevis promised.

The doctor lifted his bag from the corner of the desk. 'Well, I'd better get Duncan to take me back to the village. There's quite a few people laid up. Aye, this weather will finish a good few of the old ones. They go out to clear the snow from the peat-stack and they catch their death.'

'Is there anything I can do?' Invernevis asked.

'Well, a couple of sacks of meal wouldn't go amiss. If you sent Roddy round with them, giving out a little to the old, so that they can make porridge.' He glanced over his spectacles. 'Your father was very good at doing that sort of thing. And don't worry about Miss Laura. The bleeding should do the trick.'

When Aunt Carlotta heard why the doctor had been fetched through the snow, her reaction was predictable.

'Stuff and nonsense. She's only saying that about her head so she'll be allowed to stay in bed. It would be a very different matter if the sun was shining. Well, if she's got leeches at her throat for nothing, that will teach her.'

'Laura *isn't* well,' her nephew warned her. 'Dr MacNiven said she was to get broth and pudding. If she won't take the

190

broth, let her have pudding – with plenty of milk, to build up her strength. Tell Mrs Livingstone I want a big bowl of carrageen made. If you're going to be short, get more milk and cream from the Home Farm.' And because Aunt Carlotta was scowling: 'These are my orders, and I expect them to be carried out. And if they are not, if she doesn't get what I've asked for, I'll hold you personally responsible.'

He had taken the plunge, and was as well to proceed, keeping his eyes on her stiffening figure as he spoke, the spark of logs in the drawing-room fire a background to his level words.

'Also, I wish Roddy to put a couple of sacks of meal on the back of the gig and take them down to the village. He's to go round the doors, giving a bowlful to the old and needy.'

'I have no sacks to spare,' Aunt Carlotta said haughtily.

'Then get them,' he said harshly. 'Send Roddy down to telegraph to Glasgow. They can put them on the next train.'

'You do not seem to be aware that the trains are not getting through because of the snow. *I* have to think of these practical things.'

'All right, if there's no meal, send something else. I'll get Duncan to shoot a couple of roe-deer and you can get Mrs Livingstone to roast them. They can be cut up and taken round the doors.'

'Oh, so the kitchen is now to revolve round your sister and the village,' Aunt Carlotta said, rising in a rubbing of silk. 'Milk puddings for one, venison for the other. And where do we get seaweed for carrageen in such weather? Have you asked yourself that? Of course not. You expect me to produce stuff from thin air, at a moment's notice. I'm sick to death of this place. First your father, ordering me about as though I were a servant. I tolerated it for your mother's sake, to try and save her from that beast no girl would serve at table because his hand always went to the one place. God knows how many advertisements I put in the papers for maids. They came, and if they didn't run away they had to get money to go and have *his* child in another place. That was *your* father. He didn't die like a normal human being: he rotted away like an animal trapped in a bog. And even then he wasn't satisfied. Oh no. He's worked on this place from beyond the grave. Your mother a drunkard. Yes, my own sister, but I have to say it. And now you, bullying me as he did, caring more for the village than you do for me. The way you speak, you'd think I was trying to starve your sister. Haven't I struggled with her for years, trying to make something out of her, and meeting opposition at every turn? And as for your brother – I'm to be forced to look at the house of a drunkard and fornicator from these windows, mocking me, reminding me – as if I need reminding – that all my efforts have been in vain. Were it not for Father Macdonald's comfort, I'd have gone long ago, but I stayed to struggle against Satan. This time, however, I'm *definitely* going.'

'As you please,' Invernevis said, shrugging, not prepared to humour her any more. 'I'll advertise for a housekeeper.'

'Only this time you'll have to pay her!' she shouted, slamming the door.

He sat for a long time in the drawing-room, by the ruins of the log, thinking of his family and sighing. She had tried to shock him into revulsion about his father and the maids, but he already knew from the letters in the desk, and in a way he felt sympathy, if Carlotta was the same with his father as she was with him. As for Mama, he admitted that it was his father's fault, but there had been a weakness there already, because of her domination by Carlotta.

But Laura was the biggest worry. He couldn't help feeling that Dr MacNiven's diagnosis was faulty, that it was something serious. When he went up to look, he couldn't believe that that inert whiteness on which the leeches were already working was the same creature that had wrestled with a salmon in the Yellow Pool before South Africa brought war, death, and new responsibilities. He wanted to tear the disgusting black things from her slender throat, where a salmon scale had once clung above a moving wheel, but knew that if he did, Dr MacNiven wouldn't come again, and that would be another victory for Aunt Carlotta. The only thing to be done was to go down to the library and get tight.

When the papers got through the next morning with the milk cart from the Home Farm, churns chiming, they brought the news of Queen Victoria's death, which sent Mama into such hysterics that brandy had to be administered. Even after half a decanter she continued to lament that Invernevis would not now be visited, the accursed Campbells at Taymouth and Inveraray having usurped them. That night she suffered a stroke, and Dr MacNiven, coming by moonlight through cleared snow, warned that the choice was now between drink

192

and death. Her mouth was twisted, and he couldn't guarantee the return of speech, or power to the left hand.

Because of her sister's condition, Aunt Carlotta had her trunks hoisted back to the attic. She went through the house, putting sticky black tape round the many portraits of Queen Victoria, taking in servants' hall as well as drawing-room. Still shaky from the previous night's consumption of brandy, Invernevis watched her standing on a chair to do the dining-room portrait of the venerable Victoria in pelisse, the one that his father had wanted turned to the wall because he claimed that the unsmiling dewlapped face, more man than woman, had put him off his food. His son realized that it was the end of an age. She had brought sanity and graciousness to an Empire that was now embroiled in an unequal war, but apparently without end. For the papers that lamented the monarch's peaceful passing also informed him that General De Wet was still leading the British a merry dance across South Africa, and that diplomatic Smuts had turned soldier, having formed a commando force. Kitchener was now in command, but was he coping? And could he himself cope, with both Laura and Mama ill now, and Aunt Carlotta staying?

He was going to the library for brandy, but his aunt was in there, at the last portrait of a compulsive photographic subject.

Chapter Twelve

The thaw came, releasing the river, wheels and warmer winds turning the avenue to slush, though the lower slopes of the mountain would stay white well into spring. The first snowdrops spotted the dripping woods, and small birds were active again. Blasting resumed at the quarry across water, the rumble of falling rock making Dresden china tremble on the drawing-room tables, restored after the festivities. Men in long leather boots were now staking out the site of Alexander's house while the caped architect stood by, unrolling the preliminary plans in his gloved hands.

Laura lay behind closed curtains, listening to the liberated river. The leeches gorged, hurting her neck, but her head ached worse than ever, and when the fuse was eaten away at the quarry, the vibrating bed seemed to send her head spinning. Swimming in sour milk, the half-eaten blobs of junket floated in the cracked crested plate on her bedside table, the horn spoon protruding.

Dr MacNiven was coming up every second day, to remove the satiated leeches and attach new ones from the glass jars. She kept her eyes closed, trying not to think of the glossy black things that didn't want to leave her throat, though she had often picked up dung beetles at the stables and put them into a matchbox. She was always disappointed to find them dead, inverted. But that had to stop when Aunt Carlotta opened a box, feeling for a match.

She didn't come near her now, sending the maid up with the tray and, on Sunday nights, to sponge down her body. Laura didn't care any more if the maid saw her stripped, though more hairs were curling. The water from the enamel pail was always cold, but she liked that because of the heat in her body. It was lovely when the sponge was squeezed, and the water dripped.

Niall came up often, to sit on the edge of the bed, holding her hand, telling her how Mama's dogs were misbehaving, and how he had seen a squirrel sitting in the hole in the wishing stone. Squirrels didn't seem to matter much now, though she had gone up trees after so many, tearing her dress and feeling the weight of Aunt Carlotta's hand. Though she didn't tell Niall, she couldn't see him very clearly. One minute he was there, the next only a blur, like the time her father had let her look at the standing stones through his stalking glass, then had closed it to show her magic. She told her brother she was feeling better.

He felt more confident. Though meals were only clinking silver now, he didn't regret putting the position straight once and for all to Aunt Carlotta. He was carrying out his New Year resolution to be more firm with her, and saw he was succeeding when trays with broth and pudding started to go up to Laura. He felt he was slipping easily into the role of laird, able to speak more naturally to the servants. Alexander had now signed away his inheritance. The Edinburgh lawyers were preparing the papers.

It was the day of Alexander's wedding, which had had to be postponed because of the snow. The whole of the village had been invited, but Miss Carlotta had dared any of the servants to attend, on pain of instant dismissal. They weren't even allowed to look out of their attic windows for the arrival of the wedding party at the Home Farm, and in case her nephew the laird had any ideas about watching, his aunt pulled down the blinds in the front public rooms, though that meant early lamps, extra paraffin.

Knowing how angry she would be, and not wishing to lose her patronage, Father Macdonald hadn't wanted to conduct Nuptial Mass because of the condition of the bride. And besides, it was really Miss Carlotta's chapel. But when their horses had met head-on on the narrow road, and MacPherson had indicated the bag of potatoes and salted pork which, 'funny thing', he was just taking down to the priest, Father Macdonald intimated that he would be pleased to offer Nuptial Mass. It was now a matter of converting Miss Carlotta, and having transferred MacPherson's gifts to his own vehicle, the priest parked it at Wade's Bridge and walked up the avenue, explaining, when his patroness met him in the porch and asked if there had been an accident, that he was walking out of enjoyment. Once settled with coffee in the drawing-room, he succeeded in convincing her that it would be the triumph of good over evil if she was to offer her chapel, and he Nuptial Mass, to bring the fornicators together in

195

wedlock. She agreed that marriage was better than living in sin, and that if they were not wedded, it would serve as a dangerous example to the rest of the priest's unruly flock.

Washed and polished by the two loonies, MacPherson's gig bore the newly marrieds up the rutted track from the chapel by the shore, an old boot dragging from the back axle, a piper swaggering in front of the blinkered horses, the chill corries of the January afternoon echoing the wedding march. Alexander wore his tight black suit, with a new stiff collar and tie, which he kept tugging at. His bride wore a white satin dress, the delicate veil that had been her mother's lifted by the fitful breeze from the grey loch, revealing an expression that strangely belied the occasion. She carried a small bunch of flowers close to the swelling that the village seamstress had made no attempt to conceal.

The gig lurched and the villagers, led by MacPherson, formidable in black, with a new bowler and with his wife on his arm, walked behind, nudging and whispering, their laughter visible till MacPherson looked behind. His wife wobbled in unaccustomed shoes and held down the alien hat, but Mac-Pherson's pace did not slow. Also in black, his boots polished, Archie the eldest son followed his father, face twitching as he looked up at the man on the gig.

The reception was being held in the barn, its big doors thrown wide, cobbles hosed down, hay serving as sofas, a village band consisting mainly of fiddles stationed on a cart in a corner, lanterns on hay ropes hanging from the rafters in whose dark heights the nests of departed swallows were stuck.

While the fiddles were twanging towards harmony, mine host went among the guests, slapping backs, his shout to enjoy themselves sounding like a threat. He climbed on to the cart beside the musicians, stamped his boot for silence.

'Now I'm not a man for speeches, as you all know, so I'm going to be short. It's a great day for the wife and me, to see our Kate marry Master Alexander. A finer fellow there never was, except for his own father, and him and me were like that.' And he held up two crossed fingers in illustration. 'Oh aye, I'll very likely have to sell a few beasts to pay for this wedding, but I don't grudge a penny, seeing the son-in-law I'm getting. Now I'll be asking the young couple to lead off in the first waltz, and the rest of you better bloody join in.'

They clapped him, and then the fiddles scraped. Alexander looked sheepish, standing blinking in the bright lantern light, but his bride pulled him gently by the hand. Because of her pronounced curvature, he had to hold her at arms-length, which produced laughter here and there. Her head inclined, the veil hiding her face, she held the embroidered hem of her shining dress clear of the old swallow droppings spattering the cobbles, and because his heels were coming out of his new shoes, he stumbled and several times had to be saved by her. With her glazed dress, and his white pallor heightened by sweat, they looked like a pair of Dresden figures joined at the stomach. And then, letting her hem trail on the fouled cobbles, she lifted aside her veil and was looking into his face, with a queer sad smile, the gold wedding band gleaming on her raised hand. It was she who kissed him, and that broke the spell, bringing other couples rotating, the fiddles speeding up into more daring dances until exhausted couples dropped laughing into the fragrant hay. Soon the cobbles were crowded, and in the centre MacPherson was dancing with his daughter, spinning her round and round.

Wearing swallow-tailed coats MacPherson had given them from an old trunk, the two loonies were dancing together, clasping hands at arms-length as they had seen the bridal couple do, and, hunched, they stared down laughing at their uncontrollable booted feet.

'You should stop them,' Kate, who had stopped dancing, said to her father.

'Leave them. The poor buggers get little enough out of life,' MacPherson said. 'Like that poor wee girl lying in the big house because of the bullying of that bitch Carlotta. Has Sandy heard how she is?'

'Just the same, Roddy the coachman told him. I'd love to go and see her, with Sandy.'

'You wouldn't even get over the back doorstep, lass. Forget about that tribe because Sandy wants to forget. He needs to forget, if he's ever going to be a man.'

The food and drink had been set out on the big table in the kitchen, where Mrs MacPherson presided, an apron over her new dress as she made sure that those crossing the mire from the barn got sufficient. There was everything from home-cured pork to crowdie, and in the centre of the bare boards, the two-tiered cake which Mrs MacPherson had baked and Kate iced. It had an edible couple on the top, the groom in tall hat. The presents had been laid out in the sitting-room overlooking the river for the inspection of the females, utensils and linen for the house still to be built. There were small presents from some of the big house servants, surreptitiously taken across the river by Roddy the coachman, but on Mac-Pherson's instructions the laird's cabinet of King's Pattern cutlery had been put away, 'in case it offends those who couldn't afford to give much, but gave with a good heart'.

Back in the barn the lanterns brightened, and men too old or cynical for dancing leaned back on hay, puffing clay pipes as they watched MacPherson coming and going. Eyes twinkling, they conversed in Gaelic out of the corners of their mouths.

'Well, he went looking for a bullock and he got a stunted stirk.'

'No, no, you're wrong, it was the stirk he was after all the time. They're easier led, man.'

And when MacPherson passed, they nodded and smiled.

He was climbing on to the cart, telling the fiddlers to go for refreshments. Once again his boot on boards brought silence.

'We've had enough dancing for the time being. Let's have a Gaelic song from Murdo the smith, but nothing suggestive, Murdo.'

Usually bare to the waist, the massive black-suited man went to stand in the centre, straightening his spine and folding his arms across his chest for the 'Song to Sandy'

> '*Alasdair nan stòp*
> *Ann an Sràid a Chùil,*
> *Sin an duine còir*
> *Air am bheil mo rùn.*
>
> '*S coma leat an sile,*
> *B' annsa leat an stòp,*
> *Cha n-e sin bu docha*
> *Ach am botul mòr.*'

*

198

Sandy of the Stoups,
In the Back Wynd,
He's the good fellow
Is much to my mind.

The gill you like but little,
The mutchkin you prefer,
But with the bigger bottle
In great content you are.

MacPherson was scowling, but was forced to stand for the rest of the song till the fiddlers had returned and he could start the dancing again. But young couples who had had too much dancing and drinking had retreated into the fragrant darkness of hay beyond the lanterns, some climbing to the loonies" loft. The thrashing and moaning overhead between dances made Kate complain to her father.

'It's life, lass, and *you* know it now. I wish to God some of the beasts that eat and sleep among this hay were as keen.'

She was turning away in disgust, hem trailing, the crumpled bouquet in her fist when she felt the kicking within, as if her stomach wall was being booted down. Gasping and clutching, she managed to make the heap of hay, to sprawl there in constricting satin, the lanterns wheeling overhead, the fiddles grating, until her father found her. He towered over her, blotting out.

'I think it's coming,' was all she managed to say.

Then Alexander was kneeling beside her, with that lost, scared look, the drink showing in his eyes. They carried her through the mire to the bed, but before driving down personally for Dr MacNiven, MacPherson had another announcement to make.

'Now just because she's going into labour doesn't mean that the dance has to stop. That's her words as well as mine. So keep on enjoying yourself, and don't leave me with all that food and drink in the house, which I'll have to pay for, anyway. She's a fine healthy lass, and it can't be very often you get a wedding and a birth on the same day,' he added, laughing.

The doors of the big barn stayed wide, spilling a yellow stream which almost reached down to the Summer House

Pool. As the sound of fiddles and the whoops of the dancers reached Invernevis in the library, he felt a pang. He should really be across there, joining in the celebrations to show family solidarity, despite Alexander's mistake and Aunt Carlotta's contempt. He could slip across, but that would be cowardly; and he knew that when she pointed out his position as laird, he would be forced to agree that it wasn't in order to go. There were many privileges to the position he occupied, but one disadvantage was that he would always have to watch what he said and did. For once the laird had lost respect, he could never reclaim it, though his father had tried, going among them, drinking from the same stone jars, distributing silver medals. He had forgotten one simple fact: they needed someone distanced whom they could respect.

Stiff-spined Aunt Carlotta was at her organ, tramping out sacred music – Saul's 'Death March' – to smother the sounds of revelry from the Home Farm, to remind the house of the outrage across the river. They might be married now, but the child would still be a bastard, and the polluted blood would darken the generations to come. The house to be erected on the opposite bank of the river would mock the mansion, as a fool sometimes mocked his master. As she played she closed her eyes and prayed, feeling the vibrations through her spread fingers, all the stops pulled out.

That night the rain came in torrents, washing away the last traces of snow from the corners of the woods, adding height and speed to the river. The corries above Invernevis House became vocal, stirring boulders, and the site of Alexander's house was swamped.

Laura lay listening to the waterfalls above which seemed to spill into her aching skull, but when the golden thread of lightning zigzagged down the curtains, her eyes did not follow. Fresh leeches were feasting. They seemed to be draining her, but she did not have the strength to lift her hands and tear them away. The waterfalls were sweeping her down to the river, spinning her, head pounding stone. Oh, she wanted stillness and darkness so much, the kind that salmon got when they reached their spawning grounds.

But her brother in the library below heard a different music in the rushing water. It signalled the beginning of the spring run, big fish lurking in the river mouth, ready to come up.

By dawn they would be in *Earrach*, the Spring Pool, and he was ready for them, the rod, gaff and landing net stacked in the front hall, to be picked up at first light. And now, as he sat by the fire, he was oiling one of his father's reels, winding the handle, the moaning changing to a snarling.

At least Laura wasn't worse. She wasn't eating much, but Dr MacNiven didn't seem worried, though he was still using leeches. She *said* she was feeling better. A week's fishing, and he would risk going to Edinburgh. There was a new item on his shopping list: a governess for Laura. Not to teach, but to be with, sharing the same room and interests. And the three of them would go to South Africa after the war finished, which shouldn't be long now. He had already written to Cook's, enquiring about places. The Cape was safe, though he would like to take her across the Great Karroo, to show her the animals as well as the Modder and Magersfontein. He was keeping all this from Laura in case it excited her. For that was what she definitely needed: a change of scenery, to get away from bad weather and Aunt Carlotta's bad tempers.

Invernevis and his ghillie left the house at seven the next morning, when grey light was breaking behind the standing stones on the hill above the Home Farm. The earth had had enough of rain. Encumbered with tackle, they went down the lawn, past the wishing stone, the studded soles of Invernevis's waders leaving depressions in the sodden turf, his loose oilskin inflated by the breeze driving more rain clouds. The ghillie followed behind, gaff and landing net crossed on his back. He was wearing the high leather boots that had been habitual to his old master.

Keen anticipation showed in Invernevis's face as he swung his game leg towards the swollen river. They turned right at the summer house, the wind sniping through its splayed boards. The slatted seat where Laura had sat, watching him casting on the day he had left for the Boer War, looked cold and uninviting, and the stepping stones she had wobbled across were submerged. The going became rougher as they went downriver, past *Cruibeag*, the Small Pool, the game leg now a serious impediment among grasping ash branches, on moss that sucked at his weighted soles. The river rushed beside them, loud in its own praise, up to the level of the bank and in some places spilling over, as if seeking release from the volume the corries were sending down. At *Poll Garbh Mor*, the Big Rough Pool, Invernevis was saved from certain death by his ghillie's grasp on oilskin, when stone proved unstable.

When they reached the hundred yards of angry water that was *Earrach*, the Spring Pool, boulders showing despite the spate, the ghillie assembled the rod, the reel sounding as he threaded line, and then the big fly of bullock hair from the Home Farm fences and tinsel from the big house Christmas tree tied with a knot that was tightened with the teeth. He scanned wild water, pointed to the lee of a boulder where an ascending salmon could get some respite. Invernevis began casting, but clumsily, using the Spey method of whipping the line from the side because of overhanging trees. Line flailed, flecking foam, fly trawled, lifted away. The ghillie had removed the landing net and gaff from his back in anticipation, but Invernevis found it hard to believe that such powerful water could be a resting place for newly arrived fish.

He kept casting, however, because the desire to beat his father's record was becoming an obsession. It wouldn't prove anything to Aunt Carlotta, of course, since *any* man *had* to be better than his father. But Laura, who had wrestled with a salmon two unforgettable summers before, in the shadow of Wade's Bridge, when the world was a better place, might be impressed. At least it encouraged him to get out of the house. And, when the fly was out again, he looked upriver, to the Home Farm, strangely silent after the wedding celebrations of the night before. But MacPherson would get his grandchild, Invernevis thought wryly, casting in a new place. And in marrying and getting his site by the river, Alexander had his freedom from the big house. Social position was sometimes an encumbrance, like waders, but you had a duty to the tenants. It was like fishing, really: you had to watch every move. Alexander's site would soon dry out, and bricks and rafters loom. Young children and maturing trees. Time he himself thought of taking the plunge.

It was his ghillie who had to call his attention to the tugging, and the fact that the reel was running free. Stout wood deferring warned him it was a big one, going down into *Poll Fada*, the Long Pool, getting out of the river that had betrayed it so early, after such a long return. The way it was taking him was treacherous for his leg, so he relied on his ghillie, giving and taking line as told, moving and staying, bracing his body against his game leg. It couldn't be allowed to get into *Poll Fada*, because that gave it a long free run, and yet there wasn't much ground left. So the breaking strain of his father's green-heart would have to be tested.

The fish heaved once out of corrugated water to tantalize with its size, mint silver, but then it went down, the line twitching as it rubbed its impaled jaw against rock, trying to dislodge. The vibrations along seventeen feet of choice wood told him he was winning, and he was able to retrieve considerable line, keeping the point of the rod down as the ghillie ordered, the reel harder to turn now as the exhausted salmon was dragged through discoloured water to where the gaff was waiting, cork off the poised tip.

A foot separated steel and fish when someone shouted to Invernevis's right, startling his hand from the reel. By the time he was in control again ten yards had run away. It was the windswept figure of Maggie, waving both arms in scissor movements and pointing up to the house. And when that did not seem to shift them she cupped her hands and shouted with the last of her breath. Though the wind carried away her call to be mocked by the mountain, Invernevis heard his sister's name. The fish was into *Poll Fada* now, the biggest he had ever hooked.

'Cut the line,' he ordered, and without question the curved blade of the ghillie's clasp-knife sprung, line snaking away. Invernevis thrust the relieved rod into the ghillie's arms. 'You'd better come up as soon as you can in case you've to go to the village.'

He stumbled up the bank, getting assistance from branches, certain that his sister was dead, cursing himself for having come out, studded soles scraping rock, oilskin snagging, but jerked free, rending. He had her by the arm and was hurrying her, head inclined to hers, grimacing as the wind muffled her words.

'Miss Laura, sir. She's taken a terrible turn, sir.'

And then the heavens opened above the mountain, spattering his oilskin, the wind getting in, holding him back. He swore at the weighted waders, but there was no time to shed them.

Though his fingers were hurting Maggie's arm, she was too frightened to say. All she understood was that Miss Carlotta had gone up to see Laura and found her in a bad way, and when she told the Master this as they bent their heads into the whipping rain, she saw anxiety become anger. Her sodden black dress was clinging to her limbs because there hadn't been time to find a coat, with Miss Carlotta pushing her towards the front door because she was the youngest and, presumably, swiftest, ordering her to go as fast as she could. Her boots made embarrassing sounds as they headed up the lawn, the going getting harder as they reached the slope with the wishing stone on the summit.

Invernevis was unbuttoning his oilskin as he crunched across gravel. He let the voluminous coat slide from his arms, on to the floor of the front hall, and then he was taking the stairs, impeded by the waders, both hands on the groaning banister. As he heaved himself on to the landing, the screaming began.

Aunt Carlotta and Elsie were on either side of Laura's bed, holding her down. She squirmed and kicked, the sound of her agape mouth like an animal caught in a trap, a yelping that rang and rang.

'What in God's name's going on?' her brother shouted, studded boots scraping bare wood as he lurched towards the bed.

'I came up to see her and found her like this,' his aunt said, without letting go.

Invernevis pulled the kitchen-maid out of the way and pressed the ball of his palm against his sister's shoulder. Her eyes were on him momentarily, but then her head began to whiplash against the pillow again, between aunt and brother, screaming.

'Have you sent for the doctor?' Invernevis yelled, beside himself with panic. He knew that hysterical people could choke on their own tongues, as over-ridden horses did.

'No, I haven't. I was waiting for you.'

'For me? You fool! Get downstairs and tell someone to take a horse – this instant.'

Aunt Carlotta transmitted the order to Elsie with a movement of her head.

'No, you I meant, since *you* seem to have upset her. Now go, woman!'

She hesitated, her lips marshalling a reply, then hurried out, white-faced.

But Laura kept struggling and screaming, her ringlets dashing across her face, which was turning blue. He hated doing it, but he had to, as with Mama, when she had been drunk and querulous. He slapped her sharply, once. The head came to rest, facing him, mouth and eyes wide as she wailed:

'Oh, please, Aunt Carlotta, I didn't mean to do it!'

It was then he realized that she was blind. He sat on the edge of the bed and began to cry, not caring that the kitchen-maid was watching.

Maggie had stayed on gravel, frightened to go inside because of the Master's face, and because she could not bear another death so soon. Though it should only have been under a new moon, and by one of the Invernevis family, she turned to the wishing stone, linking her hands through the lichen-encrusted hole, helping Laura the only way she knew. And as she opened her eyes after the wish into which she had put all her being, concentrating even harder than on the Master's photograph, she saw the speeding horse on the other side of the turbulent river, as if racing it, the rider standing in the stirrups, precariously balanced above the long neck, the whip hitting. As the green blur became her father, the best horseman in the district, a lump came into her throat. It was both savage and grand, with the standing stones on one side, the river on the other, and between them, man and animal one.

Dr MacNiven put Invernevis and the kitchen-maid out of the bedroom and spent a long time with Laura, moving a lighted candle in front of her eyes. When he eventually came down to the library, where Aunt Carlotta also was, he was baffled.

'I just can't make it out. You try and make her tell you what's wrong, but she doesn't seem to be able to find words any more. And another thing – ' he looked keenly at Invernevis. 'She's not seeing. Meningitis? There are signs, but somehow it doesn't fit. But it's definitely something *inside* the head.'

'Then you know,' Invernevis said, almost with relief. 'And you'll be able to do something.'

'You don't mind if I sit?' Dr MacNiven said, taking the swivel chair and sweeping up the tails of his coat before turning it to face the fire. He indicated that Invernevis and his aunt should take the two arm-chairs. Aunt Carlotta sat suspiciously, her fists on her lap, a lace handkerchief protruding from her tight cuff.

'It's not an easy thing to put,' the doctor began, taking off his spectacles to pinch his watery eyes, leaving the small thick lenses dangling from his fingers. 'Maybe Miss Carlotta will understand better.' He paused. 'Take two dogs, a Skye terrier and a fox terrier, say. Now they *should* breed with their own kind, but nature can be strange. Supposing these two dogs mate and produce a pup, this size.' He showed with his hands. 'It's not really what the Lord intended. It's small, but it manages to survive. But it's different from other dogs, more vulnerable, because – well, it's damaged in some way, shall we say. And because of that you don't expect it to live as long as more normal dogs. And maybe it's for the best that it has a short happy life because as it grew older it would just have more and more problems. No hope of breeding, no resistance to illness or accident. You love it while you have it, but are glad to see it get peace.' He looked from one to the other. 'Do you follow me?'

Miss Carlotta nodded, but her nephew was frowning. 'Are you saying that my sister's been damaged by somebody? By being hit, for instance, because if that's it – ' He was looking murderously at his aunt.

'No, Invernevis, you misunderstood,' Dr MacNiven said, interceding with a raised hand. 'Yes, your sister's been damaged, but not by a human hand, and even before she came into the world. I wasn't happy with the pregnancy because your mother was forty, and that's a difficult age for a woman having a child. I delivered Miss Laura myself, and it was touch and go for both mother and child, I can tell you. You remember?' Aunt Carlotta nodded. 'Well, the brain was damaged in some way, but she managed to survive, to give and receive a lot of happiness. And now – ' he sighed – 'nature is signalling. Nature doesn't want Miss Laura to become a woman. There is nothing I can do, nothing anyone can do. You could bring William Macewen from Glasgow, but he wouldn't put a scalpel near her head.'

'How long do you give her?' Invernevis asked hoarsely.

'A few days at the most, because she hasn't the strength. She's quiet now, but whatever's going on in her head might make her start up again. If that happens, send for me, even though it's in the night. I'll give her something to make it easier.' He was bringing his bulk awkwardly to his feet, restoring his spectacles. 'And don't worry about having to tell her. There's no need: she already knows, inside herself.' He was looking at Miss Carlotta as he added: 'Who knows, but they know more than us, and we're supposed to be normal.' He turned at the door, black hat going to his sloping bald head. 'No doubt you've heard that there was a bit of a panic at the wedding last night. They thought Kate was due, but it'll be a few days yet. MacPherson's fretting, but as I told him, he should know the ways of nature by now.'

Aunt Carlotta went out with Dr MacNiven, strengthening Invernevis's suspicion that they were in league. The doctor must be well aware that Laura had received not one, but many blows from her aunt. Well, if his sister was going to die because of what his aunt had done to her, that would make it a matter for the constable. He would have no hesitation. Yes, his father had been right; she was a dangerous woman, a wicked woman, and she should have been kicked out long ago. That was his error as much as his father's. To hell with her money. When he remembered Laura lying in the meadow across the Summer House Pool, pleading with him not to go back to his regiment, his eyes misted. Oh God, he should have resigned his commission, even though they would have called it cowardice in the mess, with war pending. That would have stopped Mama from becoming a drunkard, and would have given Laura a few precious years of happiness. It might even have saved her life.

But her eyes: why should they go wrong? Even if she pulled through, she might not see again, and those eyes had loved life, dazzled by sunsets, saving the smallest creatures from being trampled underfoot. Blindness; muslin. Horror hurried him to the encyclopaedia shelf, to pull out the S volume, crumpling the pages as he had done on his first night home when he had seen the doctor's note to his mother. His finger went down the column, discounting what he already knew. And then, plain despite the complicated terminology: syphilis, the disease that blinded, could be transmitted to the unborn.

He found his chair again, put his face into his hands, the blackness behind the muslin drapes back again. That brutal arm that had molested so many maids had reached out from the grave to molest Laura, and perhaps Alexander and he himself. Dr MacNiven's elaborate parable of the damaged puppy could not conceal a truth he knew. His fear flowed naturally into intense anger. Aunt Carlotta had been right all along; his father had been nothing but an animal. He must have known in India that he had picked up the disease. Why therefore in God's name had he fathered not one, but three children, putting his wife at risk as well? Very probably Mama's brain was affected, hence her heavy drinking, and as for Alexander, it could explain his erratic behaviour. It was in their blood, which meant that they would pass it on to any children they might have, so the Invernevis lineage would be polluted by blindness and early death. The only solution was the self-inflicted extinction of the whole family, a horrifying thought. Only Aunt Carlotta would be left, and maybe she realized that she was the only uncontaminated one, the rock of ages.

It was the same feeling he had had, under Magersfontein Hill, when the Boer guns had blazed in the dawn, sending him staggering. First the tingling flush of fear when confronted by death, the whirling kaleidoscope of his life darkening, over in seconds, it seemed, a futile span not worth mourning, more sorrow than happiness, then brightening as the bullets failed to strike and he realized that life was an infinitely precious thing, to be held on to at all costs, clasped as Laura had clasped the salmon in the Yellow Pool, though she could not hold it for long. Man was like the salmon, moved by some inexplicable instincts to navigate the dark depths, facing all manner of hazards, continually challenging the waterfall in order to reach the bright pool of the river of its origin, to shake out spawn that the grinning pike would gobble, and yet die satisfied, leaving no traces behind. Only, his ancestor had been the large salmon, emerging out of darkness to lead the shoal, strong and confident, surmounting the waterfalls that sent others reeling, shaking off the lamprey, depositing spawn and warding off the pike, not prepared to die till succession was certain. It was all a question of guts and vigilance, not acknowledging cruives till one ran into them.

Invernevis went out to find Aunt Carlotta. She was sitting in the drawing-room, staring into a fire that was not there, her lips moving, a rosary like a limp snake in her fist. He had not come to apologize or continue the quarrel. Nor was he going to explain his discovery from the encyclopaedia. Speak-

208

ing slowly and resolutely, as he stood at her back, he issued his orders. He was going to sit up with his sister. He wanted an arm-chair moved into her room, a fire, a lamp, and his meals brought up on a tray. He wasn't to be disturbed for anything. But the ghillie was to stand by, in case Dr MacNiven had to be sent for.

Aunt Carlotta nodded meekly, and half an hour later, when he went upstairs, he found that all his demands had been satisfied, with coal catching in the grate, and a lamp gleaming on the dressing-table, reflected in the silver-backed vanity set he had given his sister for Christmas.

Laura was lying on her back, her arms stretched outside the clothes. He winced when he saw how thin they were. The leeches had gone, leaving red marks at her throat. The doll he had brought back from London lay on the carpet by the bed, but when he put it in beside her she showed no interest.

It was eerie, those sightless eyes scanning him. But the slight smile gave him hope. It was this, and the smooth white-ness of her cheeks that made him think that Dr MacNiven was wrong. Maybe she was on the mend. But why was she lying there so still, her eyes open? He did not want to drain her strength by speech, so he sat in the chair by the bedside, his hands folded on his lap, the fire to his right growing tall tongues. He was frightened of falling asleep.

Since the curtains were closed, he could not follow the progress of the day, and when the Jubilee clock chimed, he did not count the strokes. Coal shifted, the room grew hotter, the lamp more radiant, its circle seeming to expand towards the bed, revealing the dark circles round his sister's eyes. Once or twice he jerked out of near sleep, thinking that Laura had fallen asleep, but her eyes were still open, the smile still there.

The sticky heat and the stillness recalled lying among iron-stone and ant-hills, waiting to cross the Modder. The maid knocked and brought in food under a silver cover, but with-out lifting it he told her to take it away and bring coffee. He was desperate for a cigarette, but was frightened that the smoke would upset Laura. And when the coffee came in the high silver pot with the arched spout it was allowed to get cold on the circular table by his elbow.

Though his eyes were on his sister, he let his mind rove, back to time past, her running beside the big wheel as he left for war, her wrestling with explosive silver at Wade's Bridge. And her smile seemed to encourage such memories, as if their minds were identical magic lanterns. He was pursuing the black button boots through the walled garden, back to an afternoon raining crab apples, her crooked white teeth crunching, when she spoke two words.

'Where's Alexander?'

He nodded and went towards the bell she had never been allowed to use. When the maid came, he asked for the ghillie to be sent up. Seconds later he was there, and Invernevis stopped him outside the door, whispering to him to go to the Home Farm and fetch Alexander, since Laura, who was sinking, was asking for him.

The ghillie left by the back door with a lantern, without telling anyone about his mission. Maggie was at her sink, scrubbing it in the absence of dinner dishes, frightened to go upstairs because of the uncanny silence of the house, Mrs Livingstone and Elsie moving silently next door, knowing death was ascending the front stairs. The bristles stopped when Maggie saw the light on the avenue. She was shaking, but not from the coldness of the surrounding stone. For, hunched over reddening peats on rare nights of recollection after a satisfactory day's toil, her mother had told of a light flickering on the doorstep of one about to die, then moving, taking the route that the funeral would take to the cemetery. But Maggie did not wait to see if the wavering light on the avenue took the road above the river. She rushed into the bright warmth of the kitchen, where Mrs Livingstone was crying at the end of the table, the two Skye terriers lying whimpering by her swollen feet, sad eyes on the door.

The rain had stopped, but water dripped from high branches, hissing on the lantern as the ghillie hurried down the avenue, wearing the old laird's big boots and the thick socks Miss Carlotta had given him for Christmas. Once over Wade's Bridge, he crossed heaped stone and cut up hillside to the Home Farm, taking his bearings from the standing stones.

Alexander was in his sister's bedroom within half an hour, ploughman's waistcoat buttoned the wrong way, scarf knotted at the throat, and one bootlace undone. Invernevis smelt drink as they shook hands. He gestured to the chair drawn up on the other side of the bed.

Alexander's expression was asking the seriousness of it, and

210

his brother was nodding sadly. They sat in silence, each holding a hand, the white face between still with its smile, the eyes favouring Alexander, but with no word of recognition. But he knew by the pressure of her fingers.

The heat finally defeated Invernevis. He was nodding, askew in his chair, flogging dark water in dreams when a tug pulled him to consciousness. Laura turned like a salmon that had got loose, and was gone.

Book Four

Chapter Thirteen

The coffin was supported between two chairs in the centre of the drawing-room, with the lid left off so that the servants could pay their last respects. But Miss Carlotta insisted on order, even in death. As at Christmas the servants were lined up in the front hall, with Symmers the butler at the head, and at a beckoning finger from the housekeeper they filed in, shuffling, pausing at the foot of the coffin to make a sign of the cross before going round the head and out again, back to their duties.

As usual, Maggie was last in the line. When Miss Carlotta had come through to muster the procession, clapping her hands and calling for work to be left for the time being, the scullery-maid had been frightened, but could think of no excuse. Her heart had protested all the way to the drawing-room, and, now, as she entered, the dramatic effect, by design or accident, seemed to strike the breath from her body. Though it was day, Miss Carlotta had drawn the curtains, had distributed a nest of four small tables at the four corners of the coffin, and on each placed a three-pronged candelabrum from the silver safe. The effect was to make an island of light in the centre of the room. And there, trapped by the steady tongues of flame, lay Laura, in a white nightdress with long sleeves. Her hands were crossed, her shoulders hemmed in by buttoned satin.

The light on this slim whiteness dazzled Maggie, but it was

the face that stopped her. It was unreal, like the sleeping beauty's in the only picture book that her mother had ever given her, from a jumble sale. The ringlets arranged at the neck looked like looped strands of fine gold resting on white satin. And at the corners of the mouth was the cutest little smile, with the slightly crooked tooth just showing. This was not death, for Laura was smiling at her. She had faced death before, with her mother scaled down to a yellow skeleton, but here was beauty and bloom. No, she was just sleeping. But how could that be when the eyes were open, when there was no sign of breathing at throat and bust? And what had inflicted these terrible red marks at her throat, like the claws of a wild cat?

The other servants had filed out, and Maggie was alone. She was reaching out to touch the whiteness, to make sure it was not living, when Miss Carlotta's thin stern face appeared above the three peaks of the candelabrum. She snapped her fingers, and Maggie hurriedly made the sign of the cross and passed into the gloom again. But when she was outside the door she let her grief go.

Invernevis kept to the library, where the temptation to find solace in the brandy decanter had to be resisted until all necessary arrangements had been made. He loathed it, but who else was there to do it? Who more natural to do it, getting the estate joiner to take the measurements, then telegraphing them to Glasgow because the estate wood was sodden. And – so harrowing – having to go and meet it off the late train, to ride back with it on the same gig, sitting with it to steady it as they went over Wade's Bridge, to look down into the Yellow Pool where she had wrestled with life. When she had been washed by an old woman in the village and lifted into the narrow wood, it was carried downstairs to the drawing-room, where Aunt Carlotta made space for it in the centre. He took to the library, for notices had to be sent to newspapers, letters written to relatives.

He had been at his desk since dawn, using the black-bordered notepaper that had been in the rack since his father's death. He blotted the intimation for *The Times*, laid down the pen and felt the justification for an early brandy. At least the major decision had been made, he thought with relief as he sat at the fire, cradling the glass. Where was Laura to lie? It was not something he cared to discuss with Aunt Carlotta, who had taken the news of Laura's death in the small hours as a personal affront, not crying but accusing.

'You sent for your brother and ignored me when it was I who brought the girl up and gave her as much as I could. It shows what you think of me. It shows I have no place here now. However, I shall do my duty and see that the girl gets the proper rites of the Roman Catholic Church before I go. Because it was not *me* you should have sent for: it was Father Macdonald. By sending for your brother instead you denied your sister absolution. Worse: you brought wickedness to her death-bed.'

There was no point in making matters worse by telling Aunt Carlotta that Laura had had no sins to answer for, and no point in maddening her by explaining that Laura had asked for Alexander. And he was not going to discuss Laura's last resting place with her. Hadn't she broken three centuries of family tradition by burying his father outside the chieftains' enclosure when he was away at war? There were only two places left in the enclosure, presumably for himself and his wife, but Laura certainly wasn't going to lie beside the brute whose transmitted disease had probably killed her. No, Laura would have one of the spaces in the enclosure, and the other would be for himself. At least she would have the company of his dust, whatever heaven offered.

He was conscious that in putting Laura into the enclosure he was breaking tradition as much as Aunt Carlotta had done, for Laura wasn't only a female, but one without issue, a lopped shoot of the family tree. When he went up to his bedroom, the faces in the oil paintings warned, but when he crossed the hall and saw the small face among the candles, his mind was made up. He was prepared to risk the wrath of the dead.

It was like waiting, shivering in the rain, for the assault on Magersfontein Hill, knowing there was something out there he might not be able to face, wanting it over with, and at the same time wanting it abandoned. Rain drumming on bivouacs had paced the seconds; now toothed brass behind his head pushed on time. He was impressing his seal on the last black-bordered envelope when Aunt Carlotta came in to say that the coffin would be closed soon.

It was the moment he had been unconsciously dreading ever since she had come into his world, and he had seen what

214

a precious thing she was. It was going to be far worse than facing the muslin tent on the summer afternoon he had left for war. He got up, drained the glass in one gulp, and when it was circulating he began to move.

The hall seemed so small as he made for the yellow glow rayed with candles, like a grounded star, pausing at the threshold to swallow, but going on, into the gloom, his brogues muffled by carpet till bare boards came with the candles. He had been bred to cast a cold eye on death, to keep his emotions bridled, since succession was all. In the same way, shows of affection were not encouraged, even in childhood, when he and Alexander were confined to the nursery. Only at evening were the nannies allowed to carry them through to the drawing-room, to see their parents before sleep, and though his father always had a pat on the head for Alexander, he had nothing for Niall. Mama tried to compensate by holding him tighter to her bosom, but the *eau de toilette* only made him squeamish. And these strictures extended to the physical. Though the nursery was freezing, there was no hope of fire from Aunt Carlotta, and never hot water for washing. She believed this spartan training toughened up the soul.

But this was different. This was the only person he had ever really loved. As he stepped into the circle of fire, it seemed to him that he had entered the silence and stability of eternity. Satin accommodated a flawless alabaster vase, so frail that to touch was to disintegrate, a vase with gold encrusted where the neck narrowed. And yet, because light attacked, it had to be put away into darkness to be preserved, as an heirloom, but always with the comforting knowledge that it was there, in the darkness, perfect.

It had nothing to do with soiled dresses or scuffed button boots, nothing to do with damage. The wrestling with light and the blows were over. It was now too precious for the world. He felt released from a great responsibility. The object that had been in his care was going back to where it belonged, unflawed by time, more precious than ever. And it had been his only.

But as he stepped back into gloom again, he saw Maggie the scullery-maid come forward. She had removed her boots and was tiptoeing towards the coffin, breaking the cordon of candles, placing on the breast a small bunch of snowdrops, with the delicate concern of a mother at a crib. And because flowers meant mortality, he began to see and hear again stumbling boots and streaming ringlets, a wheel being raced, silver wrestled. Maggie heard the sobbing, and without waiting to find the source ran in terror from the room.

He leaned over the glass cases in the shadows, venting the emotions of years till Aunt Carlotta came in to say that it was time for him to go up and dress. And when he had gone, keeping to the shadows to conceal his grief, his aunt substituted a crucifix for the snowdrops which she thought he had placed on his sister's breast. The estate joiner then lifted on the lid and tightened the gilt bolts.

Aunt Carlotta wanted a full Mass for the dead, with chant and chalice, but Invernevis would not allow it, not only because it was too long and harrowing, but because Laura had always been bored by the unintelligible Latin of castigation, wanting to slip out into sunlight. Aunt Carlotta was shocked and accused her nephew of being a pagan, like his father, but he stood firm, though Father Macdonald supported her.

'High Mass is for those who have sinned and need repentance, but Laura has nothing to answer for,' he said. 'If she was flawed from the beginning, it wasn't her fault.' He was adamant. He would only permit one prayer, and he chose it himself, giving the priest back his Missal with the red tongue for marker. But Father Macdonald knew it by heart. Standing at the head of the closed coffin, he raised his arms and clenched his fists.

'*Deus, cui próprium est miseréri semper et párcere, te súpplices exorámus pro ánima fámulae tuae Laura, quam hódie de hoc sáeculo migráre jussisti: ut non tradas eam in manus inimici, neque obliviscáris in finem, sed júbeas eam a sanctis Angelis súscipi, et ad pátriam paradisi perdúci; ut, quia in te sperávit et crédidit, non poenas inférni sustineat, sed gáudia aetérna possideat. Per Dóminum.*' ['O God, whose nature is ever to show mercy and forbearance, we humbly entreat thee for the soul of thy servant Laura, who at thy bidding has today departed from this world. Do not deliver her into the enemy's hands, or put her out of mind for ever, but bid thy holy angels welcome her and lead her home to paradise. Let her not undergo the pains

216

of hell, for she put her hope and trust in thee, but establish her in that bliss which knows no ending through our Lord.']

Aunt Carlotta snuffed the candles, and four men led by MacPherson from the Home Farm came in to carry out the coffin. One at each corner, they easily shouldered the girl whose dancing had delighted and frightened them in that gloomy room only a few weeks before. Tenants held their hats by the brims and bowed their heads as it came out of the dim porch into the first bright day of spring, the air bracing, the sky blue, with insubstantial white clouds on the horizon above the standing stones. The coffin was slid on to the cart from the Home Farm, the plough-horse waiting with bowed head between the trams. It had often been slipped lumps of sugar by the corpse it was to carry.

And then Invernevis came out in full Highland dress, but with a black jacket and black garter tabs. He was carrying a tall cromach, its hilt a carved ram's horn, a ceremonial stick his father had used to lead funerals and the procession to the Highland games, now lapsed through war. Aunt Carlotta was also at the door, with Father Macdonald, watching her nephew take his place immediately behind the cart, standing erect, the tip of the cromach buried in gravel, staring over the coffin. A few paces in front of the horse, Farquhar the piper was adjusting his discordant drones, black ribbons dangling from his bonnet.

Farquhar's fingers had now found the tune, his brogues stamping time on crushed stone. MacPherson stepped forward to slap the horse. Its huge hooves shifted gravel, and then the cart was moving forward, the pipes full-bellied. Aunt Carlotta had been standing stiffly in black silk, staring almost defiantly at the burden on the cart, but as her nephew began to move, the tenants falling in behind, leaving a gap of a few feet, her head snapped back, unearthly screams forming into the frantic words: 'I didn't do it! Before God I didn't do it! I meant her no harm! It was for her own good!' And as she lunged towards the moving cart, clutching at brass, the gravel bit through silk to her knees, the pipes cancelling the anguish she was giving to the sky, staying on her bleeding knees till Father Macdonald raised her to the iron seat and smelling salts. But her nephew did not look back.

217

The cortège of Laura Jane Macdonald moved slowly down the avenue of Invernevis House, the pipes' lament amplified in the tunnel of trees, pigeons shedding grey feathers as they scattered, the circular iron-shod hooves sparking and ringing, the tip of Invernevis's cromach skidding into ruts as he dragged his game leg, and behind him, the crunch crunch of boots, like an army marching. Untouched by sunlight, the avenue seemed cold and endless, Invernevis conscious of his bare legs, and especially the lagging one. He remembered coming up that avenue in another season, but with his sister laughing, wet linen and not wood encasing her maturing body, and salmon scales stuck, like mother-of-pearl. The wheel of the farm cart creaked, but there was a bigger, faster wheel she had dropped away from, having thrust up the clustered, blood-flecked trumpets of the rhododendron bloom as he rode to war, leaving her to an enemy far more barbaric than the Boer, but an enemy that might now have repented. Instead of rhododendrons, the tiny white cowls of snowdrops clustered between the trees, coming up to the verge where a wheel hooped with iron crushed them. He saw the tree where his *sgian dubh* had carved their initials that last day of happiness and harmony, but the white wood was now green, like suppurating wounds. It was as if the blade was at his own heart, scoring.

It went beyond the crumbling stone pillars, by the gate flaking in grass, turning right, but having to halt because Colonel Campbell was coming in his new toy, an Argyll Voiturette, honking the horn, whisker-fringed face impassive above the tiller, goggles giving him the bulbous eyes of a fish, a high-collared cape saving his tweeds from the dust the wire wheels were disturbing. By his side sat his severe-faced lady, her big-brimmed hat tied down. They went by without acknowledgment, and without the Colonel removing his deerstalker, the horse hauling the coffin having to wait till the dust had settled.

Wade's Bridge loomed, and the horse instinctively slowed for the hump, MacPherson going forward to brace the heel of his big rough hand against the foot of the coffin, to stop it sliding off. *Linne Bhuidhe*, the Yellow Pool where Laura had wrestled with living silver, was now the colour of dirty dented pewter as the spate subsided, the bank by Deirdre's fenced-off bog minus marigolds. Her brother could not believe it was the same place where the little Italian had passed, having laid the ghost of that day on a plate.

On the other side of the bridge Alexander was waiting in the tight black suit of his wedding, and boots from which all the manure had not been brushed. The brass stud was showing at the creased collar, where the badly knotted tie slipped. He carried a black hat, but awkwardly, as if too embarrassed to wear it, and in the other hand, a wreath like a wheel. Beside him, the site of his new house was still waterlogged.

He fell into step beside his brother, and they went on in silence, the road more level now, and the river less querulous as it swung in towards the summer house, but the stepping stones still not showing. The house was white and silent, without smoke under the snow-capped mountains, the drawing-room curtains still closed, Aunt Carlotta having been helped inside. On the other side of the road, the rolling fields of the Home Farm awaiting Alexander at the spring plough, and a hand wearing a wedding band clutching muslin at a high window. Then the savage outlines of the standing stones on the summit. Ahead loomed the chain of mountains across the loch, with the open sore of the quarry at the flank. Invernevis had sent a message across, demanding no blasting on the day of his sister's burial.

Where the river began to widen for its estuary, the road divided, the village to the left, and straight on, the track leading to the chapel and ferry. Tenants too old and infirm to tackle the avenue twice were waiting there to join the procession, most of them supported by stout sticks, without coats in the chill, some veterans of India, with the old laird. Watery-eyed, they saluted the principal mourner before falling in.

The track of jagged stone barely allowed the width of the cart, and thorns tangled in the spokes as the horse began its wary descent to the shore, the coffin rocking, brass handles clanging like impatient bells, giving Invernevis the horrifying momentary idea that Laura was not dead, but trying to break out as she had had to do so many times from Aunt Carlotta's thin retentive arms, or, locked in the school-room after a grammatical error, pounding with her fists.

The loch lengthened above the sloped coffin, the road even rougher, briars becoming more tenacious as the circle of trees sheltering the chapel came into sight, and between it and blue water, the tall bare poles of the salmon netters, their inverted cobbles beached well beyond the snatch of the tide. For the last fifty yards of descent four men, including MacPherson, climbed aboard the cart and straddled its slewing wood, until the cortège came to a halt on the narrow strip of sandy turf between chapel and river mouth, where the ferry plied for the quarry. Trestles were waiting to take the load, to await Father Macdonald's arrival in the gig, since Miss Carlotta had insisted on him being driven.

Duncan the ghillie and his son Hector had taken a gig down to the morning train, to collect the wreaths sent by relatives and friends. There were very few, but the ghillie had done his best to conceal the shortage by arranging them in a circle round the trestles. Most of the mourners from the estate were bringing home-made wreaths, hoops of wire upholstered with moss and greenery, snowdrops stuck in. Hector helped his father with them, putting Master Alexander's over the brass plate. The card read:

FROM ALL AT THE HOME FARM
WITH FONDEST LOVE

The piper had stopped playing, and the mourners stood round in awkward groups, their eyes on water. Invernevis leaned on his long stick and congratulated his brother on the birth of a daughter. He asked him when he expected to have his house completed. Alexander shifted from boot to boot, and said by the summer, if the weather was fair. And while Invernevis was thinking of something else to say, Father Macdonald came down, clinging to the padded seat of the gig as Roddy shouted the two horses to a halt.

Surpliced and black-skirted, wearing boots because of the boggy ground, the priest stepped into the circle of wreaths and, raising his arms, moved his fingers to gather the mourners together before opening his Missal at the silver tongue.

'*Fratres: Nólumus vos ignoráre de dormiéntibus, ut non contristémini, sicut et céteri, qui spem non habent. Si enim crédimus quod Jesus mórtuus est et resurréxit: ita et Deus eos, qui dormíerunt per Jesum, addúcet cum eo. Hoc enim vobis dicimus in verbo Dómini, quia nos, qui vivimus, qui residui sumus in advéntum Dómini, non praeveniemus eos,*

220

qui dormiérunt. Quóniam ipse Dóminus in jussu, et in voce Archángeli, et in tuba Dei déscendet de caelo: et mórtui, qui in Christo sunt, résurgent primi. Deinde nos, qui vivimus, qui relinquimur, simul rápiemur cum illis in núbibus óbviam Christo in áera, et sic semper cum Dómino érimus. Itaque consolámini invicem in verbis istis.' ['Brethren: make no mistake about those who have gone to their rest; you are not to lament over them, as the rest of the world does, with no hope to live by. We believe, after all, that Jesus underwent death and rose again; just so, when Jesus comes back, God will bring back those who have found rest through him. This we can tell you as a message from the Lord himself; those of us who are still left alive to greet the Lord's coming shall not reach the goal before those who have gone to their rest. No, the Lord himself will come down from heaven to summon us, with an archangel crying aloud and the trumpet of God sounding; and first of all the dead will rise up, those who died in Christ. Only after that shall we, who are still left alive, be taken up into the clouds, be swept away to meet Christ in the air, and they will bear us company. And so we shall be with the Lord for ever. Tell one another this for your consolation.']

As at the house, Invernevis would only permit one prayer, and had chosen the Epistle himself, despite Aunt Carlotta's protests, supported by Father Macdonald, that it was against the edicts of Rome to fragment a Mass. Invernevis looked out over water on that perfect morning, with the mountains and their mint snow reproduced in the blue stretch, and off the jetty, a swan drifting, its neck curving back into its plumage, as if coy in the presence of man. But as the Latin promise rang out, the disturbed swan rose, thrashing water as it shifted to another silence across the loch, and Invernevis saw that one webbed foot was gone. And the faces of the mourners gathered around him showed that they still did not understand the language with which they had been bombarded, morning after morning, since Miss Carlotta came to Invernevis. The wooden chapel that she had had erected at her own expense stood near the shore, strategically sited to take the villagers away from the temptations of the Arms, the rough ride or walk down wakening them for dawn Mass.

The pipes were sounding again, a path being cleared through

221

the wreaths, the coffin shouldered, steadied, moving into the shadows of the small wood surrounding ruined stone, relic of the first Macdonald settlement at Invernevis. The chapel stood on a knoll, its pitched roof stripped centuries before by storms, the arched windows crumbling, jackdaws nesting in ivy gripping granite bonded by lime and crushed shells. Behind it, outside the wall, the family enclosure where the old laird lay with spinster aunts, dissipated uncles, stillborn children and nephews sent home wrapped in regimental standards. Aunt Carlotta considered it to be a pagan place, her proximate wooden chapel helping to call attention to the accumulated sins of centuries.

The iron grille of the chapel proper was unlocked, its twenty-foot square crowded with slabs, flat and upright, legends corroded by salt-laden wind, obscured by lichen, some so old that they looked like natural rock, and in a corner, a crude effigy stretched out, the first of Invernevis, son of Angus, Earl of Ross and Lord of the Isles, who had fought at Flodden. The tip of his massive two-handed sword rested between his deerskin-shod feet, chain-mail shirted, the visored helmet shading a grim mouth.

At the threshold, where the granite stone of John, fifteenth of Invernevis, trawled from *Casan Dubh*, tilted, the earth gaped, shells showing that the tide had receded. The coffin bearers were skirting the slope, going round the back to the family enclosure, but Invernevis's cromach pointed the true way upwards, producing gasps of surprise. MacPherson was first, polished wood compressing his cheek as his shining rump strained. But powerful hands were coming out of the crowd to heave up, boots scraping on the slope, brass clanging where wood slipped. It was steadied at the top, eased between stone and iron, then slid on to the poles across the grave. When it was balanced, and the bunched red cords jerked from brass, Invernevis was helped up, protesting that he could manage. Facing the mourners beneath, his cromach hooked over his arm, weight braced on his game leg, he brought the black-bordered cards from his sporran.

It was the moment for which they had all been waiting, since a cord conferred distinction and favour. The pipes were folded up and ears inclined as Invernevis called down, shuffling the cards with their miniature coffin motif. Himself at the head, 'my brother' at the foot. Duncan the ghillie because he

222

had always had time to stop and chat to her, helping her to identify flowers, bringing back frog spawn which Aunt Carlotta threw out because she could not bear squirming things. Farquhar the piper, who had defied Aunt Carlotta by playing a specially composed reel under Laura's window to waken her. Ranald the gardener, who had given sanctuary to the tortoise her brother had brought home as a present, but which Aunt Carlotta had banished from the house.

There were frowns, for too many cords were going to the big house. Only three left. But Invernevis was determined to honour only those who had been kind to her. That was why Roddy the coachman was scowling at the fringe of the crowd.

One for the Home Farm, but not for MacPherson, who was waiting with smug satisfaction immediately below Invernevis, his hand ready. It went to his son Archie, who delivered the milk to the big house and who had let Laura ride down the avenue on the back of the cart, among the churns. Archie came forward, nervous twitch working as he passed his father.

Dr MacNiven deserved a cord because he had brought her into the world and had watched over her health, making a joke of her measles, finding a simple explanation for the involuntary bloodletting of the beginning of womanhood which Aunt Carlotta could not bring herself to acknowledge.

There was only one card left in Invernevis's fist, and all eyes were on it, MacPherson still to the fore, the coachman still hovering. His choice caused a gasp and nudging elbows, for Dougie the cobbler, who had told her stories of the little folk as he heeled her button boots, was being called up. He pushed his way through proudly, a black frock coat in lieu of his leather apron as MacPherson went red and those behind him tittered.

The cord bearers crowded into the cramped chapel, bruising shins on protruding stones, boots slithering on fresh soil as they braced for the load, wrapping the red cords round their knuckles. There was no room for Father Macdonald. He stood in the arched doorway, pronouncing a Latin blessing, a breeze through precarious stone flicking over the gilt-edged pages of his many-tongued Missal. Then he made the sign of the cross, and released the fist of earth.

The poles were slid away, the cords straining and lowering, wood wobbling, eased to keep level, dulling as it went down. Holding the head cord, Invernevis was remembering the morning – how long ago it seemed – when the scullery-maid had come down to say that his sister had taken a bad turn, and he had ordered the line to be cut, letting the big fish – perhaps the one that would defeat his father – go free. The coffin scraped as it settled on the bottom, but his cord was still tight, though the others were relinquishing theirs, red tassels bouncing on wood.

But he could not let go. The grave below his splayed legs was a cruive, like the one in *Linne Curraigh*, and the gleam of the brass plate was a salmon that had entered the trap after the long hazardous voyage, the lamprey clamped to its side upsetting navigation in the last stretch. It could not go forward or back, and because it was weak and wounded it could not be killed. The only way was to lift it out, tear away what was draining its life blood, return it to the main stream. It would never be strong again, it would never become a big leaper, getting to the high pools to spawn, but at least it could lie, protected and at peace, in *Linne Bhuidhe*, the Yellow Pool.

It was dark and cold down there, like *Casan Dubh*, and a salmon did not like shadows and stagnation for too long, because it needed aeration and the company of its own kind. The gleam was darkening as the blackness closed in, but he had to get it out, give it life and freedom again. He was tugging frantically at the cord when Alexander crossed to take it from his hand. And the gleam was gone.

Father Macdonald helped him downhill, back to the gig, away from 'The Lament for Miss Laura' that Farquhar its creator was playing as he moved slowly among the trees, amplifying the anguish of the black drones, splayed fingers in the sky. Where the coffin had rested on trestles a table had been set up to continue the custom of dispensing a dram to those good enough to come. Duncan the ghillie had been put in charge by Invernevis, and as he opened the first stone jar Irish navvies who had crossed water on the unexpected day off, but without pay, emerged from the trees where they had hung about, leaning, sucking on broken clay pipes as the little lady who had waved to them from the other side of the river was lowered. Though they were massive men in shapeless moleskins, with red handkerchiefs knotted round their bull necks, and sinews rearing from wrestling rock, the ghillie was not going to serve them, but Alexander insisted, putting

224

glasses into their fists. And the locals had to wait till they were topped up again.

Invernevis turned, saw Alexander in their midst, with his arms round their shoulders as the gig pulled away. He did not look back and was silent on the jolting journey home, merely nodding as Father Macdonald said how upset Miss Carlotta was. And even when the priest remarked on how good his aunt had been to the dead girl, he made no reply. He was carrying home a queer image of anguish, Laura's button boots drumming on the drawing-room floor at the Hogmanay dance blurring to earth drumming on her coffin.

He did not touch the funeral lunch of baked ham lanced with cloves which good manners forced him to watch Father Macdonald consuming because Aunt Carlotta was now lying upstairs behind drawn curtains, a bottle of smelling salts at her nostrils, her knees being painted with iodine by Elsie the kitchen-maid. But as soon as he had seen the priest off in his trap, he took a bottle of brandy up to his room, shed his clothes and drank himself into a sleep without dreams.

Through the wall Mama was not in the same state. Fearing another stroke, her son had wanted Laura's death withheld from her, but Dr MacNiven had backed Aunt Carlotta, insisting that she had a right to know. The expected hadn't happened. Mama had been hysterical, of course, blaming herself for being in bed. But she hadn't asked for brandy: she had asked to be left alone, lying sobbing, biting her twisted mouth in that big bleak bedroom, as she stared at spring light coming through the gap in the curtain. The circular dance floor of the Soldiers' Garden at Kamptree was being cleared with the announcement that Captain Alexander Macdonald would dance over crossed swords to the pipes. You gasped as his pumps seemed to touch sharpened steel, but rising again, unscarred, to tap hose and floor, hose and floor as he turned in a circle, dark eyes drilling you. You were fascinated by the flexing of the stripe down the side of the tight blue trousers, the delicacy of the feet despite the brutal buttocks, the heap in the groin. You had felt the same when a pipe coaxed the flat-headed snake from wicker, to sway and sway, until you could have gone forward and stroked.

How grateful to God you had been when the 91st was recalled from India in '68. It was only to Dover, but as Carlotta said, you would go to prison for molesting a child in

225

England. And when Sandy's brother had buried his doubts in *Casan Dubh* you had come to Invernevis. You did think that Carlotta would have taken a little place for herself in the south, but she had insisted on coming too. There had been a frightful row in which Sandy had put his fist through the panel of a door, but of course Carlotta knew all about the little Indian girls because she had sometimes had to provide the money.

You would have expected it to get better, but it didn't. He spent most of his time out on his horse, on the hill or up in the village, drinking and shooting with the rifle volunteer company of which he had become Colonel. And he had got gross, seventeen stone, with a black beard that reached down his chest and made his eyes even more piercing. No woman could be expected to carry that weight, and such stamina, especially when he was tight. You heard the rasp of his spurs on the stairs, and that was your afternoon nap gone. You knew it was his right and you lay back, your eyes closed, but India had aged you, and the thought of native girls put you off *that* sort of thing.

Then he started on the maids, nothing much at first but a squeal at the table while serving, and Carlotta glaring. He had his own room, of course, so you didn't know what he got up to in the night, but it was Carlotta who noticed how big the kitchen-maid was getting. She questioned her, and it all came out, so she had to be given money and sent away. He settled with the others himself because you didn't want to know, though Carlotta kept on and on, saying what a beast he was. One day you heard a scuffling on the back stairs. You thought it was the dogs fighting and went to separate them. There he was, his spurs dug into the bare board, his shoulder cracking the plaster, and the new maid on the step above, her hands pushing the walls out, and the hem of her dress between her teeth.

What could you do but forgive if you couldn't forget? You were stuck in that big eerie house, with its bad plumbing and rats, relying more and more on Carlotta because it was all getting too much for you. Niall had arrived, then Alexander, and Carlotta was such a help because you couldn't cope with two babies, and a bigger one downstairs. Oh, he had tried to make it up to you, and that was how Laura came, though you hadn't wanted any more, because of the way they were come by.

You were forty, your ankles twice what they had been, and he was even heavier, though he hadn't the same stamina. You'd noticed that, the way he went up the stairs, and thought it was his heart, but he wouldn't hear of Dr MacNiven.

He wasn't coming near you. Not that you really wanted him in *that* way. You'd just had Laura, and it had almost killed you. The poor wee mite wasn't meant to be, so no wonder that she'd turned out the way she did. Niall was such a lovely little boy, away at school, and Carlotta so fond of him, but Alexander, who was with his father most of the time, turning out a problem, very cheeky to his aunt. Of course he heard his father speaking to her, for when Sandy had wine in him he mocked her religion, which wasn't really fair. Maybe Carlotta did carry Catholicism too far, but she was so capable with the children, and strict with the servants.

Then Sandy had asked you to order a box of carbolic, though he knew that was Carlotta's department, and she complained that a cake wasn't lasting him two days. One evening at dinner you let your knife go, noticing the backs of his hands, but you didn't dare say to Carlotta. You took your coffee for the first time with him in the library and he told you it was something he'd picked up in India. Immediately the lepers squatting by the roadside sprang to mind, and you could have screamed, but it wasn't that, he said. Probably some sort of insect from the swamps. He took trays in the library for a time, but you couldn't conceal it from Carlotta, and she swore she was out of the door if he didn't get upstairs, and stay.

What could you do, with Laura to be looked after? Niall was now in the army, against his wishes, and as for Alexander, he was at the Home Farm most of the time, coming home at all hours smelling of drink, Carlotta said, though his father wouldn't hear a word against him. And Sandy: he turned his swivel chair round and sat for hours staring into the fire, leaving his boots off, the ghost of the man you'd seen dancing over crossed steel at Kamptree. You were frightened he'd go the same way as his brother, and managed to get him upstairs.

You were so tired in the evening, having helped to turn and sponge him behind muslin, that you started taking a toddy. God knows, you needed it, because Carlotta had gone against his orders and put an organ in the drawing-room, playing it at all hours, and such mournful music. But Sandy couldn't

227

see his way downstairs. And he wanted the Jubilee clock, which took the last of your own money, stopped, but Carlotta dared. You couldn't quarrel with her because she was looking after Laura, trying to teach her something. Oh yes, they would be saying that you had neglected Laura, but they could never be told the *real* reason because just before Sandy had died, Dr MacNiven had said the word. You didn't even want it explained, just doubled your toddy.

You felt so guilty, having left it all to Carlotta, who was so capable and clever, but inclined to use her hands a bit much. Not that the girl hadn't been difficult, you quite appreciated, going down to the river and crossing Wade's Bridge when the Irishmen were about. And the way she set the dogs off, running through the house, when you were trying to sleep. Oh, they would have plenty to say in the village, but did they ever stop to think what would have become of the girl when you and Carlotta were gone? Because Niall couldn't cope. He was so patient with her, but he didn't know the ways of women, and especially one not quite right. That sounded so cruel, but as Carlotta said, you had to face up to the truth. So maybe it was for the best, a warning that you would have to try and make it up to Carlotta and Niall, be more of a help.

When she heard the cart going away over gravel, she thought she was going to need brandy, but she held on, even though someone was screaming. She hadn't had a drink since the day it had happened, and really, it was wonderful how she was managing. She would have a good sleep, a warm bath and get into fresh clothes, black they would always have to be, it seemed. Then she would go down and help, get up to the village to show them. Carlotta certainly needed a holiday, she thought as the swords of sunlight crossed.

Along the passage Miss Carlotta was gritting her teeth as Elsie applied more iodine to her bleeding knees. Now that the coffin had gone she felt better, but wouldn't be going down again that day. Mrs Livingstone had wanted to send for Dr MacNiven, but it wasn't the doctor she needed; it was Father Macdonald, if she had been able to receive him, to hear him confirm that she had done her best by the girl, trying to help her get by in a hard world. She had been wilful, whatever Niall said, and as God was her witness, there had been no blow struck. It was God's hand, because, as Dr Mac-

228

Niven had told Niall, the girl had been damaged at birth. Didn't you put a wasp out of its misery when you found it, weakly trying to ascend glass in the autumn, at its short span's end? It was the fault of that beast who had impregnated Constance when she was too old, and he knew he was diseased from the Indian girls, she thought, more iodine making her moan.

The girl was gone, and prayers were better than regrets. Perhaps now was the time to embark on her great scheme, the one the brute had denied her. Though the war had made her gold shares slump, they would rise again when the Boer was beaten, and there were other investments to liquidate. Father Macdonald agreed: pamphlets on temperance were all very well, but most of the people in the village couldn't read. They needed something more substantial to keep them on the true path. Time, therefore, to tear down the wooden chapel by the ferry and put up one in stone, in the meadow across the Summer House Pool. With a proper altar, and all the images. A chapel there would heighten the outrage of Alexander and his harlot upstream. It was one of the fields of the Home Farm, but the trustees would take it off MacPherson. Her nephew would most likely oppose, but a stained-glass window could be put in for the dead girl, who hadn't, after all said and done, had much of a chance with such a father. Because (and this was something – one of the very few things – she could not tell Father Macdonald) the brute had tried to molest her too, in India, and it was almost rape. But a chapel would help her soul also, and if Niall showed more strength as laird, he would get what money there was left. But what a comfort Elsie was, though a little too liberal with the iodine.

When the whisky for the funeral had been exhausted, Alexander accompanied the Irishmen to the village, to continue the wake in the Arms. His elbows on the counter, he put up glass after glass and shared their clay pipes as they described how they had met the 'little ledy' several times at Wade's Bridge, when they were 'lookin' at, but no' goin' after salmon, ye understand', and once they had sat on the parapet, clapping as a mouth-organ urged on her dancing boots in the dust. 'Aye, a better jig was never seen in Tipperary,' one sighed, whisky gurgling.

As the day went to darkness Alexander's lantern saw the Irishmen safely aboard the ferry. Instead of taking the track ahead, he turned left, lurching against trees, scrambling up the slope to the chapel. Stone supported his shoulder in the silence interrupted by scornful owls as he contemplated the wreaths smothering the freshly heaped soil. He left the lantern on the grave, its hot glass shrivelling petals, and made his way by occasional moonlight to the Home Farm, barging into bushes, causing rusted wire to clang. Once opposite the big house, all its windows black, he stopped, drew breath and, hands cupped round his mouth, swayed in the dust, shouting: 'Carlotta, you bloody murderer!' But the black mountain above sent back his slurred shouts, distorted, and when he climbed to the Home Farm kitchen, discovered that he had wakened the baby.

Still in the scullery, though there were no dinner dishes, Maggie was stooping to the swill bin, exhuming the snowdrops that the house-maid had tossed in, having found them on the drawing-room floor. The sweet face she'd seen by candlelight that morning was now shut away, underground. Maggie could imagine what it must be like. But she wished she was with Laura because putting in the snowdrops had only made it worse with Miss Carlotta. What a noise she'd made when the coffin had moved away, but Mrs Livingstone had said to the butler that it was only for show.

She was arranging the snowdrops in a cracked cup between the brass taps, where the Master's picture usually stood, when she heard the shouting across the river increasing to a roaring. It sounded like the Home Farm bull, but was probably a drunk Irishman who had missed the last ferry, she decided as she lifted the saucer with the candle, the snowdrops retreating into darkness.

Chapter Fourteen

Invernevis drove himself to the village in the gig on his first day out after Laura's burial, the hands holding the reins still shaky after three days' drinking in which he had shut himself in his room, refusing the trays that Mrs Livingstone had had sent up, at least on the first day, and leaving the razor in its leather case. When he had tilted water from the pitcher, it was to drink it. But though it was pleasant to lie there, Laura resurrected behind drawn blinds, running and wading, letting the tears come when they wanted, it had to stop, before it got a grip, like the woman through the wall. Apart from giving Aunt Carlotta ammunition, it would get to the village.

The world was a different place, bare and grim, the light gone from the sky. He could not believe that she had come barefoot through sunlight on that avenue, a dark silent sepulchre amplifying the iron-shod wheels beneath, the spokes shedding shadows. Something irreplaceable was gone, like the Venetian glass he had dropped on stone as a boy, his father lashing with leather to re-enforce the loss. Life was finished for him, and he wasn't yet thirty. If his father's disease had tainted his blood, there wasn't much point in worrying about an heir. Which meant that getting Alexander to agree to dis-inheritance had been futile.

He was taking the problem to Dr MacNiven, driving between thorn hedges where small birds were building, bring-ing the tiny twigs in their beaks, and yet the boys from the village would rob their nests. At least Alexander had a daughter.

He hid his hands under the desk as Dr MacNiven listened in silence, but only to dismiss his outpourings as strain follow-ing bereavement. Yes, it appeared that his father had had syphilis, but the doctor could assure the son that that hadn't been the cause of his sister's death. And he could say with equal confidence that the disease wouldn't be in the sons' blood, for transmission to future generations.

At which point Dr MacNiven rose and turned to the window, putting his hands under his tail-coat. 'You know,

231

your father had a remedy when things got too much at the big house. He went away to Edinburgh and had a damned good time. I'd advise you to do the same.' When he turned, Invernevis saw that he was smiling.

It wouldn't entirely be escape, he told himself. He could get rods, guns and tweed suits, thus allowing him to get out of doors, away from morbid thoughts and Aunt Carlotta's harrying. And he might make friends he could invite to Invernevis, to break his sense of isolation in a house with two elderly women, both difficult. Who knew but marriage might come out of it? For Dr MacNiven's denial of contamination was a tremendous relief. Before he went home he telegraphed his Edinburgh club.

Aunt Carlotta was up and about again, and when he told her of his trip, he was surprised by her approval. She seemed different, as if Laura's death had subdued her.

'It'll give me a chance to have the spring cleaning done properly. And I'm going to put your mother in Laura's room. It'll be more convenient for me, to keep an eye on her, now that she's threatening to come downstairs and get in everyone's way. God forgive me, but sometimes I feel she should just be allowed to drink herself to death. But I'll struggle on.'

The first-class compartment to himself was a necessary extravagance, allowing him to ease his game leg. When Invernevis was out of sight he settled back, uninterested in the unrolling mountains and moors, monotonous miles and miles of bleak drizzle, the only occupants hoodie crows and stags, so different from the beautiful animals of the Great Karroo. When he began to feel hungry there was the wicker hamper prepared by Mrs Livingstone, the cold game washed down with brandy from a silver hip-flask, regimental present on his forced retiral. When the bones were picked clean they were carefully wrapped in the linen napkin. A cigar completed the mobile feast, smoke swirling against rain-streaked glass as he stared, contemplating. A twisted tree threw up its bare arms and was gone, backwards.

Maybe he had misjudged his father. It couldn't have been easy, living with Aunt Carlotta's thin critical lips and that mournful organ, morning and evening. Of course that didn't excuse the molestation of the maids, the sordidness of his Indian sojourn. What *had* his father been searching for with all these women, so much lower in society, some of them

232

prostitutes, it seemed? Surely not simply physical satisfaction, because there had to be more than that to a man. Perhaps it was because he did not fit in, because there was no fixed place for him in life. Oh, he had got the estate, but that had come late, through tragedy. He could appreciate why his father had broken the strict social bonds imposed by Victoria's melancholy reign after she had lost her consort, with Mama aping the monarch's mourning style in clothes and furnishings. His father was like himself: they had both seen the world beyond Invernevis, in India and South Africa. But his father had paid a terrible price for the freedom he took. Maybe it was worth it, a few years of reckless freedom.

And a fantasy became intention in his mind. He would pick up a woman in Edinburgh, have a good time, but return to sleep at his club. It would be so discreetly done that Aunt Carlotta would never come to hear, and even if she did, what would that matter? It was his life; he was the laird. Oh yes, he was of the faith of his ancestors, but Catholicism was like devils on horseback, one of Mrs Livingstone's favourite savouries: if you were full of other things, you could leave it. And maybe after he had had a woman, he would understand his father and Alexander better.

As the clattering wheels hurried him south, he nodded into sleep, dreaming. He was casting over *Casan Dubh*, with Duncan the ghillie in attendance. The line suddenly tightened and he thought the hook with the writhing worms had snagged on dead wood at the bottom, but it was on the move, making his reel hysterical. The ghillie was yelling: 'Cut the line! For Christ's sake cut the line!' But he could not. The need to know the nature of the brute struggling so fiercely down in the black depths was too powerful. He grew so impatient with giving line that he began to reel in, chancing the breaking strain of the buckled green-heart. But when it came swirling to the surface he saw to his horror that he had hooked a giant pike, its grinning jaws gaping to show that the hook was in its guts, its beady eyes on him, daring him to land it.

The engine goring the bumpers of Edinburgh thankfully jolted him to consciousness before he could put a name to the face. Immediately he entered into the excitement of a temporary transfer from rural peace to urban bustle. A porter had to be hailed to carry his cases to the queue waiting to hire hansom cabs. In these arrangements Invernevis was in

233

competition with dozens of fellow travellers, but his Inverness cape and game leg soon brought porterage, and the first cab.

It was only a short way along Princes Street to his club, but the thoroughfare was crowded with horses hauling cabs to hotels and villas at the end of the day's business. Trams clanged, open tops packed, black-hatted travellers hemmed in by advertising boards. The pavements were crowded as the shops closed, awnings pushed back by long poles, women with hidden ankles waiting to cross on the arms of swallow-tailed escorts, with the wink of gold at waistcoat, pointed shoes peeping where stripes ended, the cane with its gold skull.

He noted all these details as his hansom swayed along because life was taking on a new interest, with all the activity of Princes Street. Some of these faces sweeping by, left at the kerb, frowning, had known sadness as he had, no matter the cut of the clothes. What was in that parcel under the man's arm, and what kind of face behind the veil hanging from the hat? And that dog darting under the wheels: would it get to the other side?

He looked left, saw the match seller slumped against the rail, the placard on his chest imploring custom because of his infirmity. And where the gardens sloped, Sir Walter Scott sat under his massive stone pinnacle, open book on his knee, deer-hound by his side, looking out with sad, almost pained eyes.

At the club he relinquished cases and cape and climbed to the smoke-room, a huge apartment with a high ornate ceiling, gas jets hissing between gloomy oils of stag and huntsman, leather sofas and chairs angled among circular tables. The fire banked high between marble columns in the form of nymphs hoisting the mantelpiece seemed incapable of heating such a space, and yet figures were sprawled, immobile in sleep, in the dim far corners.

It was like entering a house of the dead. Hide sighed as Invernevis settled, easing his game leg, ordering a large brandy. It came to him in a huge balloon, gliding to a halt by his right hand as if no human hand supported the salver.

He swirled the balloon between two fingers, mixing the brandy with the mellow light coming through the long windows above Princes Street, where hooves hurried wheels, and a vendor cried the latest on De Wet. This was the club his father had prized so much, as a place of refuge from the

234

brooding isolation, the predominantly spinsterish society of Invernevis, with Aunt Carlotta, that champion of temperance, presiding. Rumour eventually reaching Invernevis hinted that his father had done some hard drinking in the club, but his son could not see the scope for opportunity. Where the wide sofa welcomed by the fire frail hands failed to keep *The Scotsman* steady at the stock-market page, and under a gas mantle, a magnifying glass scanned *Blackwood's Magazine*. A teacup touched down silently on a saucer; two elderly gentlemen in wing collars, one with a shining ascent of skull, brooded over a chess board while, two chairs away, a kilted figure with spreadeagled brogues snored.

The match scraping for Invernevis's cigar turned heads, and the skull inclined to the queen furrowed. It was too quiet, a club for old men where, he suspected, ebullience through drink would bring suspension. It must have changed a great deal since his father's time, reverting to Victorian principles of sober order, or else the stories of his excesses had been damned lies, started by Aunt Carlotta. Or perhaps it was the wrong time of day. Perhaps it grew lively after dinner, when members became flushed with wine and brandy after a trying day in the Court of Session, or wandering arrows in the butts up at Archers' Hall. Just now it was a bitter disappointment, after the teeming life of Princes Street. The silence and dark corners made him think of the Invernevis drawing-room with its menacing organ. He smiled to imagine the confusion that Laura would cause were she suddenly to burst in, throwing the doors wide, looking around with excited anticipation, the black button boots doing their skipping circuits, leading the yapping dogs round and round.

Where its reader had fallen asleep he retrieved *The Scotsman*, turned to the entertainment advertisements.

OPERA HOUSE

CHAMBERS STREET

BESIEGED

EDISON'S ANIMATED PICTURES

THE ACKNOWLEDGED PREMIER ANIMATED PICTURE

EXHIBITION IN SCOTLAND

A SENSATIONAL AND UP-TO-DATE SERIES OF VIEWS

OF THE

235

BOER AND CHINA WARS
INCLUDING THE LATEST PICTURES FROM THE FRONT
(ACTUALLY TAKEN UNDER FIRE)
GENERAL FRENCH'S MOUNTED INFANTRY
CHASING DE WET
THE FUNERAL PROCESSIONS OF THE LATE
QUEEN VICTORIA

Or he could go and see *The Belle of New York* at the Theatre Royal. It sounded interesting, but he wouldn't go alone. He turned to the stocks page, saw that Consolidated Goldfields were down, which would put Aunt Carlotta into a bad mood.

He went in to dinner as soon as it was called, having definitely decided to go out and enjoy himself, to release the tensions that isolation, Aunt Carlotta and bereavement had caused. Dr MacNiven had given his blessing, hadn't he? Part of the satisfaction was in not knowing where he would go, but the porter was bound to know places, and would be discreet. Then a sudden thought stopped his soup spoon. That porter had also served his father; thank God he had remembered in time. It wasn't only the embarrassment of like father, like son; he didn't want any of his father's addresses because they were bound to be the lowest dives in the city, Leith docks probably, and no doubt he had left disease as well as sovereigns. But his heir now wished that he had accompanied his fellow officers on their hedonistic forays beyond gaslight when Princess Louise's Highlanders were garrisoning Edinburgh about eight years before. They had thought he was keeping to the mess because he was a new recruit, but the reason was that his father was still on his feet then, and he was frightened of meeting him. The thought that they might have shared the same woman brought sweat to his brow.

Not that he hadn't desired. Every healthy man did, though his boyhood had been made miserable by Aunt Carlotta's assurance that those who availed themselves of the pleasures of the body went to hell, and once, when the laundry maid had complained about Alexander's sheets, Aunt Carlotta had threatened to bind his hands to the bed posts, though he said it hadn't been intentional. But when Alexander had gone crying to their father, the burly man had roared with laughter, telling a baffled boy that Aunt Carlotta was only jealous.

There had been plenty of opportunities during his army service, but more than lack of confidence had held him back. He couldn't really explain it to himself, but when he thought of women, Laura always came into his mind, laughing, shaking her ringlets. Now death had darkened her, bringing the realization that he was nearing thirty, and alone in his narrow life. He was bound to get tight that night, and it wasn't a drawing-room he was looking for.

To fortify himself for the pleasures to come, he had a bottle of full-bodied claret with his game pie, and would follow that up with a brandy and cigar in the smoke-room before going out into the adventurous night, to walk until he had made contact, then life could take its course. For if you didn't sin, there was no need of Aunt Carlotta's call for repentance.

The alcohol was through his system, spreading its benevolent warmth, and his cigar down to an inch when he was hailed across the smoke-room. In the confusion of bringing his mind back to the present, he struggled to his feet, having recognized Jamie Mackay coming towards him in the poor light. Invernevis's hand was extended in delighted recognition when he noticed the Captain's right sleeve pinned across his chest. He could only spread his hands helplessly and groan.

But Jamie made it easier by clapping his other hand on his friend's shoulder. 'Well, well, this *is* a surprise.'

'But your arm – ' Invernevis said, not meaning to stare.

'I copped it soon after you, at Paardeberg, and I've been telling everybody that General Cronje himself did it, so don't you go letting me down.'

'I heard when I was out there in hospital that you'd been wounded, and that you'd got the DSO, but I didn't think it was *this* bad,' Invernevis said, having to sit.

Jamie took the opposite chair, rearranging his empty sleeve. 'Oh, I can't complain, considering what some of the poor devils got. But *you*: how's the leg?'

'I manage. I've learnt quite a few tricks.'

'You staying here?'

'Yes. And you?'

'No, I'm only in for a committee meeting. When they heard I was home, they co-opted me. It gives me an excuse to get away. Election of new members. We've been talking since lunch.' He was putting a cigarette into his mouth, holding the box between his knees as he struck the match.

'So who have we got?'

'Someone from your part of the world,' Jamie said, shaking the match out. 'Campbell of Branglin.'

'You didn't let *him* in,' Invernevis said, horrified.

'I voted for him.'

'But he's got no breeding,' Invernevis protested, remembering how the goggle-eyed brute at the tiller of the motor car had halted Laura's funeral, the first insult being Campbell's sneaky attempt to get the Disputed Pool off drink-befuddled Mama at the beginning of the war. 'He styles himself of Branglin, as if they've been there for centuries, but he only bought the place about twenty years ago, with East Indies money that came from slave plantations. You should see the monstrosity of the house he keeps adding to.'

'It's a new age, Niall,' Jamie warned. 'Edward's supposed to spell enlightenment, after his moth-eaten mother. Money buys position; it also pays for improvements.' He looked around. 'This place needs brightening up, and Campbell's promised to stand the cost of electric light, so it would have been silly not to let him in. Or would you prefer to pay double the subscription?'

'No, the gas lighting's good enough for me,' Invernevis said scrutinizing his friend's face to see if he really was being serious. 'It's the thought of a vulgar man like that coming in here, throwing his weight about, disturbing the peace, just because he's got money. He's a common trader who bought himself an estate and built a mansion. And do you know what will happen? In a generation or so everyone will think the Campbells of Branglin are an aristocratic family who've been there for generations.'

'Well, he's in, so you just have to accept it,' Jamie said firmly. 'How long are you staying?'

'About a week. I had to get away, it's been such an awful time. My sister died, you see.'

'I *am* sorry. And you were always promising to invite me to Invernevis, to meet her.'

'It was the way our leaves didn't match,' Invernevis said wistfully. 'So there's only my mother and my aunt left.'

'I wish I could say that I'd fled from female company, but my mother and sister are with me this time, in the hotel

238

across the road. It's the shops that make them brave the journey.'

'And they're both well?'

'My sister still isn't very strong, but I feel this visit's done her good. Sutherland's such a depressing place. They'd love to meet you, if you care to come across for an hour. But I can't promise that mother won't make you take a hand of cards. The only difference between us is that she doesn't play for money.'

'I'd be delighted,' Invernevis murmured. He could go out on the town later.

They crossed Princes Street and walked along the gardens to the big hotel, Invernevis wrapped in his Inverness cape against the evening chill. Jamie was wearing a big slouched felt hat, with a hole through the crown.

'Genuine Boer,' he explained. 'I picked it up at Paardeberg just before I was wounded. It brought me luck.'

'Luck? With that arm?'

'Yes, because I could have quite easily got a bullet through the head, like the poor fellow who was wearing it before me. Anyway, let's talk about *you*. You're running the place now, I presume.'

'Not very successfully, I'm afraid, but I'm hoping my brother will keep a watch on the farms. And yourself?'

'Father's been bedridden for the last two years – doesn't recognize us now – so I've more or less taken over. But I'm like you, I'm only learning. Still, I can write with my left hand now, so I *can* sign away the family money, and I do get about. I've had to learn the art of fishing all over again, trout, not salmon, because a big rod's too heavy. No, the only things that I miss are not being able to shoot or play billiards. But what the hell. I suppose one's lucky to be alive.' He sighed, the tip of his stick rattling along the railings. 'Do you remember the nights we had, when we were garrisoned here? Whisky, women, Gaelic songs. I never told you before, but I lost a thousand at cards one night and had to get my father to bale me out. I almost shot myself, but now it doesn't seem very important, the folly of youth. So long ago. Don't you feel that war's made you old?'

Invernevis stopped. 'Extraordinary, but I was just thinking the same before I met you tonight.'

239

'After you shoot a man, it's never the same again,' Jamie continued, walking again. 'And women. Strange, the way the Boer women follow their menfolk into the thick of battle as if duty comes before death. At Paardeberg Cronje was sitting in the Modder, holding his wife's hand while the bullets were whizzing. It made me laugh till I saw how obscene it was. It puts one off women. I mean, you think of them as being reasonably clean, sitting in a room or lying on a bed, waiting for you, not squatting in rags in a river in the middle of a battle.'

Invernevis wondered if his friend was trying to tell him something. Oh yes, Jamie had always left the mess with the other officers in search of women, in Dublin and Edinburgh, but no one had ever seen him with one; and there had been talk about a handsome young private he had claimed as his orderly. There was something about his looks, that too clear skin and sandy hair, that hinted. And he remembered the way his friend had watched the naked soldiers bathing in the Modder. Invernevis didn't feel revulsion, he knew such things frequently happened in regiments, but it saddened him that his friend had chosen such a dangerous path, and he the heir to a baronetcy. Look what had happened to Wilde, whom Aunt Carlotta never tired of citing as the classic example of the pervert, coupling him with her late brother-in-law.

Jamie led the way through the swing door and across the wide expanse of discreet carpeting, on whose borders obsequious porters waited. The Boer hat was handed, or rather tossed, to one of them, and having been helped from his Inverness cape, Invernevis followed through columns, speckled stone indistinguishable from marble in the dimness. The room they arrived at through double doors was bigger than the club smoke-room, but even quieter.

From the centre of the embellished ceiling chains let down a cluster of muted crystal fire for the card players sitting at half a dozen baize tables, an island in the centre surrounded by sofas and arm-chairs arranged in groups round the walls. A pair of massive gilt mirrors flanked the marble fireplace, where coal blazed.

Invernevis was affected by the stifling atmosphere as soon as he crossed the threshold, keeping his game leg clear of furniture so as not to disturb play as he followed Jamie to his mother's table. Even before he reached her, he recognized the

240

similarity of features, the long thin face, the same light hair. But age had been cruel to her. The concentrated face above the splayed cards was so heavily wrinkled that he immediately thought of a tortoise, a comparison reinforced by the way her thin neck of fluted bone poked from the frilled silk blouse, a crocheted shawl round her humped back. But it was the hands that fascinated him. As they held up the cards for consideration they seemed like jewelled claws under the chandelier.

She was playing with her daughter, who was sitting opposite, her back to Invernevis, so that as he followed Jamie forward he was only aware of a red head inclined on cream silk. But what hair. The same colour as Laura's, but spun in such quantities from a finer gold, piled on the head, wave upon wave, that it seemed the slender white neck was not capable of bearing such weight and glory. And, with her profile wheeling into sight as they approached the table, Invernevis stopped, knowing that this was the woman he was going to marry, an intuition that might have been transmitted to Jamie, for he turned to see if his friend was following.

Lady Mackay held up a hand to warn that there was to be no talk till the game was finished, so they stood there, looking down on the splayed cards, Jamie at his mother's shoulder, Invernevis at the sister's. Lady Mackay's lips were pursed as she studied, then plucked, the cameo holding her blouse closed at the scraggy throat moving with her breathing, as if her life depended on that game.

And now it was the daughter's turn to deal, the Joker set aside, shuffling the cards in long thin hands unadorned with rings, that looked to Invernevis as if they were made of light. Moving slightly, he saw a slightly upturned nose, a brow that swept without flaw up into the heaped gold, curling at the temples. She glanced up, smiled, and extracting a card, gave the game to her mother.

Which meant that introductions could now be made by Jamie, with a withdrawal to sofa and arm-chairs near the fire, Lady Mackay refusing the offer of her son's one arm in a surprisingly harsh voice, saying that she wasn't 'over the hill yet, thank you'.

'So you were at Magersfontein,' she said when she was settled, fixing her watery, almost wild eyes on Invernevis.

'I should explain that Mother's been cutting all the war

maps out of the papers and pasting them in a scrap-book,'
Jamie said. 'She's really a frustrated general.'

'I want to know what's going on,' she snapped. 'A week
after I was married, my husband went out to the Crimea, and
I didn't see him for two years. Naturally I want to know.
Now, Magersfontein: what *was* it like? I've asked Jamie, but
he's no use.'

She obviously had to have an answer, yet Invernevis was
hesitant. To tell its full horrors might shock and make him
out to be a hero. On the other hand, to play it down might
make him sound insensitive.

'It was pretty bad,' he began, his eyes on the sister. 'We
thought they'd be on the hill, not below it, so they took us by
surprise. There was a lot of confusion in the darkness.'

'Typical of the Boers,' she said contemptuously, her mouth
still working after her words were finished. 'Of course, one
never expected *them* to observe the rules of war.'

'Hang it, Mother, there aren't *any* rules, out there,' Jamie
said. 'The might of the Empire against a few thousand Boers.'

When he realized that Jamie was serious, Invernevis was
shocked. It was obviously an old argument between them, and
he didn't want to get caught in the middle.

'Cowards, you mean,' Lady Mackay said. 'They fire from
behind rocks, but as soon as they see a bayonet they jump
on their horses and take off.'

'If that's the case, why isn't the war over?' Jamie persisted,
more irritated.

'It will be, very soon,' his mother promised. 'They've had
to take to the hills.'

'But we can't catch them, can we? Look at the way General
De Wet's making a fool of Kitchener.'

'Lord Kitchener's a very great leader,' she sniffed.

'A very *cruel* leader,' her son corrected her. 'Devastating
farms and setting up concentration camps for women and
children. Now *that's* not observing the rules of war.' He shook
his head sadly. 'No, Mother, you've swallowed all the lies
the papers print. The Boers aren't savages. They don't murder
our soldiers when they take them prisoner. They're a simple,
God-fearing people, who only want to live in peace, in their
own land, only we won't let them because we're after their
gold and diamonds. Because that's what the war's really about,
no matter what the papers say.'

'There speaks a supporter of Lloyd George,' Lady Mackay informed Invernevis.

He didn't know what to make of Jamie's arguments, but they certainly were a reversal of the ones he had used before the Modder and Magersfontein. It was quite clear that it wasn't simply a case of provoking his mother; his eyes were luminous with conviction, his speech fast. Lady Mackay sounded a replica of Aunt Carlotta, but her daughter sat and said nothing, staring down at the silver bangle shackling her wrist, as though she was embarrassed by both of them.

Lady Mackay and Jamie were waiting for Invernevis to say something, and to deflect the expectant eyes he began speaking before he had thought out what he was going to say.

'I think you're wrong about Kitchener, Jamie. He has a very difficult job to do, in a very difficult country, which the Boers know like the back of their hand.'

'He's a fool,' Jamie said bitterly. 'All our leaders in South Africa are fools. Buller's a buffoon, and look at Methuen. He led the Highland Brigade into slaughter at the Modder because he hadn't even bothered to get proper maps made. Apart from not knowing there were two rivers there, he didn't even know which way they flowed. And as for Roberts, he didn't even know the strength of the enemy. The same thing happened at Magersfontein. Methuen didn't know the projection of the line of Boer trenches, and there wasn't any surprise in the attack. He made damn sure of that on the Sunday, by shelling the hill with all we had, but the only thing he hit was rock. And after the battle, he had the damned cheek to say that the Highland Brigade had stampeded and lost him the battle. I'll never forget that speech of his the day after. I wouldn't have been surprised if one of our men had shot him. No, the whole war's been bungled, from beginning to end. The sooner we pull out and leave the Boers alone, the better.'

How could Jamie defend the Boers, after what they had done to his arm at Paardeberg? Was he tight, Invernevis wondered, or trying to justify the loss of his arm by blaming it on the British? It was better to let the subject lapse, for Lady Mackay looked furious, and her daughter, who had not said a word, was fidgeting.

But Lady Mackay wasn't finished. 'My son intends to stand for parliament. As a Liberal. You are his friend; perhaps *you* can dissuade him. It's money we can't afford, and the estate's been very neglected with my husband's illness.'

'Look, Mother, we've had this out before,' Jamie said wearily. 'I've already made up my mind. I'll get a good factor.'

'Is there a chance of getting in?' Invernevis asked, but it was a mistake, for it allowed Lady Mackay to draw herself up and say majestically:

'Oh yes, there's a good chance of him getting in, provided he's prepared to follow that Welsh devil, which he apparently is. And if they get a majority they'll give the Boers everything they asked for, and the Cape as well, I shouldn't wonder.' She glared at her son.

Invernevis saw it was time to change the subject, so he asked the daughter how she was enjoying her Edinburgh visit.

She blushed as she said, 'Very much, thank you,' in a small voice, and Lady Mackay said: 'You won't get much out of her, but she takes it all in. Now tell me about yourself. I heard about your father's death.'

Invernevis looked to see if there were any implications behind the words, but the face was still set severely as she continued: 'Are you married yet?'

He had to admit that he wasn't, and that there were no prospects.

'Well, I've been giving Jamie a row about that,' she said. 'It's very important to keep the continuity of a family, especially if there's a title involved. I don't mind being the dowager, but Jamie just isn't bothering.'

'He will, in time,' Invernevis assured her, and received a pleading look from the subject.

'Time goes quicker as you get older,' she said with a sigh. And, leaning towards him, the cameo moving: 'We rely on you young men to keep our estates going. If it's not going to go on, what's the use in struggling? So you two better start looking for wives.'

Invernevis did not know if that was a hint, for as she was lecturing Lady Mackay was looking at her daughter. He looked too, but out of the corner of his eye. She sat there, shoulders hunched, blushing, as if expecting her mother's attack to be turned on her at any moment. Their eyes met momentarily, and he wanted to believe that he saw some interest in them, but her head went down again, back to the silver bangle. She really was beautiful, very like Laura in looks and build, but if there was to be any chance of making her acquaintance beyond polite conversation, her mother would have to be out of the company.

Creaking joints warned that Lady Mackay was beginning the long ascent to bed. Invernevis was trying to think of something to say, to detain her, though it would be bad manners. Too late: she was on her feet, staggering slightly, clutching her box of cards.

'Come now, girl, late nights don't do for you.' And, as she turned to Invernevis, offered her hand to show that he should retreat first: 'Well, it's very pleasant meeting someone one has heard so much about, though if you *are* the friend Jamie says you are, you'll put him off this silly parliament business.'

He took the daughter's small hand, surprised by its coldness in that stifling room, feeling the sweat on the palm. 'I hope we meet again,' he said in general, but it was meant for her.

Jamie saw to the collection of Invernevis's cape, and waited while the porter helped his arms through.

'Sorry about that argument over the war, but Mother only wants to see things *her* way. I think she expected me to come home with the VC.' He laughed, but Invernevis could see that it was no joke. And spontaneously: 'Look, why don't you come and dine with us tomorrow night? I promise you, there'll be no more talk of war and politics – at least from me. And maybe Mary Rose will have more to say.'

It was a godsend, but Invernevis did not want to show him. 'I'd be delighted, the club's so lonely. At what time?'

'Let's make it eight. I'll meet you here and we can sneak a drink before. Mother's dead against it. And another thing: smoking. She says it gets up her nose. Better put on evening clothes to show we've not gone to the dogs, eh?'

He was so dazed he went the wrong way round in the swing door, jarring his game leg. He did not see or hear the horse as he stepped off the Princes Street pavement, and as its head was jerked back, wheels grinding, the driver shouted swears. Thank God he had stayed in the club smoke-room to finish his cigar before going out to look for a woman. So near. He passed the dim windows of latest fashions, glanced up at the garrison silhouetted on rock. His breath clouded, but the evening's encounter generated warmth, put briskness into his dragging stride. A couple came towards him, their faces blue-tinged in the electric light, the woman's laughter made visible, her hands buried in a muff. The man who was holding her arm had a tall hat pushed back. He bent, whispering, and her mouth burst again. Though he did not know its substance, Invernevis shared their happiness as he passed. Oh, it was good to be alive. He raised his eyes to the columns on the Calton Hill, saw at the same time the scaffold-girded structure of the new railway hotel. So beautiful, so young, so like Laura. But wasn't the discrepancy of age a problem? And that damned leg. Still, Jamie being a soldier helped. Thank goodness he had brought his evening clothes with him, due to Aunt Carlotta insisting on formality, even away from Invernevis. But with the mother and brother to be present the next night, there wouldn't be a chance to talk, say what he *really* felt. Ask her to Invernevis? No, that wasn't done, unless Jamie brought her, and even then there was Aunt Carlotta to contend with. Now *there* was the crux of the problem he should have solved as soon as he came back from South Africa. If he had, things would have turned out very different with Laura. But this time he wasn't going to allow Aunt Carlotta to destroy. And if she complained, as she was bound to do, she would have to be told, simply, to take herself off, though he suspected that Laura's death had subdued her. Because if this was love, being in harmony with the night where stone reared to the stars, feeling years younger, with a lighter step, the air sharp as a water-ice, he wanted more of it.

Jamie was right: the club bedrooms were disgusting. The place needed sprucing up, so Campbell of Branglin could foot the bill. As he unbuttoned his shirt he kept repeating: 'Mary Rose, Mary Rose.' What a beautiful name. What a beautiful night. He would leave the window open, so that the sounds of the dawn traffic would waken him.

By eight-thirty the next morning he had a pair of kippers picked clean, and as the city clocks struck nine, was going under the Georgian fanlight of his lawyers' Charlotte Square offices. Richardson, a neat little man in starched collar and striped trousers, enquired after Miss Carlotta's health before making him comfortable on the other side of the big desk. The lawyer assured him that the disinheritance of Alexander was the wisest course. But there would have to be a trustees' meeting soon, to get certain things straightened out, Miss Carlotta having written with 'proposals' endorsed by Father Macdonald. As for Colonel Hooker, he seemed to have disappeared from the scene. Invernevis would have to watch his spending, because he hadn't much personal money. The third war budget had added another twopence to the income tax, and another, cheaper War Loan had had to be issued which patriotism had forced the trustees to take up.

He had come to Edinburgh to get rods, guns and tweed suits made, but they didn't seem to matter now. He would use his father's sporting gear, though it wasn't well balanced. But he did spend five guineas on a hundred fine Havanas. Jamie appreciated a good cigar, and that was always an aid to intimate conversation, if he could get him alone. As he limped along Princes Street to his club, he gave to hawkers without taking their goods. The sun encouraged the gardens; horses stood snorting; good-looking women swept into stores. A boy in boots trundled a hoop, almost knocking him down. How Laura would have loved staring into the windows and slipping sugar to the horses. It would be a wonderful evening, and he would try and make her laugh, but not too much, in case she thought he wasn't serious. Should he buy her flowers, from the woman with the basket? No, it wasn't time.

He lunched at his club but refused wine, wanting to keep his head clear, and there was no brandy with his cigar in the smoke-room. It was even deader than the previous evening, with only two members, each sleeping off the bilious remains of game pie. But the peace suited him, let him stock up on energy for the evening to come.

He was dozing in his chair when the telegram arrived on silver, and still dazed with sleep when he opened it.

COME HOME IMMEDIATELY. TROUBLE. CARLOTTA.

Nothing else, and only an hour to the only train that day. It *had* to be something serious, since she wouldn't have spent money otherwise. Probably to do with Alexander. By the time a reply was received to a telegram to Invernevis, demanding clarification, the train would have gone.

He was the laird, and his responsibilities lay in the north. The notepaper in the rack was all black-bordered, for Queen Victoria, as he sat at stained leather, dipping the basic nib.

My Dear Jamie,
Apologies for the paper. Dreadfully sorry I can't take up

247

yr kind invitation tonight as I've been summoned home *urgently*. Sounds serious. Apologies and kindest regards to mother and sister. Will be in touch.

He had signed it Invernevis, but it was too late to rewrite it, so he rang for a porter.

Chapter Fifteen

When the train emerged from the pass in the spring evening
he pressed against darkening glass but saw with relief no
evidence of conflagration at the big house across the river.
And when the coachman collected him, he assured him that
there had not been a serious accident or a death. 'Miss
Carlotta's very angry,' was all Roddy would say as wheels
rumbled above the river.

His aunt was in the front hall, her face grim. 'Wait in the
library,' she ordered. 'I'll be through in a minute.' And she
turned towards the servants' part.

There was a fire, but Invernevis couldn't settle. Ignoring
the unopened letters on his desk, he paced, smoking, wondering what on earth he was going to be confronted with, and if
he was going to be able to handle it.

Then Maggie the scullery-maid was pushed in by Aunt Carlotta, who laid her nephew's silver-framed photograph on his
desk.

'It was found in her room this morning, when the cleaning
started,' Aunt Carlotta said triumphantly, confronting both
with folded arms. 'Just look at the glass, and the dent in the
frame. And not only is she a thief who creeps into her master's
private room as soon as his back's turned; she's also a wicked
liar, saying that you *gave* it to her. I called you home to get
you to check this room, and the glass cases in the drawing-
room in case there's anything else missing, and others get the
blame. That was under the mattress, and I'll go through the
horse-hair myself to see if there's anything else.'

Invernevis's first reaction was one of intense anger against
his aunt for preventing him from keeping the most important
engagement of his life for something so trivial. But when he
saw the crack crossing his shaded face in the photograph lying
in front of him, he began to see the seriousness. He had
completely forgotten about the spontaneous present, and now
it had come back, damaged, to haunt him. He saw the implications all too clearly. If he admitted giving it to the girl,
Aunt Carlotta would immediately decide that there was some-

thing physical between them. And, as in the case of his father, the scandal would spread beyond Invernevis. It would provoke laughter and exaggeration over brandy and cigars in a dozen smoke-rooms, but frowning anger where needles picked and cards were turned on baize. Jamie's sister would hear an abridged version, but that would be sufficient to exclude him forever from her affections. It was a great gamble, and, as usual, Aunt Carlotta held the trump card. It was she who had put him into the position by not giving the girl a Christmas present in the first place, and as for the scullery-maid, he felt angry at her for leaving her reckless choice in such a place. But when his reproachful eyes met the girl's, he saw only utter trust, the faith that he would not let her down, would not abandon her to his aunt's tongue and the whispers and fingers of the village. And these eyes reminded him of his obligations to her dead brother, to her father, to an Invernevis family almost as old as his own. This surely was the real test of lairdship. And somehow – though he couldn't rationalize in such a critical situation – he owed it to Laura.

He would have liked a cigarette, but that would only have betrayed his nervousness, and Aunt Carlotta was waiting, smug at having her quarry cornered at last, without her nephew's protection. It was going to be a slow and satisfying extinction, a crushing out, and at the same time she intended to clear the house of father and brother.

Invernevis saw that his time was up. He kept his speech slow, the words distinct, so that there should be no mis-understanding.

'I gave it to her at Christmas because you forgot to get her a present. I asked her what she would like, and she chose that. I agreed, though I couldn't see what good it was to her.'

Aunt Carlotta looked from one to the other to see if there was spontaneous agreement of eyes. 'Not true,' she said emphatically. 'You're only saying that to save her, because you feel sorry for her; that's the position she's put you in. You *know* the little tramp stole that photograph.'

He saw that it was going to mean committing himself to a confrontation that could have several outcomes. More than Jamie's sister and the gift of a photograph were involved; there were scores to settle for his father and Laura. And though he was angry, he was also perfectly calm, facing his aunt.

250

'If nothing else will satisfy you, I'm prepared to take an oath in the presence of Father Macdonald that I gave the picture to this girl, in the circumstances I've just described. Now go back to your work,' he nodded to Maggie, 'and take this with you; it's your property now.' When he saw the door close, he continued: 'Only a wicked mind would see other things in the situation. Oh yes, you're about to remind me of the example of my father, but I'm not like that. God is my witness. And you know in your heart that ever since the girl set foot in this house you've been picking on her, finding faults where none existed. You also know that you *deliberately* didn't give her a present because you wanted to humiliate her in front of the other servants. Why you have such a spite I cannot guess. After all, she's only the scullery-maid. And if you accuse me of taking an interest in her because of her brother, I admit it, because I took him out to South Africa. But my interest *doesn't* extend beyond her well-being. So I have to say that I can't tolerate your victimization of her any longer. Because there's no question of the girl going. You might be the housekeeper, but it's *my* house, and I have final say.'

He stopped because he did not want to force the argument to the conclusion he wanted. He knew she would do that, because the face across the desk was set for battle, the mouth marshalling, the eyes bringing up the reinforcements of old scores.

'Take an oath for such a thing, and in front of Father Macdonald? I would never allow it, and *you* know it, so you think you're quite safe. No, the evidence of my eyes is enough. A man in your position doesn't give a servant a photograph of himself unless he's received some favour, though I'd use a different word to describe it. And a servant doesn't keep such a thing under her mattress unless she's stolen it, or received it for some service outwith the call of duty. So there are only two possibilities: she's stolen it or you gave it to her. Unless you've taken leave of your senses, you wouldn't incriminate yourself by such a lie just to save a scullery-maid from being dismissed. So I can only conclude that you *did* give her the photograph because – but I don't need to spell out the sordid details. But I shouldn't have expected anything different, considering your father and brother. And now, because of the sin with which this house will always be associated in my mind, I've no alternative but to go, because – ' and she spread her hands to show her helplessness – 'I too could become corrupted.'

Though it might have been yet another bluff to get him to reverse a decision, her nephew knew that he had to go through with it.

'Yes, I think it's better. I think the time's come. There's no use going on in this situation and, whatever your plans are, I'll compensate you for the years you've spent here. That much at least I'm due you.'

That she was taken aback was certain, but she was going to brazen it out. 'I assume you're referring to money,' she said stiffly. 'Oh no, you're not going to pension me off like a servant. The little I received here in the way of creature comforts I paid back many times over in enduring the insults of your brute of a father for the sake of your mother, and trying to save the maids from being ravished on the back stairs, because that's what it amounted to. You can't tell me that young girls found that diseased beast attractive. And I repaid with my sweat, trying to teach your sister, and failing miserably, I may say, because you can't work with something that doesn't exist. So I've settled my debts, and I don't need your charity. I've a little money of my own, thank God, sufficient to see me through. I had planned to do something with it, here, for the good of the village and this house, and you were to get what was left, but that's finished now. I couldn't stay anyway; my health wouldn't stand another week. I shall go to Leamington Spa, to rest.'

'A good idea.'

'I shan't be going alone,' she continued. 'Elsie from the kitchen will be coming to look after me. She knows my ways.'

Invernevis merely shrugged his assent. He had hardly noticed the kitchen-maid.

'But before I go, it's my duty to say something to you, for your own sake. I can only assume that the attraction for the scullery-maid has been purely physical. Having had your pleasure, you have no alternative but to send her away, because if she stays in this house and you continue to satisfy these animal instincts, you will end up worse than your brother, because you are the laird. And if she becomes pregnant, she will claim the child is yours, though others, like the footman, have no doubt been with her also. Because you have no wife to protect you, yours will be a far bigger scandal than your father's. That is why I will be praying for you, and so will Father Macdonald. You are fortunate in having him to watch over you, both as a spiritual adviser and trustee. He will put you on the true path in both.'

It was her parting shot, and when the door slammed Inver-nevis sat, his hand shaking towards the cigarette box. He was both frightened and pleased – frightened that she would spread a story about himself and the scullery-maid, but pleased that he had at last found the strength to stand up to her, forcing her to go. It cleared the way for the possibility of bringing a bride to Invernevis, and it was a blow struck for Laura, though she was beyond its benefit. It would mean a new life for a lot of people; it would bring brightness to a drab house, and her money didn't matter. Already his mind was dealing with the practicalities of her departure. No, a new house-keeper was an unnecessary expense; Mrs Livingstone could keep an eye as well as cook. The girl his aunt was taking from the kitchen wasn't a problem either; Maggie could be promoted, and a new scullery-maid got from the village.

Then he remembered Mama. How would she react to the departure of her sister, after so many years? She had relied a lot on Carlotta, in the bringing up of her children, the run-ning of the house, the sorrows and shame of a wayward husband. No doubt Carlotta was upstairs now, telling Mama about the scandal of the scullery-maid, shouting that the other son was just like the father. And that would make Mama turn against him, and any woman he might introduce to Inver-nevis, unless Mama was back on the bottle, in which case she would use the incident of the photograph to throw hysterics for more drink.

What a mess. What a rotten run of luck. The happiness and confidence of Edinburgh had evaporated. Since he had come into the place nothing had gone right, as though he were fated to fail, with Carlotta's organ mocking his lack of inner strength, and his father's laughter from the darkness mocking his lack of manliness. They had made him into a caricature in tweeds, a laird without power or a sense of destiny. Well, he would show them. There were going to be big changes. He would get out and about, go round the farms, go up to the village, get to know the tenants. And he was going to keep in touch with Jamie Mackay, persuade him to bring his sister to

Invernevis. The grouse shooting was a good time, but it was too far away; he would need to think up something else.

The new sense of purpose drove him to his desk, to open his letters. The accounts could no longer be passed for checking to Carlotta; he would have to do that himself, or get someone capable. That could wait, however. He'd better get through to the kitchen, to have a word with Mrs Livingstone. If he told the cook of the changes he was going to make, then Carlotta couldn't change her mind about going.

Cloth in hand, the cook was agitating at the oven. 'Oh, sir, I was waiting for Miss Carlotta to come through and tell me when you were going in to dinner. I've a nice pigeon pie here.' And she poked pastry.

'I'm not hungry, Mrs Livingstone, but I'll enjoy it tomorrow. Now sit down a minute.' He signalled to Elsie, who was doing something at the table, and she went out, scowling.

Thinking it was bad news, the cook slumped into the chair at the end of the table, the cloth still in her fist. He remained standing, but walking about, and before he began to explain he closed the scullery door.

'You've been with us so long that you're one of the family, so I know anything I say won't go out of this kitchen. The fact is, my aunt's decided to go away. The family has needed a lot of looking after, and she feels in need of a change. She's going to Leamington Spa – away for good, I mean. And she says she's going to take Elsie with her, as her maid.'

The cook's grey head jerked round at this news, but Invernevis held up a hand to prevent sidetracking.

'That means we're going to be without a housekeeper, since that's what my aunt was. Now I think you'll agree that we can manage without one, since we don't have many house-guests nowadays. Colonel Hooker won't be back; that's certain. There's my mother, of course, but I'll get a nurse. So I wonder if you would be prepared to keep an eye on the maids for me, make sure they do whatever they're supposed to do. Symmers can look after the men. Of course I appreciate you've got a lot to do in here, and that you're going to lose your helper, but what I thought of doing was: putting Maggie into the kitchen, and getting a new girl for the scullery. What do *you* think?'

Mrs Livingstone seemed to be in some kind of trance, staring, not at Invernevis, but at some invisible being standing by the stove, the fire barred by iron dimming as night drew on. Knuckles automatically knocked wood as she spoke in a low, lethargic voice.

'Going away? Oh aye, you knew that from her face when she came in here a few minutes ago. Not a word, so something was wrong, and no thought about your dinner. As you say, sir, I've been here a long time, like one of the family. I wish now that I'd spoken up because that poor wee creature might still be running about. No, she was no bother, though she was always wanting to lick the bowl when you were making a cake, or making the dogs fight under the table. But the cuffs she got. I always said that's what knocked her off because she was such a nice wee girl, so full of energy. And going to turn out a real beauty. Oh, the tinkers made *such* a fuss of her at the back door, and you can't tell me they're not the wise ones. Called her the little princess, in Gaelic, but *she* knew. Aye, she took some blows, and most of the time for nothing. I tried to come between them, but it wasn't any good, when *her* temper was up. And the tongue. The poor wee thing's better off, where she is. Then she started on Maggie. No, not hitting her, because she wouldn't dare, with Duncan about. But words can hurt just as much as a hand. And it only made the girl drop things. No Christmas present; what a dirty way to do. But not a word to Elsie. Oh no, *she* gets a dress for Christmas. Well, she's welcome to take that one with her. I never liked her. Too many airs and graces, always looking into the mirror, letting things burn. And other things too. I'm a light sleeper, and I hear things, but enough said. So good riddance. Yes, I'll take Maggie in here, give her the chance because she's keen, and if she's as good as her mother, she'll do. And you're quite right, we don't need a housekeeper. I'll give the maids a shake-up. Of course it was your aunt got them from the islands, through Father Macdonald. I'm a Catholic myself, and a good enough one, I hope, but you can go too far. Thank God we're not going to hear any more of that organ. Here you are, trying to get the mixture right, and it booming away. No, I'll keep a watch. It'll be a happier house from now on. You'll see, sir.'

Shocked to hear her confirm his fears about Laura's miserable life at the hands of his aunt, Invernevis could only mutter his thanks as he made for the door. But Mrs Livingstone wasn't done.

255

'And another thing: I hope we'll be seeing Master Alexander and his baby up here now,' she called out. 'I'm hearing she's a lovely little thing, and I thought that's what was making your aunt mad. The poor soul, he never got much of a chance, either.'

'Oh, certainly,' Invernevis said vaguely, hurrying through to the library. He didn't particularly want to see them, but there was Mama to be considered. Having a grand-daughter about might do her good. A grandson would be even better. He settled at his desk, plucked notepaper and wrote:

My Dear Jamie,

I was so sorry to have to cancel our dinner engagement through having to return home. I found that the problem was easily solved, but I shan't be returning to Edinburgh for some time, as I have much to do here. We *must* get together very soon. Men who have been in the same regiment should stick together, and especially when they share a passion for cigars! (I have an excellent stock.) So you are most welcome to come to Invernevis whenever suits, and if you can persuade your charming sister to venture into Macdonald territory, that would complete the Mackay clan for me. Instead of battle, I can promise brandy, and for your sister, some pleasant walks.

Most truly,
Niall Invernevis.

He let red wax flop and used the brass seal, pressing in the arms. By the time Jamie replied, Carlotta would be gone, and Mrs Livingstone would soon arrange rooms. But though he had tried to be hospitable, it was very vague. Jamie would have plenty to do on his big place, with his mother nagging, and Mary Rose certainly couldn't come alone. She might be going to stay elsewhere, meet someone, accept a proposal. His mind paced the possibilities. Oh, if only conventions didn't have to be followed, he could write her direct, expressing his feelings. Alexander had swept aside such barriers and gone on to claim his prize, and his was a double achievement because he had broken rank.

While her nephew awaited a reply from Jamie, Miss Carlotta was having her trunks taken down from the attic for the last time and carried to her rooms where Elsie helped to fold and pack clothes. The retiring housekeeper wasn't only clearing her wardrobe and drawers. The Dresden figures on the mantelpiece of her sitting-room had been there so long that she regarded them as being her property, though she had originally taken them from an Invernevis cupboard, acquiring the keys when her brother-in-law had gone upstairs for good, and soaping the ornaments gently with her own hands to get the dirt out of the grooves. Elsie wrapped them in several layers of newspapers to prevent the thin white hands of the flower-carrying girl and her bewigged, blue-coated escort from being snapped off.

And that was not all. Some of the big ornaments in the drawing-room had been rescued from dusty darkness and artistically spaced. She would have taken the porcelain clock encrusted with naked nymphs, forming an arch for the passage of the hours, but her nephew would miss it. She wanted to avoid present contact or future confrontation at all costs because she regarded herself as being finally finished with him. He had been such a promising little boy, and she had tried to keep him on the true path, but he had gone and had carnal knowledge of a scullery-maid. Worse: he was vain enough to buy his silence with a self-portrait, and he had taken the slut's side against his own aunt's. Just like his father. Like his amoral war-mongering ancestors who flaunted their weapons and physiques on the landing, a barbaric tribe that claimed Catholic allegiance, but violated everything sacred. She was glad to be done with them, even with her own sister, because you had to face up to it, Constance was nothing but a drunkard, a weak woman who had never been able to take a stand against evil, and who had succumbed in the end. Now Alexander had started a bastard sept, and was going to live with his harlot within sight of the house. No, she couldn't defile stone by building a chapel on the river bank, and though she seriously considered taking a hammer to the organ she had paid for out of her own money, it would be wrong to punish God for the sins of men. The organ would remain, dominating the drawing-room, the silent monument to her disappointment, its pipes like a giant hand held up, calling a halt to sin.

Thank God for Elsie, the only one who was loyal, and such a help, kneeling by the gaping trunk, folding silk so that it would not crease, swaddling the crucifix from the head of the bed in a nightdress, so careful to cover the Saviour's feet of yellow ivory punctured by nails. Carlotta was quite overcome, watching her, the legs splayed, the blonde hair let down. And when she turned her head to take the Italian art books, her mistress thought she really was beautiful, with such fine sensitive features, a body without coarseness. She could not resist stooping to kiss her lightly on the neck, to murmur: 'Dear child.' Oh, it really was good to be getting away from Invernevis. They would take connecting rooms in Leamington Spa for a time, so that she could get her strength back through the waters, and then they would look for a place in the country. A small place, but with a cook and a maid, so that Elsie could be her companion. They would keep to themselves, and she would try to soften Elsie's somewhat harsh Glasgow accent, make up the deficiencies of her schooldays. The material was there; it only required working on, and Elsie would become a worthy companion for the later years. And, of course, she would get what little money Carlotta had to leave.

It was now assumed by the servants that Miss Carlotta and Elsie had deserted the kitchen for good, though Mrs Livingstone refused to confirm it. The imminent departures were producing feelings of relief, manifested in the laughter of the maids, the whistling of the men. Maggie was by far the most thankful. When Mrs Livingstone had sworn her to secrecy by telling her that she was coming into the kitchen, she could have gone down on her knees, for by the Master's preoccupied face in the past few days she was certain that her carelessness over the picture had caused a huge row between him and his aunt, a row in which he had been the loser. She had been put out of the library at the beginning of the quarrel, but she knew that Miss Carlotta was going to accuse the Master of something awful involving herself. The implications astonished her. It was inconceivable, and yet she had heard whispers – her mother talking to her father by firelight – that it had happened before in the big house. The vague idea shocked as well as giving her a frightening thrill.

But it was going to be all right. She had the picture back, and Miss Carlotta was leaving, taking the horrid Elsie with her. That meant not only a job in the kitchen, but the bedroom to herself till the new scullery-maid came from the village. She would learn to cook, as her mother had wanted her to, and one day she might be the Master's cook. That was why it was going to be essential to do everything Mrs Livingstone told her, and to give her full attention.

The knowledge of the changes to come made dish washing almost a pleasant activity. The sun streamed down on her face, running water sparkled as it struck china, the crested blue plate was stacked, another exhumed from the warm water. The Master's photograph now stood on *her* dresser upstairs, and no one could take it away. But then an appalling thought spun a plate from her slippery fingers, to smash by her boots, the pieces lying there. Suppose that Miss Carlotta committed a final act of spite by going to her father and telling him that the picture concealed something sordid? It wasn't that she was afraid of her father's belt, which she had felt on her bare buttocks before. It was the look that came into his eyes when something that she had done disappointed him. It was worse than pain; it was a hard contempt accompanied by a silence that could go on for days. If Miss Carlotta told about the picture, he would never speak to her again. Her hands were in lukewarm water as she prayed aloud: 'Oh, please, God, take her away without saying anything to my father.'

Miss Carlotta had no intention of having further communication with the servants. Nor was she prepared to announce the day and time of her departure. She was certainly not going to suffer the indignity of departing on an Invernevis gig. She'd been in touch with Father Macdonald. Elsie had carried the letter to the village, and the reply from her spiritual adviser intimated that he would hire the Arms gig, and take the reins himself. But she and Elsie didn't have the strength to drag the trunks down to the front hall. That was done by the ghillie and the gardener, but via Elsie. And when the brass-bound corners tore the stair carpet that the housekeeper had had repaired, year after year, it didn't matter.

The three big strapped trunks still plastered with the labels of Carlotta's return from India with her sister and hated brother-in-law were piled by the front door, an annoying enigma to her nephew as he came and went. Though he was still looking for a letter from Jamie, two other things were preoccupying him. Firstly, there hadn't been any response to his call at the Hogmanay dance for recruits for South Africa. Though it was true that they weren't really needed, with the war nearly over, it rankled with him because he knew that if the call had come from his father, most of the young men of the village would have trooped up the avenue. Hadn't his rifle volunteer company enlisted, almost to a man, at the outbreak of war, though their Colonel was confined to bed, dying, and weren't there quite a few able-bodied young who had come of age since then?

The second problem was an anonymous letter from the village, claiming that the Irishmen from the quarry were drinking and brawling in the Arms to the extent that local lives were at risk. The writer implored the laird 'in the name of God' to do something, and added: 'Your own brother is often in their company.'

It put Invernevis into a quandary. Was the solution to revoke the lease, close down the quarry? But it was bringing in a big rent, and the village store, not to mention the Arms, was getting a share of the rations for the camp across water. Should he ask the trustees to put Carmichael out of the Arms on the grounds that he was running disorderly licensed premises to the danger of the community? But then, the next tenant would be tempted by the lure of big takings from the thirsty Irishmen. No, the solution was to thrash it out with the quarry manager, get him to stop the navvies coming over.

The meeting took place in the library, with Morgan the manager, massive-handed, a face that had come off badly in fights and granite dust in his crumpled jacket, hearing Invernevis out, but staying on his feet to say his piece.

'There's nothing on the other side for them, and you can't expect men who have worked bloody hard all week to stay in their beds at the weekend. Once they get their wages, they want a bit of relaxation, to see other faces. No, if I tried to keep them in camp all weekend there would be a riot, and we both want the quarry to go on working, don't we?' Seeing Invernevis's face, he knew he was going to have to concede something. 'I'll tell you what I'll do. I'll give a couple of the foremen a bit extra, make them responsible for their behaviour while they're over here. But I don't believe it's as bad as this letter makes out.' He tossed it on the desk. 'Shebeen be damned. Probably the work of some fellow who's had his girl taken from him by one of my men. Well, all's fair in love and war. Good day to you.' He turned at the door, putting his cap on. 'There'll be a big blast tomorrow morning.'

Though Invernevis was angry with the manager's offhand

manner, he felt it was a reasonable solution. He would go down himself and caution Carmichael to keep a more orderly house, or else. As for Alexander drinking with the Irishmen, the only reason that he had got the site by the river was because he'd vowed he was going to settle down. The foundations had set, ready to receive the walls, and he had a daughter, yet he was still the same irresponsible person. He would need a talking to, to point out that he hadn't kept his word.

The next morning, as the neglected clocks failed to concord at seven, Invernevis was shaving at his wash-stand, the honed steel of his ivory-handled razor making china clink. He was wondering if there would be anything in the morning post when he heard wheels arriving, and was at the window before he remembered that Johnnie the post always walked from the village and went to the back door. It was too early, anyway.

He was looking down on the rounded hat of Father Macdonald, sitting holding the reins of the Arms gig while two unidentified men hoisted up Carlotta's trunks. Invernevis turned to go down in his dressing-gown. No, damn it, that was what she wanted, to insult him in front of the priest. He felt angry as he parted the curtains, watching Father Macdonald's boot feeling for gravel as two floral hats came out from under the ivy. His own hat tilted as he helped them up, Carlotta first, her pointed shoe on iron, the springs settling, then the kitchen-maid, showing a substantial calf. They made room for the priest.

The last trunk was aboard, and the two men in cloth caps and scarves climbed up to steady them. The brightening day was bringing the standing stones above the Home Farm into focus, where Alexander's infant slept, protected as Laura had never been. She lay where the river gaped. No, he would not knock glass. Let her go.

He cleaned hair from steel as the priest plucked the limp whip from the socket, and as the gig jolted out of view the window shook with the blast from the quarry, gravel rattling.

Book Five

Chapter Sixteen

The day after Carlotta departed, Mama came downstairs for the first time in months, supported between the ghillie and gardener. Her son found her in the drawing-room, propped up with cushions on the big sofa in front of the climbing fire. A walking-stick lay along her swollen leg, its horned handle within easy reach. She wore the shapeless black that had become perpetual mourning for husband and monarch, but the body underneath had been cleansed by the two house-maids, one holding her under the armpits in tin, the other scrubbing. A combination of alcohol and heart condition had shocked her hair into permanent white. It was now too fine for braiding, and was crudely bunched at the back, a wispy ball transfixed by pearl-headed pins. Her mouth was still slightly twisted, giving her a crazy look as her lined face stared at fire, the fingers of her left hand seeking power again, folded over a ball of wool.

She was thinking that the satisfaction of not having been near the bottle for five days was somehow diminished by her sister's departure. Carlotta had stormed into her bedroom, shouting that she was definitely going this time, accusing her nephew of a succession of sins his mother couldn't possibly assimilate, having been jolted from a dream of Victoria at Invernevis. But there was something about a servant girl and a photograph. Before she could get that explained, Carlotta had started up again (did she ever stop?), accusing Invernevis of having wasted her life. House, family, servants, village – all had been futile devotion. Niall was going to turn out as big a brute as his father, with the same low tastes. As for Alexander's baby, it was an 'utter disgrace'.

Her sister thought it best to let the storm spend itself, but that wasn't wise, apparently, for Carlotta rounded on her too, accusing her of having been far too weak with her husband, and now with the bottle. It was all old stuff, but more viciously said than ever before, and it made her sit up in bed. But there wasn't much point in explaining to Carlotta, who had never been married. After all, it was Carlotta's precious church that made you keep to the vows, and he had had to get his conjugal rights, though you knew he had been at the maids again, and with that dreadful disease already working on him. Of course Sandy was really a big boy, when all said and done. If she could forgive, why couldn't Carlotta, who hadn't known him in *that* way? Or maybe that was the trouble. There was some truth in what Sandy was always saying about frustrated spinsters.

Better to go. It was now up to her as the mother to help Niall as much as possible. She knew quite a lot about the house and the estate, and could advise him. But you couldn't do that from a bed. She'd have to give herself a shake, come downstairs, keep out of temptation's way. Of course it was hard, and she wasn't going to say that she wouldn't have a toddy from time to time, when she was tired, but certainly she wouldn't be touching any when she came downstairs. And once the strength came back into her leg and arm, she'd keep on the move, to make sure the servants were working.

Her son was not manifestly happy to see her in the drawing-room. No sooner had he solved the problem of Carlotta than here was another, threatening the peace. He had hoped to get the house quiet and in order for a visit from Jamie and his sister. He could see how it was going to be: helped down in the morning, getting tight throughout the day, having to be carried back up. It couldn't be allowed, when Jamie and his sister came.

But Mama was patting the sofa with her good hand, to show that he was to sit beside her. 'Well, here I am. I won't be much help till I get the power back into my hand, but at least I won't be a bother in bed.' And, seeing the scepticism in his face: 'There won't be any more trouble with *that*, I promise you. I don't need it now.' She gripped his sleeve. 'There's only the two of us now, son. We've got to keep things going.'

'There's Alexander.'

'Yes, but he's not much help,' she said, her decisive tone lost in the slurring caused by the stroke, and which was going to make it hard to tell. 'And he's gone and made me a grandmother,' she said with obvious satisfaction. 'I hope he'll bring the baby up. Not that I'm suggesting you allow him to come and go here, as he pleases. He'll have his own home soon. You have to start as you intend to finish; that was one of Carlotta's favourite sayings.' Her head turned. 'I wish she'd taken that awful organ with her. It spoils the room. Mind you, you could get a good price for it.'

But Invernevis wasn't interested in the organ. As he went through to the library he was applying himself to the problem of Alexander. The granite blocks from the quarry across the loch had been hauled from the ferry by a Home Farm horse and cart, and they were stacked, awaiting the masons. It would soon be ready for rafters and slates, and when it echoed with children, it would be warm and intimate, like the big house could never be. Alexander was lucky; he had defined his limits, staked off what he was responsible for, and had privacy, which his brother could never have. But what would he do with himself all day? He had never been one for books, and the occasional cast and shot seemed to satisfy him. Surely he wasn't going to spend his days in the Arms, putting up drinks for local worthies and Irish navvies?

Invernevis sent for him. They met in the library on an afternoon of clearing clouds, with the first daffodils sprouting on the lawns. Alexander's clothes showed that he had come straight from ploughing, and his boots were muddy, though he had tried to knock them clean on the front step. His brother gave him a whisky and a chair, enquired after his daughter, was told she was 'doing fine, and no trouble at all in the night'. Invernevis didn't know what to ask next, so he said: 'I think Mama would like to see her. She's down, now that Carlotta's gone.'

'And good riddance,' Alexander said, swallowing whisky with ease. 'I heard in the Arms that she's taken one of the maids away with her.' He looked knowingly at his brother. 'Now that was queer, wasn't it?'

264

'I don't know anything about the girl,' Invernevis said brusquely. 'I asked you here because I want to put a proposition to you. As you know, MacKenzie the factor hasn't functioned for years, though he's still getting paid by the lawyers, and a free house. I need help in running this place – someone to go around, looking after the farms. Purely supervisory, of course, and you would get paid. I really would appreciate your help, and I'm sure the trustees will agree.'

'But the tenants are responsible for their own places,' Alexander said, eyeing his brother as he set down his empty glass. 'They'd accuse me of spying.'

'No, no, you don't see what I have in mind,' Invernevis said hastily. 'I simply want you to go round and see that things are in order. For instance, if a storm damaged one of the Home Farm steadings, you would go and see how it was to be put right, and what it would cost.'

But Alexander was already shaking his head. 'It wouldn't work. It would only cause bad feeling. Things are better left as they are.'

'But how *are* you going to pass your time?' Invernevis wanted to know as his brother got to his feet.

'Oh, I'll find plenty to do,' Alexander assured him. 'I can always give a help out at the Home Farm. MacPherson's been good to me. He put a roof over my head, and just because I'm building my own house is no reason to break with him. Besides, he *is* my father-in-law. Anyway, I'd better go and get on with the ploughing. It's all right, I'll see myself out, now that Carlotta's no longer lurking. Oh yes, I almost forgot.' He turned at the door. 'We were thinking of calling the girl Laura. You wouldn't mind, would you?'

'No, no, it's a nice thought,' Invernevis said, completely taken aback.

'Good. And Mama can be godmother, if that's allowed,' he said, shutting the door.

Invernevis slumped back in his swivel chair, inhaling the cigarette with rapid puffs. He was hurt and angry at Alexander's rejection of his offer, and saw it as retaliation for being forced to disinherit himself to get his house site. But he was also apprehensive. The new house evidently wasn't going to bring about a reformation in his lifestyle, and the Arms and Home Farm would still be the places where he could be found. And there was something twisted in wanting

265

to name his daughter after a sister he had never bothered about. By making Mama godmother, was he trying to get back into the good graces of the big house, prompted, no doubt, by MacPherson? Alexander must know that his brother would want to use the name Laura if he had a daughter. And his fraternizing with the Irish navvies in the Arms was only to embarrass his brother, the laird.

Within an hour of his brother's visit, Invernevis went out for fresh air and saw him back in the field under the standing stones, steering the plough the pair of Clydesdales were pulling, the earth opening behind him like a black book, and the seagulls swooping and crying as the worms were exposed. Carlotta had been right about one thing at least: he shouldn't have been allowed to build by the river because it wasn't going to reform him. More than a stretch of water would always divide the brothers.

Something occurred to him to send him indoors to brood by the brandy decanter. Though she was out of the district, Carlotta would still exercise her power from afar, getting Father Macdonald and Richardson the lawyer to veto schemes that he wished to implement. She was even more dangerous away than at home.

Still no word from Jamie, and the house so quiet after Carlotta, with, amazingly, Mama staying sober, being helped down each morning at ten and sitting the day out on the drawing-room sofa, her good hand holding up to her failing eyes the accounts that Mrs Livingstone brought through while the spring sun threw on the faded Indian carpet the silhouettes of Carlotta's organ pipes, like a cattle grid.

Laura was brought back to him by the tinkers, now at their traditional site by the standing stones, a place shunned by the locals, especially at sunset. Saplings were stuck into the ground and curved into hoops, to be clad with canvas, ropes lashed round the standing stones to save their shelters from the storms the loch threw up. They came down to the back door of the big house to trade brooms and milk-cans for food, to repair kettles while talking to Mrs Livingstone in their impeccable Gaelic. Miss Carlotta had tried to drive them away, but the cook was too conscious of their powers to give offence. Besides, she wanted the tea leaves in her cup read, and when told she would meet a tall dark stranger, laughed like a young thing. The previous spring, when her son was still in a South

African hospital, Mama had come through tight and given the tinkers the entire contents of the larder. Though her son did not share the local awe of their powers, he had no wish to stop them coming to Invernevis, provided they did not make a nuisance of themselves. He knew their weakness was drink, and he was worried about confrontations with the Irish navvies in the Arms at the weekends, when both races had money to spend, the Irish from splitting rock, the tinkers from telling eerie stories at crofts.

They seemed to know that 'the little princess' was dead, and that the lady of the house was on the long road to recovery. They sat at the back door, along the wall, the stumps of clay pipes inverted in their mouths, caps over their eyes, thumbs hooked in the pockets of their assorted waistcoats as they waited for their tea to come out in the tin cans they had sent in. Maggie carried the clustered cans of black brew, strong and sweet, and Mrs Livingstone the hot buttered scones wrapped in a cloth. An old woman with a deeply wrinkled face and a small gold hoop in her right ear-lobe offered to read Maggie's palm. The scullery-maid was frightened, but the cook encouraged. Maggie knelt beside the old woman, who took the clay pipe from her mouth, spat, and spread the fingers of her subject. She seemed to take a long time, muttering in Gaelic, her grimy nail tracing the lines on a hand roughened by hot water. Maggie had seen the same eyes and skin, in a newt balanced, blinded by light, on the edge of the iron trough behind their croft.

'It'll be a good few years before you get a man, and something will come out of it that will cause you trouble for a time,' the old woman said in Gaelic, turning to drink tea from tin with hands like claws.

Mrs Livingstone's shadow was at Maggie's feet, the hard granite of the house against her back. She wanted to run indoors, up to her room. Her mother had believed implicitly in the tinkers' prophecies, and always gave them something, but her father said it was stuff and nonsense, a way of scaring folks to get free food. She stayed to question the old woman further, but the tea can was empty, the gleaming sides spattered with leaves. The old woman was holding out her hand, and Mrs Livingstone had to nudge Maggie, struck into stone in the sun.

'You've to cross her palm with silver,' she muttered. 'Run

267

inside and you'll find a sixpence on the shelf above the stove.'

Several evenings later, as he was at the window, dressing for dinner, fiddling with an awkward stud and surveying the darkening river, Invernevis saw fire leaping between the standing stones. That was not controlled heather-burning by the Home Farm, he decided, because that was the best grouse moor and was burnt only on the laird's orders. Still in his shirt-sleeves, he hurried down and out on to gravel.

Having licked stone, the crimson tongues were now swallowing the tinkers' tents which collapsed in showers of sparks, dark shapes running, shouting, a pony neighing. It tore through the dry heather with a cruel crackling sound which reached him across the river where he stood horrified by the wishing stone. The hill was luminous, like Magersfontein, the stones tilted into the glow like the black barrels of big guns, smoke billowing, the tinkers beating with the brooms they had made themselves, the women folk stumbling with bundles. It was now guzzling gorse, going downhill towards the Home Farm where figures with buckets formed a line to halt it. On the horizon game birds rose squawking, blundering into the polluted sky. The chain of slopping buckets being passed up from the Home Farm did not seem to be stopping it on that side of the hill. It was sending sparks in the direction of the hay-loft, where they gleamed on slates before fading, to be replaced by new ones. Where Alexander's plough had inverted grass, it ran round the corner of the field, turning fence posts into beacons in its search for a way down.

Invernevis was struck into indecision by the enormity of the consequences. He should get the gig, go over to direct operations. But Alexander would be there. No, the real threat was to the village, if the fire got across the moor. What was needed was as many hands as possible, and since it was a Saturday night the Arms would be crowded with Irishmen, dressed for the job in big boots and shirt-sleeves.

He went to the library, scratched a note to Carmichael to send up as many as possible, took the note through to the servants' hall, telling the ghillie to take the gig, but to come back for him. Mrs Livingstone was to muster the other male servants, tell them to get down as quickly as possible, taking brooms and damp sacks, anything that would beat out fire. Invernevis returned to the front of the house, to watch it leaping dykes and having a grand time in the bracken below the Home Farm. The road stopped it, but only momentarily. It ran along the verge, showering sparks which died in the dust, but some got across because the breeze was backing it now. It was fanning down the meadow towards the river, blackening the short grass, consuming whatever came.

Invernevis was now anxious about his house as he stood on gravel, still in shirt-sleeves, seeing night being turned back into day. The wall of fire would soon reach its old enemy, water, but would the Summer House Pool stop it? Sparks could get across in a breeze strengthening into wind, invade the lawn which hadn't been sheared since the autumn. Shouldn't he start getting the oil paintings stripped from the walls before they turned the house into a tinder-box, never mind the rotting brocade, the suspect rafters? No, these were panic measures. The fire was meeting its match among nettles, but its source on the skyline above the Home Farm was massive now, so fierce that Invernevis had to shield his eyes with an arm. It had been beaten back from the hay-loft, but only to spread over the moor in a front two hundred yards wide, and increasing every second. Damn it: he had planned to shoot that moor in August as an excuse for getting Jamie and his sister to Invernevis, but there would be no heather left for the grouse to feed on. Everything seemed to be going wrong, as if a family curse was working, as if the crackling flames across the river were laughing at his efforts to be a laird. His father would have been across there, fighting in the front line, stripped to the waist, no doubt, but his son's game leg wouldn't permit.

Fast wheels on gravel signalled the ghillie's return, with a verbal message from Carmichael. The few Irishmen who weren't too far gone to fire-fight refused because the tinkers had been riling them, mocking their Irish Gaelic. Carmichael had offered the incentive of free bottles, but men with no money left wouldn't work beside the tinkers.

'I saw the foremen being offered sovereigns by Carmichael, but that wouldn't shift them,' the ghillie said.

It would take too long to send a boat across the loch for the quarry manager.

'What about the people in the village?' Invernevis asked.

'Oh, all the able-bodied ones are up on the moor, the women as well, but it's a big fire, sir, and the wind's turned, taking it towards the village. Well, I'd better get down and lend a hand. They need everybody they can get.'

'Wait,' Invernevis ordered, staying the horses. 'Maybe Father Macdonald could make the Irishmen go up.'

'Carmichael thought of that, sir. He sent a message up earlier, but Father Macdonald said he wouldn't go down to the Arms, after what happened, the last time.' He hesitated, then added: 'He said a funny thing, sir. He said the fire was a punishment.'

Invernevis detected Carlotta's abiding influence' in the remark, but there was no time for anger. 'Give me a minute to get a coat, and I'll come down with you.'

Wade's Bridge and *Linne Bhuidhe* were lit by the glare from the hillside, giving the area a supernatural aura so that the horses had to be whipped across. Though the ghillie advised against, Invernevis began to climb the slope, the tip of his' cromach testing, brogues bogging in the soft sphagnum but going higher, past the Home Farm, the slates glistening where a hose had protected, but the fruit trees behind blackened skeletons. The heat of the scorched slope was coming up through his thick soles now, the burnt heather springing at his ankles as he climbed towards the brightening glow.

When he went over the top the vista burned itself indelibly into memory. Against the black negative of the sky was a wall of fire, and beyond it, flailing figures spread out, brooms hoisted like witches engaged in some hellish rite. The noise from fire and fighter was deafening, grating to the nerves, a roaring advancing against shouting, and in some places screaming where the flames consumed the brooms that were beating them out. Between Invernevis and the fire was a smoking waste, a blackness lit by the flares of burning clumps, like Magersfontein when the rifles opened up.

There was no way round to the fire-fighters unless he went back down to the road, and took the gig to the village. To walk on was folly because of the increasing heat of the ground, the ploughed ash smoking on his brogues, discolouring leather. He stood by the standing stones, watching, unconsciously putting up a hand as prop but dropping it with a swear because of the scorching pillar, the halter of the tinkers' tent ropes still clinging, smouldering. It was no use; he would only get in the way. Far better to go back to the house, send round a gig with as much beer as the cellar would yield, as much food as the larder contained, because it was going to be a night-long struggle to stop it getting to the village.

He went down to take the gig back to the house, get Mrs Livingstone to muster the maids. They hadn't gone to bed; they were all out on the front lawn, watching the glow in the sky in fear and wonderment. When the cook prodded the banked stove and called them inside, to help prepare food for the fire-fighters, there was much excitement, as if it was the Hogmanay dance. A lantern brought back cold meat from the larder, and as Mrs Livingstone sliced it to the bone, Maggie made thick pieces, smearing the butter. A maid supervised a large pot of boiling eggs; another was dividing a cheese from the Home Farm, while Symmers unbuckled the game hampers on the table, ready to pack the food. Meantime, Invernevis stooped in the cellar with the ghillie, a lantern on a dusty shelf depleted by Mama as they manhandled the extra barrel of beer that Carlotta would not allow to the Hogmanay dance. Invernevis's leg ached with the night's activities, but he helped to roll the rumbling barrel along the passage to the back door, where the gig was waiting. They gripped the rims, heaved after a count of three. The springs protested, but the barrel was aboard. And while Invernevis went back for a few bottles of whisky, the food hampers were loaded on.

Though the maids wanted to come down to distribute the food, Invernevis considered it too dangerous. Besides, as Mrs Livingstone said, they would have to get up as usual in the morning. But Maggie would be handy, and her father would keep an eye on her.

Sitting between the Master and her father, who had the reins, she went down the avenue, the gig's redundant lamps gleaming on the flanks of the horses that had been pulling on that route since they were young, but never such a cargo. It was the most exciting night of Maggie's life. The tree trunks were twisted grey ghosts, but she was secure between the two men she liked the most in the world. Wade's Bridge was still lit by the glare, the air pungent with burning heather that billowed, obscuring the stars, silencing the owls. The Yellow Pool now took its name from the fire on the hill. They rumbled above the river, its blackness undefined by the flames that had gone down to die, and between the Summer House Pool and the few lights of the big house, the peaked outline of Laura's summer house. When they passed the family croft, its small window black, chimney cold, Maggie tugged her

271

shawl tighter. After her mother's death she had wanted her father to give up the croft and move into the big house with her brother Hector, but he was too independent, and besides, Miss Carlotta would never have allowed. Though the two of them went home to cold beds and a cold grate, at least they got their food at the big house.

The gig moved on towards the village, lamps left to guard children where men and women were up on the moor, fighting for their future. Bottles clinked in the back and wheels groaned as the horses took the long haul, her father keeping the whip at the ready. Over the bridge, with the dull rails running back, into the glare, and on the other side, the hooded station. A gig lamp momentarily made the window of the village store flare, showing a black-bordered card.

They turned left, past the granite school that the late laird had given ground to build, its small tower slatted to prevent pigeons fouling the iron bell. And then, after the priest's house and the stones of the cemetery where her mother lay, the moor on fire.

It dazzled her, like the magic lantern show that had come to the school. The flames were about two hundred yards away from the first houses, and men and women were beating with brooms and sodden sacks, the fires stifled, but springing up again. It both frightened and fascinated Maggie. She wanted to stand up on her high seat and shout at it to go back. She wanted to be out there, wielding a broom, with the flames licking at her boots, to step back and thrash them into submission. But she didn't want to leave the Master's warm presence, his thigh pressing against hers, far more thrilling than looking at his photograph.

Her father had already jumped down, to show that there was work to be done, the game hampers slid off, the barrel of beer bumped down on a cushion of heather. Alexander was coming towards them through the smoke, trailing a broom, its twigs alight, his face blackened, the bottoms of his ploughing trousers nibbled, the seams of his boots opened. Maggie stared down at the open waistcoat, the shirt-sleeves rolled up, showing the muscular arms. He was so different from his Inverness-caped brother above, and yet he seemed more vital, like her dead brother had looked after ploughing the croft. Somehow she knew that Alexander would master the fire.

His white teeth showing as he leaned by the gig lamp, he

272

was warning that the fighters couldn't leave the fire for food. 'The wind's with it,' he said bitterly, watching the beaters walking backwards. 'It's taking some stopping.'

'I presume the tinkers were drunk and dropped a candle or something,' Invernevis said grimly. 'Well, that's the last time they'll camp in these parts.'

'I wouldn't blame the poor buggers,' Alexander said.

'Watch your language; there's a young woman present,' his brother warned.

Alexander shrugged and was gone, to take his place in the line, shouting encouragement. Maggie felt herself getting hot, but it wasn't the fire. The Master had got on to his brother for swearing when she was there, and he had called her a 'young woman'. Miss Carlotta's mode of address had usually been 'girl', or if she was very angry, 'little slut'. He must have some feeling for her, she thought. Oh no, it wasn't possible; he was only being polite. But Master Alexander had married a girl from the village. It wasn't because he had got her into trouble, Mrs Livingstone had said, but because he loved her. She was thinking of the Master, but Alexander's blackened hands kept intruding, touching.

From the high place she could now recognize some of the fire-fighters as they came closer, boys as well as burly-shouldered villagers, small shawled women with their skirts hitched up, and the tinkers in their motley clothes. Beside her the Master availed himself of a hip-flask, but turning away from her as he drank. It was no use, the fire would soon be with them. It would get a grip on the school, and then go down into the village. He shuddered at the implications beyond the realms of insurance. He would be ruined, since rebuilding was out of the question. The trustees would sell land, which hadn't been done since they came to Invernevis. He might have to marry an ample fortune for the sake of the village. Jamie's sister? A wealthy family, but not *that* sort of money, and she was only the daughter. And there was Alexander directing operations, while he sat on the gig, confined by the game leg. He couldn't watch such ruin, like seeing the massacre of the Highland Brigade under Magersfontein Hill in the bursts of Boer fire. He was about to tell the ghillie to take them home, to leave the food where it was, when the sky began to spit on the back of his hand. It couldn't be, but it was, spots and then a steady drizzle, a sizzling sound as the wall of fire began to sink. Within minutes it was a downpour, but he sat on, savouring the satisfaction.

They were cheering, throwing away their brooms and sacks, and, led by Alexander, running, but when they saw their laird they plucked off their sooty caps and stood awkwardly round the gig. Having thanked them in an emotional voice for their efforts, he directed their attention to the food. The barrel of beer was wedged on the dry-stane dyke, the bung sprung with a blade. It gushed into the enamel jug Maggie held, and when it was overflowing Alexander took it away. Beer soaked Maggie's boots before she could get another jug to the cascade.

Dawn was breaking behind the mountain. MacPherson had milked cows early, and now his gig was coming up the rutted track beside the cemetery, two churns colliding on the back. He filled pails he had brought and passed them round. Maggie had never seen anything like it. The fire-fighters were like ravenous animals, holding the pails between their paws, tilting frothing whiteness to blackened faces. She watched Alexander cracking an egg on piled stone, peeling the shell, pushing the gleaming oval into his mouth, washing it down straight from the bottle that his brother had passed down to him. As his white teeth sank into the softness Maggie knew it was wrong to have such thoughts, with her mother lying at her back.

Invernevis had passed the bottle to his brother without thinking. He was not pleased by MacPherson's arrival, making such a fuss over a few pails of milk, too familiar when he shouted up: 'Aye, well, we had the Lord on our side, for once, eh?' Why hadn't he come up earlier, to help save the village, when others had helped to save the Home Farm?

But Invernevis's immediate concern was getting at the source of the fire. He called out for Mungo, the leader of the tinkers, a small old man with clay pipe and twisted skip to his cap. He came to stand by the big wheel of the gig, putting his hand on his heart, eyes closed.

'I swear by the little princess that's gone, sir, that it wasn't one of us that started it. It was one of them Irish fellows. We had a bit of a quarrel in the Arms last night and he told us he would get us out of the district. He came over the moor, pulled a stick from the fire and threw it into a tent before we could stop him.'

'That's a very unlikely story,' Invernevis scorned. 'What was the fellow's name?'

274

'They're all called Paddy,' the tinker said, which made the people laugh.

But Alexander, who was still swigging whisky, spoke up. 'He's speaking the truth. I was in the Arms when the fellow came in, out of breath. I've got enough Gaelic now to know what he was telling his friends. That's why they wouldn't come up to help.'

Invernevis was answering when MacPherson interrupted him. 'You may be right, Sandy, but they're not camping near my place again.' He stared defiantly up at Invernevis. 'And as for those Irish navvies, if you don't get them out of the district, there's going to be a tragedy. I'm warning you.'

Though Invernevis was shaking with anger, there was a general murmur of agreement from the weary villagers.

Chapter Seventeen

In the harsh light the moor was like the morning after the Modder, the rails buckled, and millions of charred shoots twisting up from the scorched earth, grotesque fingers clutching at the sky. Invernevis touched the blackened standing stone, found that it was still hot. Filled with ashes, the sacrificial circle of an iron hoop from a tinkers' cart wheel lay at his brogues. Blackened tea cans were strewn, like spent shells. The pall of smoke after the rain was for the ruin of a grouse season that had promised to be memorable, with Mary Rose's golden head among the wicker and white spread of the moorland luncheon party. He felt the same as after the Modder, a sickening sense of unnecessary wastage, of promise not fulfilled.

He wrote an angry letter to the quarry manager, demanding an immediate interview. And the tinkers had to be given old tarpaulins and permission to cut saplings to pitch a new camp on the shore by the iron furnace, since MacPherson flatly refused to allow them on the only other suitable site, the unscathed part of the meadow across the Summer House Pool, near Alexander's rearing house. The ghillie was sent out to find another moor where the grouse were reasonable, so that Jamie could be written.

But the quarry manager did not come, and there was no alternative moor. Invernevis had to find a new excuse, so he sat in the library with cigarettes, his thought processes disturbed by clanging metal as men from the railway company replaced the buckled rails and burnt sleepers so that trains could get through again. Fishing? No use because Jamie couldn't hold a salmon rod. A social visit? But that was too vague, and besides, with her beauty, they were bound to be invited elsewhere. The railway hammers kept intruding, reminding him of the growing menace across water and at the Arms. MacPherson had been insolent, but right. The settlement of the internecine war was the first priority, though he didn't know how to go about it.

And when the railway hammers rested there was a new

sound to perplex him, the groan of wood as blocks of granite for Alexander's house were hoisted into place, the scrape of trowels as they were bedded, the Gaelic songs of the masons. It would be ready for occupation at the summer's end, he thought bitterly, staying away from the front windows. Alexander would have a manageable residence, children – these things his brother prized so much but which fate seemed to push out of reach, like a salmon rising for the lure, then shifting to the shadow of stone.

But though it was well advanced, the new house wasn't making any difference to Alexander's behaviour, as he himself had promised it would when he had come to beg the site. He was still in the Arms six nights a week, drinking with the Irishmen who had fired the moor but whom Carmichael refused to ban because profit was all. During the week Alexander drank and talked with his crofting cronies, and some nights stood at the counter, reading the war progress from the newspaper to a pub hushed, not out of respect for reader or General De Wit's brilliant avoiding tactics, but because so few of them could understand English. But when a local brought in a War Office telegram, getting fewer as the fight petered out, it meant free drinks for him all that evening, Alexander contributing with the locals so that toasts could be drunk to the deceased. By closing time he was a hero who had slain a dozen Boers in hand-to-hand combat, instead of a boy hit by a sniper's bullet and dying of homesickness as well as blood poisoning in a stifling hospital.

Alexander went home tight each night to the Home Farm where, though Kate complained about the child being disturbed, her father had no words of reproach because his guest was in the byre at first light, refusing to acknowledge the hangover that his pale face showed so clearly against the dappled flank of the cow, his fingers clasped round the udders to conceal the tremors, the warm milk squirting into enamel between his caked boots. Or else he was in the fields, a sack slung by his side, throwing fistfuls of seed to wind and stone.

And so spring moved into summer, with the lambs that Alexander had helped to deliver finding their legs. As the countryside coloured, the crofters were busy at their modest cultivation, lending horse and plough, receiving in return the services of strong hands because the only son was fertilizer for the sterile soil of the *veld*.

The hedges burst with life, and girls began to go up into the hills with boys anxious to prove that they were men. The barnacles were scraped from the hull of *The Maid of Invernevis* for her summer cruises to the head of the loch, and the morning train began to bring day trippers from Glasgow, men in black suits and bowlers, women in long dresses and big hats, hoisting parasols against the Invernevis sun. They walked arm in arm through the dusty village, only to find that Carmichael would not serve a pot of tea, far less lunch, so they were directed down the brae, to bang the doors of wayside crofts and make signs for bread, cheese and a cup of milk. The toothless old woman without a word of English smiled and nodded, and would take no payment for the produce she brought out on chipped plates, in cracked cups. The trippers sat munching and swigging by the roadside, bowlers pushed back, big hats on laps, savouring the sour manna of crowdie and frothing milk, while watching the acrobatics of butterflies, a horse shackled by sunlight to dust. In the late afternoon they went down to the shore. Trousers rolled up, dresses hitched, they stood with their feet in the cold brine, walking arm in arm like vaudeville characters. When the late train for Glasgow pulled away from the sunset they acknowledged that Invernevis wasn't a bad place.

In the evening, when the day's crofting was done, old men who had no stomach or money for the Arms sat in the sterns of drifting boats, oars shipped off the quarry as they trawled almost bare hooks for the greedy mackerel to guzzle, and when the multi-hooked line was tugging, they brained fish after fish on the gunwale, rowing home in darkness, silver slapping round their buried boots. Surplus fish were sent round the doors of widows.

And there was also fish in the river. But Invernevis would not go down in the morning, when it was cool, with shadows, because he was watching for the post, awaiting a letter from Jamie. Days, weeks went by, with no reply, and he was beginning to think that they had gone abroad when he was brought a letter on a silver tray to say that 'my sister and I will be delighted to come to Invernevis on first September, for a week, if we may. Hard luck about your grouse moor. Ours looks promising, though I don't know about the future, because the Head Keeper went and got himself killed in SA.'

In his excitement Invernevis rushed through to the kitchen,

and it was several minutes before Mrs Livingstone understood what he was saying. It was an occasion for a cup of tea, which she took, standing up by the stove, while he went on and on about getting the house ready, Maggie standing at the big table, face red as her fingers fumbled. When she had managed to get Invernevis to go back through to the library, with the promise of a cup of coffee to calm him, Mrs Livingstone sought out the ghillie in the servants' hall, where he was sorting flies.

'For God's sake take that man down to the river and give his hands something to do, otherwise he's going to have a stroke, rushing about.'

The ghillie advised crossing the standing stones and going upriver, to *Linne Bhuidhe*, the Yellow Pool, but Invernevis insisted on staying on his own side. He could not bear to walk the charred meadow where he had lain with Laura, and he did not want to pass Alexander's almost completed house.

He stood, with the sun in his face, arms rising and falling, but unable to concentrate on his casting because of the morning's news. How wonderful it was, Mary Rose coming to Invernevis, for a whole week! And Jamie too, of course. After Mrs Livingstone he had told Mama, but warning her that she must be 'good', which had made her sulk. But it was essential that nothing should spoil the visit.

His fly snagged on a bush, and as the ghillie worked it free gently, he was watching his master quizzically, because that hadn't happened to him since he was a boy.

Then there was a diversion, the gate into the meadow across the river groaning open, and shimmering darkness in the heat-haze manifesting into MacPherson leading in a mare, followed by the massive Clydesdale stallion that Morgan, a diminutive Aberdonian, brought round the district to service the mares in summer. Alexander was with Morgan, because they were drinking companions in the Arms, and though the small man's skill entitled him to bed and board *free gratis* at the farms at which he was asked to call, he preferred to make his own arrangements. At closing time he staggered out of the Arms and up main street, to where he had parked his stallion in front of the village store. He curled up in the dust and the stallion came to stand over him, its belly a protective arch, staying on its feet throughout the night but turning slowly, hooves stamping, head high, showing its teeth grotesquely and whinnying, should any nocturnal prowler dare disturb the small sleeper under it. Yet those turning shoes the size of dinner plates never once touched Morgan.

Invernevis watched, fascinated, as MacPherson halted the mare. It stood submissively, head down, tail to the side, as the stallion was brought forward, snorting, Morgan almost lifted off his feet as he clung to its harness. The Home Farm was always first in the district because MacPherson believed that the worth of the stallion's seed was diminished by inferior local mares. Also, timing was of the utmost importance. The gestation period was eleven months, and it was better to bring the mare to the stallion not more than nine days after the delivery of the foal, which kept the mare in constant pregnancy. It had to be done right, because the service fee was five pounds, rising to ten if there was a foal, which there nearly always was, with Morgan's stallion.

The great circular hooves lifted each side of the shining flanks, the telescopic organ, thick as a salmon rod butt, emerging, the stallion's back legs steadying for balance, disturbing the dark ash of the burnt meadow. MacPherson was instructing Alexander on how to hold the head of the mare, preventing it from going forward as the stallion thrust and whimpered, shoes grazing the flanks it straddled. There was something magnificent as well as obscene in the spectacle, and across the river Invernevis could not send out the fly again. But as the stallion was shuddering towards climax, squirming shoes raising more and more dark ash, the mare turned suddenly in Alexander's grip, and the seed spilled over stone. MacPherson was slapping the mare, shouting that it would have to be repeated, 'and that's another five pounds, bugger it!'

Alexander looked so sheepish, MacPherson so angry, that Invernevis began to laugh, which carried across and made the farmer shake his fist. And then Invernevis raised his eyes to the Home Farm and saw, in front of its porch, high on the hill, a woman sitting, feeding wool to a flickering wheel, her free foot rocking wicker.

He didn't feel like fishing, and besides, they weren't taking, so he went back up to the house, not looking back as stallion and mare were brought together again, this time successfully, judging by MacPherson's shout. His euphoria was changing to anxiety as his shadow went before him, his brogues avoiding the daisies because they had been his sister's favourite flower. It wasn't simply a matter of coaxing Mary Rose to Invernevis: something had to come out of it. More than marriage. An heir. But wasn't there something violent and calculated in that ambition, like the two horses below him? Where was the place for love in this pandering to tradition, the continuation of the pure strain? But maybe one could have both, he thought as he gave his rod to the ghillie.

Mama was in the drawing-room, blinking in the sunlight, full of the news about the guests. As far as he could tell, she hadn't touched a drop since coming downstairs the day after Carlotta's departure. It was miraculous, really. As her mouth straightened, her speech improved, and the leg was less swollen, allowing her to get about with the assistance of a stick. If she continued to make such progress, she wouldn't be requiring a nurse. She now had the serene face and whitening hair of a contented old lady, her husband and Carlotta having taken her shadow away. And she was displaying an interest in domestic matters she had never shown before. Her son passed on the accounts from the morning post to Mrs Livingstone, and punctually at eleven, she had to take them through, ticked off, to the drawing-room desk which Mama occupied in succession to her sister. Her spectacles were now strengthened by a magnifying glass, and when prices were up, or too much of one thing was being used, she wanted to know why.

'A halfpenny on the milk? That man at the Home Farm's nothing but a robber. And look what he's charging for cream. Well, we can do with less of that. He's just taking advantage because his daughter managed to catch Master Alexander. Have *you* seen the baby yet? No, well I do wish he'd bring it up because they're saying it's like me.' And turning to Mrs Livingstone, her voice dropping confidentially, while the cook kept a straight face: 'Now, my son tells me we're to have two house-guests in early September, a friend from the regiment. Brother and sister. From Sutherland. I know there's plenty of time, but we must make arrangements. We haven't had anyone for *such* a long time, not since Colonel Hooker, and between ourselves, he was a bit of a nuisance. My sister's friend, you understand. Anyway, these two friends of my son's are coming. The lady can have the Blue Room, which, I might say, I was keeping in case the Queen came. But that's finished now. And we'll put him – **Captain Mackay**, it is – into the Green Room. You'll see them comfortable, I'm sure, but give the beds a good airing; you know the way feathers collect damp.' (And other things, Mrs Livingstone thought to herself.) 'Now from what I can gather from my son, though he gets embarrassed, the young lady is very pretty. And one last thing: how is Maggie getting on in the kitchen? My son takes an interest in her because of her brother, you understand, and I liked her mother.'

Released from the greasy tedium of the sink, Maggie was blooming, as if the heat from the oven she stooped to was bringing her to maturity, like the tray of scones she was lifting out. Her face was fuller, less pale, the top of her apron jutting.

'Well, I think these can go through for tea this afternoon,' Mrs Livingstone pronounced, prodding the scones. 'We'll see if the Master approves.'

Maggie was so glad that Elsie had gone with Miss Carlotta, and though she was now sharing her room with Annie, the new scullery-maid from the village, the Master's picture stood on a doily in the centre of the dresser, protected by the new glass that Ranald the gardener had cut for her, though she hadn't told him what it was for. The Master had been so nice to her on the night of the heather fire, so worried that she would catch cold, and when they had driven home in the dawn she had gone straight to the kitchen, singing as she raked the warm ashes from the stove. If she stuck in, she might get the cook's job when Mrs Livingstone eventually carried out her threat to retire, and then there would only be the Master and his mother to look after.

The rest of the staff were relaxed after Miss Carlotta's departure. The laughter didn't die in the servants' hall when the door handle was turned, and the leakage of gossip had stopped with Elsie. Though he was still at school, Maggie's young brother Hector was learning now to be a hall-boy in the evenings, putting out the cracked white plates so that Mrs Livingstone could serve supper. The food had improved enormously, the scrag going straight out to the dogs. And Maggie's father seemed more at ease, smiling as he sampled her cooking at the long table.

But Laura was sadly missed, and none of the maids would go near her bedroom, though Mrs Livingstone wanted it cleared. She did it herself, with Maggie's help, opening the stiff window to let the summer in. But the lack of fire had mildewed the button boots under the wash-stand, and when her wardrobe door was opened the sweet sickening scent of mothballs escaped.

Mrs Livingstone lifted down the few dresses hanging on the corroded rail, dumped them into Maggie's arms.

'Here. You may as well have them. She didn't die of any disease, like her father, and there's no sense in good stuff going to the fire. They're nothing great, mark you; you could spit peas through them because Miss Carlotta could never believe that anyone could feel cold. Never be too proud to take cast-offs from them, girl; even if you were being paid as a cook, you'd be grateful for little extras.'

Surprise and the mothball reek so close to her mouth kept Maggie from speaking.

'And these boots,' Mrs Livingstone was saying, stooping, a hand on her arthritic knee: 'Look how the poor wee thing wore the heels away before she went. Well, they're for the bin.'

Something made Maggie blurt out through the armful of dresses: 'No, I'll take them.'

Mrs Livingstone looked at her in surprise as she placed the boots on top of the pile of clothes her assistant was carrying. 'But you don't even know if they'll fit you.'

'Yes, I do. The boots I'm wearing just now were an old pair she gave me. I didn't want to take them in case she got into trouble with Miss Carlotta. And they fit fine. I'll get new heels put on them.'

Under the bed they found the rolled-up corset with its whalebone stays and steel-tipped laces.

'You won't be wanting this,' Mrs Livingstone said quietly, throwing it among the stuff to go out to the fire.

Maggie bore the boots and clothing up to her room, dropped them on the bed and turned the key. It took her a few seconds to slip out of black, step into cotton, both hands fumbling excitedly with the bow at her back. She surveyed herself in the long narrow mirror of the wardrobe, standing with her back to the door to get all her body in. A perfect fit. The first dress she had ever owned, and such fine material, for summer or dancing. What was that gleaming at the bust? Mother-of-pearl? She picked with a nail, and the dried salmon scale floated to the dark floor. Now to see if the boots fitted.

tugging them on, disregarding the mildew. She stood up, stamped in them, felt the dampness, went back to stand in front of the mirror.

The candle on the dresser, beside the Master's picture, was keeping her face in shadow. She began to feel frightened, standing in the lilac dress and button boots as if the simple assumption of clothes had made her the dead girl. And yet she could not leave her own reflection. It was like being rooted in a dark tunnel, not knowing which way to run, calling, with the mouth open, the mind void of words. But as the candle shortened, the flame gleaming on the dented silver of the photograph, she knew he was out there, waiting, watching, to step down from sandstone.

The scullery-maid rapping on the door, shouting that Mrs Livingstone wanted her down to start the dinner, broke her dream, hurried her into drab black again, to touch the mouth on the photograph before she went down to her duties, her heart going round with the whisk, the whites frothing. When the cook asked her to pluck a fowl for the next day's dinner, she sat on the stool by the open door, staring up at the stars, her fingers automatically tugging the soft feathers, dropping them to drift and accumulate round her boots, the scrawny neck dangling. The night breeze cooled the flush on her face, and before she realized that she was singing a Gaelic song, rocking the fowl on her lap, the cook had joined in, standing by the fierce stove, stirring the porridge pot. It made Maggie want to run out into the night, down the avenue, finding wings to take her above the trees.

When she was finished for the night she didn't like going to the servants' hall with the other girls for a cup of tea and chat before the climb, though they were more friendly now. Since Miss Carlotta had left, Frank the footman had got more and more familiar. The Master had granted permission for the moustache that Miss Carlotta had denied, and it moved above the white rim of the cup as he watched her, so that she was forced to scrutinize wood. When her father had gone home for the night he started winking, jerking his head to signal that he wanted to see her outside. She didn't dare leave the other girls' presence, but when Mrs Livingstone rose to indicate that it was time for all to retire, he gripped her ankle under the table, held on till the others were out of the room. On the first night she managed to kick free, but when it happened a second time he was at the door, barring her way, demanding a kiss. She used her boot and then her teeth.

'Oh, so I'm not good enough for you, is that it? Keeping yourself for the Master, eh? Oh, don't think that I haven't noticed. Well, if he's anything like his father you'd better watch out.' He saw he had touched the soft spot, and he pressed harder. 'His class are all like that. They're all after the one thing, and when they get it, they'll kick you out. And there'll be two of you.'

'Such disgusting talk,' she said sadly, because there was no denying that the moustache made him even more handsome.

He saw what he was doing, and tried to mend it. 'Look: I'm different from the rest of them here. I don't come from these parts, so I don't need to go touching my forelock. It's a job, that's all. But you have to start somewhere. I'll get some experience here, then go for a butler's post in London. You could do the same. A couple of years under Mrs Livingstone, then a cook in London.' He leaned over the table, his hands helping his words. 'Think of it. The theatres, the pubs, the dinner parties for royalty, where you can get a sovereign a night if you watch yourself. One of my mates did, from the King, when he was Prince of Wales. So listen.' He gripped her wrist. 'Let's get engaged. I haven't any money for a ring, but that can wait. We take an oath to stick it out together, here, for a couple of years, then we go to London to get married. We can be as good as married here.'

She was studying him because she no longer felt frightened. His eyes got bigger and bluer as he became more excited, talking about the gold that could be picked up from under plates in London. His hair was neatly parted at the side, trimmed well clear of his collar, and the moustache was even above his lip. Maybe it didn't really suit him; maybe it made him look boyish. It certainly wasn't as mature a face as the Master's, and not such a nice voice. But with his way of talking, he wouldn't have any difficulty in getting a butler's post.

'And is that what you also told Elsie?' she asked quietly.

He struck the table with his palm and stood up to lean across. 'To hell with Elsie. Who are you kidding? You shared a room with her. You must have known the type she was. Or maybe you were asleep when she went down to the holy ghost's room to brush out her hair.' And seeing her puzzled look: 'Oh yes, you have them in the Highlands as well as everywhere else, because there's nothing special about this place, though you people would like to think so. My God, you're either very stupid or very cunning, and I think it's cunning because you couldn't possibly have shared a room without knowing. Or has your precious Master given you money to keep quiet about it, for the sake of his family name? He's certainly given you *something*.'

Though she still didn't understand about Elsie, she slapped him for his reference to the Master.

'You'll be sorry for that, you little bitch,' he hissed, touching his cheek as he headed for the door.

She sat on with her cold tea, hand stinging, glad she had broken the spell at last. He would never know that if only he hadn't said such things about the Master, he might have had his way, because he was a good-looker who could say nice things, and all the other maids, who had been so nasty to her when she was scullery-maid, were after him. But she could never leave Invernevis for London, no matter how many gold coins there were beneath plates, and it wasn't only because of her father and brother.

She was making a new friend in the house. When her scones were still warm Mrs Livingstone made her take one through on the afternoon tea tray, not because she wanted her promising assistant to get the Mistress's praise, but because she knew the old lady was lonely. After this had happened a couple of times, Mama didn't want the regular maid bringing through the tray. She had taken a fancy to Maggie because she was the daughter of a trusted servant who had helped to lift and wash her husband in his horrifying illness, and whose mother had shown promise in the kitchen, but more especially because the girl was a good listener. Kept in check by Carlotta for so many years, all she wanted was for someone to listen without interruption while she slurred out random reminiscences. Of course one had to remember that the girl was young, and a servant, so she couldn't be told of Sandy's indiscretions with little Indian girls, Carlotta's cutting tongue, the cross of Laura's infirmity, and Alexander's disgrace. But there was no harm in the girl hearing of how the place was in the old days, when she came back from India with such expectations, but alas, also Carlotta. She had been pretty then, with red hair and a waist Sandy could easily get his arm round.

'Yes, red hair, but of course it had to be cut in India

because of the heat. You might think the kitchen's hot, but you'll never know such heat. And the insects.' Her good hand scuffed faded linen. 'Now about this baby of Master Alexander's. Tell Mrs Livingstone that I'm waiting for it to be brought up till I see who it looks like. Someone told me it had a slightly snubbed nose, which makes it a Macdonald all right. Now you will remember? And another thing: has Mrs Livingstone started getting the rooms ready for the two guests, the Captain and his sister? Because it's not long now. They say she's very beautiful. You *will* ask?'

Maggie nodded, but she wasn't really taking in what the Mistress was saying. Standing respectfully in the bay window, but not watching the old lady breaking up the scone in shaky fingers, as Mrs Livingstone. had warned her, she was mesmerized by the tip of the Master's rod rising and falling above the dazzling hole of the wishing stone. In front of him, the stepping stones zigzagged like fire across to the blackened meadow where Master Alexander walked, casting fistfuls of seed from a sack slung by his side. And below the scorched standing stones, in front of the Home Farm, wicker was being rocked where a wheel flickered on whitewash.

It was such a beautiful day. Maggie decided she was going to save up for a camera.

End of this Chronicle.